Monkey Tales
Around the World

ALSO BY TERRY L. NORTON
AND FROM MCFARLAND

*Trickster Tales of Southeastern Native Americans:
Stories from the Creek, Natchez, Seminole, Catawba,
Cherokee and Other Nations* (2023)

Cherokee Myths and Legends: Thirty Tales Retold (2015)

Monkey Tales Around the World
A Folklore Anthology

Terry L. Norton

McFarland & Company, Inc., Publishers
Jefferson, North Carolina

ISBN (print) 978-1-4766-9542-6
ISBN (ebook) 978-1-4766-5452-2

LIBRARY OF CONGRESS AND BRITISH LIBRARY
CATALOGUING DATA ARE AVAILABLE

Library of Congress Control Number 2024037497

© 2024 Terry L. Norton. All rights reserved

No part of this book may be reproduced or transmitted in any form or by any means, electronic or mechanical, including photocopying or recording, or by any information storage and retrieval system, without permission in writing from the publisher.

Front cover images *(top to bottom)*: "A Monkey Speaking to a Fox"; "A Bear Eating a Young Monkey," unknown, third quarter of 15th century, medium: Pen and black ink and colored washes, dimensions: 28.7 × 20.6 cm, Germany, object numbers: 83.MR.171.27 and 83.MR.171.15v (digital images courtesy of Getty's Open Content Program).

Printed in the United States of America

McFarland & Company, Inc., Publishers
Box 611, Jefferson, North Carolina 28640
www.mcfarlandpub.com

We have merged with animals through magic, metaphor, or fantasy, growing their fangs and putting on their feathers, to become deities, sages, tricksters, devils, clowns, companions, lovers, and far more.
—Boria Sax, *The Mythological Zoo*

We are just an advanced breed of monkeys on a minor planet of a very average star. But we can understand the universe. That makes us something very special.
—Stephen Hawking quoted in *USA Today*

Table of Contents

Preface
- Purpose — 1
- Organization — 2
- Adaptation Techniques — 2
- Supplemental Analyses: Commentaries — 4
- A Note on Monkeys Versus Apes — 4
- Acknowledgments — 5

Introduction: Some Meanings of Monkeys and Apes
- People and Animals — 7
- Perceptions of Monkeys and Apes in the Ancient Western World — 8
- Some Views from the Middle Ages Through the Modern Era — 10
- Disquieting Simians in the Middle East — 11
- Mesoamerica and South America — 12
- Mixed Portrayals in South Asia — 12
- Major Monkeys: Old Monkey of China and Hanuman of India — 14
- Conclusion and Invitation to the Reader — 15

The Middle East and India
- The Origin of Monkeys — 17
- The Greedy Monkeys — 18
- The Monkey and the Necklace — 19
- The Monkeys Assigned to Water the Trees — 22
- The Vile Monkey and the Patient Buffalo — 23
- The Brahmin and the Monkey — 24
- The Heroic Monkey's Self-Sacrifice — 25
- The Monkey Who Outwitted a Water Ogre — 28
- The Lessons of the Meddling Monkey and the Unheeded Bird — 29
- The Story of Prince Rama — 34
- The Monkey and the Elephant — 75

The Monkey and the Mirror	77
The Monkey Prince	77
The Men Who Became Monkeys	86
The Children Who Were Turned into Monkeys	87
How the Langur Got Its Tail	88
The Monkey Husband	89
The Monkey Nursemaid	92
The Sultan's Daughter and the Baboon	95

Africa

The Monkey and the Shark	99
Monkeys and People	102
The Monkey and the Jackal	103
The Fiddling Monkey	105
Why Old Baboon Has That Kink in His Tail	107
Old Jackal and Young Baboon	111
Leopard and Monkey	117
The Baboons and ǁXabbitenǁXabbiten	120
The Boy and the Baboons	122
The Truthful Monkey	124
The Woman, the Monkey, and the Child	125
How Twins Entered the World	128
How the Tail of the Colobus Monkey Became White	130

Western Europe

AN AESOP SAMPLER — 134

The King of the Apes	134
The Ape and the Fox	135
The Lion and the Ape	135
The Monkey and the Fox	136
Jupiter and the Monkey	136
The Monkeys and Their Mother	137
The Dancing Monkeys	137
The Monkey and the Dolphin	137

VOLTAIRE — 140

Candide, the Girls, and the Two Monkeys	140

Tibet, Korea, Southeast Asia, and China

The Two Monkeys	143
The Monkeys Saved from Death	144
The Monkeys and the Moon	146

The Monkey's Judgment	147
Why Monkeys and People Do Not Live Together	148
The Adventures of the Monkey King	150
The Cruel Rich Couple	173

Japan and the Philippines
The Fox, the Otter, and the Monkey	176
Raw Monkey Relish	178
The Monkey, the Crab, and the Persimmons	179
The Monkey and the Wise Boar	181
The Monkeys and the Dragonflies	188
How Children Became Monkeys	189
The First Monkey	191
The Story of a Monkey	192
The Monkey and the Turtle	194

The Caribbean, South America, and North America
Irraweka and the Flood	197
How Monkey Became a Trickster	201
The Fox and Monkey Thieves	202
The Woman and the Monkey	205
The Monkey Who Begged for Misery	208
The Monkey Girl	209
The Signifying Monkey and the Lion	211

Chapter Notes	217
Bibliography	229
Index	239

Preface

Purpose

Whether traditional or modern, stories about animals fall into three categories: tales in which animals act like people; those in which they act like themselves; and those in which they act according to their own natures but possess human speech.[1] These groupings, of course, apply to tales about monkeys and apes as well.

While making no claim to being a definitive assemblage of stories, this book brings together a significant number of narratives concerning our simian kin. Yet, despite the title of this book exclusively using the word "monkey," its collection of stories is not just about them. It is about us also—monkeys, apes and people, all members of the primate family tree.

Gathered from print versions of folktales and from works based on or connected to this literature from the oral tradition, the sixty-three selections reveal human interactions with and perceptions about our closest genetic relatives over time and across cultures. As scholar Boria Sax has observed in *The Mythological Zoo*, people find some characteristics in animals that they wish to appropriate and others that they attempt to reject as a way to construct what it means to be human.[2]

The foregoing idea resonates throughout the tales collected and retold here about monkeys and apes. Among the positive features of simians, world-renowned zoologist Desmond Morris highlights their playful inquisitiveness and suggests that we owe much to them "as our remote ancestors" since their "inborn urge to explore things became the bedrock of our sophisticated innovations."[3] Morris also notes that this trait of intense curiosity can result in their being seen as a "destructive nuisance."[4] This anthology reveals these kinds of positive and negative sides of primates, humans included, although less flattering portraits of monkeys and apes predominate.

Organization

The tales come from every continent where humans and primates have interacted with one another. Not only are the obvious land masses like South America, Asia, and Africa represented, but Europe and North America are included as well. The exceptions are Antarctica and Australia, although the later, along with New Guinea and other nearby smaller islands, has the cuscus, sometimes referred to as a "monkey," probably because of the prehensile tail of the common spotted, or white, variety. However, the cuscus is a marsupial, not a primate, and like the opossum, the female has a pouch.[5]

Arrangement of the narratives is by geographical location, with the first story a Palestinian tale selected because it gives an explanation, although somewhat disturbing, about how monkeys originated. Beneath the title of each selection is a parenthetical indication of its place of origin if cited in the source from which I adapted it. If a source has specified the ethnic group from which a tale derived, I have provided this information as well.

Adaptation Techniques

In his classic work *Storyteller*, Ramon Ross devotes much attention to describing how oral storytelling brings people together in more intimate ways than does the written word. One reason for this closer communication is that storytellers do not have the printed page coming between their performance and the audience.[6] This same limitation holds true for written versions of works that have their genesis in the oral tradition whether they are read silently by individuals or read aloud to an audience.

For a storyteller, however, a print rendition of a folktale should not be considered its final form. It has simply been frozen on the page, and, according to librarian, folklorist, and storyteller Margaret Read MacDonald, is thawed out "as it meanders from teller to teller."[7] Although the veneration bestowed on tales from the oral tradition often spurs the teller to enshrined them in unchanged form, such a doctrinaire approach, as scholar Christine Jenkins has suggested, "ignores the enduring and fluid nature of the stories themselves."[8]

While no written version can capture the special qualities of an oral presentation, since each telling is different, even if it is of the same story, in some of my print adaptations I have nonetheless incorporated suggestions from storytelling authorities. For instance, I have often changed indirect dialogue into direct conversation to "strengthen the overall effect and credibility" of the selections.[9] As in the case of oral presentations, this modification is designed to inject added vitality into print renditions by enhancing a tale's tempo and dramatic quality, features absent in indirect dialogue.[10]

The foregoing changes in speech are also part of making a tale one's own, another recommendation for effective storytelling.[11] A further means by which storytellers achieve this goal is to relate the selection in their own words rather than in the exact words of the print source.[12] In following this recommendation, I have lowered the readability levels of some of more intricate narratives such as "The Story of Prince Rama" and "The Adventures of the Monkey King." This alteration causes the narratives to more closely approximate oral renditions which generally have shorter, less complex sentences than those found in written versions. At the same time, however, if a tale has more of a literary flair, I have tried to maintain it in the retellings.

Although conveying through print oral aspects of a presenter's style can be a difficult, nearly "insurmountable" task,[13] I have occasionally used a few typographical cues as suggested by MacDonald to specify emphasis in the voice of a storyteller.[14] Words in all capital letters in direct dialogue designate that a character speaks in a loud voice, while those capitalized and in italics indicate both volume and sound effects for a storyteller when relating narrative portions of a tale.

In addition to suggestions for storytelling, I have sometimes amplified the content of a tale to make it more accessible to today's readers. This process creates what literacy experts refer to as "considerate texts."[15] For instance, in "Irraweka and the Flood," a Carib folktale set in the country of Guyana of northeastern South American, I have added details about the land's watery environment and its plethora of animals and plants. This kind of amplification, embedded within the story and intended not to be overdone, boosts the background knowledge of readers and thereby enhances their comprehension by providing information that original audiences inherently possessed.

Although I have expanded here and there within the texts, I have not altered their essential plot, another recommendation for oral performances.[16] Even in the two longer pieces adapted from *The Ramayana* and *Journey to the West*, where I have abridged expendable material not necessary for their main storylines, I have attempted to keep to the spirit of the originals as much as possible.

Supplemental Analyses: Commentaries

A commentary follows each tale or cluster of tales as in the case of the seven fables selected from sources associated with the legendary Aesop. Each commentary provides background on the narratives and may include such information as the predominant folktale type or types a story falls under, significant motifs it contains, descriptions of the culture and geographical area from which it came, discussion of linguistic components like the pronunciation of certain words or their meanings, details about the collectors or adapters who rendered the tales into print, and comparisons and contrasts to other story parallels and variants.

A Note on Monkeys Versus Apes

I retelling stories about our simian kin, I have adhered to the earlier custom of using the word "monkey" interchangeably with "ape."[17] There is, however, a scientific distinction between the two despite their being seen throughout most of history as synonymous.[18] Both groups are *anthropoids*, just as humans are, but have various body sizes, geographical locations, and behaviors and generally share features such as "flat faces, small ears, and relatively large, complex brains."[19] Notable exceptions to the flat faces of monkeys, however, are baboons and mandrills which have prominent muzzles.[20]

The most pronounced physical difference, though, is that apes do not have tails whereas monkeys do,[21] with the main exception being the Barbary macaques of the coast of Northwest Africa and the British colony of Gibraltar where they were introduced and now have their population regulated. Sometimes referred to as Barbary apes, they are nonetheless monkeys with "vestigial" tails.[22]

An additional physical difference is that apes tend to be larger than monkeys and have chests comparable to humans.[23] Yet some monkeys like baboons and mandrills can be as big as certain species of apes.[24]

Although the evidence has been elusive, fossil research indicates that monkeys, like baboons and macaques, diverged at an earlier date from hominids (humans) than did apes.[25] This circumstance may account for another key difference between monkeys and apes: namely, the latter are genetically more closely related to people and have a bigger brain capacity than other simians.[26] Indeed, humans and the great apes of sub–Saharan Africa (gorillas, chimpanzees, and bonobos) have "a closer kinship bond with one another than the African apes have with orangutans or other primates," with chimpanzees and bonobos being our closest relatives.[27]

As for orangutans, they are great apes found in only Borneo and Sumatra because of loss of habitat.[28] The lesser apes include gibbons and siamangs, which inhabit tropical regions of Southeast Asia.[29] Along with orangutans, they are more arboreal than the African great apes.[30]

As to the number of monkey species, estimates vary. Morris cites a 1991 source as giving one hundred and seventy-three species although he states there might be more if local variations were counted.[31] *Britannica Online* in its 2023 entry "Monkey" puts the number of tailed monkeys, including those having a nubby remnant, at two hundred.[32] The website for Monkey Worlds gives two hundred and sixty species, ranging in weight from four ounces to seventy-seven pounds.[33]

Acknowledgments

The preparation of this book has benefited from critical comments on ways to improve it from the following members of the York County Chapter of the South Carolina Writers Association: Chuck Brite, Joe Creech, Lisa Dunn, Craig Farris, Bobbie Harrison, Brodie Lowe, Daniel McGregor, Bruce Nims, Evelyn Eickmeyer Quinones, and Donna Wiley. In addition, the librarians and staffs of the Ida Jane Dacus Library at Winthrop University and of the York County Library provided much appreciated assistance in my obtaining many of the sources.

Introduction: Some Meanings of Monkeys and Apes

People and Animals

Our early ancestors lived in close contact with wild animals and not only hunted and feared them but also revered them and their powers as well.[1] A consequence of this connection is that from time out of mind people have told stories about animals, whether real or imagined. Handed down over generations, these traditional tales sometimes used them to represent human characteristics, and sometimes the stories explored the relationships between people and animals.

Later stories with "a clear literary origin" traceable to a known writer, contained the same considerations and became "folk property."[2] For instance, Hans Christian Andersen's literary fairy tale "The Ugly Duckling" presents the kind of truth generations of people handed down in folklore, for it shows the all too often human impulse to reject what is different. The gangly, awkward little swan, born in a duck's nest, suffers from both physical and verbal abuse by the other barnyard animals. Indeed, as literature professor David Russell has noted, perhaps through experiencing the behavior of animals in such stories, "we can learn something about ourselves and humanity in general."[3]

If animals can teach us something about the human condition, a question that arises is which animal is most like us. Known for his writings about the cultural connection between humans and animals, Boria Sax indicates that the answer is not universal and has varied over time. Non-western cultures, of course, have had their leading candidates, but in the Western world, the ancients of the classical era considered the bear the most human. After all, it can stand fully erect and walk like a person, things which anthropoid apes cannot do.[4] Of course, the bear's similarity to humans is not limited to the Old World. Native Americans of the Southeastern United States considered the bear falling into both human and animals categories because it can walk on two legs like humans as well as on four legs like other four-footed creatures and because it often eats the same foods consumed by people.[5]

Regarding other animals, peasants of the Middle Ages found the pig to be the most human animal and regarded it as a member of their families.[6] During the eighteenth and nineteenth centuries, people believed the beaver closest to humans as European explorers in the New World, awed by its construction skills, told tales of beavers building expansive lodges.[7] Because of its long-standing connection with people throughout many cultures, another candidate might be the dog. Only with the advent of Darwin and the theory of evolution did primates attain the position of being the animal most like people.[8]

Perceptions of Monkeys and Apes in the Ancient Western World

And yet, whether they are most like us or not, our primate relatives have had from the beginnings of human history a close connection to us in art and literature. Among the most venerated gods of ancient Egypt was Thoth, depicted with either the head of an ibis or a baboon and having among his many attributes those of fairness and even-handed justice.[9] Other Egyptian artifacts contain realistic portrayals of the humorous side of monkeys, especially their bent to imitate us by dancing and performing tricks. Occasionally, they were honored as loyal friends, even accompanying the dead on their journey to the afterlife. In the Valley of the Kings, Pharaoh Thutmose III (1479–1429 BCE) was buried with his favorite baboon, and a high priestess of Amun was embalmed with a small baboon which experts once thought was her little girl.[10] Some utilitarian art objects suggest an association between monkeys and the rejuvenating power of women's cosmetics. Alabaster vessels containing such beauty aids were "delicately carved in the shape of mother monkeys holding their young."[11]

From the limited evidence available, the Greeks and Romans had mixed views on primates, although the bias bends toward the negative. Like the ancient Egyptians, the Greek physician Hippocrates associated monkeys and apes with humans. In his treatise *On the Nature of Man*, he discusses the four humors that govern personality and wellness. Active, enthusiastic, and of pleasant mind, the sanguine individual had linkages with the horse, peacock, and the monkey.[12]

And yet this more positive view of monkeys seems not to have been dominant among the ancient Greeks, who overall found monkeys to be ugly, their bottoms being one of their least attractive features. British zoologist Desmond Morris indicates that the Greeks considered the rough patches of calloused skin off-putting and immodest. They saw as even more glaringly unsightly the periodic and prominent swellings of the female's endometrium during estrus. Such physical repulsiveness surely signaled the worst kind of evil nature.[13]

Like Hippocrates with the Greeks, Pliny the Elder (23/24 CE to 79 CE) was an outlier with the Romans in his description of monkeys. In his *Natural History* of the first century CE, he praises their similarity to humans, noting their "wonderful shrewdness" and their ability to imitate people. Revealing his penchant for accepting incredulous claims and writing about what he never observed, Pliny cites Mutianus and says that monkeys have even "played at chess." He follows this fantastic statement with the observation that those kept as pets will eagerly display their new-born, sometimes dandling and embracing their offspring so much that they inadvertently kill them.[14] This belief about maternal primate behavior, along with its deadly consequence, appears to have been common both before and after Pliny's description. The same notion occurs in "The Monkey and Her Two Children,"[15] a fable attributed to the Thracian slave Aesop who supposedly lived on the Greek island of Samos some five hundred years before Pliny. The Roman fabulist Babrius, who probably composed his work one or two decades after Pliny's death, rendered the story into Greek verse by the late first or early second century.[16] As for other observations about monkeys, Pliny regards the baboon as "the most savage," whereas other species he affirms as "most gentle."[17]

Insofar as additional Aesopic fables on monkeys are concerned, whether by Babrius or other classical fabulists, these narratives commonly cast their talking simians as symbols for human foibles. For instance, in "The Fox, the Monkey, and His Ancestors," a monkey, puffed with pride, attempts to make himself seem important by falsely claiming the tombstones beside a road held his ancestors.[18] In "The Monkey and the Dolphin," false pride and lying result in death by drowning for the story's primate.[19]

Even so, fables occasionally occur which do not follow this penchant for the disparagement of simians. In "The Beauty Contest of the Animals,"[20] a monkey mother presents her infant to the gods as a candidate for the most beautiful animal baby. Finding herself ridiculed by the Olympians, she nonetheless affirms that, at least in her eyes, her little one should be the contest winner, a feeling which the story suggests is common to all mothers. These fables on monkeys along with several others are retold herein under the heading "An Aesop Sampler."

Writing specifically about the Romans, though offering only anecdotal evidence, Morris asserts that they generally associated monkeys with wickedness, especially in their role as debased caricatures of humans.[21] Indeed, one of the most severe Roman punishments in which monkeys figured, because of their sinfulness, was reserved for individuals who murdered their fathers. After being flogged, the criminal was sewn up in a sack with a monkey and other animals, then thrown into a river to drown.[22] In *The Golden Ass*, written in the second century CE, Apuleius relates the story of a trial involving patricide. Though the accused is innocent, the narrator states that he must be sentenced "as the Law provided, to be sewn up in a leather sack with four living creatures—a dog, a cock, a viper, and an ape—emblems of the four deadly sins, and cast into a river."[23]

Some Views from the Middle Ages Through the Modern Era

With the coming of Christianity, the perception of primates sank even further, although the evidence is sketchy like that from the Greeks and Romans. Early Christians in their art associated these animals with demons[24] as did later medieval bestiaries which depicted tailless monkeys to symbolize their connection with Satan. The Latin word *cauda* can refer to both tail and codex (book) and signified that monkeys without tails were like the Prince of Darkness in that they had no book, or scripture, to guide them and that they possessed the characteristics of malice, cunning, and base desire.[25] Indeed, the Catholic church of the medieval era regarded great Lucifer himself as "God's Monkey."[26]

The later Middle Ages as well as the Renaissance began to depict monkeys as symbols of art itself because of their ability to imitate or "ape."[27] In *The Medieval Menagerie*, Janetta Benton describes a beaker from fifteenth-century Burgundy that portrays, among other things, monkeys robbing a peddler and using hounds to pursue a stag, thereby mimicking the behavior of thieves and hunters.[28] James Hall relates that Flemish painters of the 1600s sometimes rendered the artist as an ape at work on a female portrait, thus giving a humorously literal interpretation to the expression *Ars simia Naturae*—"art is the ape of nature—"[29] and initiating the rise of the artistic genre of the *singerie* (French for "monkey trick"). Indeed, from the Latin *simia*, we derive the English word *simian*, a synonym for ape and monkey. The word can also mean possessing their characteristics and suggests a closeness to humans.

At first, these early instances of monkeys wearing clothes and mimicking human activities were a light satire of the lower classes aping their betters.[30] With later French painters of the late 1600s and early 1700s, the *singerie* broadened to a more extended satirical portrayal of human behavior[31] and would eventually become a parody of human activities such as playing a musical instrument or a game of cards.[32] One facet of the genre, the *singe peintre*, or the "monkey painter," sometimes ridiculed the belief that humans considered themselves superior to animals.[33] Harsher depictions used monkeys as symbols of human "shamelessness and imbecilic behavior."[34] However, painters like Antoine Watteau (1684–1721) took a gentler approach. In his 1710 painting, *The Monkey Sculptor*, Watteau's monkey, dressed in the clothing of the time, appears as a "mindless imitator of an artist."[35] As he readies his chisel to strike his sculpture of a woman, the bust humorously turns aside her face in fear of her destruction from the blow of the inept monkey.[36] In contrast to portrayals of the mindless monkey, later painters such as Alexandre Gabriel Decamps rendered their subjects in a more serious vein. His *Monkey Painter* (1833) gives his subject a "sense of soulfulness and introspection."[37] Scholar Jean H. Duffy characterizes twentieth-century versions of singeries by artists like Pablo Picasso, Frank Kupla, and Oskar Kokoschla as preoccupied by an uncomfortable and droll self-mockery which suggests "a modernist ambivalence about the act of representation," for according to expert on French art Theodore Reff, monkeys have often been associated with the circus stunts and clowns.[38]

Disquieting Simians in the Middle East

If the European painters of "monkey tricks" found humor in the resemblance of their subjects to humans, the Islamic world, in the estimation of Boria Sax, found the similarity disturbing.[39] The slim evidence presented by Sax indicates that early civilizations of the Middle East lacked the fondness for monkeys that the ancient Egyptians had. Like the Greeks and Romans, these cultures regarded them as debased human beings. In one Jewish tale, the overreaching people who constructed the Tower of Babel were punished by being turned into apes, while another story relates that the fallen Adam had a tail. The Zoroastrians of Persia considered apes and monkeys the lowest type of humans created by the all-wise and good god Ahura Mazda.[40] This negative outlook resonates in the first story in the present collection, "The Origin of Monkeys," retold from a Palestinian folktale.

Yet Western societies can find the similarity disquieting also, for to engage in "monkey business" is to lack self-control, to be disorderly, and to be unfaithful. As art historian Martin Kemp has observed, monkeys are emblems of what results when people act "in a debased way," indulging in animalistic behavior.[41] Indeed, in *Monkey*, Morris indicates that there are approximately ninety-four slang expressions in English that use the word "monkey" in a derogatory sense to signal "meddlesome, irritatingly playful, destructive, sexually animalistic, or subhuman."[42] He cites nearly two dozen of the more commonly known terms. Among those of sexual import are "Spank the monkey," which refers to male masturbation, and "Her monkey," which refers to female genitals. Morris explains that this later expression is "presumably based on the extreme obtrusiveness of the genitals of female monkeys of many species when they come into heat."[43]

Mesoamerica and South America

The Aztecs of central Mexico appear to have shared a similar contempt for simians. According to art historians Rowena and Rupert Shepherd, this indigenous group saw monkeys as mischievous and sexually unrestrained.[44] In contrast, Hope B. Werness presents modest findings that some Mayan societies may have held an elevated respect for monkeys because of their "free, irreverent, unconventional, even chaotic, and playful approach" to life—traits the local cultures may have considered inherent in artistic creativity.[45] Werness also notes findings suggesting Mayan belief that spider monkeys were devoid of sexual restraint.[46] She recounts that this behavior still expresses itself in Highland festivals of today's Mayan descendants. During these celebrations, men wear monkey masks and imitate licentiousness and sexual aggression.[47]

Mixed Portrayals in South Asia

By contrast, the southern Asian cultures of the Indian subcontinent have historically offered mixed portrayals of primates. In traditional Hindu lore through the character of Hanuman, monkeys reached their most venerated level. Morris describes him as "a monkey god who is seen as a noble hero, a provider of courage, hope, knowledge, intellect, and devotion, and a symbol of physical strength and perseverance."[48] The Indian epic the *Ramayana*, which is abridged and retold in the present anthology and which may have originated around 1300 BCE, recounts Hanuman's larger-than-life exploits as he aids Prince Rama, the narrative's protagonist.

Composed originally in Sanskrit, the *Fables of Bidpai*, on the other hand, casts monkeys in a much less admirable role than Hanuman. For instance, in the two fables retold here as "The Lessons of the Meddling Monkey and the Unheeded Bird," the first monkey, a carpenter's pet, fails painfully in his attempts to imitate his master in splitting a log, while the second monkey foolishly tries to start a fire from a glowworm.

Other ancient tales from South Asia in which monkeys figure prominently are the *Jatakas*, credited as the oldest surviving collection of Buddhist folklore. Although the exact time of origin is uncertain, the written stories were in existence by the fifth century CE, while stone carvings of story components date from the early second and third centuries BCE.[49] The several thousand tales relate instances from the life of Gautama Siddhartha in which he had been reincarnated in either human or animal form before he eventually awoke from the sleep of ignorance and attained enlightenment as Buddha.[50] However, most of the narratives are adaptations of Hindi stories that predate Buddhism, according to Sanskrit scholars and translators Francis and Thomas.[51]

Regarding the *Jatakas* and monkeys, Sax says the tales depict them as "sensible animals."[52] And yet anyone who reads the original stories or the adaptations given here would hardly reach this conclusion. The primates of these tales are sometimes foolish or malicious. At other times, they are clever and mischievous. Only when depicted as an animal reincarnation of Buddha do they exhibit the compassion and other moral and spiritual qualities like those of Hanuman in the *Ramayana*.

For example, in my adaptations "The Vile Monkey and the Patient Buffalo" and "The Brahmin and the Monkey," the monkeys engage in the nasty behavior of dropping their feces on others. Here, the monkeys are actual primates, whereas in "The Heroic Monkey's Self Sacrifice" and "The Monkeys Who Outwitted a Water-Ogre," they are simian kings who represent rebirths of Buddha and exhibit altruistic behaviors toward each one's eighty thousand subjects. (See commentaries following each of these retellings for additional information.)

In other cultures of Asia where Buddhism spread, monkeys have also had a long connection with religion and the arts. In the Chinese Zodiac, which originated around 1100 BCE, six hundred years before Gautama Siddhartha's birth in India, the monkey or *hou* is the ninth of the twelve animals. Individuals born in the Year of the Monkey are supposed to be "clever, competitive, selfish, and lovable."[53]

Major Monkeys: Old Monkey of China and Hanuman of India

As both positive and negative symbols, monkeys have a widespread significance in Buddhist lore of China. Their incessant chatter suggests the random, unfocused mind in need of discipline through meditation to become loyal and intelligent.[54] The character of Old Monkey, one of the most enduring folk figures in China, exemplifies this lesson which is embodied in the early sixteenth-century novel *The Journey to the West*. Written during the Ming dynasty, supposedly by Wu Cheng'en, the novel derives from the journey of the Chinese monk Xuanzang (c. 596–664 CE) who traveled to India in 627 to procure sacred Buddhist texts. As translator Anthony C. Yu remarks, the setting is at a time when Buddhism experienced "remarkable growth" under the patronage of the Sui and Tang dynasties.[55] The story, however, commingles historical events with Chinese folklore and aspects of Eastern religion and philosophy so that the final product is "a tale of supernatural deeds and fantastic adventures, of mythical beings and animal spirits, of fearsome battles with monsters and miraculous deliverance from dreadful calamities."[56]

The first seven of the novel's one hundred chapters relate the story of Sun Wu-kung, or Old Monkey, whose extraordinary feats cause his followers to proclaim him the Monkey King. Yet his origins, before his appearance in *The Journey to the West*, remain obscure, with his character likely derived from both Chinese lore and the Indian monkey god Hanuman, though various scholars disagree as to the exact details.[57]

Yu suggests that Hanuman of the *Ramayana* predates the Monkey King who may have made his way into Chinese culture through its contact with Buddhist India, although "traces" of the *Ramayana* are at best "fragmentary" in "early popular Chinese literature."[58] Yet both characters have striking similarities. Broad parallels noted between the two characters include their abilities to shapeshift, their enormous physical powers, and their immortality.[59]

More specific parallels also link Hanuman and the Monkey King. The *Ramayana* often refers to Hanuman as the Son of the Wind, a sobriquet derived from the fact that his father is Vayu, the god of the wind. In comparison, Sun Wu-kung's birth results from a stone egg which the winds of heaven and earth fanned into life as an embryonic monkey and from which he hatched. Both characters possess magical powers in altering their form and flying. Hanuman can shrink or grow larger. Old Monkey can change into seventy-two shapes. Hanuman can leap (or fly) great distances at a single bound. The Monkey King can cloud somersault across wide seas or the world itself. Both characters protect and defend their respective leaders. The Son of the Wind helps Rama defeat his chief foe, the demon king Ravana, and is instrumental in saving Sita, Rama's wife. After the initial chapters of *Journey to the West*, Sun Wu-kung guides and defends the Buddhist monk from monsters that beset their arduous pilgrimage to India.

Yet an essential difference separates Hanuman from Old Monkey. Considered the exemplar of heroism, Hanuman is the humble, devoted servant who uses his powers always in the service of others. Without his essential aid, Prince Rama could never save Sita from the demon Ravana, thus rendering Hanuman the epic's "most important character" to many readers.[60]

By contrast, even though the Monkey King is fearless like Hanuman, his exploits in the initial chapters of the novel are devoted to creating chaos and confusion. As such, he is no mere mischievous primate. For like all tricksters, he is a deceiver and violator of boundaries who sows the seeds of disorder even in the eternal, unchanging realm of the Jade Emperor and other celestial Immortals. Referring to a description given by Wittman Ah Sing, the main character of Maxine Hong Kingston's novel, *Tripmaster Monkey: His Fake Book,* Lewis Hyde humorously notes in his study of the trickster, that the Monkey King eats everything at the heavenly Peach Banquet, topples its tables, and pees in the wine.[61] Through his mayhem, Monkey as a trickster injects new energy and life into a social and cosmic order that is staid, static, and ultimately moribund.

Conclusion and Invitation to the Reader

As suggested in the foregoing survey of how various times and places have viewed monkeys and apes, the chief difficulty with any proposed generalization is that it stems from anecdotal, artistic, and archeological evidence of an often scattered and fragmentary type. Yet, despite this deficiency, the conclusion tendered by Morris appears the least dubious. He submits that across cultures, people have regarded monkeys and apes as "essentially mischievous beings."[62] While this perception may connote an overall negativity, the inquisitive, prying, curious traits involved in their mischief-making have a positive side. In the words of Morris, "Their urge to explore things became the bedrock of our sophisticated innovations. Their love of activity became our industrious pursuit of knowledge."[63]

However, no matter what perceptions humans have had of simians or what people have projected onto them, whether the projections run the gamut from negative to positive characteristics, we can learn much about ourselves. I, therefore, invite readers of this book to explore their own natures as they delve into its stories about our primate relatives.

The Middle East and India

The Origin of Monkeys
(from Palestine)

At one time, people and monkeys looked the same. For both were descendants of Adam, the first man. In fact, they both looked just like people today. But then a terrible accident occurred that made monkeys appear different.

A woman was once baking bread in her clay oven. As she was arranging the dough to bake, her young son suddenly squatted on the floor, let loose his bowels, and made a huge mess. This behavior angered the mother so much that she yelled harsh, sharp words at the boy. Because she did not have anything at hand with which to clean him, she cried out, "Oh, help me, God!" God heard her cry and let fall from heaven seven silk handkerchiefs to wipe the boy.

Yet the mother considered to herself, "These silk handkerchiefs are much too fine and precious to use this way." So she grabbed the nearest thing she had. This happened to be a flat cake that she had just taken out of the oven. The bread was still piping hot, but in her frustration, she swiped her son's behind with it.

That very instant, the hot cake turned his bottom a scarlet red like the leaves of autumn. He also flattened and wrinkle his face in pain. And from that time forward, monkeys have had a red bottom and a flat, wrinkled face. May God in His wisdom guard us from any such further curse.

COMMENTARY: Adapted from Inea Bushnaq's collection, *Arab Folktales*,[1] this story is a *pourquoi* which explains how monkeys came into being, yet its greater significance lies in the change the baby boy undergoes from human to monkey. Many traditional stories about animals and humans involve such transformations. Animals may change into people, or people may change into animals. Ovid's well-known *Metamorphoses* retells Greek and Roman myths about people whom the gods transform into either animals, plants, or even monsters.

In these kinds of stories, when humans control the change, as shamans sometimes do in Native American folktales, the transformation signals power and the human and animal world working together. But when the change is uncontrolled, it often comes as a punishment or a sign of woe, as in the famous episode in *The Odyssey* when the enchantress Circe turns a party of Odysseus' men into swine and other animals. Not trusting that she will keep her promise and change them back into men, Eurylochus, the only one who escaped the enchantment, warns Odysseus and the remaining shipmates as they head toward her palace to aid their stricken comrades. "Poor fools, where are you going? Why are you so in love with misery that you will go to Circe's hall and let her turn us all into swine and wolves and lions...?"[2]

In the instance of the Palestinian folktale retold here, the child in the story is accidentally turned into a monkey. Though the change is not necessarily a punishment, the teller of the tale is horror-stricken at what has happened to the boy and invokes God to protect humans from other curses of this kind. The story appears to confirm Sax's assertion that in the Muslim world the resemblance of primates to people has been perceived as disturbing.[3]

Yet the same reaction occurs in the Chinese story I have retold as "The Cruel Rich Couple." (See the last story in the section "Tibet, Korea, Southeast Asia, and China.") Transformation as punishment occurs as the cruel old man and woman in the tale are turned into monkeys after they have taken and misappropriated the magic cloth given to their slave girl by an Immortal. The couple's horror is magnified through their awareness of the change as they behold themselves in a mirror and flee into a wasteland, thus forfeiting their wealth.

The term *therianthropy* is most often used to indicate a transformation from human to animal. It is usually applied to situations in which a person has the power to make the change but can be used to describe instances in which the change is imposed as in the episode with Circe. *Zoanthropy* is sometimes substituted as a synonym.

The Greedy Monkeys
(from India)

A troop of wild macaques had long pestered the people of a village. The monkeys would squeak and grunt and hoot throughout the day and night. As if these shenanigans were not bad enough, they frequently passed their time in stealing food, and what they most liked to steal were the juicy mangoes that grew nearby.

The theft became so outrageous that the villagers might as well have had no mango trees at all. For no one could taste a single bite of the sweet fruit, until a wise elder solved the problem.

The old man gave each person a hard, ripe coconut and said, "Bore a hole through the shell just large enough for a monkey to slide a paw inside. Pull out the meat, and fill your coconuts with the pulp mixed with rice. Set these on the ground as presents for the monkeys. Then hide." The villagers did as the elder instructed.

The colony now thronged upon the ground, running and chattering here and there, sometimes fighting with one another over a coconut. Impatiently sticking in their paws, the macaques each grasped as much of the sweet treat as their fists could hold.

At the elder's signal, the people rushed from their hiding places to attack the monkeys. Yet the monkeys refused to let go of the prize and could not pull their balled-up paws out of the coconuts. The villagers tossed blankets over monkeys' heads and led them off to prison. If the greedy macaques had not grabbed such huge portions, perhaps they could have avoided being captured.

COMMENTARY: This selection is based on an untitled anecdote in *Reminiscences of Sport in India* (1885). Its author, E.F. Burton, indicates that "in the interests of veracity," he did not personally witness the greed of the macaques or the clever way in which the natives captured them.[4] Although omitting the motif of the trickster, a similar tale from Pakistan recounted by Swynnerton (1892) has a single monkey greedily put its paw into a small rock crevice to obtain a fistful of wheat. Refusing to be content with a smaller amount, it leaves hungry, having gotten none of the grain.[5] In Jones' 1912 translation of *Aesop's Fables*, "The Boy and the Filberts" tells of a lad who thrusts his hand into a jar of nuts. His fist is so full he cannot pull it out. A bystander advises him to be satisfied with half a handful. Veering away from the theme of excessive greed, the stated moral is "Do not attempt too much at once."[6] The fable's plot lends added weight to the claim of folklorist Joseph Jacobs that "a goodly number of the fables that pass under the name of the Samian slave, Aesop, were derived from India, probably from the same source whence the same tales were utilized in the *Jatakas*, or Birth-stories of Buddha."[7]

The Monkey and the Necklace
(from India)

There was once a king who owned a garden, and the garden had a lake where he and his family often swam when the weather was hot. One day, he took a walk in the woods and was gone for quite a while. When he returned, he sent for his family to join him in a refreshing swim.

The queen and her ladies came down to the lake, but before they entered the water, they removed their jewels to leave them with the servants. The queen handed over a necklace of pearls which an attendant put into a jewel-box. As she did, a girl monkey watched her from a nearby tree. The monkey wanted the pearls and hoped that the servant guarding them would fall asleep. The woman soon nodded and dozed off.

As fast as the wind, the monkey dropped from her perch, scooted over to the sleeping woman, opened the box, and took the string of pearls. Then just as quickly, the monkey scampered up the tree and tried on the necklace. Afraid that the other servants in the garden might see her, she stashed the pearls in a hole in the tree. Sitting motionless on her limb, she pretended nothing had occurred.

After a short while, the servant woke up. She saw that the lid to the box was open. One glance told her the necklace was gone. She shouted, "Someone has stolen the queen's pearls!"

The guards stationed around the garden ran to the woman at once. She said, "I have been here the whole time with the queen's pearls and the jewel-box where she put them. But as the day was hot, I must have nodded off, and when I awoke, the necklace was gone."

The guards told the king what had happened. "Find whoever stole the pearls," he commanded. Off they went, searching here and there for the thief.

Once the king left, however, the captain of the guards thought, "Something odd is going on. The pearls were in the jewel-box and disappeared from it here in the garden. The garden is surrounded by a high wall. The only way inside is through the gate. The gate has a strong guard stationed there so that no can enter or leave without being seen. Yet there are many monkeys that live and play here. Perhaps one of them took the necklace."

The captain then thought of a way to find out whether a monkey had stolen the pearls. He left and went to a nearby marketplace where he bought many strings of brightly colored glass beads. Waiting until it was dark, he went into the garden and here and there hung the beads on bushes that grew beneath the trees.

When the sun rose the next morning, the monkeys saw the glittering glass, climbed down the trees, and ran to grab the necklaces. And yet the girl monkey, who had stolen the queen's pearls, remained on her limb beside the hole where she had hidden them.

The other monkeys could not have been happier with their strings of glass beads. They chattered to one another about how pleased they were, but to the girl monkey they said, "Too bad you do not have a necklace."

While they prattled and talky-talked in this way, the girl monkey remained silent, saying nothing. At last, she could bear no more and took the queen's string of pearls out of the hole and put it around her neck. She dropped to the ground and proudly said, "Your necklaces are of glass, but mine is one of pearls."

The captain of the guards had hidden nearby and saw everything that happened. He caught the girl monkey and took her to the king. "Your Highness, this girl monkey stole the queen's string of pearls."

The king was, of course, happy to have the pearls returned, but he was curious how the captain had discovered who stole them.

"Your Highness," replied the captain, "because of the high wall, no one could enter the garden except by the gate, which had a strong guard posted. Therefore, one of the garden monkeys must have taken the pearls." He then told the king about the trick with the glass beads.

When the captain had finished speaking, the king thanked him many times over and said, "Though I might search long and hard, I could never find a better man than you to fulfill his duties."

COMMENTARY: Ellen Babbitt's "The Girl Monkey and the String of Pearls" in *More Jataka Tales*[8] provides the basis for this retelling. Babbitt, in turn, took her selection from a framed narrative within "Mahasara-Jataka."[9] According to the text, the King of Kosala discovers that the jewel from his turban is missing. The king's wives think he suspects one of them as a thief and fear repercussions. Buddha's favorite disciple and the wives' teacher, Ananda, lifts the king's suspicions by telling him a story illustrating how a queen's valuable string of pearls was stolen by an animal. In Babbitt's version, the captain of the guards solves the problem of who took the necklace, whereas in the original Jataka, a Bodhisattva exposes the thief. (In Buddhism, a *bodhisattva* is an individual who can attain enlightenment but who delays doing so to allay the suffering of others here on earth.)

In their 1916 collection of Jatakas "of most interest both intrinsically, and also from the point of view of the folklorist,"[10] Francis and Thomas include "Mahasara-Jataka" under the title of "The Stolen Jewels."[11] Their selections come from the multivolume work under the editorship of Cowell for whom Francis and Thomas served as Sanskrit translators.

The Monkeys Assigned to Water the Trees
(from India)

Long ago, a king granted a holiday to one of his cities and provided a great festival for the people's entertainment. His gardener, however, could not go because he had to water the young trees in the king's garden. A tribe of monkeys lived there.

The man said to himself, "All my friends have gone to the festival, and I could go as well if I did not have to water my master's trees."

As he considered how he might enjoy himself in the city, he watched the monkeys playing all around him. Suddenly, a thought came to him. "The monkeys can water the young trees while I am away."

So the gardener went to the head monkey. "You and your band are fortunate to live in this lovely place. Here you can scamper about and eat the foods the trees provide—fruits, nuts, and young, tender shoots. No work is required, and you can play as much as you like. My friends are on holiday in the city, and I want to join them. Would you be so kind as to water the young trees so that I can go also?"

"Of course," said the monkey chief. "We are happy to help."

"Oh, thank you," said the gardener. "Be sure to water the trees when the sun sets. Give them plenty of water, but do not over water them." He then showed the head monkey and his troop where the watering pots were and left for the festival.

As soon as the sun set, the monkeys filled the watering pots and started to attend to the young trees. "See that you give each one enough water but not too much," said their leader.

"How will we know what is enough for each tree?" the other monkeys asked.

The head monkey thought for a moment. He then said, "We must examine their roots. Pull up each tree. Give more water to those with the longer roots and less to those with the shorter ones." The monkeys did just as their leader said.

The next day, when the gardener returned from the city, all the young trees were dead.

COMMENTARY: In *More Jataka Tales*, Babbitt titles this story "The Stupid Monkeys."[12] Volume 1 of Cowell's *The Jataka* lists the story as "Aramadusaka-Jataka."[13] After the monkeys have foolishly pulled up the young trees, this Jataka gives the reflections of a wise man, an event omitted by Babbitt. The sage admonishes the troop with a moral to the effect that good intentions without sufficient knowledge are not enough because they often lead to harm as in the killing of the trees. Volume 2 contains another, briefer version, "Arama-Dusa-Jataka."[14] This version offers wisdom from a Bodhisattva:

> Monkeys, I have no blame for you,
> Nor those who range the woodlands through.
> The monarch is a fool to say
> "Please tend my trees while I'm away."[15]

Translators Francis and Thomas (1916) give the story the title of "The Stupid Monkeys."[16] Perhaps Babbitt obtained her title from theirs.

The Vile Monkey and the Patient Buffalo
(from India)

There was once a large and powerful old buffalo that ranged over the countryside—up and down hills and mountains, in cool dark caves, and through overgrown and tangled forests. One day he found a tree where he thought he could relax beneath its shade and browse the grass in peace.

Suddenly, a brash monkey dropped from the tree onto the buffalo's back where he squatted and dropped a nasty mess. Then twisting his tail around one of the buffalo's horns, the monkey swung to the ground and capered and danced and made ugly faces as if what he had done were a great joke. Being patient and kind, the buffalo, however, paid no attention to this rude behavior. Over and over, the monkey acted the same way whenever the buffalo rested beneath the tree.

One day, the spirit that lived within the tree appeared outside its trunk and asked, "Buffalo, why do you endure the behavior of this hateful monkey? You could easily put a stop to his antics by goring him with your horns or crushing him beneath your hooves."

The buffalo quietly replied, "Ah, Spirit of the Tree, if another buffalo should take my place, the monkey would act the same, believing the new buffalo would be as patient and enduring as I. But if he behaves this way to a fierce buffalo, then the monkey will receive his just reward. Thus, when another destroys him, I shall be free not only from the monkey's insults but also from any blame for ending his life."

A few days later, the old buffalo happened to go elsewhere to browse, and another one came and stood beneath the tree. Believing him to be same buffalo, the monkey climbed down, squatted on his back, and behaved just as he had before. But the new buffalo shook himself violently and, when the monkey fell to the ground, drove a sharp horn through his heart and trampled him to pieces with hard hooves.

COMMENTARY: The source for this retelling is "Mahisa-Jataka."[17] The Bodhisattva has been reborn as a buffalo and teaches the Buddhist concept of dharma or acting in accordance with one's role in life and accepting it as the basis for one's actions. The old buffalo acts in accordance with his nature of patience and kindness, and the new, fierce buffalo acts in accordance with his. Thus, each fulfills the moral law of the universe, and justice is brought to the insolent monkey who has implicitly fulfilled his role as well.

The Brahmin and the Monkey
(from India)

Long ago, there was a man from a devout family who followed the Brahmin practices of goodness and mercy. Along the roadside near his village was a deep well where people went to draw water by a long rope with a bucket. A dense forest filled with monkeys and other wild animals surrounded the village.

Because the well was the only source of water for many miles around, the custom was that those who went there, after refreshing themselves with water, would pour some in a trough so that the animals might have something to drink. Unfortunately, the water in the well ran low and remained that way for several days so that the trough stood empty and the animals had nothing to quench their thirst.

During this time, the Brahmin passed by the well on his way to complete some errand, and being thirsty, drew enough water for himself to drink and wash his hands. Off to his side, he noticed a monkey eyeing his actions. Thinking the creature thirsty, he kindly brought up more water and poured it into the trough. He then sat under a nearby tree to watch what the monkey would do. The monkey ran to the trough, and, having satisfied his thirst, climbed onto a limb, looked down at the Brahmin, and made an awful face, baring sharp fangs to frighten him.

"Ah, you ungrateful monkey," said the Brahmin. "I relieved your thirst, and now you chatter and make threatening faces at me. I should have known how a miserable rogue like you would thank me for my help."

The monkey continued to stare and make faces, before he answered, "There is yet more that I can do."

Hearing the beast's spiteful words, the Brahmin rose to leave. But at that very moment, the monkey let his rank droppings fall upon the man's head, then jumped off the branch, and ran into the forest, loudly shrieking as he called out these words:

> Before you gave me water, well you knew
> What I, as a monkey, was apt to do.

COMMENTARY: This fable derives from "Dubhiya-Makkata-Jataka."[18] Here, the Bodhisattva was reborn as a virtuous Brahmin. His archenemy, Devadatta, who is also his cousin and brother-in-law, returns as the insolent monkey. Devadatta figures in several Jatakas. His attempts to become an *arhat* (an enlightened one) came to naught so that he could not attain nirvana. He, therefore, tried to divide the *sangha*, or brotherhood of believers, against the Master.

As in the previous Jataka about the kind old buffalo, the Brahmin this time is the recipient of the monkey's dropped feces and, like the buffalo, interprets the action as disrespectful. However, according to an article in the online publication *TheGunZone*, certain real monkeys will throw their feces for a variety of reasons, whether to defend themselves, to mark territory, to establish dominance, or to cope with stress and fear. The article notes that, in regard to people, this behavior occurs when monkeys are in captivity. While the practice is unpleasant and unsanitary, it is not necessarily harmful.[19]

The Heroic Monkey's Self-Sacrifice
(from India)

A powerful and worthy monkey king with eighty thousand followers once lived in the Himalayas near the Ganges River. Along its banks grew an enormous mango tree with a canopy of thick branches and leaves the size of a mountaintop. The scent of its flavorful, sweet fruit, as large as water pots, filled the air. From one branch, the mangoes fell on the ground. From a second, they dropped into the river, and from a third, they lodged into the two main trunks. From this great tree, the troop feasted.

One day, the monkey king thought, "Eventually, danger will come upon us because of the fruit that falls into the water." He, therefore, commanded his followers to leave no fruit upon this branch and to destroy its flowers when they bloomed so that no mangoes might grow there. Yet one ripe fruit, hidden in the foliage, escaped the eyes of the monkeys and dropped into the river where it floated downstream.

Eventually, the mango became caught in a net above where the King of Benares was bathing for relaxation. When he had finished that evening, his servants pulled in the net and found the mango. No one knew what kind of fruit it was because none of them had ever seen it before. When they showed it to the king, he asked, "What kind of fruit is this?"

"We do not know, your majesty, but perhaps your servants who tend the forest can tell us."

So the king had his foresters called, and they told him the fruit was a mango. The king then took his knife and sliced it open, but before eating the fruit, he had his foresters and some of the members of his court sample it. As no one became sick or died, the king tasted it. The flavor seemed to fill his entire body with sweetness.

Wanting more, the king asked his foresters, "Where is the tree that bears such delicious fruit?"

"It stands up the sacred river in the region of the Himalayas," they answered.

The king then ordered many rafts lashed together, and he with his court and a large section of his army sailed upstream. When they came to the gigantic tree, they landed and walked beneath its shade. There, the king ate to his heart's delight, and when he could eat no more, he rested on a bed his servants had prepared. When night fell, the soldiers built a fire and posted guards around the camp. The guards' eyes soon grew heavy with drowsiness as sleep cast its spell over the camp.

At midnight, the monkey ruler and his troop of eighty thousand moved silently from branch to branch and began to devour the mangoes. Suddenly, the King of Benares awoke and beheld by the dim firelight the host above his head. Rousing his men, he commanded his archers, "Surround these beasts so that none may escape. Tomorrow, we shall dine on mangoes and monkey flesh!" The archers obeyed and, with their arrows ready, surrounded the tree.

Seeing what occurred, the monkeys knew they could not escape. In fear, they went to their leader and trembling said, "Sire, the archers stand ready to kill us at first light. What are we to do?"

The monkey king replied, "Fear not. I will save you."

So saying, he climbed a limb that rose straight up, then went along another branch that stretched over the Ganges. Jumping from it, he landed on the opposite bank and noted the length he had leapt. "That is how far I have jumped," he said to himself and cut down a thick bamboo shoot the length he judged the distance to be. One end he tied to his waist with a braided vine.

Leaving the other end secured to the bank, the monkey king jumped back across the river toward the outstretched branch. Unfortunately, he had misjudged the distance by forgetting to add the length of bamboo attached to his waist and could only reach the limb of the mango tree with his front paws. He realized his mistake and held on to the branch tightly with his hands. However, he called out to his followers, "Run quickly along my back until you reach the safety of the opposite bank." Doing as their king requested, the eighty thousand monkeys escaped across the river. Yet their treading upon his back caused their leader almost unbearable pain.

Watching from below, the King of Benares in the dim pre-dawn light saw everything that took place and said to the men around him, "This monkey, not thinking of his own life, has saved his followers."

When dawn broke, so pleased was the king with the leader of the monkeys, he thought, "It would be wrong to destroy this animal. I must somehow rescue him and see that he is cared for."

So the King of Benares had a raft placed under the limb from where the monkey still clung and had a platform built to reach him. The king then had his servants gently bring the monkey down, wash him in the Ganges, give him sugared water to drink, and clothe him in a silken yellow robe.

The king next had the monkey placed on a soft bed where he could rest. Sitting beside him, the king said, "You made yourself a bridge so that your herd could escape my archers' arrows. What are you to your followers and they to you for you do such a thing?"

In a weak voice, the monkey answered, "Great king, you have conquered me. Yet know that, as leader of my troop, my only concern was to protect them in their fear. Even though death should be my reward, my sole concern was their happiness and safety." So saying, the monkey king died.

On hearing these words, the King of Benares called his chief men together and ordered that the monkey should be given all burial rites and honors due to a noble ruler. So, in a royal manner, the king and his court mourned for seven days. They built a magnificent shrine to house the monkey's remains. They hung garlands of flowers and burned torches and incense both day and night. And for the rest of his days, the King of Benares followed the monkey's example, performing worthy deeds for his people's happiness and living a life of goodness and lovingkindness.

COMMENTARY: Unlike many of the other monkey fables in the *Jatakas*, this selection portrays a monkey as having the same noble qualities of character displayed by Hanuman in the *Ramayana*. As I have suggested in the introduction, the reason for this depiction is that the monkey king is one of the animal rebirths of Gautama Siddhartha on his way to breaking the cycle of death and rebirth before he achieves final enlightenment as Buddha. Like the patient old buffalo in one of the previous stories, the monkey acts in accord with important moral virtues and provides an example of right living for others. "Mahakapi-Jataka" is the source for this adaptation.[20]

The Monkey Who Outwitted a Water Ogre
(from India)

Long ago, a dense forest surrounded a lake, and in the lake lived a water ogre who ate everyone who went into the water to drink. This forest was also home to a band of eighty thousand monkeys and their king, who was really Buddha. He had come to life as their as their leader and protector.

The king often cautioned his subjects, "My friends, within this forest are poisonous trees and lakes where ogres lie in wait to devour anyone who drinks the water. Be sure to advise me before you eat any fruit or drink from any lake you have not previously sampled."

One day, the king and his troop wandered into the part of the forest where the lake of the water ogre was. They had never been there before. As the monkeys had traveled for a long time, they were thirsty, but recalling their leader's words, they refused to drink and waited for his counsel.

"My friends," said the monkey king, "you are wise to wait." He then walked around the shore and looked at the footprints. "Truly," he mused, "an ogre lives within the lake." On returning to his subjects, he again praised their caution. "You were indeed right not to drink, for the water is haunted by an ogre. Many footprints go into the water, but none come out."

From the lake's depths, the ogre spied upon the monkeys and realized that they would not enter his realm. He, therefore, changed into a terrible monster with a white face, a blue belly, and red hands and feet and came out of the lake to challenge them. "Why do you wait and not enter and drink?" he asked.

The monkey king replied, "Are you not the ogre of the lake, and do you not prey upon all those who enter to drink from it?"

"Yes," came the answer. "From the smallest birds to the largest beasts, I devour anything that comes down to my water. And I will eat all of you as well. Just drink, and you shall see!"

The monkey king responded, "We will drink your water, but you will not eat us."

"Foolish monkey! How do you propose to drink and defy my power?"

"Before this day is over, you will see how eighty thousand monkeys will drink and never enter the lake at all. You will never eat us," the monkey king calmly said.

"I will wait for you in my lair," and so saying, the ogre returned to the water and disappeared.

The monkey king now called for his subjects to bring him bamboo canes that grew beside the lake. Taking one, he blew down its length, and it became completely hollow without a single knot to interrupt the flow of his breath. He did the same with another cane and yet another until there were enough hollow canes for his entire troop.

The king next sat on the lakeshore with one end of a cane in his hands and the other end in the water. As they gazed upon their leader, his followers did likewise. The moment that he drew water through his cane, they did the same with theirs. Thus, sitting safely on the bank, they satisfied their thirst.

As for the outwitted water ogre, he withdrew in a rage to the middle of the lake. In this way, the monkey king provided for his subjects.

COMMENTARY: This adaptation comes from "Nalapana-Jataka."[21] As with other Jatakas, the clever main character is Buddha reincarnated and thus does not display the negative traits of monkeys when they are portrayed as animals that lack the moral and spiritual qualities of the Enlightened One. In Francis and Thomas' 1916 collection, the title appears as "The Monkeys and the Ogre."[22]

The Lessons of the Meddling Monkey and the Unheeded Bird
(from the Panchatantra of India and the Middle East)

There was once a lion that ruled all the wild animals of a local forest and the isolated valley within it. He was a proud ruler and preferred to rely on his own advice above all others.

Into this kingdom, a powerful bull named Shanzabeh had wandered to eat the tall sweet grass growing along the banks of the river that flowed through the valley. From his grazing, the bull grew even larger and stronger, his sleek neck thick with muscle and fat.

Because no other bulls or cows were there to keep him company, Shanzabeh would bellow so loudly that the noise echoed up and down the river and throughout the surrounding woods and hills. During these moments of loneliness, he would also stick his horns here and there as he pawed and stabbed at the ground. King Lion had never seen a bull before, much less heard such a frightful din. He decided, therefore, to remain within his cave to avoid whatever beast it was that made these terrible sounds.

Among the animals that served the lion were two jackals, both clever brothers named Kalila and Dimna. Because the lion now kept within his den, they grew concerned for his welfare. One day, as they warmed themselves in the morning sun, Dimna asked Kalila, "Why does our king never venture out as he once did? Is it not odd that he no longer leaves his lair to prowl and hunt?"

Kalila answered, "As the king's servants, our concern is to attend him and to follow his commands, not to meddle in his private business."

"Yes," said Dimna, "but I fear he refuses to leave his den because he is afraid of the huge beast that now roams the valley and bellows fiercely. Should we not offer the king our advice in the matter?"

Kalila responded with questions of his own. "Brother, have you lost your senses? In truth, have you little or no concern for your own life? We live here in comfort in the lion's cave. Let us not delve into why he acts as he does or disturb him with our counsel. You are like that monkey who meddled in what he did not understand and who suffered for his actions."

Dimna replied, "I do not know this tale. How does it go?" And here Kalila proceeded to tell his brother the monkey's story.

A pet monkey watched a carpenter who sat on a thick log and worked to split it in half. With a heavy mallet, he drove small wooden wedges into the log to make it crack a bit along its length. He stood up, inserted some larger wedges to keep the log from closing again, and knocked out the smaller ones. With his sledgehammer, he then pounded the bigger wedges into the log so that it split completely apart.

In this way, the carpenter halved several logs until he was tired and stopped to go and eat his midday meal. But before going, he left behind a log partially split, having driven into it two smaller wedges along one end. The monkey now came forward and straddled the log just as he had seen the man do. With his back to the crack and his face toward the wedges, his legs rested on each side while his behind sat snugly on the log and his tail hung down in the middle of the gap.

The monkey then grabbed the mallet and raised it over his head. But it was so heavy he could barely control it and clumsily sent the wedges flying out of the split. The log suddenly closed, crushing his tail along with his vital parts. At once, the monkey fell back howling as if suffering the most hideous tortures. Hearing the uproar, the monkey's master ran back, saw what the beast had done, and straightway gave him such a severe thrashing for his stupid meddling that the poor creature fainted from the pain.

When Kalila ended his story, Dimna paid not the least attention to the wisdom it contained. He left to worm his way into the king's confidence and obtained his permission to bring Shanzabeh to court to give an account of himself as a stranger in the realm. To the jackal's surprise and dismay, when the bull arrived, he instantly became friends with King Lion. In fact, the king liked his new friend so much that he bestowed upon him great honors and high titles. Over time, the bonds between the two grew stronger, making the jackal extremely jealous. He could think of nothing but how to destroy the bull.

When any private chance arose, Dimna began to tell falsehoods about Shanzabeh, at first only small ones to sow doubt in the king's mind. These became bigger and bigger until the jackal claimed the bull's secret purpose was to overthrow the kingdom, murder its rightful ruler, and become king himself. The lion eventually believed the crafty jackal's lies and started to see his grass-eating friend as a deadly menace.

Despite Dimna's continued attempts to destroy Shanzabeh, Kalila still counseled his brother to cease his evil plot. One day, as Kalila sat upon his haunches, he said to Dimna, "I am not sure why I bother to caution you against your scheming. My words are like dust blown away by the slightest wind. They are as useless as the advice of the bird who tried to help a stupid monkey."

Dimna bared his teeth and snarled slightly. "I fear you are about to tell me another story."

"Yes, that is my intention," Kalila said, "although its message will likely be wasted as with the one before."

"If you must," Dimna answered and scratched with his hind leg at an annoying flea biting his left ear as Kalila began.

> A band of monkeys once lived happily enough on a forested mountainside. They had plenty of nuts, fruits, roots, insects, and other kinds of monkey food to eat—that is, until winter came. Its bitter winds left them hungry, cold, and miserable.
>
> As the monkeys huddled together for warmth, one of the larger members of the troop spied a tiny light in a nearby bush. Being curious, he went to find out what it was. Although it was only a glowworm, he thought it an ember from which he could start a fire to keep himself and the others warm. So he slapped at the glowworm, knocked it to the ground, and started to pile dry leaves on top of it. His fellow simians saw what he did and trooped over jibber-jabbering noisily.
>
> Observing them from a tree close by, a bird piped out, "You silly monkeys, that's no way to light a fire. It's a glowworm, not a glowing ember."
>
> The monkeys paid not the least attention to the bird and ran here and there, gathering more dead leaves and twigs to pile on the little worm. As they did, the big monkey huffed and puffed, blowing as hard as he could to

kindle a flame. With their hopes raised, his companions stood around the pile and held out their paws expecting to be warmed.

Such ignorance proved too much for the nosy bird. He fluttered down from the tree and landed beside the big panting monkey. "As I said before, you can't make a fire from a glowworm. It's a shiny bug, not a hot coal. It just won't work."

The monkey ceased huffing and puffing and cocked his head sideways, staring at the scolding busybody. Then reaching out, he grabbed the bird in one hand and with the other twisted his neck until his head popped off.

When Kalila finished his fable, Dimna turned his head and began biting at another flea along his side, all the while snapping furiously as he tried to kill it. He then got up and walked away toward the lion's den to spread further lies.

Now convinced more than ever of Shanzabeh's plot against him, the king waited for the right moment to destroy the bull. This came one day when the lion had summoned Shanzabeh to meet him beside a huge banyan tree that grew in the valley.

As the bull drew near, King Lion pounced. He barely missed one of Shanzabeh's great horns and landed on his back, roaring in rage as he clawed and bit deeply into the bull's flesh. Running toward a tree, Shanzabeh scraped the lion against an overhanging limb and sent him tumbling to the ground. Yet the king of beasts quickly recovered and sprang again, this time clamping his teeth in a deadly grip over Shanzabeh's muzzle. Struggling for air, the bull grew dizzy, stood trembling for several minutes, then toppled over, the light slowly fading from his eyes as he suffocated.

Kalila witnessed the entire spectacle. Thoroughly disgusted at Dimna's lies and the evil they had brought about, he could bear the presence of his brother no longer and parted from him, never to see him again. As for the lion, he soon came to regret what he had done and mourned the killing of his friend Shanzabeh.

In time, the meddlesome deceit of Dimna became known to the king. He had the jackal put in heavy chains and thrown into a narrow prison cell. There, he received neither food nor water and slowly starved to death.

COMMENTARY: This adaptation of these two stories comes from the first book of the ancient Sanskrit text *The Panchatantra* which means "five treatises." Paul Lunde says that it was "a bestseller for almost two thousand years" and is "still read with pleasure all over the Arab world."[23] Its structure and the fables within it have great overlap with another ancient Sanskrit work, *The Hitopadesa*, meaning the "book of good counsels."

Although the original Sanskrit version of *The Panchatantra* appeared in Kashmir around 300 to 200 BCE, the stories compiled and arranged within it are much older and like the *Jatakas* come from the oral tradition of India. Translated many times over the millennia in many countries, *The Panchatantra* was intended as a guidebook of practical wisdom for princes and potentates. *Kalila and Dimna*, the longest of its five books, was translated into Arabic around 750 CE from Pahlavi, or Old Persian, and became a major source for translations that found their way into Europe through the Muslims of Spain.

Among the three sources consulted for the adaptation "The Lessons of the Meddlesome Monkey and the Unheeded Bird" is Sir Thomas North's 1570 translation of *The Fables of Bidpai*, which was the earliest version to appear in English.[24] North based it on Anton Francesco Doni's Italian rendition of a Latin translation printed in 1480. This book, in turn, derived from Rabbi Joel's translation into Hebrew of the 750 Arabic version *Kalila and Dimna*. According to Doris Lessing, North's book was "popular reading" in renaissance England.[25]

The second version examined is I.G.N. Keith-Falconer's translation titled *Kalilah and Dimnah or The Fables of Bidpai*. A Scottish missionary to Aden on the Arabian peninsula, Keith-Falconer was also a scholar of the Semitic languages of Hebrew, Arabic, and Syriac. His career as professor of Arabic at Cambridge was all too brief as a result of his contracting malaria while in Aden. He died in 1887 at the age of thirty-one.[26] As for his translation of *Kalilah and Dimnah or the Fables of Bidpai*, he describes it as "a literal rendering" from Syriac based on the Arabic version.[27] Its first selection is "The Story of the Lion and the Ox." Embedded within it are the two fables that I have retold.[28]

The third source consulted for my adaptations is Ramsey Wood's *Kalila and Dimna: Selected Fables of Bidpai* published in 1980.[29] Wood indicates that he based his retelling on eight earlier versions rendered into English and gives particular credit to the translation of Sir Thomas North, as edited and introduced by Joseph Jacobs, and to supplemental information in Keith-Falconer's work.[30]

In "The Story of the Lion and the Ox," the jackal brothers, Kalila and Dimna, appear as servants and advisers to a lion king. Kalila is the more restrained and wiser of the two, while Dimna is one of the more odious tricksters in folklore. Through vicious deceit and treachery, he successfully finagles to destroy the friendship between the lion king and the ox or bull, Shanzabeh, much to the horror of Kalila, who, early in the narrative, relates the story of a meddlesome monkey as a warning about what happens to those who intrude themselves into affairs beyond their capabilities.

Recounting other fables, Kalila attempts to impart additional wisdom to his brother. One of these stories is about a nosy bird that offers advice to a troop of monkeys. His words go unheeded, and one of the big monkeys kills the intrusive bird despite his informative efforts. Like the big monkey, Dimna, too, never heeds Kalila's counsel and throughout the larger narrative interposes fables of own as counter arguments.

I have retained the framing of the stories about the meddling monkey and unheeded bird within the larger narrative about Kalila and Dimna to impart the original structure surrounding the two embedded fables. When adapted for younger readers, the stories are usually rendered as stand-alone folktales and exclude the more intricate structural aspects of *The Fables of Bidpai*. For instance, Wiggin and Smith's adaptations of eleven of its fables in *The Talking Beasts* follows this streamlined format. However, their retellings do embed morals at the end of each, occasionally in verse form, much like the arrangement of the ancient texts. "The Hermit, the Thief, and the Demon" closes with the following didactic couplet:

> When the two hostile armies fall to strife,
> Then from the sheath what need to draw the knife.[31]

The Story of Prince Rama
(from the Ramayana of India)

The Birth of Rama and His Brothers

In India, the beautiful city of Ayodhya once stood along the banks of a wide river. The tall spires of its magnificent temples rose so high into the air they seemed to kiss the heavens. A wide moat surrounded the city and protected its people who lived together in peace, with each person working in harmony for the common good. The priests devoted themselves to studying and teaching the wisdom of the ancient scriptures. The farmers provided abundant food. The merchants sold all the goods the inhabitants needed or wished to buy. The warriors safeguarded them, and the magistrates ruled with fairness and justice for everyone.

Yet, despite these circumstances that would seem to make life perfect, the king of Ayodhya was not happy. For even though he had reigned many years, he had no son to take his place when he should die.

One day the king summoned his chief priest and said, "I am growing old and wish more than anything for a son to inherit my throne."

The priest understood his master's need and replied, "Oh, King, you will indeed have many sons. But you must first go to the temple and perform a sacred ceremony of sacrificial fire that will make the gods pleased to grant your wish."

Overjoyed by these words, the king hurried to his three wives to share the good news, saying to them, "Sons shall be mine at last."

Meanwhile, as these events occurred, the gods' anger had increased against Ravana, the cruel lord of the demons and ruler of the large island of Lanka south of India. With ten heads and twenty arms, the Demon King possessed great powers, and now he and his subjects were using these to keep the holy men from their prayers.

Aware of these evil deeds, Vishnu, the guardian of the universe and protector of all that is in it, decided that the Demon King must be destroyed. To kill this monster, however, would be no easy task. For Ravana had a special gift that allowed him to defend himself against the gods. He had never considered humans or monkeys as a threat. So Vishnu cleverly decided that he would be born as a human being and that in this form he would destroy the wicked demon. But first Vishnu would send the Fire God, Agni, as a messenger to Ayodhya.

At the very moment that the king was performing the fire ceremony and praying for children, Agni arrived. Radiant in appearance, he stepped from the firepit and offered the king a bowl of sweetened milk and rice. "Give this to each of your wives," said the Fire God, "and each of your wives will bear you sons." The magnificent figure then vanished.

The king did as Agni instructed, and when his wives drank the potion, they each glowed from the life of a child growing within. The eldest queen gave birth to Rama, the first son. The second queen gave birth to the twin boys, Lakshmana and Shatrughna. And the third queen, who was the youngest and the king's favorite, bore a fourth son, Bharata. The father's heart filled with joy, and there was great rejoicing throughout the land.

As the four sons grew, they became tall, strong, handsome, and brave princes. Each was intelligent and applied himself readily to the study of the sacred writings. The brothers respected the elders and the holy men, and the welfare of the people was always their foremost concern. The twins, Lakshmana and Shatrughna, were especially close to each other and seemed like two people who inhabited the same body. Although the king loved his four sons dearly, Rama, his firstborn, was his favorite, so much so that the father could not bear to be parted from him even for a brief time.

Rama's Early Adventures

When Rama was nearly sixteen years of age, one of the country's wise men came to visit the king. The monarch held the utmost respect for the great sage. "Welcome, oh, Wise One," said the king. "Tell me why you honor us with your visit."

Pleased with this greeting, the man replied, "You are known far and wide for keeping your word. I have come to ask a favor."

"State your request, and it shall be granted," said the king.

"I have been trying to perform a sacred fire ceremony. But two demons under Ravana's rule disturb the ritual. With blood and human flesh, they pollute the firepit, but as a holy man, I cannot cast a curse on them. I ask that you permit me to take Prince Rama with me for ten days so that he might destroy the demons. Only then can I perform the rite of the sacred fire."

The king listened thoughtfully and paused before he answered. "Great Sage, Rama is not yet sixteen years old. He is still a boy. Let me send my soldiers to fight these demons. I will lead the warriors myself, and if need be, I shall battle the demons with my own weapons. But please do not ask for Rama alone to go with you. I cannot live without him even for a few moments." So saying, the father began to weep.

The sage felt the king's heartbreak, but he had no other choice, for the holy man knew that Rama was really Vishnu who had come to earth as a human being. The sage also knew that only the god in human form could destroy Ravana and put an end to the demon's evils. So in his wisdom, the sage responded, "Oh, Great King, no one but Rama can help me. Do not go back on your promise."

At first the king was unwilling to grant the request, but eventually he agreed to send Rama as well as Lakshmana who wanted to go with his brother. They departed with the holy man. Like him, the brothers walked barefooted to show their respect. They crossed one wide river, then another. During the long journey with their guide, the brothers learned valuable skills in the art of how to kill demons.

After many days, the party entered a gloomy forest. Here the sage explained, "This country was once beautiful and thrived in plenty. But now the she-demon, Taraka, has laid waste to it. She kills all who enter here."

Unafraid, Prince Rama nocked his bow, and he and his brother followed the holy man into the forest depths. Mysterious and frightful sounds attended their every step. All of a sudden, they heard a terrible roar that froze them in their tracks. Then a huge boulder fell from the sky straight toward them. Rama drew his bow just as the rock was about to strike. His mighty arrow cut the rock in half, and the pieces broke apart, hurting no one.

Then the trees began to shake with a violent motion, and coming toward the three was the gigantic she-demon, Taraka, hideous beyond words. A human skull hung from her neck. Long, sharp talons adorned her fingers. A low, deep growl issued from her throat. She charged immediately at Rama, but his brother was ready. Lakshmana fired an arrow and severely wounded the monster.

Feeling the arrowhead cut through her flesh, Taraka covered the wound with her hand and groaned, "What man has done this?" And before she could say more, Rama aimed his bow at Taraka's heart and killed her. At once the heavens poured down lotus blossoms on Rama and blessed him.

The three travelers continued their journey. With the sage's help, Rama and Lakshmana killed many other demons within the forest and further honed their battle skills. Finally, the little band had rid the forest of evil so that the sage and the other holy men there were able to perform the sacred fire ceremony. Yet it was one thing to destroy Ravana's subjects. It would be quite another to kill the Demon King himself.

The Shiva Bow and Princess Sita

At last, Rama and the others left the forest and entered another realm. Its king knew the sage who had guided Rama thus far, and on greeting the holy man asked him, "Have you heard of my daughter?"

"No," responded the sage, "but I would like to learn about her."

So the king told about his beautiful daughter Sita. "When she was a child, I found her in a plowed field and adopted her as my own. She was a gift from the gods. She has grown into a beautiful young woman with much strength of heart and holiness. Now that she has become old enough to marry, I have announced a contest. Whoever can string the ancient bow of the great god Shiva—he who destroys but also recreates—will win her hand."

The sage turned to Prince Rama, "I would like for you to lift the bow and bend it to the string."

The king thought to himself, "Many have tried, and all have failed. Even Ravana came here and failed. Like all the others, when he attempted to pick up the bow, he could not lift it and collapsed, then quickly left in shame." Yet the king would not deny Rama a chance because he could see the young man's noble bearing.

Rama entered a magnificent hall, filled with thousands of princes and nobles. Many of these had tried to lift the bow. They watched as

Rama approached it. He looked at the weapon and noted its beautiful design. He next rubbed his hand over it, admiring it still more. Then with a heart empty of pride, without the least effort, he hoisted the mighty Shiva bow and began to string it. Suddenly, like a child's plaything, it snapped in two and fell to the floor. The onlookers turned pale in awe. They could not believe what they had seen. At once, everyone cheered and chanted, "Rama! Rama! Rama!"

The king announced, "Princess Sita has found her spouse. Send a messenger to Rama's father to tell him that his son will wed my daughter."

Delighted to hear the news, Rama's father came with his wives and other members of his court to attend the wedding. Not only did Rama wed Sita, but Lakshmana and the other two brothers took wives as well. A grand feast was held for people from all over the kingdom, and everyone offered blessings to the newly married couples.

Along with his brothers and their wives, Rama and Sita left for his homeland, and when they arrived, its citizens celebrated the weddings anew. Sita was a devoted wife, and she and Rama seemed to be meant for each other. The people loved Rama and his brothers, but they especially loved Rama, and in this knowledge, the heart of his father rejoiced.

A Reversal of Fortune

Rama continued to grow in goodness. Though he could do nothing but what was right, he was patient when others did wrong. He respected the elders and honored the sages. He learned and applied their wisdom drawn from the holy books. He possessed great intelligence and untold courage. As a warrior, he knew when to take up arms and when to lay them aside. In truth, he was becoming the perfect man.

After several years, Rama's father realized that the time had come to choose a successor. He spoke to his advisors, and they agreed wholeheartedly with his decision that Rama should take his place. The king immediately announced his choice to the people. "It is my wish to crown my eldest son." Great rejoicing spread throughout the land at the news, and elaborate preparations began at once for the coronation.

During this time, Rama's brothers Bharata and Shatrugna were away from the city and were unaware of their father's announcement. Rama's mother and the king's other wives were delighted that Rama was soon to be crowned. However, the youngest queen's old nursemaid, Manthara, worked to poison her mistress against Rama.

"My queen, do you not recall that you, too, have a son? Does not Bharata deserve a share in the kingdom? Once Rama is crowned, the old queen, his mother, in her pride will consider herself above you. You will be a servant to her, and Rama will be lord over your son, Bharata. Is it fair that you, the king's favorite wife, should suffer such treatment?"

"Why should this matter concern me?" answered the young queen. "Is not Rama the first born? Is he not a strong, brave, and good man, full of wisdom? Besides, the people love Rama, and to be honest, I love him more dearly than my own son."

But Manthara refused to halt her plea. With sweet words, she said, "I am old. My years have made me wise enough to know how the world works. Your love for Rama is misplaced. If he becomes king, his mother will control him, and your position as favorite will end. Awake from your dream and act. Convince the old king that your son should rule."

The young queen thought about her servant's words. She did not mind that Rama might become king, but she could not bear to have his mother placed above her. She replied to Manthara, "How can I prevent Rama from being crowned?"

The old nurse answered, "Have your husband send him away from the palace and into the forest."

"Yet how?" asked the queen.

"Recall that years ago the king was hurt in a war against his enemies and lay wounded in his chariot. You drove him from the field of battle and saved his life. He then offered to grant you two wishes. Now you must ask for them," Manthara urged. "Demand that Bharata be made king and that Rama be sent away."

The night before Rama's coronation, the king came to his youngest wife to share his happiness about his son's succeeding him. As they talked, she began to speak of the past. "My husband, do you recall that grim day when I saved your life after you had fallen in your chariot? How I stopped your runaway horses and took you to safety?"

"Yes, my beloved," said the king. "I recall."

"And do you remember what you promised me that day?" Without pausing, she continued, "Oh, great king and husband, you promised me two wishes. I ask that you grant them now."

"Have no doubt I will keep my word," he replied.

"First, place our son Bharata upon the throne. And after that, send Rama into the forest and forbid him to return for fourteen years. Otherwise, my life must end."

With dismay, the king heard his young wife's requests. He dropped to his knees before her, the color draining from his face. "Do not hold me to these terrible wishes," he pled. "Surely, this must be a joke of some kind."

"No, I am serious," said the queen and laughed cruelly.

Overcome with emotion, the king fainted, and when he revived, he pled once more. "My queen, give up these dreadful requests. Long have you said that you love Rama as if he were your own. How can I ask Rama to forsake the crown and go into the forest? There, no soft bed invites sleep, thorns fill the paths, and savage tigers and panthers roam. I cannot bear to be away from my son for fourteen years. Do not torture me in my old age. Let me crown Bharata king, but do not separate me from my firstborn for such a long time."

All night the king remained in the young queen's chamber. Despite his pleas, she would not change her mind. The morning dawned, with the whole city preparing for the coronation. The king sent for Rama, and when he came, his father whispered through his tears, "Rama, Rama, my beloved son," but the grief-stricken old man could say no more.

Quietly, Rama asked, "Father, why do I find you pale and speechless?" The old king could not reply, so his young wife answered for him and told Rama about the two wishes and his father's decision.

The prince did not argue and offered comfort. "Father, your word is sacred. I shall do as you bid. For it is my duty to respect and obey you." To the young queen, he said, "Have Bharata return to the city, and I shall go to the forest today to live the life of a hermit. I request that you give me enough time to tell my mother and my wife." So saying, he knelt before his father and the queen and touched their feet with respect. He then left the room.

When Rama told his mother the news, she begged him to take her to live with him in the forest, but he refused. The reaction of his brother Lakshmana, who was also present, was quite different. He became enraged and shouted, "Why is our father banishing you for fourteen years? If he fears Bharata and his supporters, I will rid the earth of them."

With clear and simple words, Rama replied, "Our father must keep his word. My duty is to respect and obey him so that he can fulfill his promises. Neither you nor I would be worthy to be called his sons should we disobey."

"Your words are true, my brother, but if you must leave the city, I will go with you," vowed Lakshmana.

Rama then went to inform Sita. On hearing that Bharata would be crowned king and that her husband was to be banished, she tried to set him at ease. "My lord, I am your shadow. I go wherever you go. Life within this palace is nothing if I am not with you." Though Rama wished her to remain behind, Sita was determined to follow him wherever he might go and however difficult the journey.

Before Rama, Sita, and Lakhmana left the palace, they laid aside their soft royal robes and put on the rough clothes of the poor and holy, though the brothers took their weapons of swords, bows, and arrows for protection. The news of the departure had already spread throughout the city. As the three walked, barefooted and dressed as hermits, the people wept at the sad scene. "How cruel is fate," they thought. "How can only three face the dangers of the savage forest?"

As the little band passed from his sight, the old king cried out in a feeble voice, "Rama, my son, do not leave me!" At that moment, the will to live left him. His heart could not bear the loss, and he later died.

Bharata's Search for Rama

After several days of walking, Rama, Sita, and Lakshmana came to the Ganges River and crossed it. Hoping to disappear so that no one could find them, they soon reached a place with many trees and waterways. There, they built a little hut beside a slow-moving, peaceful stream. Paradise seemed to surround them. Delicious fruits grew abundantly on every vine. Beautiful sounds of songbirds enchanted their ears. The scent of fragrant flowers and the sight of bright butterflies filled the air.

One day, as Lakshmana hunted in the forest, he felt the earth tremble with the pounding hooves of countless horses. Believing that a great army approached, he climbed a tree. To his surprise, he saw that the front rider carried the royal flag of Ayodhya. Lakshmana's mind raced, and he said to himself, "This must be the army of Bharata. He has come to kill us."

Lakshmana at once reported to Rama. "A large army led by Bharata approaches. He has come to make certain you will never be king. We must prepare to fight, and I must kill him first, or he will surely kill you."

Rama calmly answered, "Lakshmana, you are mistaken. Bharata has likely come here to ask that I return to the palace. We must welcome him, for he is our brother and our king."

As Bharata neared, he called out, "My brothers and Sita, my dear sister, my heart is heavy with sadness and shame." And running to them, he embraced them and said, "Our noble father is dead from a broken heart." On hearing this news, their eyes filled with tears.

Bharata then told how he had discovered the wrong his mother had committed against Rama. "I learned how my mother's servant, Manthara, had poisoned my mother against you. Our brother Shatrugna wanted me to punish the old woman. And yet I could not treat her cruelly. And though my mother has repented of her action, I came here to set right her evil deed of sending you away for fourteen years. I ask that each of you return home with me. Rama is our true king."

"I cannot go back and break my word," said Rama. "Only after my exile of fourteen years is completed can I return." Although Bharata continued to plead, nothing could sway the prince.

At last, Bharata realized that Rama would not break his promises, so he begged his brother for the sandals he still carried with him. "These will be a sign that I rule the kingdom in your name and that I represent you only. If you do not come back when your exile is over, I shall walk into a fire and die."

Rama agreed to this request, and with great reverence, Bharata took the sandals back to the capital. There he placed them upon the throne and ruled in Rama's name. Bharata refused to stay in the palace and lived as one who possesses nothing, eager for the moment when his brother would return as rightful king.

The Dandaka Forest

After several days had lapsed, Rama, Sita, and Lakshmana journeyed southwest. They lived in various places for a few months and sometimes for a year. During this time, Lakshmana found many suitable sites to build shelters for them before they continued their travels. In this manner, thirteen years of Rama's exile passed.

During the summer of the fourteenth year, they arrived at the forest of Dandaka. It was the frontier of Ravana, the Demon King. Once a beautiful place, it was now a thirsty, dry jungle, littered with dead and dying trees. A hot wind seemed to warn anyone who approached it not to enter, and anyone who did enter had to be on constant guard, especially at night. For when the sun set, blood-drinking and flesh-eating Rakshasas prowled the land.

Despite these horrors, wise and holy men still lived in Dandaka. These Rishis had given up all the comforts of the world and become hermits. They told of the evil deeds of the Rakshasas, and Rama and Lakshmana vowed to free the forest from the night-wandering demons.

One afternoon, as the two brothers and Sita made their way through Dandaka, the air became wavy and unbearably hot. The trees looked like columns of dead wood with twisted branches holding a few dry and brittle leaves. The wind blew in scorching gusts. Sita opened her mouth to speak. Before she could say a word, a long hairy red arm reached out from the trees, wrapped around her waist, and pulled her away.

Rama and Lakshmana chased after her. Yet the arm that held Sita was so long they could not see its body. On and on, they pursued it through thick, thorny trees wrapped with dead vines. When they came to a clearing, a tall Rakshasa stood before them. Coarse red bristles covered his body. Hollow green eyes sunk in his face. A wide mouth spread from ear to ear, and these looked like sharp pointed spears. In one hand, he held Sita and in the other an iron spit where he had stuck the head of an elephant along with three lions and four deer, now limp and dead. The open eyes of the elephant's bloody head stared at Rama and Lakshmana.

"Scum! Your weapons cannot kill me!" bellowed the demon as his outstretched arm placed Sita high in a tree. "How dare you and this woman travel though my land! Before I marry her, I will first drink your blood!"

So saying, the Rakshasa ran toward Rama and Lakshmana, and toward the monster sharp arrows sped from the brothers' bows. And though the arrows injured the demon severely, they could not kill him. He yawned, and the arrows fell from his flesh. Then with a snort and roar, he picked up each brother and walked off, leaving Sita alone in the tree and out of sight.

Yet before the beast had gone too far, Rama broke one of the demon's arms and Lakshmana the other. With a loud noise, the Rakshasa collapsed, and as Rama held him down by the throat, Lakshmana crushed all the monster's bones. He next dug a deep pit where they tossed their defeated foe and covered him with earth and rocks. They piled huge boulders on top so that escape was impossible. The pair then went back and rescued Sita out of the tree.

The She-Demon Surpanakha

Rama, Sita, and Lakshmana continued their journey south through the forest until they reached a river. They came to a lovely spot where a grove of five whispering trees grew along its bank and where everything seemed peaceful. There Lakshmana built a shelter a little distance from a hillside cave.

One morning, soon after their arrival, they sat in the open air near the shelter. As Rama was telling a story, the demoness Surpanakha emerged from the surrounding forest. Sister of Ravana, she was hideously ugly and cruel. Her skin was yellow and so heavily wrinkled it looked like a road washed out and deeply rutted by the monsoon rains. Long claws grew from her fingers and toes. Her fat belly jiggled as she walked, and her flat ears flapped like an elephant's fanning away stinging insects. Peering here and there, her eyes squinted through a tangle of coarse red hair that hung down her face.

As she approached, the demoness gnawed on a bone and flung it away. At that moment, she spied the handsome Rama and called out with a voice that made the forest shake. "Who are you?"

"I am Rama," he answered.

"And I am Surpanakha, sister to Ravana. Our brother, the mighty Khara, commands the demon forces of this forest. You are to be my husband, and we shall be very happy. I can turn myself into a beautiful woman and provide everything you need." Instantly, the ugly creature changed. No longer a hideous she-demon, she looked like a gorgeous princess.

"But I am already married to this beautiful woman," the prince replied, pointing to Sita. "To have one wife is joy, but to have two would be misery."

Surpanakha then fixed her gaze on Lakshmana. He quickly said, "You don't want me! Rama is my master, and I am his servant. Why settle for second best?"

"Oh, don't be shy. You should do quite well as my husband. My hugs will fill you with joy," said the she-demon as she smiled, flicked her dagger-like tongue, and winked at Lakshmana.

To save his brother, Rama answered, "Though his wife is not here, my brother is also married and cannot wed you."

"I think I see the problem!" Surpanakha shouted. Changing back into her original form, she flashed her long claws and charged toward Sita. At once, Lakshmana unsheathed his sword and sliced off the monster's ears and nose.

Howling with pain, Surpanakha ran to seek her brother General Khara. She found him in his fortress, fell at his feet, and looked up at him. When he saw his dear sister's bloody face, he flew into a violent rage. "Who has dared to wound you?" he cried, his voice like the low, deep rumble of thunder rolling over a mountainside.

"Two men and their woman attacked me!" Surpanakha moaned.

"Sound the alarm!" yelled Khara, and before the words were out of his mouth, a Rakshasa soldier struck a huge brass gong. A great troop of demons, ready for war, assembled before the general.

The soldiers marched out of the fortress. As they took flight in Rama's direction, Surpanakha called after them, "Bring me the woman's blood to drink and the heads of the two men!"

Meanwhile, Rama stared in the direction where the demoness had fled and to Lakshmana declared, "We have enraged the she-demon, and she will unleash her brother and his forces against us. We must be prepared."

No sooner had the prince spoken than the sky above the trees filled with flying Rakshasas led by General Khara.

"Stop or die!" shouted Rama.

"Surrender!" cried Khara.

"We live here in peace and hurt no one willingly," replied Rama.

"We will destroy you!" fumed the general and attacked.

His bow already strung, Rama took three steps back to steady his aim. Lakshmana stood guard by Sita. Like swift lightning, the golden arrows of Rama swept the sky clear of demons, and that day he slew the whole host of General Khara.

From a safe distance, Surpanakha watched what occurred. She dove into the ground and by her evil powers passed through earth and stone and beneath the Indian ocean. She arose to the surface just outside Ravana's palace on his island kingdom of Lanka. With ear-splitting screams, she ran inside repeating over and over, "Rama! Rama! Rama!"

Ravana's Revenge

The Demon King sat on his throne holding court. Everyone fell silent as Surpanakha entered, her bloody hand pressing against her stub of a nose.

Ravana saw his sister's wounds. "Who has defaced you, my sister?" he asked and rose in anger, the golden crowns on his ten heads brightly gleaming.

"Two princes driven out of their own country. The one called Rama has a beautiful wife named Sita. I wanted to bring her here as a present to you," the demoness lied. "Rama refused and in his anger ordered his brother Lakshmana to cut off my ears and nose."

"You suffered these horrible wounds just to bring me a gift, sweet sister?"

"Yes, and our brother General Khara and countless Rakshasa warriors under his command died in trying to help me," she replied. Then to stir Ravana's anger further, she urged, "Capture Sita and keep her, and so take your revenge on Rama for what he has done to us."

Ravana remembered the lovely Sita from the time he had tried to bend the Shiva bow and had failed to win her hand in marriage. He also recalled how Rama had strung the great bow and hurt the pride of the many princes, including himself, who had attempted the task.

Now at the urging of Surpanakha, the wicked Ravana plotted revenge. The next morning the king mounted his pushpak. Pulled by mules with the faces of devils, the flying chariot resembled a swift moving cloud and, as it sped across the sky, glistened like the sun. When he landed, Ravana had reached the home of Maricha, his uncle as well as the father of Taraka, the she-demon Rama had killed in his youth.

Maricha sat alone in a clearing and wore only a black deerskin. Not only was he a demon, but he was also a powerful magician. He could change himself into any shape and mimic the exact sound of whatever creature he became. When he heard Ravana tell what had happened to Surpanakha, Maricha trembled with fear. He had faced Rama's power before.

The demon wizard told his nephew, "Do not speak that name to me. Fear of him has turned me into a hermit. He wounded me once. I still carry the scar from his arrow, and for that reason I hide here in the forest."

"You must help me," Ravana insisted. "I will have Sita as my bride. For she is at the height of her beauty."

Maricha eyed his nephew sadly. "What enemy has said Sita's name to you and filled you with desire. Whoever it is wants to destroy you."

"My sister, Surpanakha. She was attacked for no reason."

"Ah," said Maricha. "Your sister's words spell doom. She will be the cause of your end and the demon race." Nothing, however, could sway Ravana. He would lose everything to have Sita.

After much argument, along with the threat of death, Maricha agreed to help. "I will turn into a golden deer and wander in front of Sita's hut. She will ask her husband and his brother to catch me. I will swiftly flee. When they give chase and are far away, you can kidnap the princess. And yet you will be drinking your own poison and die, and I, too, will die by Rama's hand. Better, though, for a good man to kill me than an evil thing like you."

Princess Sita Kidnapped

With Ravana, Maricha mounted the chariot, and the two flew until they landed some distance from Sita's hut. Maricha changed himself into a deer. His antlers were ivory-tipped and studded with pearls, and his hair a golden hue with silver spots that flashed along his sides. Sensing him a Rakshasa in disguise, even the tigers ceased roaring and slunk away in fear while the other deer fled as he approached the dwelling. Rama, Lakshmana, and Sita were resting inside.

Once there, Maricha browsed the grass, then trotted past, stopped, and lay down to nibble fallen leaves. Sita saw the beautiful creature and called to her husband, "Look, Rama. Come quickly. Please catch him for me."

"How beautiful!" exclaimed Rama.

Yet, when Lakshmana beheld the deer, he warned, "I must be dreaming. No animal like this exists on earth. See how it glimmers in the sunlight and loses its shape as its edges blur. Surely this deer is a demon's trick."

Wishing to please his wife, Rama brushed aside his brother's doubt and strung his bow with one arrow. "You and Sita wait here. If possible, I will catch him. If he is a Rakshasa, I will kill him. Take care of Sita until I return."

As Rama approached, the deer rose and walked toward him. Then backing away, it jumped and sprang toward the forest. At the edge of the clearing, it stopped, turned, and pricked up its ears as it looked back before bounding into the trees.

Rama sprinted in pursuit. Sometimes the deer appeared to grow tired, but just as Rama drew near, it swiftly outdistanced him. In this way, the sly Maricha teased his pursuer deeper and deeper into the Dandaka wilderness far from Lakshmana and Sita.

Realizing he could not catch the deer, Rama decided to shoot it. A golden arrow pierced the beautiful animal through its heart. It leapt high into the air and landed on its back. As it lay struggling for life, Maricha became a black demon once again. Throwing back his head and imitating Rama's voice, he breathed his last words, "Help me!"

Much louder than any human shout, Maricha's plea echoed throughout the forest and made Rama tremble with fear. He knew the sound would easily reach his wife and brother.

When Sita heard the voice, she said to Lakshmana, "You must go to my husband, your brother. He is calling for help. Go! Now go!"

"But he told me not to leave you, dear sister."

Yet Sita insisted that Lakshmana go, so worried that she even threatened to kill herself if he did not leave. At last, he yielded, but to protect her he drew a circle around their shelter. "Sita, you must stay within this circle. Its magic will keep you safe as long as you do not step beyond it." Then gathering his bow and quiver, he ran toward Rama's voice.

The Rakshasa King had been watching the whole time. He turned himself into a holy beggar, and walking toward the hut, he called for food for his bowl. Sita opened the door but did not cross the circle.

To Ravana, the princess appeared more beautiful than he remembered, making him want to have her at all costs. Pretending to sound weak with hunger, he begged, "Dear lady, would you please give an old man food for his bowl?"

Her heart melted at the beggar's plight. She held out a gift of food, for she had always fed the poor. Yet she remained within the magic circle.

When Ravana saw her hesitation, he said, "As a holy beggar in the service of God, I cannot enter your home or approach it too closely. You must bring your kind offering to me."

"How can I refuse this holy man?" thought Sita. "I must do my duty." Ignoring Lakshmana's warning, she stepped outside the circle.

The demon lord at once clapped his hands and stood before Sita in his true form. Twenty red eyes glowed from his ten faces. Sharp tongues of fire darted from the many mouths filled with yellow fangs. A long ivory bow hung from his shoulder; along his back, a quiver made from human skins.

No wind stirred the leaves of the forest, and the light of the sun faded as it beheld the Evil One. Two of Ravana's twenty arms seized the princess as his pushpak floated down. Holding her tightly, he stepped within. The chariot rose above the trees.

An Attempted Rescue

As they sped south toward the Rakshasa Kingdom, Sita silently prayed to the gods of the rivers and the trees and to the deer and birds of Dandaka. *Tell Rama! Tell Rama!* Glancing below, she saw Jatayu, the Vulture King and Lord of the Forest Birds, asleep high in his nest. He heard her plea, and with his great green eyes, he saw Ravana's pushpak pass across the sky. He took flight and glided after, soon overtaking the chariot and soaring above it.

The Lord of the Air called down, "King Ravana, I forbid you to do evil in my sight. Do not carry Sita away to be your wife. She already has a husband, and Rama is his name!" Ravana continued his flight.

His warning ignored, Jatayu attacked Ravana's chariot and hooked it with a talon as long as an elephant's tusk. The pushpak shook violently, causing the demon to loosen his grip on Sita. Jatayu lifted her out, and settling to earth, he gently placed her unharmed beneath a tree and flew aloft again.

Ravana shouted in a rage, "You are nothing!" He aimed an arrow and charged toward the Vulture King.

But Jatayu was ready. His claws tore the armor from the demon's back, and from Ravana's heads, his beak ripped out thick tufts of hair. His mighty wings blasted the chariot and sent it spinning toward earth where it crashed.

Ravana lay stunned, and Jatayu shrieked in triumph. Yet the old Vulture King was exhausted. His eyes dimmed until he became blind, and though he searched carefully, he could not find the Demon King. Dropping lower and lower, Jatayu searched by sound only. Ravana saw his weakness, and rising from the ground, he drew a sword and sliced off the great bird's wings and feet.

The Lord of the Air tumbled to the earth. Sita rushed to comfort him, but Ravana snatched her away. With his magic, he restored his pushpak, and he and his captive rose once again into the air.

Though helpless, Sita said, "Wicked king, you will pay for your evil with death. My husband is the bravest of the brave and unequaled in the art of war. His bow is like no other, and he will slay you with a single arrow."

Unmindful of her warning, Ravana continued south, as the shadow of his pushpak raced over the land below and crossed a wide river. Peering down, Sita saw two monkeys on a hill beside a lake. Shading their eyes, they looked at the chariot above them. Sita quickly loosened her jewels, necklace, bracelets, and bells she had received as gifts during the long exile. The monkeys watched as these fell to earth with a dainty noise. Focusing on his flight, Ravana noticed nothing.

Rama's Search for Sita

As Rama hurried toward the forest dwelling, he met Lakshmana rushing to find him. Beholding his brother, Rama knew at once Sita was in grave danger. Much troubled, he asked, "Why have you left my wife alone?"

"We heard your mournful call, and at Sita's urging, I ran to help you," answered Lakshmana.

"We have been tricked! The golden deer was the demon Maricha! We must find Sita!" cried Rama. Both ran back to the hut, but she was not there.

Heartbroken, Rama fell to his knees and wept. For a while, he wandered aimlessly, searching for his wife and calling her name. Then gathering his strength at last, he and Lakshmana headed toward Lanka. For Rama believed that the Demon King had had a hand in Sita's disappearance.

As the two made their way south, they came upon Jatayu slowly bleeding to death. Thinking the Vulture King a Rakshasa in disguise, Rama nocked his bow. At that moment, Jatayu spoke in a feeble voice. "She is alive. Sita yet lives." Rama rushed to comfort him.

"Prince Rama, Ravana has taken your wife. I tried to rescue her, but he wounded me so that I was unable to save her." Blood ran from Jatayu's beak, the light went from his eyes, and the Lord of the Air died in Rama's arms. Before leaving, Rama and Lakshmana mourned his passing and gave him a proper funeral.

Traveling toward Lanka, the brothers soon came across the paths cut by the shadows of Rakshasas flying back and forth from Lanka in the south to General Khara's fortress in the north. Once teeming with animals, the land lay wasted with only scorched trees and packs of starving wild dogs.

Throughout the journey, Rama's mind churned with constant thoughts of Sita. He could barely eat, and sleep was almost impossible. Yet Lakshmana ever offered encouragement. "Dear brother," he would say, "do not give up. We are sure to find Sita and set her free."

In the Land of the Monkeys

The pair at last reached the end of Dandaka, and after crossing a wide river, they entered the kingdom of the monkeys and came to a large lake by a steep hill. Here, Sugriva, the monkey ruler, lived with his followers. The way to Sugriva's camp was guarded by his friend, the powerful Hanuman.

As Rama and Lakshmana climbed the hill, they met a poor woodcutter who greeted them. "For what reason have two men, who glow with splendor like mighty lions, come to this remote hillside?"

Rama saw through the woodcutter's disguise. "It is you, Hanuman."

Upon hearing these words, the woodcutter shook himself, turning back into his true form. White, shiny fur covered his body. A long tail curved and flicked like a whip, and long, thin arms rippled with well-defined muscles. His face glowed with a red sheen, and his mouth revealed two rows of bright teeth. Golden earrings dangled from his ears. Eyes of a light, yellow hue sparkled with intelligence.

"I have heard of you, Prince Rama," said the white monkey. "What do you seek from me?"

Rama introduced his brother and said, "We come in peace. The Demon King has taken Sita, my wife. We seek the help of Sugriva, your leader."

"We saw her fly overhead—a captive in Ravana's pushpak. Climb upon my shoulders, and I will carry you to Sugriva." As he spoke, Hanuman grew larger and with a single bound landed at the top of the hill.

The golden monkey, Sugriva, sat alone by a small fire. When he saw Hanuman with the brothers, he rose and welcomed them. They told him of their adventures in Dandaka during nearly fourteen years of exile from their homeland—about their struggles to free the forest from demons, about Ravana's trickery, and about his capture of Sita.

When they had finished their story, Sugriva said, "I also am an exile. Vali, my oldest brother, was our king. I went with him once to battle a Rakshasa. After a long struggle, he drove the demon into a deep cave. I waited patiently by its entrance for many days for Vali to reappear. My worry knew no end. Then I heard the Rakshasa's roar and saw blood seep from the cave's mouth. I lost all hope, for I believed the demon had killed my brother. So I sealed the opening with huge rocks and returned home."

Sugriva paused in sadness before he spoke again. "Because we had no ruler, the monkeys crowned me king. Yet one day Vali suddenly appeared at the palace. He had learned that I had taken his place, and his anger knew no bounds. Thinking I had stolen his throne, he drove me out of the kingdom and kept my wife. With my followers, I fled here to these wild hills and remote valleys beyond the reach of his power. So, as you can see, Prince Rama, your story of exile is my story as well."

Sugriva stopped, his eyes moist in the flickering firelight and his voice choking with emotion. Continuing, he said, "Hanuman and I saw these things fall on our hill." The Monkey King then showed his guests the objects Sita had dropped from Ravana's chariot.

Rama recognized them as belonging to his wife and swore, "I will destroy this demon who has taken my beloved wife from me."

Sugriva wept inwardly at the prince's loss and offered comfort. "Take heart, my friend. Together, we will find your dearest Sita and kill Ravana. My troops are yours to command." In return for this offer, Rama and Lakshmana promised to help Sugriva rescue his wife from Vali and regain his throne.

Even though the Monkey King was grateful for the offer, he was unaware of Rama's tremendous courage and fighting ability. "My friend," he warned, "I am thankful for your help, but Vali is powerful beyond all imagining. I have seen him, with one shot of his bow, send crashing a line of strong trees. Can you do the same?" Without answering, Rama drew his bow and knocked down seven trees with a single arrow.

Convinced of Rama's skill, Sugriva set out for the monkey palace of his brother to challenge him. Vali's wife warned her husband that Rama, Lakshmana, Hanuman, and a small party of warriors had been spotted hiding in the nearby forest, but Vali did not believe her. "Sugriva is a coward," he said. "No one would help him."

To his regret, Vali recklessly ignored his wife and left the palace. Rama saw him, and his arrow found its mark. It pierced the king's heart and left him stunned and sprawling on the ground where he died.

Sugriva thus regained his wife and his kingdom through Rama's aid. Yet now that his riches had been restored, he began to live a life of ease in the city where Vali once ruled. Then came the heavy monsoon rains when nothing can be done for months. The Golden Monkey King forgot the bitter and hard years he had suffered in exile. He gave no thought of his promise to help find Sita.

Week after week passed as the unending downpours continued. Rama grew sadder and sadder, longing for his dear wife and living in a cave on the hilltop where he had first met Sugriva. Lakshmana saw his brother's grief and finally could bear it no more. In anger, he vowed that he would go to Sugriva and force him to honor his word. When the rains ceased, Lakshmana took his bow and set out for the monkey capital. Upon reaching the walls of the city, he called out to the guards, "Let the king know that Lakshmana comes armed and waits at the gate for him to keep his promise."

Hanuman heard the call. He ran to Sugriva to inform him but found him asleep from too much drinking. "Awake, my king! Lakshmana is armed and at the gate. He comes in Rama's name. Everyone despises a promise-breaker, especially an angry friend. Should you not show your gratitude to Rama and repay his friendship? Perhaps then Lakshmana will spare your life."

Regaining his senses and recognizing his failure to honor his word, Sugriva roused himself and met with Lakshmana to cool the prince's anger. "Take my hand in friendship," said the Golden Monkey King, and the two climbed a long winding stairway to the top of a high watchtower.

"Look down at the valleys below us." Sugriva nodded in every direction, and everywhere Lakshmana gazed, he saw troops of monkeys, apes, and huge shaggy bears. "See how they speed toward the palace. I have commanded my warriors and my friends the bears to gather so that they can begin to hunt for Sita. I have also sent Hanuman to inform Rama and bring him here."

The Quest to Free Sita

As Lakshmana and Sugriva beheld the four quarters of the earth, the king declared, "No place can escape our reach." He then ordered his forces divided into four armies. A gray monkey commanded the army of the east, a red monkey that of the west, and a white bear that of the north.

"Because we saw Ravana fly toward Lanka," said Sugriva, "my nephew, the crown prince himself, will lead the army of the south. He and the other generals have one month to complete their search."

As the Monkey King finished speaking, Hanuman entered with Rama. Sugriva greeted them and said, "I would like for Lakshmana and Rama to remain with me in the palace." Then pulling a scroll from his robes, he added, "Hanuman, you will go south with the crown prince, but you will have a special mission as well. Memorize the message on this scroll, and if you meet the Demon King, give it to him."

The armies departed and began a thorough search—up high mountains, down deep valleys, through thick jungles, over burning deserts. They questioned all the animals they met, whether growling tigers, crawling snakes, flitting butterflies, or skittish village cats. They especially thought the high-flying birds, who see in all directions, might have news of Sita.

None of Sugriva's forces could locate the princess. After two weeks, Hanuman and the army of the south, still unlucky, reached a craggy cliff beside the Indian Ocean. Perched high among the rocks was an ancient vulture, the brother of Jatayu.

Though age had dimmed his once keen eyes, the hulking creature saw the monkeys and bears. He took flight from his crag, slowly glided down toward them, and landed with a heavy thud upon the beach. "My name is Sampati," he said. "Why do you come with such large numbers to this remote shore?"

Their troops standing ready, Hanuman and the crown prince introduced themselves and informed Sampati about Sita's capture and their failure to find her. As their story unfolded, they told of the brave deeds of the Vulture King. "Lord Jatayu almost killed the evil Ravana but in the end lost his life to the Demon King," said Hanuman.

"Jatayu was my brother. This news is the first I have received of his death," replied Sampati in sadness, his voice nearly failing him. "I should kill Ravana for what he has done. But now I am old, my eyesight faint, and my flight clumsy. Yet know this. I saw Ravana cross the ocean with a beautiful lady in his chariot. He flew toward the island of Lanka. Strong walls surround its capital, and no one can scale them without being seen by its many guards."

The army rejoiced on learning of Sita's whereabouts. Yet the warriors wondered how they could cross the mighty ocean. One soldier said in sorrow, "We have failed and must return home." Others whispered in agreement.

Jambavan, one of the leaders of the bears, turned to Hanuman. "Only you have the power to fly over the ocean to Lanka and save Sita."

Hanuman took heart from these words and started to pray. As his chest swelled with a deep breath, he grew larger and larger. In his mind, he already saw himself sailing through the sky. Then with a shout, he jumped and soared above the great vulture and the army. A mighty roar rose from everyone on the ground to greet his ears as he sped toward Lanka.

Hanuman's Search

Nothing could stop Hanuman. He hurled through the air until he soon saw the green hills of Lanka and its beautiful city set on a wide plain. A tall mountain with three peaks rose behind it, and blue rivers watered and made fruitful the surrounding countryside.

Hanuman landed on an overlooking hill to plan what to do next. For despite its beauty, the city of Lanka had thick walls that bristled with high towers, and a ring of forts protected it. No matter where the white monkey looked, Rakshasa archers stood guard to prevent strangers from entering.

How could anyone approach such a strongly defended city? Yet when twilight came, Hanuman shrank to the size of a long-haired silver housecat. He hung Rama's ring around his neck and under the cover of darkness leapt over the city walls and slipped past the guards. He peered into this house and peeped into that one but found only demons lurking within. Some were pretty and handsome. Others were gruesomely ugly.

Hanuman gradually worked his way to the middle of the city. Here another wall surrounded the palace of Ravana. Hanuman jumped over this wall and with catlike silence padded through the many rooms of the palace, but he could find no sign of Sita.

Still in the form of a cat, he went outside and followed a path through a large park filled with hundreds of trees. The sound of waking birds told of the coming dawn. The early light filtered through the branches to reveal a beautiful lady who sat beneath one of the trees. Her clothes were torn and faded, and her face pale and care-worn, thin from grief and fasting.

Hanuman recognized her as the woman he saw fly overhead in Ravana's pushpak. He paused as his heart filled with warring emotions—sorrow for what Sita had endured and happiness that she was still alive.

The rustling of dry leaves brought Hanuman back to himself. He feared that a Rakshasa might be approaching. So he shrank even further into a little white monkey no bigger than a man's hand. Leaping into a tree, he hid among its branches. From his perch, he saw that Ravana had entered the park and was walking toward Sita.

The Demon King bowed before Sita, smiled at her with his many lips, and spoke. "Dear lady, do not be afraid. I am helpless before you. Reward my love, and you will rule my city and my other wives. For you, I will do anything, even turn from evil to good."

"If you truly love me," said Sita, "you would return me to my husband. Rama would then not lift a finger against you. But keep me here as prisoner, and he will save me. That day will be your last. Now leave me to my sorrow."

His anger swelling within him, Ravana flew into a rage. His twenty eyes rolled and spun in different directions. His royal robes whirled like opposing winds over a storm-tossed sea. His ten mouths foamed as he snapped and bit at the empty air. Before stalking off, he roared, "The kinder I am to you, the crueler you are to me. You have one month to decide."

Hanuman quaked in his tree. "What a terrible temper," he thought. "Does he have these love fits every day? How exhausting."

The she-demons who prowled through the park as guards witnessed Ravana's fury. They came to Sita and tortured her with mocking words. "Good luck kisses your face. Our glorious ruler is in love with you. Forget Rama. He lives among animals. Submit to our king's charms, and the world is yours."

Refusing to listen, Sita turned away. Her tormenters howled angrily, "We have been too patient with you!" They bared their fangs, flashed sharp knives, and shouted, "We should carve her up and eat her and let the crows pick her bones!"

In horror, Hanuman drew a deep breath and nearly jumped out of the tree to defend Sita. But at that moment, an ancient she-demon named Trijata stepped forward. She looked like a sweet old woman with braided white hair, even though her eyes were as big as saucers and rolled inward toward her nose.

"Cease your shouts and shrieks," she ordered. Everyone fell silent. "Last night I had a dream. I saw Ravana clothed in red. He drank foul oil, and the hair was shaved from his ten heads. Laughing and crying like one insane, he rode on the back of a huge hog and was fleeing south. As he fled, our city sank into the sea behind him. It was the end of the Rakshasa Kingdom."

On hearing Trijata's dream, the she-demons trembled and one by one slunk away to guard the gates and walls of the park and palace. "Here is my chance," thought Hanuman.

Yet he feared to speak, for Sita might think that he, too, was a demon in the form of a little monkey. Hidden by the leaves, he began to recite softly the deeds that only a friend would know. How Rama had bent the great Shiva bow to win her as his bride. How he had shot Maricha, the golden deer. How Ravana, disguised as a holy beggar, had tricked her. How she had been whisked away in his flying chariot to Lanka.

Then Hanuman whispered, "I am your friend. I leapt over the ocean to find you. I am hiding in the branches above."

Looking up, Sita saw a little red face smiling at her through the leaves. "Who are you?" she asked.

"I am Hanuman, Son of the Wind," he said before dropping to the ground. "I serve your husband. This is his ring."

Holding the ring, Sita quietly began to cry as she read the name on the gold band. *Rama, Rama, Rama.* "Oh, my sweet monkey. You are like medicine to one nearly dead. And yet my husband and I have been apart for many months." Then with a sadness in her voice, Sita asked, "Tell me, Hanuman, does Rama still love me?"

"Dear princess, you fill his thoughts day and night, and his heart so yearns for you that he eats little and sleeps less. Now climb upon my shoulders, and I will take you to him." Hanuman grew larger as he spoke.

"Doubts still haunt my mind. Rama is free to have any wife he wants. Yet your words give me hope," said Sita. "Return to him, and tell him I am a captive in Lanka. Give him this as a sign that I still live." She handed Hanuman her last remaining jewel, a pearl from her wedding. "I will wait for him to come, if he will. Yet know that at the end of the year Ravana will kill me."

"Princess, time cannot dim Rama's love for you," said Hanuman, and he solemnly promised, "Once he is certain you are here, he will rouse himself from his sorrow, and with a mighty army he will come to save you."

"Faithful friend, you have stirred my hope. Now stay with me this day before you leave. Surrounded by evil things, I have no one here to comfort me. Tomorrow will be soon enough for you to go. Then we shall say farewell."

Hanuman's Revenge

The white monkey did as Sita commanded. Yet before he left Lanka, he decided to punish Ravana for the misery he had caused her. "I will not harm the park where Sita stays, but as for the rest.... Yes! Yes! It's only fair!"

Hanuman shot like an arrow from Rama's bow. He pulled up the flowers in Ravana's gardens, clawed up the lawns, tossed bricks and benches through the palace windows, and splattered the guards with mud. Proud horses panicked, war elephants ran amuck, and tame deer jumped over the walls.

The noise of destruction reached Ravana as he sat upon his throne. Before he could bark out any orders, his palace guards sprang into action, thinking a powerful enemy or the gods themselves attacked Lanka.

"Victory to the Monkey King!" roared Hanuman.

"What monkey king?" shouted the guards.

"Why my Lord Sugriva, of course!" yelled Hanuman, growing bigger and bigger. Snatching an iron bar from a broken gate, he hammered them all to death. The ground trembled from his fury.

Hanuman jumped over the palace walls to spread ruin throughout the city. The fierceness of his flight was like a mighty wind. Leaves rose in green clouds, grand houses collapsed, and temples burst into flame.

Through a window, Ravana saw destruction everywhere. He quickly turned and ran down some narrow stairs and entered a tunnel. It led beyond the city walls to a wooded hillside. Beneath a tree sat his son, Indrajit, who lived the life of a hermit. Wrapped in only a deerskin, he had once been a powerful warrior, but now he was thin and pale from eating little and praying much.

"My son," pled Ravana, "stop your prayers, and study war. Return to my world of sight and sound, of pleasure and pain. I need you now. An animal is loose in Lanka and destroying everything. Take him by trick, or take him by force, but stop his rampage."

Indrajit smiled. "The animal is Hanuman. Whether I stop him matters little. For this life is not even a grain of sand on the shore, a drop of water in the ocean, a snowflake melting in the sun. Yet I will do as you wish."

Indrajit's body immediately changed. No longer lean, colorless, and fragile with thinning white hair, he stood before Ravana as a warrior with glowing skin and keen eyes that glanced here and there. His hair was dark and shiny; his clothes, of blue and yellow silk. In one hand, he held a large round shield, and in the other, a long curved bow. A quiver full of arrows hung over his back, and along his side, a sword in a silver sheath.

Knowing Hanuman could not be killed, Indrajit cast a spell on an arrow. It would snare its victim in a noose making escape impossible. He saw the white monkey sitting among the ruins of Lanka and fired his shot. Hanuman reeled and fell, tied hand and foot by an invisible rope.

And yet before Indrajit could reach the helpless monkey, a swarm of demons ran to Hanuman, and in the twinkling of an eye, they wrapped him in chains. "They know nothing," said Indrajit. "The spell works only once, and it fails if its victim is tied by other means. Why did I leave my peaceful hillside grove for this world of fools!" He spoke no more and went back to fast and pray.

The Rakshasas hauled the stunned and bound Hanuman into the palace. Vibhishana, brother of the Demon King, asked, "Who are you, and why have you come casting ruin throughout Lanka?"

"My name is Hanuman, and I have a message for your king."

Ravana leaned forward and stared into the monkey's eyes. "What message?"

"I am Rama's servant and the servant of Sugriva, King of the

Monkeys and Bears. They sent me to find Sita. You kidnapped her in Dandaka Forest. She is Rama's wife. Return her, and live unharmed. If you do not—"

"And how did you get to Lanka?" interrupted Ravana.

"I jumped across the ocean, and I could jump back again and take Sita with me, but my mission was to find her. Rama himself will rescue her. I beg you not to risk your own destruction by keeping his wife."

Ravana sneered. "You are too amusing, but I am not in the mood to laugh."

"Then don't!" snapped Hanuman.

The Demon King's twenty eyes glared in anger, and he ordered Vibhishana to cut off the monkey's head. But his brother cautioned, "Even though a sassy monkey, he is a messenger from another ruler. It would, therefore, be wrong to remove his head. Shave him or brand him, but do not kill him."

"My brother, you are not a very good demon. You are aware that I've killed messengers before. Anyway, monkeys are proud of their tails. Set fire to the tail of this tiresome little beast and carry him throughout the city. Then toss him out."

Several Rakshasas held Hanuman. As others wrapped his tail in oily rags, it grew longer and longer, and the more they wrapped, the longer it grew. "Set it on fire!" Ravana shouted.

Hanuman broke his chains and with his flaming tail whipped the Rakshasas of Ravana's court. Then bursting from the throne room, he darted into the sky. He flew over Lanka and set temples, palaces, houses, and gardens ablaze. The entire city looked like a smoldering ruin. Only the park where Sita remained was spared the monkey's wrath.

Satisfied that he had punished the Demon King enough, Hanuman doused his tail in the ocean and leapt toward home. The warriors greeted his return as they had his leaving. Triumphant shouts and great rejoicing echoed along the beach and through the surrounding hills.

The crown prince, Hanuman, and the army of the south hurried to tell Sugriva and Rama of the monkey's return. When Rama saw them, his spirits lifted, for he had lost all hope of ever seeing Sita again. He ran toward Hanuman, who shouted for everyone to hear, "The princess lives!" At these words, Rama, Lakshmana, Sugriva, and the animals who had remained at court gave thanks.

"I gave her your ring, and in return she sent you this," said Hanuman, and he handed Rama the wedding pearl.

His charred tail twitching, Hanuman next related what he had learned. "The year will be up in one month, and then Ravana will kill Sita if she does not give herself to him. Yet at this moment, surrounded by evil, Sita is slowly dying. Though her beauty remains, her waist grows thin like a crescent moon, and her shoulders stoop from the weight of her cares and her longing for you. You must act. You must kill Ravana."

To Hanuman's advice, Sugriva added, "Put away your grief, Rama. It will only prevent you from doing what you must. Look around you. Here is your brother. See how he and all your friends stand ready to help you. Only say the word, and we march on Lanka."

Preparing for War

His friends' support now stirred Rama to act, and he called for a council of war. Hanuman told about the defenses of Lanka—its strong gates, its wide moats, its thick walls and high towers, its loyal demon soldiers who never sheathe their swords. He concluded by saying, "Despite the dangers, the Demon King cannot defeat the monkey people and the bear tribes, nor can he stop Lakshmana as long as Rama is our leader." Armed with this information, the council formed its plan of attack.

At noon the next day, Rama's forces headed south toward Lanka. They cleared trees, drained swamps, cut through hills, and removed boulders to make a road to take them to the sea. After three days, they could smell the salt air. They arrived on the white shore as the sun was setting. The sky looked like the ocean, and the ocean like the sky, all one vast space without end.

Rama said to Sugriva, "Make camp nearby, and post guards to watch for strangers. I will wait here a while." The prince then lay down, his head resting on his arms. He listened to the silvery waves falling endlessly upon the beach, one after the other, and he wept, wondering whether he could cross the wide ocean and whether he would see Sita again.

As these thoughts clouded Rama's mind, the Lord of the Ocean appeared and spoke to him. "Prince Rama, I am your friend. My heart is as large as the sky above us, and I will help you. In your army is the monkey Nala. He was born with the gift that whatever he tosses on the water will not sink. Anything he puts on my surface I will support. Let him build you a floating bridge to Lanka." The Sea Lord then sank into his depths.

Rama found Nala. The monkey first studied the hills above the shore. He then looked south in the direction of Ravana's island. For a long time, he gazed at the sand and drew lines. The other animals watched his work, but he took no notice. When he finally raised his head, he gave orders for them to build a bridge hundreds of miles long.

Meanwhile in Lanka, the demons prepared for war. Though

Hanuman had left much of the city in ashes, Ravana had them rebuild and strengthen it.

Still the Rakshasas shook in fear and laughed nervously. For they had seen the destruction caused by one monkey, and they trembled even more at what an army of them might do. To give themselves courage, the demons boasted, "We will squash Rama and his bears and monkeys like insects."

Only a few voices called for peace. "Do not destroy Lanka, but save your kingdom from Rama's anger," urged Vibhishana. "Reject evil, and do what is right. Let Sita return to her husband."

"I fear no one," Ravana replied angrily. "If I let Sita go, all the demons and the gods will mock me. I will not turn from my path. The woman is mine."

"Then I must leave," answered his brother. "May you save yourself."

"My kingdom has no place for the fearful and weak," Ravana hissed. "Now go."

Vibhishana left the palace and flew in his pushpak across the ocean to Rama's camp. "I am Vibhishana, brother of the Demon King," he told the prince. "When I asked Ravana to return your wife, he banished me from Lanka. I have come in friendship."

Rama replied, "You have chosen to follow good and are welcome here. Add your strength to ours, and you shall have your brother's kingdom."

Vibhishana eagerly agreed to serve Rama's cause. Yet Sugriva and other leaders suspected this offer might be a trick and Vibhishana a spy. They warned, "He is a Rakshasa from the enemy's camp. Consider well before you accept his aid."

Hanuman spoke next. "Rama, I urge you to accept Vibhishana into our ranks. When his brother would have killed me, Vibhishana defended me as a messenger and saved my life. Let him take Ravana's place as King of Lanka once you have put an end to the Evil One. Make a faithful ally of Vibhishana. Help him to win his kingdom as you helped Sugriva win his."

Rama agreed with Hanuman. "I befriend all who seek my friendship. Vibhishana will provide valuable aid to our cause. He may join our ranks."

At these words, Vibhishana fell before the prince and thanked him. He also provided information about Ravana. "The battle before you will not be easy. My brother has a vast force of demons armed to the teeth, and to his own magical powers, he has added those of his son Indrajit."

The prince then closely questioned Vibhishana about Lanka's defenses and learned much that was new about its strength. When Rama had finished, he embraced his new-found friend and promised him that he would be King of Lanka.

Rama Reaches Lanka

During this time, Nala and his crew of beasts had been building the bridge of logs and stones. After five days, their work was complete. Shouting with excitement, the animal army marched over the ocean at night and reached the demon kingdom the next morning. There, Rama divided his forces and placed troops at key locations. The whole island echoed with the blasts of conch shells and rang with the stringing of bows. Like trembling leaves, the Rakshasas shook in fear.

Anxious to know Rama's plans, Ravana summoned two of his demons. "Turn into monkeys, and move among the animal army to gather what news you can," he ordered.

"Our sole joy is to obey you, Great King," they responded, and bowing low and licking the dust before Ravana's feet, they changed into monkeys as commanded.

Yet when these spies entered the enemy camp, Vibhishana recognized them as demons and brought them before Rama. The prince, however, refused to punish them and sent back with a message for Ravana. "Tell your master I have come to rescue my wife and to slay him."

This message enraged Ravana. He decided to try a new trick and called upon another demon who had once seen Rama in the forest of Dandaka. "Make a head that looks exactly like Rama's, and bring it to me," he said.

The demon did as bidden, and when he brought Ravana the head, the king took it to Sita sitting alone in her grove. He smiled at her. "Dear lady, Rama is dead, and his army destroyed. Here is his head as proof, covered in sand and blood. Give up your foolish hope of rescue, and become my bride and queen."

Wailing, the princess fell to the ground at the gory sight. "Oh, my husband, you have done all that you could to save me, even giving your own life. I cannot live without you. The pain is too much." And the sound of her sobbing filled Ravana's gardens and palace.

Seeing the depth of her love for Rama, the Demon King stormed out of the grove and summoned his entire force to defend the walls and towers of the city. For four days, the two armies stood poised against each other.

The Battle for Lanka Begins

On the fifth day at dawn, the battle for Lanka began. "Let the young warriors fight first," said Ravana. The north gate of the city opened, and one third of the demon force swarmed out to attack. But the sunlight diminished the power of the Rakshasas, for their tricks could be more easily seen.

The leaders of the animal army and their troops fought bravely. Strong bears shattered enemy chariots. Long-armed apes grabbed demons and squeezed them to death. Nimble monkeys chopped others to pieces with axes and swords. When dusk fell, the beaten demons retreated inside the walls of the city.

That night, however, veteran Rakshasas poured out of Lanka to allow the younger warriors to rest. Conch shells blared out-of-tune notes. Chariots dashed forward, pulled by gigantic scorpions, toads, lizards, hogs, or grinning rats the size of mules. The soldiers' battle cries rolled over the plain and echoed back from distant mountains.

The demon champion, General Prahasta himself, led the charge, and each time he drew his bow, an arrow killed five or six animals of Rama's army. With the general's onslaught, the monkeys and bears broke their ranks and fled.

Only Nala the Bridge Builder remained to confront Prahasta. The monkey dodged arrows as the general's chariot bore down upon him, the long knives on its golden wheels spinning to carve up any who stood too close to its sides. Just as the chariot almost overran him, Nala cast a large stone under one of its wheels and leapt to the side, barely avoiding the whirring blades.

The axle snapped as the chariot bounced high into the air and overturned, throwing Prahasta onto the ground. Holding a spiked club in one hand, the general stood up and charged toward Nala. Yet the monkey was too quick for him and sidestepped the blow. Rushing to the broken chariot, Nala pulled off one of the wheels and hurled it against Prahasta's chest. His breastplate gave way, and life left the Rakshasa champion's body.

With Prahasta's death, the first day of fighting ended. The monkeys and bears gathered their fallen and hid them in a forest to await proper burial. The demons carried off their dead as well and threw their bodies into the ocean where they disappeared with the outgoing tide.

A New Rakshasa Champion

Neither side had gained advantage over the other. But the death toll was higher among the forces of Lanka and caused Ravana's courage to fail. "If I lose my kingdom, my desire for Sita matters little," he brooded. "If I cannot kill Rama, then I welcome death."

As these dark thoughts filled his mind, Ravana heard a quiet voice behind him. "Oh, Father, dismiss your doubts and sorrows." He turned, and there stood his son, Indrajit, dressed in golden armor and looking every inch a magnificent warrior.

"My king, be of good cheer. Drink wine, and sleep. I can take the form of a hundred and eight false shapes. I will do a son's duty and return to the fight. Know that your foes already lie dead in the dust and that Sita shall be yours."

Ravana replied, "I am in a deep hole and cannot climb out—"

"My lord," Indrajit interrupted, "your foe does not know me. I will be a flame in dry grass that Rama fans. My fire will burst forth and consume him and his whole army."

"To kill Rama and Lakshmana is enough," said Ravana. "Their troops will melt away if those two are destroyed."

"So be it," answered Indrajit, and he turned and left the palace. Going to his secret grove outside the city, he built an altar and on it lit a small fire where seven flames flickered. Indrajit next lifted a bowl of buttery oil and doused it on the flames which blazed into a red and golden light. There, a dazzling chariot appeared, adorned with the golden faces of demons along its sides and pulled by four green-eyed tigers. An enormous bow and a quiver of magic arrows dipped in poison lay within it. If he shot one, another would instantly replace it.

Indrajit stepped into his fire-born chariot and tied back his long black hair. Then waving his left arm and hand around his head, he vanished.

On the field of battle the next morning, Vibhishana stood beside Rama and gazed at the blue sky, clear except for a few puffs of small white clouds. A look of worry came over his face, and he said to Rama, "Though I cannot see him, Ravana's son, Indrajit, rides to attack us. I hear the creaking of his chariot in the distance. He has fashioned it from fire, and while he remains within it, he cannot be defeated. We are deer fighting a lion. He will destroy us."

The little white clouds grew heavy and dark, and Rama and his army soon heard the chariot's terrible rattle and its tigers' growls. Lightning arced across the sky, thunder cracked, and a fiery axe came hurtling from the now black clouds and headed straight toward Rama. Sugriva saw it fall and threw himself in front of his friend. The axe struck through the Monkey King's brave heart and killed him at once.

From behind the beyond, Indrajit rained down arrows in a torrent of death. The crown prince of the Monkey Kingdom dropped, and his blood stained his golden fur bright red. An iron hook caught Nala the Bridge Builder in the chest, and he fell coughing, strangling, dying. An iron spear passed through Vibhishana's shoulder and fastened him to the ground. Everywhere the cries of the dying rose toward heaven.

Indrajit, terrible and invisible in war, furiously drove his chariot onward. As Hanuman leapt into the clouds to try to stop him, a sword flew toward the monkey champion. He grabbed it, but it became a beautiful young woman who cried in fright, "Release me! It is wrong to hold a woman against her will!" On hearing the word *wrong*, the just and noble Hanuman let her go.

Demon warriors now streamed from the gates of Lanka, and the animals withdrew in panic, many killed as they fled. Only Rama and Lakshmana remained on the field. They fired their arrows at the sky, but these could not hit their unseen target and dropped back to earth. The poisoned arrows of Indrajit, however, pierced the brothers' golden armor, with each receiving many wounds.

Rama sank to the earth first and collapsed, unconscious among the rolling heads and broken bodies of monkeys and bears. When Lakshmana saw his brother, he could not believe his eyes and wept. As he blinked to clear away the tears, several more arrows struck him, and he fell, his sight growing dimmer until the poison also wrapped him in darkness and he lay still.

Thinking he had killed Rama and Lakshmana, Indrajit returned to his hidden hillside grove outside Lanka and became visible once more. He called his servant and sent a message to Ravana to tell him the brothers were dead. Then shedding his golden armor, the mighty Rakshasa champion stepped from his chariot as it and his tigers vanished in smoke and flame. Now covered in only a deerskin, he sat beneath a tree, slowly breathing in and breathing out—a thin, pale figure at prayer, cut off from the savage world around him as darkness fell.

Hanuman's Great Deed

Though pinned to the ground, Vibhishana began to stir, and raising his head, he saw around him thousands of monkeys and apes and bears dead or dying. As his eyes cleared, he noticed at a distance a white shape move slightly. He pulled the spear from his shoulder, carefully stood, and went to find out what it was. He recognized Hanuman sitting on the ground, alive but bleeding from many sword slashes.

As Vibhishana drew closer, he saw lying near the white monkey Jambavan, the old bear chief—heavily wounded, groaning, and barely breathing. Vibhishana went to him first and offered water. "Great Bear Chief, you still live, despite the arrows in your side."

"I am blind from battle and pain," groaned Jambavan. "But tell me. Does Hanuman yet breathe?"

"He cannot be killed, and though sliced by Indrajit's sword, he walks toward us even as we speak," Vibhishana replied. "Why do you ask?"

"While he lives, we live. If he dies, we all die."

Hanuman now stood beside Jambavan and heard his words. "I am here next to you," he said, and he took the wounded chief in his arms to comfort him.

"And what of Indrajit?" Jambavan asked, barely able to speak.

Vibhishana said, "Earlier this day, he killed Rama and Lakshmana and left the battle. He has likely returned to his secret grove to escape earthly cares and to pray."

"Time is crucial," said the old bear. "Our army is scattered, and many are dead or terribly injured. But grief for the fallen must come later."

"What do you mean?" Hanuman asked.

Breathing heavily, Jambavan whispered, "I mean you, Son of the Wind. You are our only hope. Swiftly fly back over the sea, and head north. Go to the Himalayas, the source of the water of life. There, the holy River Ganges begins. Gather the mountains' healing plants and bring them here. Even their scent can heal us."

Hanuman crouched low, vaulted toward the sky, and sped to the snow-capped mountains. In less than three shakes of his tail, he plucked as many life-giving herbs as his arms could hold and headed back toward Lanka faster than a shooting star. In the swiftness of his flight, the plants became hot and steamy, causing their vapor to drift over the battlefield as he neared.

As Jambavan had predicted, the healing fragrance restored the wounded. It caused dead apes, monkeys, and bears to come back to life. Only the slain Rakshasas, thrown into the sea by their comrades and now underneath its waves, remained beyond the vapor's reach.

Nala awoke from his eternal sleep, and Jambavan stood and looked up. Laughing and crying at the same time, he called to Hanuman, "We are saved! We are saved!"

Sugriva next rose from death and with cool water bathed the blood-stained faces of Rama and Lakshmana until the brothers revived. The Monkey King rejoiced. "Look at what Hanuman has done. You and I live, and our army is restored."

Hanuman dropped from the sky and landed beside Rama. The prince embraced him and said, "I am blessed to see all of you alive again. But I do not want you harmed further. King Sugriva, I ask you to return home with your army. Let there be no more dying for my sake."

"How can we leave you after all we have been through?" asked the king.

Before Sugriva could say more, Hanuman interrupted, "Rama, we are your fast friends and have suffered with you and will suffer more if need be. We animals came before you, and you are our child. We will not desert you. Our days together must be without number."

With Hanuman's promise, the second day of the war concluded.

Ravana's False Hope

Ravana slept well that night, but when he awoke the next morning before dawn, the guards on the city walls told him that Rama had overcome death. The king hurried beyond the city to his son's grove and softly pled, "Help me yet again."

"Father and King," Indrajit said, "each of us has the power to choose right or wrong. The second has been your choice, and your wrongs are a fire that burns us to ashes. Though not readily seen, the world moves ever toward Goodness. It is on Rama's side, and you cannot stop its path."

"Save your talk. I do not care," said Ravana. "You are my greatest warrior, and I need you now."

"You are chasing nothing real, only shadows. But I will do as you request. You are my father, and I owe you a son's duty," Indrajit answered and followed Ravana back to the palace.

Searching for Sita in the park, Indrajit found her asleep under her tree—beautiful, yet thin and sad. He molded an exact copy of her and breathed life into it. Then calling for a flying chariot, he climbed aboard, carrying in one arm the figure he had made.

The pushpak rose and flew over Lanka's walls and hovered low near the animals' camp. Hanuman and many monkeys saw the false Sita as the figure cried, "Rama! Lakshmana!" and burst into tears.

"What is this?" shouted Hanuman.

Indrajit replied, "Anything to cause you torment." He grinned and drew his sword. A loud scream tore through the air as the Demon Prince sliced the fake Sita in two from her left shoulder to her right hip. One-half of the body he held while the other half tumbled to the pushpak floor.

A hopeless wail filled the air when the monkeys saw what occurred. Indrajit wiped the blood off his blade on Sita's hair, then let the half that he held also fall into his chariot. He circled slowly around, flew back over the walls of Lanka, and vanished.

Joined by Jambavan and Lakshmana, Hanuman told them what had happened, and they ran to find Rama. Vibhishana suddenly appeared. "Why do you run with terror on your faces?"

"Indrajit has killed Sita, slicing her in two!" the white monkey told him.

"Do not believe your eyes," said Vibhishana. "What you saw was not real."

"How can it be false?" asked Hanuman.

Vibhishana twisted his face, and its flesh broke into a thousand pieces, falling at his feet. His eyes, too, shattered like glass, leaving two empty holes in their place. The eyeless skull said, "Like me, Monkey, you are blind."

While Hanuman, Lakshmana, and Jambavan looked on in disbelief, the flesh and eyes returned, and Vibhishana reappeared, looking exactly the same as before. "What you just saw never happened. It was all a demon's trick. Now listen carefully. Indrajit let you see him because he did not ride in his tiger pushpak. Only within it is he invisible. To defeat us, he will again offer his fire sacrifice and summon his magic chariot to his secret grove. I will lead you to it, but we must hurry. Lakshmana, gather your bow and arrows. Jambavan, summon your bears."

Night had now fallen and wrapped the land in a blanket of darkness. Vibhishana and Lakshmana spotted a fire glowing through ancient trees. With his back to them, Indrajit stood before the altar and fed its flames from an iron pot filled with liquid butter. A black goat lay dead in a pool of blood beside him along with piles of spears. Indrajit mumbled, and the earth split open. Snakes slithered from the cracks and spread their poison over the tips of the spears.

By this time, Hanuman, Jambavan, and his bears had surrounded the grove. Fire danced on the altar. Indrajit had one more offering of butter to pour over it. Already a chariot had started to take shape within the flames, and the outlines of tigers clawed the hot air.

"Shoot," said Vibhishana, and a bolt sped from Lakshmana's bow, breaking the iron pot in Indrajit's hand. The vipers crawled back into the ground, and the tiger pushpak sank in the altar's blaze. His black hair floating in the air and the firelight glinting in his eyes, the Rakshasa prince whirled around. He drew his sword and twirled it above his head. But a second arrow from Lakshmana broke the blade in two. A third arrow with a razor-sharp edge in the shape of a crescent moon sliced through Indrajit's neck. For a moment, he paused where he stood as his head teetered, then toppled to the ground with his lifeless body. The mighty and glorious warrior disappeared, and in his stead lay a hideous demon, its rotten flesh covered with flies.

Hanuman hoisted Lakshmana onto his shoulders and took him to Rama. The prince praised his brother. "This war was lost while Indrajit lived. We are all grateful to you."

The animals cheered, "Hail Lakshmana! Victory to Rama!" And the third day of fighting ended.

The Demon King's Last Stand

The next morning, the news of his son's death plunged Ravana into deep despair, not because the king was sad but because he feared defeat. The citizens of Lanka trembled as well and cast about for blame, for death and destruction had come to every household. Some thought the she-demon Surpanakha at fault for persuading her brother to kidnap Sita. Others blamed Ravana for the costly war and his desire for Sita.

Alone now in his palace, the Demon King decided that he himself must take the fight to Rama and kill him. Armed with powerful weapons and drunk with the fever of war, Ravana mounted his pushpak and flew over the walls of Lanka ahead of what remained of his army. Hovering in mid-air, he saw Rama and the animal warriors marching toward the city's northern gate.

The signs did not favor a demon victory. Thunder rumbled through the dark gray sky, the ground quaked, and the mountains behind Lanka shook. Ravana's troops hung their heads low and moved without spirit. Yet the king plunged onward, advancing ever closer to death.

The Evil One sounded his conch shell, and the front lines of monkeys and bears scattered, unable to withstand the force of his charge. His bow string constantly twanging, he rained a shower of arrows at Rama, and though a few struck the prince, his own arrows stopped the rest of Ravana's in mid-flight.

Angrily, Ravana cursed the gods and exclaimed, "Why waste more arrows? I shall seize him and dash him to bits!" Yet he continued to shower Rama with missiles, though now the prince's bow met each one, arrow for arrow, and split them apart.

Powerless to move, both armies watched the battle between their leaders rage for two days. As the wounds made by Ravana took their toll, Rama felt his strength drain from his body. His courageous heart, however, wanted to fight on. Though his arms and legs ached, his spirit spurred him to take the last and largest arrow from his quiver.

Holding his breath, the prince took three steps back to steady his aim. Ravana jumped from his chariot and rushed toward him—a sword in one hand and a club studded with brightly flashing jewels in the other. The king himself glowed like a god, a halo surrounding him.

Rama fired. The arrow hit Ravana's breastplate, pierced the armor, and lodged in his chest where it burst his heart. As the Evil

One staggered, halted, and fell dead, a loud cry of thanksgiving rose to heaven from the monkeys and bears.

Carrying a small bundle, Hanuman came quickly to Rama's side. "What do you have, Monkey?" asked the prince.

"These are the precious things Sita dropped on our hill when Sugriva and I first saw her."

"At last she is saved, and we can be together again." Rama looked down at the blood-soaked ground, then up at the cloudless sky. "Beauty will come once more into my life. Find Sita, and tell her we have won." Hanuman sprang from the battlefield and reached Sita's grove beside the palace in Lanka.

In the meantime, Vibhishana had run to the body of Ravana and knelt beside it. With tears trickling from his eyes, he softly whispered, "Why did you not heed my warnings? Your lust for power and your desire for another man's wife have brought you to this end."

Rama went to Vibhishana and touched his shoulder. "Ravana was your brother and a valiant warrior. He lured me here and died, thus escaping the shifting shapes and shadows of this world and of time. No one can know what he might have achieved if he had not filled his heart with evil. Your duty is to honor him with a proper funeral. The battle for Lanka is over. Now kneel, Demon Prince."

Rama took water and poured it over the head of Vibhishana. "Arise, King of Lanka."

The new king stood and promised, "Fear us no more, Rama. Heaven created us all. We Rakshasas will do no more harm to those who are good. We will protect the temples, and we will dwell in peace."

At Vibhishana's command, some Rakshasa warriors carried away the dead Ravana and washed off the blood. Gently, they laid him on logs over which they had put soft deer hides. They placed a bow and sword beside him. Then covering him with a golden cloth and fresh flowers, they doused the logs in oil and burned the body. And so Ravana returned to the earth from which he was made.

Rama and Sita Reunited

While the warriors prepared Ravana for burial, Hanuman returned with Sita. In her grief, she had neglected her appearance, so she prepared herself, dressing as finely as she could, before she met her husband. When she arrived, the army gathered around Rama on the plain before Lanka. He stood ready to meet her.

After months of separation and loneliness, Sita felt awkward seeing her husband again before such a vast crowd and with his brother

Lakshmana and his friends Hanuman, Sugriva, Jambavan, and Vibhishana at his side. She approached Rama but noticed he seemed distant and cold, his mind far away. As she knelt before him, she thought, "What invisible wall stands between us?"

Rama remained silent for a long while before he spoke. "I rejoice that you are safe from Ravana, but you have been his captive for a year. When we return home and I am crowned king, the people will murmur against me. The worst will laugh and say, 'How can Rama accept a wife who lived with another man? She is unfit to be his queen.'"

The prince then turned to Lakshmana and said, "Should not a king be better than others, not subject to doubt and laughter? How can I rule without the respect of my people? How can I take Sita back?"

Not believing what she heard, the princess burst into tears. Through them, she said, "I am blameless. The Demon King kidnapped me and brought me here against my wishes. During my captivity, one name alone occupied my thoughts. Rama! Rama! Rama!"

Indeed, Sita's grief was so great she decided life was not worth living. Speaking to Lakshmana, she begged, "Prepare a fire so that I may throw myself into it and end my life in the purity of its flames."

Lakshmana paused and looked toward Rama, but the prince gave no sign to deny Sita's request. Ever loyal to his brother, Lakshmana gathered wood and soon readied a roaring fire. Horror-stricken by what was happening, the host of monkeys and bears watched the flames rise, licking higher and higher into the air. Rama stood as still as a statue and said nothing.

Sita stepped around her husband and approached the blaze. Kneeling and touching her head to the ground, she prayed to the Fire God. "Lord Agni, bear witness to my faithfulness to Rama. Save me if I have been pure." She then jumped into the center of the flames.

In the heart of the fire rose the beautiful Agni, clothed in bright red robes. From his eyes, pure drops of liquid gold dripped upon the ground. Taking Sita in his arms, he stepped from the blaze and set her unharmed before Rama.

"Oh, prince," said the Fire God, "I live within all life and am never deceived. You have acted in an all too human way, suspecting your wife of betrayal, though she remains loyal and innocent. Remember that our aim is to be like the Supreme Being, never letting jealousies and doubts cloud our minds. Accept your true nature by accepting your wife as she accepts you. Sita is one with you. You are one with Sita. All is one with God."

"My brother, heed Lord Agni," Lakshmana urged. "Do not grow old believing truth is what people think about others. Our life is like a mist on a lake. It vanishes quickly in the morning sun, and we must do the most good while we can. Sita, your loving wife, stands ready to take your hand."

"Speak no more," answered Rama, put to shame by the fiery trial of his faithful wife. "Sita is True Love, and I am hers, if she will have me."

With joy, the Fire God placed Sita's hand in Rama's. Then gently touching his face, Sita embraced Rama and whispered, "Oh, my husband, you are my one love." At these words, the animals on the plain of Lanka bowed before her, soft voices sang hymns of thanksgiving in the air, and sweet-smelling flowers fell from Heaven to signal approval.

Lord Agni said to the reunited couple, "Tomorrow ends your fourteen years of exile. You must go back to your home. Worry will torment your brother Bharata if you do not return."

Turning to Vibhishana, Rama asked, "Can you help us reach Ayodhya within a day?"

Vibhishana ordered Ravana's flying chariot brought to Rama and Sita. "Here is Ravana's pushpak. Say the time you wish to return, and it will carry you wherever you want to go."

The Return Home

Along with Hanuman, Sugriva, Jambavan, and Lakshmana, the couple mounted the pushpak and commanded it to take them home. They crossed the ocean and flew over mountains, forests, and rivers—places familiar to them from their adventures—and landed some distance from Ayodhya.

Outside the city in a small village, Bharata counted the hours as he waited. Throughout the fourteen years of his brother's exile, he had kept Rama's sandals to return them as promised. They were with him now.

Yet without any news or any sign of Rama, Bharata was becoming more and more worried. He called for their brother Shatrughna to come to him and said, "I do not know what has happened to Rama—whether he is alive or dead. I promised to govern in his name for fourteen years. The time is nearly over, and I have no right to reign in his stead. You must—"

Before Bharata could finish, Hanuman fell from the sky and landed with a bounce. Bowing first to Rama's sandals and then to the two brothers, the white monkey said, "I saw you as I flew above. My name is Hanuman, and I am the Son of the Wind and friend of Rama. Why do you stand here doing nothing? Rama, Sita, and Lakshmana have returned and will meet you in the capital tomorrow."

At the news, Bharata and Shatrughna wept tears of joy. Bharata sent runners to the capital and ordered signal fires lit to inform the villages and countryside. "Go and have the people prepare a welcome." As dusk fell, he said to Hanuman, "Stay with us tonight and rest."

Hanuman agreed, and after feasting on fruits and nuts, he sat by a fire's soft glow and told the story of how Ravana stole Sita, of the war in Lanka, and of Rama's victory. And when, late in the night, Hanuman had finished, Bharata and those with him gave thanks and blessed the monkeys and bears.

The next morning, two rows of painted elephants lined the road outside the gates of the Ayodhya, silk flags and banners flapped from its high walls and towers, music filled the streets, and people dressed in their brightest clothes—all to welcome Rama, Sita, and Lakshmana. Everything seemed peaceful, fresh, and new.

In the east, the pushpak came into view, gleaming in the early light of the sun and growing closer. It slowly descended but did not land. A ladder laced with flowers dropped to the ground, and Bharata led forward an elephant holding his brother's sandals. He took hold of the ladder and climbed into the chariot. Kneeling before Rama, Bharata put the sandals on his brother's feet.

Bharata rose and smiled and looked into Rama's eyes. "King of Ayodhya! I am blessed to see you and to return everything you left in my care. Take back this land you left in my trust." And turning to Sita and Lakshmana, he said, "I am doubly blessed that all of you are now safely home."

Bharata then faced Sugriva and Jambavan. "King of Monkeys and Lord of Bears, Hanuman has told me your story. Without you, faithful friends, this joyous day would not be possible, and for it we give thanks. I am your loyal servant always."

The party descended from the pushpak, and met by the men and women of Ayodhya, they entered the city in a celebration of song and dance. At the palace, the three mothers of Rama knelt to greet him and Sita. "Rise," said the prince to the three queens. "Be at peace, all of you, and know that the world always, if sometimes slowly, moves toward Goodness."

"We are all well," responded the oldest queen, Rama's true mother. "And by all that is Good, we see you again, safely returned to us." She then embraced her son.

At that moment, the chief priest and sage, who had been advisor to Rama's father, entered the room. To the youngest queen, he said, "Though you did not know it at the time, when your words and deeds sent Rama into exile, you saved the world from demon rule."

The old priest next addressed the mother of Lakshmana. "In his quiet way, your son has always been the support of Rama. His twin Shatrughna is also Bharata's strong and silent friend, and you and the other queens are friends with one another. Our hours and days are blessed indeed."

Then placing his hands upon Rama's shoulders, the sage declared, "Rule your city and your lands well, as far as they extend."

"Yes," said the prince.

Going to a balcony overlooking the city, the priest shouted to the people gathered below, "He will! He will!" At his words, a roar rose from the streets, and the palace shook with a tremendous noise. All the city rejoiced.

The next day, bright ribbons hung from the trees of Ayodhya, and its priests blessed everyone they met. When evening came, candles lit the outdoors like countless flowers of light. The night was crystal clear, and the stars glistened above. While Rama slept peacefully in his room, Sita sat in the palace garden by a fountain and listened to the soothing music of its water.

The old servant Manthara approached. She knelt before the princess. "Forgive me for causing your exile and your suffering."

Sita replied, "The evil Ravana once held the world in his hands, but now it is free from his grip. Rama killed him because of your words."

Manthara bowed her head and answered, "Princess! I am your servant always."

The Coronation

The stars soon fled from the sky, and the sun glowed a glorious red. The throne of Ayodhya sat in a wide park beside the palace where everyone could see Rama crowned king. With Sita by his side, the prince sat on the throne and faced the rising sun. The chief priest stood before them, and taking water drawn from the east and west, north and south, he poured it over Rama's head to make him king and Sita his queen. The people and animals clapped and cheered, "May your rule last forever!"

That day, Rama gave many presents to his followers, but to Sita he presented a necklace of perfectly round and shimmering pearls. As she held them, she looked at her husband, then at the pearls, and then at the monkeys and bears. "Give them to whomever you wish," Rama said.

Sita paused before she nodded for Hanuman to come forward. He knelt, and she circled the pearls around his neck. They glistened like small moons against his white fur. Smiling, she said, "When I had no one to comfort me in Lanka, you came and offered hope. These pearls, my friend, are for your courage, loyalty, help, and skill."

Throughout that day, celebrations continued in Ayodhya. When night fell, the king and queen entered their private rooms within the palace.

And so began Rama's long and prosperous reign. The world was kind, and the good earth provided food for everyone. Peace filled the land, and men and women lived to ripe old ages, surrounded by their loving families. And in truth, at no time before or after, was there ever a king as great as Rama or a queen as full of lovingkindness as Sita.

COMMENTARY: Along with the *Mahabharata*, the *Ramayana* (or *Rama's Way*) is one of the two spectacular epics of ancient India. Regarding its composition, dates vary, with it perhaps having been composed sometime in the first century BCE.[32] However, the date could range over a roughly four hundred year span between 200 BCE to 200 CE.[33] The authorship is attributed to the Sanskrit sage and poet Valmiki, a legendary figure who was once a robber but who later "converted to a virtuous life."[34] According to *Ramayana* scholar Robert P. Goldman, Valmiki was said to have "created the world's first true poetry in a spontaneous utterance" spurred by "his compassion for the mate of a bird struck down by a hunter."[35] Whoever may have been the author, he likely drew from numerous popular tales about his narrative's hero and synthesized them into a grand epic containing various "exotic and fabulous incidents."[36]

The work's influence on the people of India cannot be overstated. For two millennia, the adventures of Rama have been commemorated in sacred ceremonies and in public and private celebrations, and the story has inspired scores of other literary compositions.[37] In describing his own abridged retelling of a version by the eleventh-century Tamil poet Kamban of southern India, novelist R.K. Narayan notes that Valmiki's text has been the source of numerous adaptations where such languages as Hindi, Bengali, Tamil, and others regionally predominate.[38] Indeed, it is little wonder that an authority like Goldman finds the *Ramayana* to be among "the most enduring, widely diffused, and popular narratives in all of human history."[39]

The moral universe in which the *Ramayana* takes place revolves around the Hindu concept of *dharma*—that is, living a life of righteousness according to eternal moral law.[40] In fulfilling this duty, humans may attain ever higher planes of existence through reincarnation and prevent themselves from regressing to lower levels as a result of not following the cosmic code of justice.[41] As B.A. van Nooten points out, both Prince Rama and Princess Sita are exemplars of adherence to their *dharma* and thereby secure for themselves "a more agreeable position in the next life."[42] They have thus put into effect Hinduism's law of *karma*, the inviolable moral law of cause and effect which for them is reward for virtuous thought and behavior. For individuals who violate their *dharma*, retribution follows. As philosophy of religion professor Huston Smith describes *karma*, a related concept of Hinduism, individuals have "complete personal responsibility" in the moral universe and each decision freely made "must have its inexorable consequences."[43]

Much of the story focuses on the battle between the forces of Rama and those of Ravana for the demon capital of Lanka. One interpretation of the battle is that it "represents a glorified account" of the triumph of a more advanced Aryan culture from northern India over the less developed Dravidian people of the south as symbolized by the demon Rakshasas of Lanka. Based on archeological discoveries, this speculation is likely spurious since such findings indicate that advanced civilizations flourished in the southern regions of India for nearly as long as those occupied by the Aryans of the north.[44]

The sources for my abridgement and adaptation are both adaptations themselves. Rather than offering a work of precise scholarship, William Buck's 1976 rendering of the *Ramayana* trims the repetitions and digressions of the ancient sources to concentrate on the essential plot, characters, and settings to make the narrative more accessible to modern readers.[45] Among the more significant changes Buck made in his retelling is his omission of Rama's rejection of Sita when she returns to him after the defeat of the Rakshasas. The prince considers her virtue undermined by her long stay in Lanka with Ravana after he had abducted her. She, therefore, attempts to commit suttee to demonstrate that her honor is intact, but Lord Agni, the Fire God, rescues her from the flames of self-immolation and presents her to Rama as his still chaste wife. I have retained this episode and followed its presentation as given in the second source used, Narayan's 1972 retelling of Kamban's Tamil version of the epic. Like Buck, Narayan makes clear his rendition is not a literal translation. He terms it a "literary product."[46]

For commentary on Hanuman, the langur monkey who is Rama's loyal servitor and helper, see the heading "Old Monkey of China and Hanuman of India" in the introduction. The discussion there compares the connection between these two famous primates of Asian folk literature.

The Monkey and the Elephant
(from India)

Grand Tusk the elephant and Nimble the monkey were friends. Proud of how large he was, Grand Tusk one day said, "Look at me! Behold my strength and size!"

Nimble replied, "Look at me! I am quick and clever!"

"How much better to be large and powerful than quick and clever," the elephant answered.

"I think not," said the monkey. "To be quick and clever is much better than large and powerful."

So the two started to quarrel.

At last, Nimble said, "Let us not argue further with each other, but go to Dark Sage, the wise old owl, and have him settle the dispute." Grand Tusk agreed, and off they went.

Dark Sage lived in the dim twilight of an ancient tower. He heeded carefully what the monkey and elephant told him before he spoke. "You must do exactly as I say. Only then will I tell you who is better." Both agreed.

"Now look to the other side of the river that flows below my tower," said Dark Sage. "Behold yonder the great tree. Go across and bring me the mangoes that grow there."

Off went the two friends, but when they got to the river, it was broad and deep. Nimble cried out in fear, "We must turn back! I will never be able to cross so wide a stream!"

Grand Tusk laughed at the little monkey. "Did I not say large and powerful is better than quick and clever? The stream is nothing for me to swim across. Climb on my truck." And with it, he lifted Nimble onto his wide back and easily swam across the river.

In a short while, they reached the great tree, but it was far too tall for Grand Tusk to gather mangoes with his trunk, no matter how long he stretched it out. So he tried with all his might to push the tree down, but its roots held fast in the ground.

"I can't reach the mangoes," he finally admitted. "We will have to return without any."

Now it was Nimble's turn to laugh. "Did I not say quick and clever is better than large and powerful? I will get the fruit."

He swiftly scrambled up the tree and tossed down enough mangoes to fill a whole basket. Grand Tusk gathered them up, and as before, with Nimble upon his back, he swam across the river. They soon reached the tower of Dark Sage. "Here are the mangoes," declared the elephant. "Now give us your judgment as to which one is better—large and powerful or quick and clever."

The wise owl said, "Is not the answer obvious? You swam across the river, and your friend got the fruit. Sometimes it is better to be one, and sometimes it is better to be the other. Each gift has its place."

"How true," replied Grand Tusk.

"Even so," answered Nimble.

With that, the two left, and from that time forward, their friendship was stronger than ever.

COMMENTARY: From P.V. Ramaswami Raju's 1901 *Indian Fables*, "The Elephant and the Ape" is the source for this adaptation.[47] Bryce's 1910 *Fables from Afar* has the same talking beast story word-for-word as its opening selection.[48] The story contains the folk motif of a stark contrast between the elephant, Grand Tusk, and the monkey, Nimble.

The Monkey and the Mirror
(from India)

A monkey once came across a mirror in the forest and decided to show it to the different animals he knew.

When the bear saw his reflection, he said, "How sad. My face is so ugly."

When the wolf saw his, he declared, "I would prefer my face were like the stag's, crowned with majestic antlers."

And so it was that every animal that looked at its reflection found fault with its own face or preferred that of another.

Then the monkey took the mirror to the wise owl who had been watching everything. When the monkey offered to hold it up, the owl said, "I refuse to look into it. In my case, as with the others, to know would cause pain."

On hearing these words, the other animals exclaimed, "You are indeed right. Knowledge *is* painful."

COMMENTARY: "This very short fable is also from Raju."[49] As a matter of curiosity, it seems likely that the famed Victorian painter of landscapes and animals, Sir Edwin Henry Landseer (1802–1873), knew of this fable from an earlier source. Done between 1820 and 1829, some seventy years before *Indian Fables* appeared, Landseer's painting *The Reflection, the Monkey and the Looking Glass* has nearly the same title as Raju's story. Yet Landseer provides a different twist. In the Indian tale, the monkey gets other animals to look in the mirror. In Landseer's work, however, the monkey beholds itself, crouching and grimacing with an expression of surprised abhorrence at its own reflection, perhaps offering a satiric comment on the human condition.

The Monkey Prince
(from India)

There was once a king who had seven wives but no children. This matter troubled him so greatly that he became very angry. "I have married seven women, but God has not seen fit to give me a single child," he said one day. "I will go into the forest and die all alone, for there is no hope." His wives begged him to stay with them, but he refused, and off he went.

Journeying deep into the forest, the king met an ancient holy man who lived on only what people gave him. As he leaned on his staff, this fakir asked, "Why have you come here where tigers may kill and eat you? Tell me what you want, and I will give it to you."

At first, the king refused to answer, but finally he said, "Though I have seven wives, I have no children. So I came to the forest to die alone."

The old man replied, "Here, take my staff. Walk just a little farther until you come to a mango tree hanging with fruit. With one hand, throw the staff against its limbs, and with the other hand, catch the mangoes as they fall. When you have caught seven, go home and give one to each of your wives to eat."

So the king did as the fakir said, knocked down seven mangoes from the tree, and caught them. He then returned to the palace and began to hand out the fruit, but before he could give a mango to his seventh and youngest wife, the other six ate it because theirs had been so delicious. All she got was a seed, so she ate it instead.

Several months passed, and the six wives each had a son. But the seventh, who had eaten the mango seed, gave birth to a monkey. Although he was really a boy with a monkey-skin covering him, no one knew any better, so everybody called him Prince Monkey. Even worse, his six brothers hated the child. When they grew older, they attended school, but he was not allowed to go. He, therefore, went underground, and unbeknown to his mother, the fairies taught him. Even though he was the cleverest one of his brothers, she thought he did nothing but play in the forest and swing from trees.

In another realm far away lived a beautiful princess. Her father the king wanted more than anything to have her marry a very strong husband and thus had a huge iron ball made. He then sent letters to all the kings and princes near and far to tell them that anyone who wanted to marry his daughter would have to pick up the ball, toss it at the princess, and hit her. Many came to try their luck, but not one could even lift it, much less strike her.

The six brothers of the Monkey Prince heard about the challenge and decided they would try to win the hand of the princess. "Surely, I will be able to do what others have not," each one said to himself, and together they set out by land on the long journey.

The Monkey Prince, too, heard about the competition. Laughing quietly, he said, "I know I can succeed. I will go also."

But before the boy left, he went into the forest and removed his monkey-skin. At once, God gave him a fine horse and the rich clothes of a king to wear. The boy then followed his brothers, and when he caught up with them, he offered them flowers and betel leaf to chew to show his respect.

The brothers exclaimed, "Who is this lovely boy? His father must be a great prince!" But the youth said nothing and galloped off a short distance so that they could not see him. He removed his fine clothes, laid them over his mount, and again dressed in his monkey-skin. As his brothers renewed their journey, his horse rose above the trees, and the Monkey Prince secretly followed their path.

When the party reached the king's palace, the six brothers pitched their tents in a park within its walls. The monkey brother arrived soon thereafter covered by his skin. Even before the brothers had gotten to the competition, each evening the princess would stand on her high balcony, her long golden hair floating and flowing around her. The many suitors who had come earlier to seek her hand had tried to lift and throw the heavy iron ball and hit her. However, no one had yet succeeded. Each of the brothers, though, was certain he could complete the task. Before they left their camp, they said to the monkey boy, "Mind our tents while we are gone, and be sure to prepare a good dinner for us. If it is not ready when we return, we will give you a thrashing you will not soon forget."

As soon as they left, the monkey boy took some gold coins he had brought with him. Just outside the palace walls was a resting house for travelers. He went there, told the owner to prepare a grand meal, and paid him with the gold. The boy then took the food back to his brothers' tents, went into the forest, and removed his monkey-skin. Once again, God provided him beautiful clothes and a spirited horse. He dressed himself, mounted the grand steed, and rode back to the palace. He paid not the slightest attention to the king, the princess, the iron ball, or any of the suitors trying to lift it.

When the boy respectfully presented his brothers betel-leaf and beautiful flowers, everyone stared at him and whispered, "Who is this stranger so splendidly dressed? Where is he from? Was there ever a royal youth as handsome as this prince?"

As the princess beheld the stranger, she thought, "I do not care whether he lifts the iron ball or not. This is the prince I will wed."

As soon as the Monkey Prince had bestowed his gifts upon his brothers, he galloped back to the forest, removed his finery, and placed it upon his horse. This time, it rose into the air and disappeared into heaven. Putting on his monkey-skin, he returned to the tents and went to sleep.

When his brothers arrived, all their talk concerned the handsome stranger. Even as they ate, they spoke of nothing else other than this prince.

For ten days, the same event occurred with one exception. Each time the unknown prince appeared, he wore different clothes. The princess still made the same promise to herself. "Whether he can toss the ball or not, this is the prince I will wed."

However, on the eleventh day, having given his gifts to his six brothers, the stranger addressed the gathered suitors, the king, and the attending servants. "I want all of you to withdraw to a far distance, for I intend to throw the ball."

"No! No!" they shouted together. "We wish to stand here so as to see you better."

"But the heavy ball might land among you," the handsome prince answered. "You will be safer at a distance." So the crowd retired to watch him from afar.

Dusk had now fallen, and the Monkey Prince raised the ball with one hand, as if it weighed nothing, and tossed it at the balcony railing. The ball fell short of its target. With that, he galloped into the forest.

The next evening, he returned. When he threw the ball this time, it lightly hit the clothes of the princess and caused no harm.

On the third evening, the ball dropped on her left foot and bruised her little toe. The princess now became angry. Here was this handsome prince, whom no one knew and who had thrown the ball at her three times, hit her twice, and on the third try had hurt her little toe. Yet after each attempt, he rode off as fast as he could without speaking to anyone, much less her father the king.

The princess decided the next day would be different. She, therefore, had a bow and arrow brought to her and vowed that, when the unknown prince arrived, she would shoot him if he hit her again. Because she loved him, though, she would not kill him but only fire an arrow.

When the Monkey Prince threw the ball on the following evening, it hit the other foot of the princess, this time bruising her big toe. Seeing what happened, he was sorry and said, "I did not mean to throw the ball so hard as to hurt you."

The princess did not answer but shot her arrow and wounded the prince's leg so badly that blood spurted from it. He immediately jumped on his horse and galloped off. However, he did not remove his royal clothes but wrapped his monkey-skin over them. His horse rose heavenward, and he returned to his brothers' tents.

In the meantime, the princess had ordered a servant to go into town. "If you hear anyone or anything moaning in pain, whether man or beast, bring him to me," she instructed.

As night had fallen, the brothers had gone to sleep in their tents, but the monkey boy could not rest because of his leg wound. Returning from town, the servant walked through the park and heard something crying. He seized what he thought was a wounded monkey and brought him to the princess.

The next morning, the princess took the monkey to her father and proclaimed in front of him and his court, "This is the one I will wed."

"What!" shouted the king. "That monkey! No! No! No! How dare you think you can marry a filthy monkey?"

Yet, despite her father's rage and protests, the princess insisted. "I love this monkey and will marry him."

After much back and forth, the king at last gave in. "Though I have never heard of such a thing, if it is your will, then marry the nasty creature."

On the wedding day, while the bride appeared in her most beautiful clothes and adorned in her finest jewels, the groom wore his monkey-skin. But that night, he cast aside his covering and lay beside the princess. When she saw that her husband had now become the handsome prince, her heart rejoiced.

"Why do you dress in a monkey-skin?" the princess asked.

"I wear it to protect myself. You must tell no one who I really am. If my brothers knew, they would kill me for spite."

After the wedding, the prince and princess lived with her father the king for six months. They were very happy. His six older brothers continued to reside there as well, and each day they despised their younger brother more and more. For he had married a beautiful wife, and they had wed no one.

It so happened one night that Prince Monkey remembered his mother, and to his wife he remarked, "I have been away from my mother for a long time. Perhaps she is sad and longs to see me. Let us return to my own land and visit her." The princess readily agreed, and the next day the couple received permission from her father to travel there.

When the six brothers heard about the request, they intruded, "We will go, too. We can travel by water on two large boats, one for the happy couple and one for us. That way, it should only take six days to reach our father's kingdom. When we came here by land, our journey took six months"

The plan seemed well-considered, so the Monkey Prince agreed. Yet that night, the princess passed by a chamber where she heard the brothers whispering. The eldest said, "On our way, we will throw the monkey overboard and let him drown. When we come to our country, our father can then decide which one of us will marry the princess."

At first stunned by what she heard, the princess composed herself and wisely ran to her father. "I beg you, Father, have prepared for my journey six large mattresses stuffed full of cotton."

"As you wish, my daughter," said the king. "But for what purpose do you want them?"

"I want to be comfortable when I travel," the princess replied. Thereupon, the king had the mattresses made, well-stuffed with cotton, and put aboard her vessel.

The princess next informed her husband of the plot against him. "Do not approach your brothers or speak to them," she cautioned. "They plan to kill you."

Everything thus readied, the couple boarded their boat, and the six brothers theirs. On the first day of the voyage, they called from their vessel to the prince, "Will you fetch us some salt?"

Old habits die hard. Being used to his brothers' commands and ignoring his wife's warning, Prince Monkey said, "No, but my wife will bring you some."

"That would be unseemly for your wife," the six returned, for they still considered their brother beneath them because he wore his monkey-skin. "No, you must fetch it." They then tossed a rope from their boat to his, and he started to walk across. When he was midway, they untied the rope, and their brother fell into the water.

The princess saw what happened and in alarm shouted, "My husband cannot swim and will drown!" Thinking fast, she tossed a mattress overboard. The monkey climbed on it and buoyed on the surface, floated back to his wife and boat where the sailors pulled him up.

The second day, the brothers ordered the monkey to fetch them water and dropped a board from their vessel to his. Despite his wife's pleas, he began to cross, but they tipped the board over, and the prince again fell into the water. The princess quickly threw him a mattress.

Over the next four days, the brothers tried their same trick. They would command the monkey to bring them food or drink by crossing a rope or plank and then cause him to fall into the water. He would have drowned, indeed, had not his wife thrown him a mattress each time.

When Prince Monkey and his brothers reached their father's kingdom, the eldest ran ahead of the rest to his mother's house on the grounds of the palace. Bowing, he pressed his hands together and said, "Mother, I wish to present to you the beautiful bride I have brought home. Ready your palanquin so that the servants may carry her here from my boat."

The news delighted the mother, and she told the other wives, "I am so happy that my son has married a beautiful bride. Oh, how happy I am."

On hearing these words, the youngest wife started to weep bitter tears. "Oh, my son," she cried. "He is only a monkey and will never marry anyone."

With the palanquin prepared, the seven wives and the eldest son left to get the princess. She had already landed and stood by the water with her monkey. When the ladies saw her, they murmured, "How lovely. How beautiful." The eldest wife rejoiced more than ever, and the youngest wept even more.

The princess stepped onto the palanquin, her monkey still beside her. "Why is that beast with you?" the eldest son demanded. "Put him out now!"

Yet the princess refused. "No, this is my husband whom I dearly love. I will not put him out."

"What?" cried the others. "You have a nasty monkey for a husband!"

"Yes, indeed."

"Then remove yourself from my palanquin this instant," the eldest wife ordered. "You may not ride in it with that filthy creature."

Beholding the scene, the youngest wife's heart leapt in joy. "My monkey son has a beautiful bride," she said to herself.

Hugging her monkey husband in her arms, the princess stepped from the palanquin and went straight to his mother's house, and there the couple lived for some time. The mother still had no idea that her son was really a handsome man, for she had seen him in only his monkey-skin. The princess never told her who he really was because of his request not to reveal his true nature to anyone for fear of his brothers.

One evening, the servants in the palace held a grand nautch on the grounds, and the king, his six sons, and various princes from surrounding kingdoms came to the dance. The monkey brother decided that he, too, would attend the dance. He removed his monkey-skin and placed it under his wife's pillow. He then dressed in the fine clothes he wore when he last tossed the ball at his wife. He had kept these and never placed them on the back of his steed when he had last put on his monkey-skin.

Looking like the handsome prince that he was, he walked over the grounds where the nautch was being held. Great crowds of royalty and common people attended, and when the prince passed among them, they exclaimed in awe, "Who is this handsome young man with golden hair and fine clothes?" After observing the dance for a while, he returned to his mother's house and to his wife, and when the rosy-fingered dawn appeared, he removed his finery and put on his monkey-skin.

During all this time, the monkey prince's mother, even though she was happy he had married a beautiful wife, remained puzzled over what her daughter-in-law saw in him. After all, he was a monkey. "How could you wed such a creature?" his mother would ask the princess.

And the answer always came back, "Because I wanted to marry him."

"Are you really happy with a monkey?" the mother would then query.

"Of course," said the princess. "I love him."

These replies never satisfied the mother and only deepened her wonder at it all.

The servants soon held another nautch. Leaving his monkey-skin under his wife's pillow, the monkey prince attended it as well. This time, however, when he left the house, the princess called to her mother-in-law, "Come. I will prove to you your son is not a monkey but an exceedingly handsome man. In beauty, he has no equal."

The mother could not believe her ears but became convinced when the princess lifted her pillow to reveal her husband's monkey-skin as she added, "Your son becomes a monkey when he wears this, but as soon as he takes it off, he turns into a handsome man. I feel he has worn it long enough and should remain a man. I am going to burn his disguise. What do you think?"

Concerned, the mother replied, "Yet he may be hurt if you set fire to his skin. He might even die."

"No, no, my beautiful husband will not die. Shall I put the skin in the fire?"

"Yes, put it in the fire," his mother said.

So the princess placed the monkey-skin on the flames, and it slowly burned to ashes.

As Prince Monkey sat watching the dance, in his mind's eye he saw his wife burning his skin. He sprang to his feet and ran home, and there what he had imagined turned out to be real. In his anger, all he could say to his wife was "Why have you destroyed my skin?" Indeed, his ire was so great that he stormed out of the room and went straight to bed.

When the sun rose the next morning, while the prince was still asleep, the princess got up and tiptoed to his mother. "Come and look at your handsome son."

"No, I cannot. He is a monkey. I fear my shame is too great."

"What nonsense! What shame is there is seeing your own son!"

"Come," said the princess.

Urged thus by her daughter-in-law, the mother went into her son's room, and when she saw his loveliness, her heart grew glad. As she gazed in the golden rays of the early morning sun, the prince awoke, beheld his mother, and kissed her.

The house servants heard of the wonderful change in Prince Monkey, and the news quickly spread throughout the confines of the palace. Everyone there came to look for themselves. When they saw his beauty, with his hair all gold, they fell down in awe, including his father the king.

Prince Monkey raised the old man up and said, "Father, you must not bow before me, for I am your son, and you are my father."

And rising to his feet, the king asked, "Why did you clothe yourself as a monkey?"

And the prince answered, "My mother ate a mango seed and not the sweet fruit itself. God thus ordered that I should be born in a monkey-skin and fated to wear it until I found a wife."

Then the prince's brothers marveled, "Who would think that such beauty as yours resided within it. The ways of God are beyond understanding." And from that moment, they ceased to hate the monkey boy and loved the prince as one of their own.

Throughout the realm, there was much feasting, attended with great rejoicing. And the six elder brothers lived happily with their father and Prince Monkey, though not one of them ever found himself a wife.

COMMENTARY: This folktale comes from *Indian Fairy Tales*, translated into English by Maive Stokes and first published in 1879.[50] As a child, Stokes listened to its thirty stories as they were told to her in Hindustani by three household servants working for her family in India. She credits her young nursemaid, Dunkni, as the source of "The Monkey Prince."[51]

Dunkni's very fine narrative contains many common components of folklore: the magical transformations back and forth of the title character from monkey to handsome prince; the stark contrasts between the monkey boy and his grasping elder brothers; his quest to find a human bride and the accompanying task with the iron ball to win her hand; the supernatural helpers—the fakir, or holy man, who helps the king obtain children, and God, who helps the monkey boy overcome various obstacles to obtain a wife; the human helper when his wife tosses him mattresses to prevent him from drowning; and the ultimate triumph of the underdog as embodied in Prince Monkey.

The story also has the eternal literary theme of appearance versus reality as epitomized by the protagonist who to others seems to be a nasty monkey but who is really a handsome man. However, lest any reader perceive in this tale a positive portrayal of simians, the Monkey Prince is despised by everyone, except his wife and mother, when he wears his monkey-skin. His true worth is recognized and accepted only when he makes his final transformation from beast to beauty.

The Men Who Became Monkeys
(from the Lotha of India)

Once upon a time, a man named Kimothang went to the husbands of his sisters. He gave the men some rice beer before he made a request. "I've chopped down a tung tree to use as a post for sacrifices. I want you to drag it here but be sure no leaf falls off."

The men then went and started to drag the tree. The leaves, though, had already withered, and they kept dropping to the ground. Before dragging the tree further, the men tied onto its stems the remaining leaves to prevent any others from falling.

Despite these efforts, the leaves kept dropping until the tree had not a single leaf remaining. Too ashamed to go to Kimothang and tell him what had happened, the men slipped off into the jungle where they turned into myna birds. "Kyon! Kyon! Men! Men!" they called and trilled.

Back in the village, the men's wives heard their cries and ground up rice for flour and beer. When the women walked into the jungle, the men called out "Woka! Woka!"

The women rubbed some of the rice flour onto the birds' heads. This time, the men turned into gibbons, and ever since these monkeys have had a white circle around their faces.

COMMENTARY: This tale and the two that follow it are *pourquoi* stories which explain either a physical or behavioral trait of monkeys such as the white hair that encircles the faces of gibbons. Published in 1922 by J.P. Mills in *The Lhota Nagas*, all three narratives derive from the Lotha (or Lhota) and other related tribes that lived in the Naga Hills of the far northeastern part of India in the state of Nagaland which borders modern-day Myanmar (formerly Burma). About two million Nagas live in Nagaland, and approximately one hundred thousand in northern Myanmar.[52] As with other Nagas tribes, the origins of the Lotha are uncertain. Because of population growth, the Nagas migrated from Central Asia and eventually arrived in their present location. As to the specifics of migration by the Lotha, they supposedly traversed the Himalayan foothills before they resettled. Prior to British colonization, the Lotha lived a solitary existence in isolated communities—"a life that was in tune with nature and reminiscent of the old ways."[53] Along with the stories Mills collected, he also gathered ethnographic information on the Lotha before their traditional religious and other communal ceremonies were overly affected by outside contact with Baptist missionaries to the north and Hindu influences south of the region.[54]

Mills titles this particular story "How Men Were Turned into Gibbons."[55] Based on Howard E. Hutton's note in Mills, the men's transformation appears to be a satire on two Lotha clans whom other groups in the tribe "despised" and regarded as gibbon clans.[56] A note by Mills indicates that *kyon* means "man."[57] As for the word *woka*, I have been unable to find an English equivalent. Perhaps the Lotha used it to signify a sound made by gibbons like the *wu-wu* chatter of the monkeys in the following tale.

The tung tree in the story is a small tree of Asia. From its nuts, tung oil is extracted for use in furniture finishes. An early use for the oil was in lamps.[58]

The Children Who Were Turned into Monkeys
(from the Lotha of India)

A husband and wife had a son and daughter. The wife died, so the man took a new bride. Now this woman did not care at all for her husband's children and treated them badly. Things got worse and worse.

One day, the new wife told the children, "Go down and watch the fields. Don't bother to come home. Stay there, and I will send you food."

Instead of food, though, she sent the boy and girl rat turds, chicken droppings, and rice husks, all stirred together and bundled up in leaves. When the children untied them, they realized the woman had given them only filth to eat. So they began to pick and eat berries from the jungle. Eventually, they forgot what real food was like.

One day, their father went down to the fields to see his son and daughter and to bring them human food. "Come and eat," he called.

When the children saw what he had brought, they said, "Father, it has been so long since we ate human food we don't remember what it is like."

As soon as they said these words, the boy and girl began to chatter "Wu-Wu! Wu-Wu! Wu-Wu!" again and again. Hair grew all over their bodies, and they each grew a long tail. They had turned into monkeys.

Their father said to them, "You are now monkeys. You will wait for *emong* when our people gather together to rest from work. Then, when no one is around, you will go into the fields, and you will dig up the roots and seeds we have planted."

Even so today, when people keep *emong*, monkeys enter the fields and scratch up the seeds and roots.

COMMENTARY: This story of magical transformation also appears in Mills[59] and explains why monkeys dig up plantings when the villagers are keeping *emong*, a word meaning "gathered together."[60] Each year in November, the Lotha of Nagaland celebrate Tokhu Emong, as a time to express thanksgiving, relax, and enjoy the fruits of their labor. This grand harvest festival of "dazzling ambience" lasts nine days and among other activities includes song and dance and inviting friends and family into homes for food and drink.[61]

How the Langur Got Its Tail
(from the Lotha of India)

Sometimes called Hanuman monkeys, langurs are gray with dark tails and faces. These body parts were burned black when the Rakshasas of Lanka set Hanuman on fire. Long ago, however, before Hanuman's time, langurs did not have long tails. Here is how they got them.

In the old days, the animals were not that different from one another, and the big sambar deer and langurs were close companions, having sworn friendship to one another. At that time, the sambar had very long tails, but the langurs had none whatsoever.

One day, a langur asked a sambar for his tail. "My friend, I would like to try out your tail to see how it looks on me. Would you let me borrow it for a while?"

The sambar willingly agreed. "Here, friend, take my tail, and see if it becomes you," and the deer gave the langur his tail.

Yet, as soon as the monkey put it on, he scooted up a tree. After a while, the sambar thought he should have his tail returned. "Climb down, friend," he said, "so that I can have my tail again." But the langur ignored him.

The sambar could do nothing, but he still wanted a tail. So he removed his liver to make a shorter one. People today say this is the reason sambar tail is good to eat. It tastes just like liver.

COMMENTARY: This third *pourquoi* from *The Lhota Nagas* is adapted from "The Sambhur and the Hanuman Monkey."[62] The story associates the sambar's long black tail with that of the langur, or hanuman monkey, here cast in the role of trickster.

Sambhur is a variant spelling for sambar, a deer of southern Asia not quite the size of an elk. Large males can weigh up to twelve hundred pounds. The species' population is in serious decline because of hunting and loss of habitat.⁶³ These deer have been introduced into New Zealand, Australia, and the United States in Florida and Texas for purposes of preservation and hunting. Rapid population growth of the sambar in parts of Australia has resulted in problems in biodiversity. Some states in Australia now consider the species a pest and allow hunting year round with no limit on kills. In Texas, the deer are part of exotic big game imports.⁶⁴ As such, they are hunted in both confined areas and on free ranges.⁶⁵

The Monkey Husband
(from the Santhal of India)

One hot day, some children went to a place where water pooled in a stream. Leaving their clothes on the bank, they splashed in the water to cool off. A langur watched them, grabbed a cloth of one of the girls, scurried up a tree, and quickly vanished.

When the children got out and dressed, they found one of the cloths had disappeared. Looking here and there, they saw the langur sitting on a limb and holding it in his paw. "Give us back the cloth," they pled.

"I will," replied the monkey, "but only if the girl who owns it will marry me."

The children could not believe what they heard and began to fling sticks and rocks at the monkey. But he just climbed out of the way to a higher limb.

Seeing that their actions were useless, the children ran to the girl's parents and told them about the monkey. The parents then called to their neighbors for help, and soon a large crowd gathered with bows and arrows. When they got to the tree, they threatened to shoot the monkey if he did not return the girl's cloth.

"I will give it back if she will marry me," the langur repeated.

So the people shot arrows at him, but not a single one hit the mark. With that, the neighbors concluded, "It can't be helped. Your daughter must marry the monkey. That's why all of our arrows missed him."

Greatly distressed, the mother and father started to cry and chant, "Monkey boy, give our daughter her silk cloth. Give the girl her cloth."

But the monkey repeated his demand, this time in a verse:

> If she agrees to marry me,
> I'll place the cloth within her hand,
> Your daughter, though, must first agree
> That she will marry none but me.

Back and forth went the pleas of the parents and the demands of the monkey. After a while, the father's younger brother and his wife joined in the chant begging the monkey to return the cloth. Then the girl began to plead as well. When the langur heard her, he lowered the end of the stolen cloth. The girl caught hold of it, and when she did, the monkey pulled her up to his perch, wrapped the cloth around her, and scampered off with her clinging to his back.

The girl seemed happy to run away with the beast. For she called down to her mother and father, "Don't worry about me. I'm going off with the monkey."

The langur and the girl escaped to the mountains where he found a cave, and each day he would leave and shake down from the nearby trees whatever fruit was ripe for her to eat. However, if she saw any bite marks on it, she pretended to be full. For she refused to eat after a monkey.

One day, the girl said, "I've had enough. I'm tired of eating only fruit. I want some rice." So the langur set out with her to a bazaar in a village that was close by. Leaving her on its outskirts, he entered the stalls where goods were being sold. There he stole some pots, salt, rice, and spices and returned to the girl where she was sitting under a tree. She built a fire and cooked the rice.

After tasting the rice, the monkey decided he liked prepared food and said, "I want you to cook for me every day." The two continued in this manner for a while, the langur stealing food and the girl cooking what he stole.

After a while, the girl decided she wanted some new clothes, and the monkey went to the bazaar to steal them, too. By now, though, the vendors, having gotten wise to his thefts, were on the lookout and drove him off.

After this turn of events, the girl said to her husband, "I'm tired of living outside and sleeping under a tree."

So the pair returned to the cave, and as before the monkey gathered mangoes and other ripe fruit. But this time he told the girl to take it to the bazaar and sell it. "With the money you make, you'll be able to buy some clothes."

The girl did as the langur said, but upon selling the fruit, she remained in the village. There, a well-off merchant hired her to work in his shop. Though the monkey waited for her to return, she never did, and though he searched for her at the bazaar, he never found her and in sorrow at last went back to the cave in the mountains. As for the girl, she eventually married one of the men in the village.

COMMENTARY: The original appears under the same title in Cecil Henry Bompas' 1909 *Folklore of the Santal Parganas*.[66] The Scandinavian minister O. Bodding first compiled the collection and had the stories transcribed in the language of the Santhal (or Santal) which Bompas later translated into English during the British Raj. Parganas is a district in the state of West Bengal where Bompas worked in the Indian Civil Service and where many of the Santhal still live. This ethnic group today numbers over five million in eastern India. Besides West Bengal, the Santhal population is found throughout the states of Bihar, Jharkhand, and Orissa. Approximately two hundred thousand live in Bangladesh and ten thousand in Nepal.[67] Bompas indicates that his collection preserves the integrity of Santhal folktales before they were unduly affected by outside influences from Europe and other parts of India.[68]

"The Monkey Husband" is one of three tales in Bompas' collection in which a monkey seeks to wed a woman. Less detailed than this story in which the girl resists a langur's advances, "The Monkey and the Girl"[69] offers an interesting comparison. In this version, to her parents' chagrin, the girl from the outset willingly wishes to wed a langur. Aided by his fellow villagers, the angry father shoots the monkey. They then decide to cremate the body as if it were a human being. The girl diverts their attention from the blaze and throws herself onto the pyre, thus committing suttee, a traditional practice whereby an Indian wife kills herself to join her husband in death. The girl's act upsets her father and brothers who declare she must have had a "monkey's soul."[70] Thereupon, they purify themselves with a ritual bath and go home.

"The Monkey Boy" is a third, more detailed version of a girl marrying a monkey[71] but with significant differences. It begins with a wife who has borne her husband eight children. A ninth is on the way, but the husband dies. When the child arrives, he turns out to be a monkey. Although her relatives and fellow villagers advise her not to keep him, she decides to rear the child anyway. Her choice results in banishment to a hut on the outskirts of the village. As the monkey boy grows up, he learns to talk like a human being. His siblings, however, laugh at their brother and generally have little to do with him. Through hard work and his wits, he successfully grows an abundant crop of rice and in a horse race wins a bet against his brothers. He eventually becomes rich and seeks a wife. As in the "Monkey Husband" and "The Monkey and the Girl," the monkey boy steals a cloth from a girl who is bathing. He similarly promises to return it if she will marry him. Bewitched by his conversation, she agrees, whereupon he pulls her by the hair into his tree and the pair abscond. Again, as in the other two tales, the girl's father and relatives seek to kill the monkey boy with their bows and arrows, but he cannot be found. In contrast to the other two variants, he and the girl return to the village, her family accepts him, the couple officially wed, and both live happily ever after.

"The Monkey Boy" contains several character motifs frequently found in folktales. Living on the fringes of the village in his early life, the protagonist is an outcast who is belittled by his older siblings. They also perceive him as a simpleton when he plants pumpkin seeds and says he has grown rice. And yet he turns out to be a wise fool because inside the pumpkins is an abundance of rice to feed him and the members of his family who scoffed at his efforts at farming. Through use of his wits as an adult, he becomes a trickster who deceives a horse dealer into selling him the fastest mare of his stock which he later uses to outrace the horses purchased by his arrogant human brothers and gain a small fortune, thus putting him on the road to marriage and much success in life. The ironic upshot of the story is that the lowly monkey boy, once rejected and scorned, not only achieves acceptance but also greater success than his proud brothers, a further example of a stark contrast often embedded in traditional narratives.

The Monkey Nursemaid
(from the Santhal of India)

There were once seven brothers who lived together in the same house. All had married and had one child apiece. To help with the children, the brothers decided they would hire a boy to carry the children from place to place.

When the boy arrived for work, the brothers thought they should first test him to see whether he had enough strength for the job. So they baked a loaf of bread the size of a door and asked him to carry it off and eat it. Unfortunately, he could not lift the loaf and thus proved himself not strong enough for the expected work.

While the brothers were testing the boy, a langur in a nearby tree had observed everything. When the boy failed to pick up the loaf, the monkey dropped from his limb, picked up the bread, and ate it as if it were nothing. Upon seeing the langur's strength, the brothers' wives hired him at once to help with the children. In fact, he proved to be so strong that he would carry all seven on his back at the same time.

One day, as the children ran about and hindered the housework, the mothers fussed at the langur for not minding the boys and girls better. The beast then began to pout and not long after, taking the wages he had earned thus far, sneaked away with the children to a hill some distance from the village.

When the monkey did not return with them at dusk, the mothers were worried sick over their children's whereabouts. But the other villagers, on hearing about the incident that evening, made a big joke. "How could anyone be so foolish," they laughed, "as to hire a monkey instead of another person to mind children!"

Then someone said, "Oh, the monkey probably took the children to a hill some distance from here and hid them."

Now the mothers became even more upset. For one hill in particular was home to a rakhas, or ogre. Boys and girls were among his favorite foods. Yet, for the moment, nothing could be done as it was too late and too dark to go in search for the children.

Meanwhile, having caught sight of the rakhas and fearing the danger posed, the langur carried the children up a tall palm tree. Fast on his tail, the rakhas tried to scale the tree as well, but the monkey pelted him so hard with toddy palm fruit that the brute ran off.

Fearing the ogre might return, the monkey still felt himself to be in a fix, so at first light, he took his money and hurried to a blacksmith's shop he had passed on his way to the hill. There, he bought sharp knives and tied them to the palm tree.

Sure enough, the ogre came back and tried to climb up, but the knives cut his hands and feet so much that he toppled to the ground. *Kerplunk!* He landed heavily with the wind knocked out and lay completely still.

Ever so cautiously, the langur climbed down. Unable to rise, the rakhas groaned and begged, "Oh, monkey, please help me. I am cut so badly I must surely die."

"Rahkas, I will cure your wounds, but you must give me new clothes for the children."

"Yes, anything you want. But cure me first," whimpered the ogre.

So the monkey chanted some time-honored spells:

> Murmuring, whispering sesamum,
> Seven cords to tie the waist
> For seven dhotis the legs to grace—
> Give us these, oh, sesamum,
> To cure the rakhas' bloody wounds!

He then recited further verses that spoke of seven coats, seven pairs of shoes, seven caps, seven horses, and seven hogs.

As the monkey chanted, he blew his breath on the ogre and listed all the things he must give. Yet, when the monkey mentioned the seven hogs, the rakhas balked, declaring the number too many and that one hog would have to do.

"I will not be greedy," said the langur. "Though I will not take seven hogs, you must give me two for you to be healed. With two, I will be content. You must further promise not to eat any of the children or their parents."

With this agreement, the *rakhas* was cured and left to fetch the gifts. As promised, the next day he returned with seven waist cords, seven dhotis, seven coats, seven pairs of shoes, seven caps, seven horses, and two hogs. The monkey dressed the boys and girls in their new finery and sat each one on a horse. He and the ogre then mounted the hogs, and they all set out for the village.

Frightened at first, the mothers beheld the parade headed their way, but on seeing their children, they rejoiced. The langur dismounted from his hog and presented the boys and girls to their parents who were so delighted that they feasted both the monkey and the ogre.

When the festivities ended, the ogre left for his hill. As for the langur, he gave up his position as nursemaid and departed as well, sent on his way amid the good wishes by all for his future health and good fortune.

COMMENTARY: Another story adapted from Bompas' collection about a langur interacting with people, this time as a caregiver for some village children.[72] The plot presents vivid contrasts, here between monkey and monster. Although not a genuine trickster, the weaker langur is clever enough to outwit and neutralize a stronger but not very intelligent ogre who is bloodthirsty like all his kind. However, with his promise not to eat the children or their parents, the tale softens his nature.

The langur's magic chant contains two words that may not be familiar to the reader. *Sesamum* is an erect annual flowering plant that dates from antiquity and that produces sesame seeds and cooking oil. The plant's height runs from two to nine feet.[73] Like all bushes, its leaves will rustle in the wind and produce a murmuring, whispering sound. *Dhoti* refers to baggy pants sometimes worn by either sex in India and surrounding countries but often thought of as "common to the subcontinental men of India."[74] The pants are made by winding a long strip of cloth around the legs and waist. A drawstring is often used to hold dhotis in place. Deemed by the ancient Greek historian Herodotus to be "exceedingly beautiful," the dhoti is considered "ideal to wear during the hot summer months as it provides ventilation."[75]

As for the toddy palm fruit, sometimes called Palmyra fruit, with which the langur pelts the ogre, nearly all parts of the tree have benefits for people. For instance, the fruit contains vitamins and minerals, and its ripe inner flesh is sweet like coconut water.[76] Writing for *Medical News Today,* Karen Veazey says that one of its products, jaggery, is a "superfood sweetener" much better for consumption than refined sugar. She describes jaggery, also known gur, as having a golden yellow color and tasting similar to brown sugar or molasses.[77]

The Sultan's Daughter and the Baboon
(from the Middle East)

The daughter of the Sultan of Bagdad fell in love, not with a man of royal birth, but with someone far below her station. The man who moved her heart was a black slave of her father's court. In her passionate addiction to the amorous affair, the young sultana lost her maidenhead. Indeed, she could not endure to be parted from her lover for more than an hour, yet to consummate their bliss was often difficult.

As a consequence of thwarted desire, the sultana gave vent to her frustration to her closest handmaiden. The servant informed her mistress that she might find an equal or greater satisfaction in the embraces of an ape. Said the woman knowingly, "No living creature can perform what you require with greater alacrity than a baboon."

Soon thereafter, it serendipitously happened that a monkey keeper with a large baboon in his train passed beneath the sultana's lattice. The princess unveiled her face and with her eyes suggested to the beast she willingly would be his. He thereupon broke his bonds, untethered his head, and clambered up the side of the palace where he entered the young lady's boudoir. From wayward eyes and babbling tongues, the sultana immediately concealed the creature in an alcove over which hung an arras. Day and night, he abode in her chamber, all the while eating, drinking, and clicketing endlessly with his mistress.

Eventually, a gossip discovered the situation and revealed to the sultan his daughter's frenzied, sybaritic spree. Alas! He doomed the young woman to die. Rumor, however, intervened and carried the news to the princess of her father's intent. Heeding the alarm, she disguised herself as a bondsman, gathered gold, jewels, and other precious pickings, and loaded down two mules. Then, in the dead of night, she took horse beneath a thin sliver of a crescent moon, sallied from the city with her hirsute lover, and fled east to Cairo. There, she and her paramour took residence in an abode outside the city walls.

Each day, still clad as a slave, the sultana bought meat from a butcher. Yet she went to his stall, not early in the morning, but at midday when almost no one was about. Along with her pale face, her distressed and disordered appearance aroused the suspicions of the young man. "This slave bodes some mystery," he said to himself.

One day, when she made her late excursion, he vowed to follow her at a distance and thereby remain unseen. As he trailed her from place to place, he mused, "How curious that this slave takes a roundabout way to an old house outside the city gate."

On observing her enter her dwelling, he decided, even though the hour was late, to spy through a cranny to discover what might unfold. He saw the bondsman kindle a fire, cook the meat, then eat her fill. The remainder she offered to a large baboon who sat nearby upon his haunches. Once he had eaten, she removed her slave's raiment and arrayed herself in rich silks and jewels meant for high-born ladies.

"Ah," murmured the knacker, "I knew she was no male."

In her finery, the woman set out wine and two glasses from which both she and the ape drank. As surprising as this scene of dining and drinking was, what shocked the young man most was, after the pair had drained several glasses, the magenta-bottomed beast leapt from where he sat and served his mistress nearly a dozen times, after which she fainted away. Then, to hide the prostrate lady's nakedness, the simian tossed over her a silken coverlet and returned to his seated post where he scratched his hair-covered haunches and feet.

Aghast, the butcher barged into the midst of the room. The alarmed ape bared his yellow fangs and would have sent him to his death had he not swiftly removed his sharp knife from his belt and slit the creature's heavy paunch. The commotion roused the princess from her stupor, and when she had regained her senses, trembling and horror-stricken, she beheld the plight of her baboon and shrieked so loudly the young man well-nigh believed her spirit had left her body.

She collapsed in a swoon again, and once again her senses returned as she cried, "Why did you kill my dear baboon? In the name of the Prophet, I bid you slay me that I may join him!"

But the butcher spoke fair words to her. "Let me in clicketing stand in your monkey's stead so that your pressing troubles may subside and you become my wife."

Yet, when he tried the ape's exertions, his clicketer fell short in its performance. He, therefore, sought the aid of a wise old woman to cure the sultana and ease his burden. The crone instructed him, "Fetch me a large cooking pot filled nearly to the brim with virgin vinegar, and from an apothecary, bring me a pound of pyrethrum ground from the dead-heads of chrysanthemums."

So he brought the old woman what she requested, and she mixed the pesticide into the pot of vinegar and set it over a fire to heat. And when it had boiled briskly for a time, she enjoined the young man, "Serve a portion to your lady."

He did as directed, and instantly the lusty princess fainted on her couch. Yet the old woman lifted her up and set her thighs above the remainder of the bubbling potion so that its vapors entered her nether parts and suffused them with curative powers. There then fell from her thatched cottage two tiny dragons, one black and one yellow.

"Methinks," declared the beldame, "the embraces of her former lover, the slave, engendered the black dragon while those of the baboon bred the yellow."

By now, the sultana had recovered. She agreed to the proposal of the lowly knacker, and he took her to wife. Like one newly borne, she was no longer afflicted with her former insatiable yearnings, for God Most High had curbed her appetite. In gratitude, she took the crone to be as to her a mother. Thereafter, the old woman, the butcher, and his wife lived out their days in joy and lovingkindness until at last the Sunderer of Life ended their long years.

COMMENTARY: Adapted from the anonymous *One Thousand and One Nights*, also known as the *Arabian Nights*, the story depicts the long-held folk conception of what Morris calls the "despised" or "sinful" monkey.[78] He contends that, although rumors of "lewd and lustful" monkeys had existed for centuries long before the collection appeared in the ninth century, this particular tale, boosted their reputation for lasciviousness.[79] Titled "The King's Daughter and the Ape," in John Payne's 1901 translation[80] as well as in others, the selection recounts how the protagonist craves intercourse so much that, once her slave lover is no longer available, she finds an ape to satisfy her needs. Morris asserts that the primate "in question is almost certainly a baboon."[81]

The representation of the creature's sexual prowess is akin to the portrayal of the two monkey lovers in chapter 16 of *Candide*.[82] (A retelling of this episode with additional commentary is in the present collection in the section containing narratives from Western Europe.) An interesting aspect of both stories is that the male characters despise the monkeys and "look upon them as brutal lechers" while the females "adore" their paramours and "are distraught at losing them."[83]

In my version of Payne's translation of "The King's Daughter and the Ape," I have put the point of view consistently in third person. In the original, as rendered by Payne, the tale begins in third person then shifts to first, with the butcher giving a personal account of his encounter with the sultan's daughter, the baboon, and the wise crone who cures the sultana of her nymphomania. In retelling the tale, I have echoed the flavor of Payne's formal diction.

Despite the unusual content, this selection is both a magical and romantic tale of the happily-ever-after kind. The crone, or wise woman, is a magical helper who possesses the knowledge to create a potion that heals the sultana of her overcharged libido. This antidote leads to the marriage of the princess and the butcher and their long life of felicity with the motherly old lady who aided them.

In describing the archetype of the crone, Barbara G. Walker says that, in the ancient world, women were considered "very wise" once they ceased menstruating or stopped shedding the lunar blood of wisdom and instead retained it within. As a result, the crone (also hag) became associated with such goddesses of wisdom as Athena, Minerva, and Sophia.[84] Today, "hagiology" refers to "the study of holy matters and saints," although negative connotations have attached themselves to its root.[85]

Africa

The Monkey and the Shark
(from the Kamba of East Africa)

A monkey once lived beside the shore. One day, as he sat in the top of his tree, he saw the shadow of a shark swim by, and to draw his attention, the monkey tossed into the water some figs. Though figs were not what the shark usually ate, he gulped them down on the spot. For several days, the same thing occurred—the monkey throwing figs to the shark and the shark eating them.

Gradually, a friendship began to form between the two until at last the shark became comfortable enough to say, "Because you have been kind enough to share your food with me, I would like to invite you to my home here in the ocean. I have already informed my parents, and they will provide you with a delicious feast, neglecting nothing to please you."

On hearing this invitation, the monkey paused for a moment, then asked, "My friend, I am flattered by your request, but how will I get to your home? I don't know how to stay under water."

"Oh, that's not a problem at all," answered the shark. "Just climb on my back, and I'll glide over the ocean. You won't even get one paw wet."

The monkey, however, still hesitated and probed the shark further. "I'm not sure how you'll be able to carry me. Your back looks slick and slippery, and I might slide into the water."

"My dear friend," said the shark, "permit me to put all your fears to rest. I'll swim so slowly that you won't fall off. You'll be perfectly safe." These words finally soothed the monkey's anxiety, and he climbed onto the shark's back.

The pair soon got far out in the ocean when the shark casually noted, "My friend, there's something I have to tell you before we reach my home. My father is extremely sick, and there is nothing—no, not a single pill—that can restore his health except, of course, a monkey's heart. Therefore, when we arrive to dine—this really pains me to tell you—your heart is mine."

Though the monkey showed no sign of fear when he heard these words, he sighed to himself, "Alas! There will be no feast, my friend has lied, and I must soon give up my life to save an old and ailing shark."

After some thought, the monkey said, "I hate your father's health is so fragile. I wish you had told me before we left. I could have prepared to help him." Tears now trickled down the monkey's face. "You see, we monkeys never take our hearts with us when we travel. We always leave them at home."

"You mean your heart's not here!" exclaimed the shark surprised.

"Alas, no. My heart's at home. It's nowhere near."

Then pausing briefly, the monkey suddenly added, "But wait! I have a solution. We could, if it's not any trouble, go back and fetch my heart for your dear father. But please don't disappoint me again after you've asked me to a feast."

Without another word, the shark spun around and headed for the shore. As he neared land, the monkey jumped off his back into the shallow water and scurried up the closet tree. Grabbing a large loose limb, he hurled it at his former friend's head and yelled, "*THERE'S MY HEART! NOW TAKE IT!*"

COMMENTARY: Here the trickster is tricked in this story having many interesting variants, the oldest ones likely originating in India and later making their way into other lands. Promising a feast, the shark persuades the monkey to hop upon his back. Out at sea, the shark admits he only wants to give his ailing father the monkey's heart as a cure. The monkey claims his heart is at home and tricks the shark to return him to the shore.

The chief sources for this adaptation are "The Monkey and the Shark"[1] from Vincent Kitutu's *East African Folktales*, a 1997 collection from Kenya, and the much older Swahili versions told by the natives around the area of Zanzibar to the south and translated into English, first by Edward Steere in *Swahili Tales* (1870) and later by George W. Bateman in *Zanzibar Tales* (1901). Steere's version of the tale is titled "The Washerwoman's Donkey"[2] which contains within it the story of the monkey and the shark. Bateman's story is "The Monkey, the Shark, and the Washerwoman's Daughter."[3] With only minor differences, the monkey and shark episode in each is essentially the same as Kitutu's. In his 1910 *The Lilac Fairy Book*, the last of his rainbow folktale series, Andrew Lang titled the selection "The Heart of a Monkey" and indicated Steere's *Swahili Tales* as his source.[4]

A.K. Ramanujan included a variant in his 1991 *Folktales from*

India.[5] Instead of a shark, the monkey makes friends with a crocodile by feeding him rose apples. The crocodile tricks the monkey onto his back because the crocodile's wife wants the monkey's heart. However, unlike the shark in the African story, the crocodile has pangs of conscience that will not allow him to betray his monkey friend.

A variant in *Jataka Tales*, retold by Ellen C. Babbitt, is divided into two sections.[6] In the first part of "The Monkey and the Crocodile," a female crocodile asks her son to fetch the monkey's heart for her. He tempts the monkey onto his back with the prospect of ripe fruit across a river. But the son is something of a dimwit and through the monkey's trickery goes back to his tree where the monkey claims he left his heart. In the second part, the monkey has moved down river and jumps onto a large rock to reach fruit trees growing on an island. Aware that the monkey must go back across the river, the son waits on the rock and lies perfectly still. The monkey recognizes the trick and calls, "Hello, Rock!" After the third call, the crocodile answers, and the monkey offers to jump into his mouth. Knowing that crocodiles shut their eyes when they open their mouths, the monkey leaps onto the crocodile's head and vaults back safely to the river bank, thus outwitting his adversary.

Babbitt took her *Jataka Tales* and its companion book, *More Jataka Tales* from the multi-volume translations of the stories made between 1895 and 1913 under the general editorship of E.B. Cowell at the University of Cambridge. The first volume of *The Jataka or Stories of the Buddha's Former Births* contains "Vanarinda-Jataka" in which a female crocodile, "being with young," craves a monkey's heart to eat. The male crocodile pretends to be a rock to trick a monkey into stepping on him but is outwitted.[7] "Sumsumara-Jataka" in the second volume[8] and "Vanara-Jataka" in the third[9] are additional variants.

Making its way into Japan from Indian sources in the eleventh century, the tale is known as "The Monkey's Liver."[10] The pregnant daughter of the dragon god of the sea kingdom of Neinya is ill. A priest determines the cause and says she can only be cured by eating the "fresh raw liver of a monkey."[11] The god sends a dog to a faraway island to fetch one. Hanging onto the dog, the monkey arrives in the dragon kingdom and is well-entertained for a time but later learns from an octopus and a spined shellfish that he is in "a terrible fix."[12] As in other variants, the monkey says he left his vital organ at home. Sent to retrieve it, he wisely disappears. Discovering that the octopus and the shellfish had warned the monkey of his fate, the dragon god orders the bones of the octopus pulled out and the spiny shellfish beaten until his bones stick out. With these additions to the plot, this trickster tale also becomes a *pourquoi* as it explains certain physical characteristics of the two sea creatures.

"The Jelly Fish and the Monkey" is yet another variant included by Osaki in her collection of Japanese folktales.[13] In this story, the Dragon King of the Sea sends a jelly fish to retrieve a monkey's liver to cure his new bride who has become ill. The jelly fish tricks the monkey into coming to view the wonders and splendors of the king's palace. Halfway there, the jelly fish reveals that the king's doctor needs the monkey's liver for medical purposes. As in "The Monkey and the Shark," the monkey outwits his adversary by claiming the liver is still at home on the Island of the Monkeys and they must return to get it. When they do, the monkey escapes up a pine tree. Unfortunately for the jelly fish, the Dragon King of the Sea has him deboned and beaten flat for his failed mission. The elaborate narrative thus depicts the trickster out tricked and, as a *pourquoi*, describes why jelly fish are flat and boneless "just as you see them today thrown up by the waves high on the shores of Japan."[14]

Monkeys and People
(from the Kamba of East Africa)

In times long past monkeys lived here on the ground with people until a locust famine came. The monkeys decided to live in the trees and began to change how they lived, eating whatever they could find, especially when people left their houses. Then the monkeys would raid the barns and sheds and eat what the people had stored for themselves.

It so happened that a farmer captured a monkey and took it home to play with his children. Yet, when he went to tend his crops, the monkey would leave the children and sneak into his barn to eat the sorghum he stored there.

One morning, the farmer went to his barn and found some of his grain scattered on the floor. Clearly, a monkey had been inside. The man thought, "I will catch this thief." So he made a slipknot in a rope and tied it to the sorghum bin to snare the monkey when it stuck its paw inside.

The next morning, the monkey waited until the farmer left for his field. It then scampered away from the children and went to the barn where it thrust its hand through a gap in the bin to eat as it had before. When it tried to pull out, the slipknot fastened tightly around its wrist.

That evening, the man checked his sorghum. And what did he see? His own monkey was the thief. Looking at his pet, he said, "A monkey is a monkey."

Moral

Mosquitos, hornets, wasps, and bees
Will sting without as you suppose.
But ants and spiders, ticks and fleas
Will sting or bite within your clothes.

COMMENTARY: Along with "The Fox and Monkey Thieves," "The Monkey and the Jackal," "How Twins Entered the World," "The Greedy Monkeys," "The Greedy Monkey and the Pearl Necklace," "The Two Monkeys," and "The Monkey, the Crab, and the Persimmons," this story, adapted from Kitutu's collection,[15] presents monkeys as pests with reputations for stealing, especially food. In several anecdotes in *The Land I Lost: Adventures of a Boy in Vietnam,* Huynh Quang Nhuong attests to their thieving of crops as well as to the more malicious features of their nature.[16]

The Monkey and the Jackal
(from the Bushmen and Boers of South Africa)

Every evening in the veldt's twilight, a farmer would gather within his kraal his lambs and sheep so that they could safely sleep during the night. Yet once the sun had surrendered its last beams, a jackal would silently steal through the gate of the enclosure and take a tender young lamb to eat.

The theft occurred off and on for several nights until the farmer devised a trap. Taking a long lithe limb, he fixed one end in the ground, bent the other end, and held it in place by a notched stake. Around the bent limb, he tied a cord that had a noose at the opposite end. If an animal stepped on a trigger stick, the limb would spring back, ensnare the thief in the noose, and leave him dangling in the air.

That night, the jackal returned to the gate of the kraal. *ZIP* went the whip. The noose tightened around the jackal's body and left him swinging and swaying aloft.

The dark slowly turned to dawn. Not far away, resting upon a stone outcropping, a baboon saw the ill-disposed jackal and heard his yelps. Sauntering down from his high perch, the monkey approached to sneer and mock at the other's plight. "Dear friend," he said in monkey chatter, "it seems you've finally been caught, wound up tight in a springle."

"What's that? I caught? Oh, no. I'm swaying in the sun and warming myself. If you knew how pleasant it is, you would do the same and never want the sport to end."

Back and forth, the two talked until at last the jackal convinced the baboon to scamper over and take his place. Climbing into the loosened noose, the monkey tightened it snugly under his arms and around his chest while the jackal held the whip. When he released the limb, the monkey swung to and fro above the ground.

"HA HA!" laughed the jackal as if in a fit. "YOU FOOL, YOU'RE IN THE WHIP!" Then he whispered, "But listen! Over the veldt, I hear feet drumming. I think the farmer fast approaches. Rock a while in your noose and enjoy yourself. I see him now with his gun. Goodbye, my friend, goodbye." So saying, the jackal ran off, leaving the baboon swinging.

When he arrived, the farmer said, "You, Monkey, have killed my lambs, but now you dangle in the noose sprung from my springle."

"Oh, no!" the baboon barked. "Not I but Jackal made a sweet feast of them."

"Oh, Monkey, no. You're not too good to do the deed. I know you. You were the one. Right?" The man then cocked rifle. "Just wait. Just wait."

The baboon could barely stammer as the farmer raised his gun and shot the poor beast dead.

COMMENTARY: Assembled by physician James Honey, *South-African Folk-Tales* is the source from which this story is retold.[17] Honey's introduction indicates that the tales derived primarily from the Bushmen, whom he describes as a small-statured nomadic people of southern Africa, although other ethnic groups had an impact on the folklore.[18] This trickster tale about a monkey and jackal shows strong influences from the Boers (descendants of Dutch farmers) who settled in South Africa in the 1600s. The story contains several words from Afrikaans, the language that developed from their original South Holland roots. *Veldt* refers to a large, open field; *kraal*, to an enclosure for livestock; and *wip*, to a trap or snare with a noose for catching animals.

Like foxes and monkeys, jackals are often portrayed in folk stories as wily and deceitful. Discussing various animal tricksters of Africa such as Ananse the spider and Zomo the rabbit, storyteller Oyekan Owomoyela notes that jackals are commonly depicted as tricksters in the cultures of southern Africa.[19] Jackals also assume this role in stories from India. F.A. Steel and R.C. Temple's 1884 collection, *Wide-awake Stories*, reveals jackals as tricksters in stories like "Lambikin" and "The Jackal and the Crocodile."[20] Joseph Jacobs' *Indian Fairy Tales* of 1892 includes "Lambikin" as well.[21] Having delightful rhymes repeated at intervals, this folktale depicts how a clever jackal sees through a fat little lamb's disguise as a "Drumikin" and eats him.

Numerous Jataka stories from India present jackals in the same vein. In "Manoja-Jataka," a bodhisattva, who is a lion, warns his son

Manoja that "jackals are wicked and sinners and give wrong advice."[22] Unheedful of his father's counsel, Manoja befriends a jackal who tricks him into eating the horses of a king. The king's ace archer eventually shoots Manoja. Knowing about the lethal wound, the jackal abandons the lion to his death. His father, mother, sister, and wife react to his end in the following verse:

> This, or worse than this, his fate
> Who is high but trusts the low,
> See, 'tis thus from kingly state
> He has fallen to the bow.[23]

Despite the differences in the two stories, "Manoja-Jataka" has some obvious parallels to the selection adapted here. The most notable is that, like the unfortunate Manoja the lion, the monkey in the South African tale is shot and killed because of a jackal's deceit, although it is the jackal, not the monkey, that has killed the farmer's lambs.

Joel Chandler Harris refuses to present such a dire conclusion in the Uncle Remus story "In Some Lady's Garden."[24] As a result of stealing vegetables from Mr. Man's garden, Brer Rabbit is trapped in a box. He faces his likely end, but while Mr. Man is away for a few moments, along comes Brer Fox. Brer Rabbit claims Mr. Man has been fattening him up with mutton and thus persuades Brer Fox into getting inside the box. The trick completed, Brer Rabbit "tuck'n gallop off in de woods, en he laff en laff twel he hatten hug a tree fer ter keep fum drappin' on de groun'."[25] The little boy, listening to Uncle Remus tell the story, asks what happened to Brer Fox, but Uncle Remus deftly changes the subject.

Lest anyone think the farmer in "The Monkey and the Jackal" falsely suspicious in accusing the monkey of killing lambs, Nhuong relates a true story of a Vietnamese butcher who owned a monkey that watched him cut up meat each day. When the owner and his wife visited a neighbor, the monkey escaped from its chain and imitated the way it had seen the man cut up hogs. It butchered their two-year-old daughter who was sleeping alone in the house.[26]

The Fiddling Monkey
(from the Bushmen and Boers of South Africa)

The food in Monkey's country was no more, nothing left—not even bulbs, scorpions, and bugs. Because of nothing to eat and his intense hunger, Monkey forsook his land and sought work from afar. His great uncle, the one called Orangutan, took him in and gave him shelter.

After working for a time, Monkey longed to return to his own land. As payment, Orangutan offered him an enchanted fiddle along with a bow and arrows. He told his nephew, "With your bow, you can kill food you would like to eat. With your fiddle, you can force any animal to dance."

On returning home, Monkey first met Wolf who reported all that had happened while Monkey was away. The old fellow also added, "Since early this morning, I have stalked a deer but to no avail."

Monkey then informed Wolf about the power of the bow and arrows. "If I see the deer, I will shoot it for you."

They traveled together for a while, and Wolf pointed to the deer. True to his word, Monkey brought it down, and the two ate together. Yet Wolf was not contented with the meal but was jealous of Monkey's power. "Please, let me have your bow and arrows," he begged. Monkey refused. Wolf now threatened Monkey, for he feared his greater strength.

At that moment, Jackal happened to pass by. Wolf called to him, "Monkey has stolen my bow and arrows."

Jackal listened to Wolf's claim, then asked for Monkey's side of the story. Unsure who was telling the truth, Jackal said, "I do not know which one of you to believe. I think we should take the case to court and let Lion, Tiger, and all the other animals decide. While we wait, though, let me keep safe the cause of your dispute." So he took the bow and arrows and immediately slaughtered everything to eat in the vicinity before the court could rule.

When the three finally arrived at court for the animals to hear the case, Monkey made a mess of his evidence, and the judges found him a thief. "You are hereby sentenced to hang," they declared.

Monkey, however, still had his fiddle. Removing it from his back, he asked, "Before you hang me, as a last request, may I play you a tune?"

Monkey was a masterful fiddler and fiddled all the better because of his charmed instrument. When he hit the first note of "Cockcrow," Lion lashed his tail, Tiger shot into the air, and all the other animals jumped to their feet. As Monkey continued to play the old waltz, they started to dance as if caught in a whirlwind.

Over and over, faster and faster, "Cockcrow" sounded on the strings until some of the dancers collapsed on the ground. Although they lay exhausted, they still moved their legs uncontrollably, beating the air, while Monkey's eyes remained closed as he fiddled on and on, keeping time with his foot.

The first to cry for mercy, Wolf pled, "I beg you to stop, Cousin. PLEASE! PLEASE! STOP!" But Monkey heard nothing as the waltz swirled along.

No one knows how many times Lion and his wife rounded near Monkey in the endless dance, but as the couple drew near him yet again, Lion gave a feeble growl. "Cease fiddling and my kingdom is yours."

"KEEP IT!" cried Monkey. "ONLY WITHDRAW THE SENTENCE AND RETURN MY BOW AND ARROWS!" He then shouted, "WOLF! YOU STOLE THEM FROM ME! CONFESS YOUR CRIME!"

"I CONFESS! I CONFESS!" yelled Wolf.

At the same instant, Lion managed to roar, "I WITHDRAW THE SENTENCE!"

Before Monkey stopped, however, he played a few more turns of the tune. Jackal dropped the bow and arrows. Then, gathering his things, Monkey scurried high up the nearest thorn tree. Still concerned that he might begin anew, the breathless court of animals trembled in fear, and for this reason, they hastily dispersed to other parts of the world.

COMMENTARY: This selection also comes from Honey's *South-African Folk-Tales*.[27] In contrast to the previous story, the monkey is a triumphant trickster instead of a hapless victim. One interesting facet of the tale is that it implies all animals occupy the same geographical area even though some like Great Uncle Orangutang live a good distance from Monkey. As the archetypal helper, he provides Monkey with the charmed fiddle by which he overcomes his adversary Wolf and forces Lion to retract the death sentence. As with other folktales, the stark contrast in this one demonstrates how the weak can prevail over the strong.

Why Old Baboon Has That Kink in His Tail
(from the Khoekhoe of South Africa)

Wolf had grown tired of Jackal's mischief. His last prank had nearly gotten Wolf killed by King Lion. So Wolf said to himself, "I'm going to get even with Jackal," and off he went to one of the many koppies, those rocky rises dotting the flat savannahs of southern Africa. There, Old Baboon's troop had gathered, nearly a hundred strong, so that they might keep a watchful eye on predators in the surrounding countryside.

"Good morning, Chief," greeted Wolf.

"Morning, Uncle," returned the baboon leader.

"Been pretty dry lately. You think we'll get some rain soon?"

Old Baboon just scratched his back and chewed the bark off a thin stick he was holding. "It might rain by-and-by. This koppie's done got pretty hot this morning."

With the ground now cleared by polite small talk, Wolf asked, "You remember that rascal Jackal, the one who never paid for all that lamb and goat meat you gave him?"

"Don't I, though," said the old chief, puckering his eyebrows tight before he grabbed a fresh twig and ripped the bark off with one snatch of his sharp teeth.

"Well, it's got to where I can't stand Jackal. He's done one thing after another, and I want to get even. You know he never bothered to pay me for the hindquarters of an eland he took from me. So I vote you and I put an end to all his shenanigans and tricks and such. What if we gave him such a licking he won't show his face around here till this time next year?"

Old Baboon gazed up at a tiny bird on a limb above his head and down on a bright little lizard sprawled on a rock. Then he stared back at Wolf before he looked around again. His eye caught a scorpion's tail sticking out from under a stone. He jumped, grabbed it faster than blue lightning, and began to eat it.

At last, Old Baboon said, "But how do I know you won't streak off as soon as Jackal prances out to meet us?"

Wolf puffed himself up. "Why would I streak off? Do you think I'd run away from a no-good like Jackal? I sure ain't afraid of him."

Old Baboon scratched his left haunch and then munched on what remained of the scorpion's tail. "If you're so brave, what do you need me for?"

Wolf paused. He had to think fast. "If I'm the only one who takes on Jackal, people might say it's just a quarrel I started. But if we both go, they'll say, 'He must have done something bad for those two to tangle with him.' That's why I need your help."

Old Baboon twisted this way and that on his backside as he watched a fly light on Wolf's nose. "Look here, Uncle Wolf. You convince me you won't light out, and then I'll listen. If Jackal tries to do something, you can run off and escape, but I can't because there're no trees for me to scoot up out there where he lives."

Wolf scratched his left ear with his hind paw, and Baboon rubbed his stomach with his right hand. "Now listen, Uncle Wolf. Here's how I see it. You let me tie your tail to mine, tight, so it won't slip loose. That way, I'll be sure you can't leave me high and dry when we meet Jackal. Say yes, and I'll help you."

Old Wolf laughed, pleased as could be. "That's a deal sure enough. I couldn't come up with a better one myself cause I know you can't skip out on me either. Here's my tail. Tie it to yours tight as you please, Chief."

Now Jackal knew Wolf was angry about the eland's stolen

hindquarters and had laid low at home on the lookout. That morning, the prankster happened to be out in front of his house chopping kindling. His sharp axe glinted brightly in the sun with every chop and chip. All the while, he kept eyeing the horizon when, in the distance, he spotted two figures headed his way. The closer they got, the more awkward they looked trying to walk, wobbling and stumbling beside each other with their tails tied together.

Jackal stuck his tail straight out, cocked one ear out to the side, and turned his nose up. "Well, if that ain't the funniest sight I ever seen. They must be looking for me," he said to himself. And while he studied on the situation for a moment, his tail started to wilt. "What am I going to do?" he thought. "They're coming after me."

Jackal scratched one ear and then the other, and his tail shot back out. "Oh, Missus," he called out over his shoulder, and his wife stuck the tip of her nose out the door.

"Yes, Daddy, what you want?"

"Now listen here and listen carefully. I'm going to start chopping again, and the minute I stop, you pinch the baby just as hard as you can. Pinch her till she bawls. And when I tell you to stop her squalling and carrying on, you yell back, 'It's your fault. You've done nothing but feed that child wolf meat, and now you want her to stop bawling for more.' You got what I say? Don't forget," Jackal shouted.

"Yeah, I got it just as you say," said the missus and left the door cracked wide.

By now, Old Baboon and Wolf had gotten closer. "What's that flashing worse than heat lightning in Jackal's hand?" Wolf asked, trembling slightly.

"Why he's just chopping kindling with his axe," Baboon said. "You're not about to turn tail on me, are you?"

"I ain't afraid, but that does look like an awfully sh-sh-sharp axe he's got." Wolf moved slower and slower. "Looks to me like he'd use an old rusty axe with a blade full of nicks and gaps the way other folks do when chopping kindling. I believe he's got more than an axe."

"Don't be backing out now," Old Baboon grunted.

"Didn't you tie my tail to yours yourself," grumbled Wolf, now almost completely stopped.

Old Baboon gave a tug. "Let's get moving."

"I am moving." Wolf took no more than half a step to lessen the pull on his tail, and the two began fussing. Old Jackal raised his head and quit chopping. With that signal, the missus pinched the baby so hard she started bawling till her eyes shut tight and looked like two wet slits. You could hear that child all over the country.

Jackal yelled, "If you don't stop that girl from squalling, I'm coming in there to give her something to squall about."

"It's all your doing," screamed the missus. "You reared our child on nothing but wolf meat, and then you start to carry on when she's crying and hungry for more."

"Don't worry none," Jackal shouted back. "I sent Old Baboon out three days ago to fetch some, and I just now saw him coming this way with a scrawny, scraggly fellow with flies buzzing all around him. I suppose some meat's better than none." Jackal lifted his axe and swung it around his head as if he was about to chop something up.

Wolf had heard and seen enough. He jumped around so fast his head landed where his tail had been. "So that's why you tied my tail to yours," he cried, and he bucked and jerked from side to side like a water buffalo with a lion on his back.

"OH! YOU FATHEAD! YOU CRAZY FATHEAD!" yelled Old Baboon yanking on Wolf's tail to turn him around toward Jackal. "He's just trying to scare you."

Just then, Wolf looked up and saw Jackal waving his axe and running as fast as he could toward Baboon and him. Terrified, he jerked his tail so hard both he and Old Baboon rolled over and hit the ground, and before they could get up, Jackal was on them. He jumped this way, and he hopped that way, all the time flashing his axe and calling out, "Move over a bit, Chief, so I can take a clear swing at him. Just shift your head a little, and I'll gap him one."

But the more Baboon tried to shift out of the way, the more Wolf pulled on his tail to dodge the axe. He finally yanked the chief up in the air and streaked out toward the koppies, towing Old Baboon by his tail behind him all the way.

Before the dust and hair could settle, Jackal said to himself, "I think I've seen about the last of that lot for a while." And to this day, Old Baboon's tail hasn't straightened and still has a kink in it. You can see it whenever he gets up to walk or run.

COMMENTARY: Derived from Captain Arthur Owen Vaughan's 1904 *Old Hendrik's Tales*, this story[28] and the one that follows present conflicts between a jackal trickster and other animals of the South African savannahs. Each story is a droll *pourquoi* that explains various physical features of baboons.

Like the earlier "The Monkey and the Jackal," adapted from James Honey's anthology, this selection depicts a monkey that once again falls victim to a jackal's ruse. Vaughan's original version is two stories in one. The first part, omitted here but briefly alluded to in the adaptation, focuses on how Old Jackal cheats Old Wolf out of the hindquarters of an eland and how the trickster nearly caused King Lion to kill the dimwitted Wolf. Although my rendition uses Vaughan's title, it concentrates on the second part of the narrative where Old Baboon has a significant role. The story also provides a stark contrast between the slow-witted wolf and the clever jackal.

Old Jackal and Young Baboon
(from the Khoekhoe of South Africa)

That time Old Jackal came at Wolf with the axe, Old Baboon thought Wolf never would stop streaking across the savannah with their tails tied together. When Wolf finally did stop, Old Baboon just stared at him, let loose their tails, and crawled off. Never even whispered a single word. Decided he'd let Wolf think about what he did and stew a while.

A couple of days later, Jackal thought it safe to go out to the koppies—sneaking around here and slinking around there. As he walked under a tree, WHACK, a rock hit him in the ribs. He peered around, and WHACK. Another rock smacked his behind. He took off as fast as he could—BOOGEDY, BOOGEDY, BOOGEDY, BOOGEDY, BOOGEDY—to get away from that tree, and when he stopped to look back, what should he see but Old Baboon's youngest son, Leelikie, sticking his head and shoulders out of the leaves and barking and yelping and hollering. "I guess you think you're pretty smart with all your tricks and such, but I'll teach you to play them on the baboons."

When Jackal saw that smart-mouth squirt squawking, he felt like chunking the biggest rock he could find. But he knew he needed to sweet talk the young'un first. So Jackal grinned from ear to ear and acted surprised. "What have I ever done to you?" he asked, rubbing his bruised ribs.

"Jackal, you ain't done nothing to me, cause I'm too smart to fall for your monkey business. But you fooled my old daddy, and I ain't about to stand for it."

"What's that you say?" whimpered Jackal, wriggling as if he couldn't keep still because of his sore side.

"Why, you flimflammed Uncle Wolf until he couldn't take any more of your cheating. So he begged my daddy to help work you over. But when my old daddy got back home, his tail had such a kink and was so sore all he could do was sit and nurse it and growl. And when he feels bad, he wants gum and sends my brother and me to shinny up an acacia tree to get some. The problem, though, is I like to eat gum, too. But if I do, Daddy shambokkin me so hard I have to yell and carry on so as folks think he's killing me before he stops."

Jackal eyed Leelikie up and down. "Let me get this straight. The only thing wrong with you is you got to give your daddy all the gum you gathered? Is that right?"

"Yep, or else I get whacked for the few little scrapings I stick in my mouth."

"Well, ain't that a shame," Jackal said with a slight sneer. "If it was me, I'd eat all the gum I want and still give your daddy all he wants. I know you think you're pretty smart, but I'd be smarter than what you just told me." Then Jackal stuck his nose up in the air.

"My daddy always said talk don't mean a thing," sassed Leelikie. "I bet you can't show me how I can eat all the gum I want and give Daddy all he can eat, too."

Jackal smiled. "Young'un, you ain't getting me that easy. But here's what I'll do. Meet me back here in the morning with some good clear gum, and I'll tell you how you can keep all you want and let your brother get all the shambokkins instead of you."

"Now, that sounds like a bargain, Uncle Jackal. You be here in the morning, and I'll be here with the gum. Don't forget."

"Oh, I won't," said Jackal leaving and winking at every bush along the way.

The next day, when Jackal returned, there was Young Baboon already waiting in the same tree as before. "Now what's this game you got in mind?" he yelled down as Jackal looked up.

"Show me the gum."

"See. Here it is. Now tell me the plan you got planned."

"Hold on," chuckled Jackal. "Give me the gum first so I know it's good and clear."

"Here, watch me," Leelikie said, and he bit off a chunk of gum, all the while smacking his mouth like an old bull water buffalo pulling its hooves out of deep-sucking mud.

"Whoa, young'un!" yelled Jackal riled up. "Why are you eating all my gum?"

"Since you ain't sure, I just wanted to show you how good it is. Besides, it's still my gum till you tell me what trick you got in mind."

"So that's how it is, my little friend. You don't trust me."

"Look here, Jackal. I got the gum. I know it's good. But I don't know if what you got is any good. So I'll keep what I got." So saying, Leelikie opened his mouth as wide as he could and flopped out his tongue while he rubbed his stomach with one hand and with his other hand stretched out the gum toward Jackal. "Yum, yum, yum. That sure is good gum."

"Well, by cracky, ain't you a right smart fellow," said Jackal as he scratched the ground and stirred up some dust. "I guess I better go find your brother. He ain't likely to cheat me out of my gum." Jackal turned as if to leave.

"Go on then and see if I care. I'll just sit up here and eat this gum all by myself."

Jackal paused. "You still don't trust me I see." By now, he knew he was on the wrong side of the fence. "I suppose we'll have to figure something out. What if I stand back a ways and you lay the gum on this flat rock down here by the tree root? Then I'll tell you the plan."

"Now you're talking." Leelikie swung down and planted the gum on the rock. But he stood right there and didn't leave.

"All right. Here's what you do," Jackal finally confessed. "When you and your brother go fetch the gum in your gourds, you eat all that's in yours. Then, when your brother ain't looking, you swap your gourd for his. That way, when you give the gum to your old daddy, he'll shambok your brother and not you."

"That does sound like a smart trick," Leelikie admired. "But what if—" As he spoke, Jackal made a dive toward him and the gum. Too late, though. The young baboon grabbed the gum and scooted up the tree out of sight.

"Tee-hee," he tittered with sweet gum running down his chin. "Thank you, Uncle Jackal. Here I was thinking I had to pay my gum for your advice, but now I get to keep it for myself."

"Didn't I tell you what I promised?"

"You sure did, but my brother ain't no fool. He's always looking, so there ain't no swapping gourds with him. Why, he'd whack all the hair off my hide the first time I tried that trick."

"Don't matter anyway," Jackal sneered. "I still got you. You have to climb out of that tree sometime, and I'll be right here waiting."

"I hate to tell you, but in just a bit my daddy and the rest of the baboons are heading this way. You might end up staying here longer than you want."

Jackal jumped around to look behind him where he caught a glimpse of the scruffy old scout who leads the baboons when they feed. He decided to slink off over a rise and stay out of sight so he could think about how to deal with the little one's game. As soon as Jackal disappeared, Leelikie swung down to join the rest of his clan and look for scorpions, tarantulas, and other food.

Soon the troop came to some tall thorn trees with thick fine sap oozing out. Leelikie looked up at the gum, and then he looked at his daddy. Leelikie thought, "Here's my chance for gum if I can work it right." He studied a while, then picked off a few legs on a tarantula to munch on. Finally, he slapped his ribs. "I got it."

"Daddy," he called out, "you see all this gum. Here's your chance to get even. If you take it and smear it all over me, right thick like, and put a big chunk in my hand and set me on a stone in the hot sun, while the rest of you go off feeding over that rise there, I'll nab Old Jackal for you."

"How's that you say?" asked Old Baboon. "What you got in mind?"

"Watch and you'll see. Just come scooting back here fast as you can when I holler."

Old Baboon eyed his son up and down, scratched one ear and then the other, while he pondered the plan. But when Leelikie happened to bump against his father's sore tail, that settled everything. "Son, that's the best plan I ever heard planned to catch Jackal. You're about the smartest baboon out here in the koppies."

So the baboons gathered gum and plastered it all over Leelikie. Then they sat him on the stone and put a big chunk in his palm.

By volunteering, Old Baboon's son expected he'd have all the gum he could eat—the piece in his hand and what he could scrape off himself. He hadn't figured on the hot African sun beaming down on him and heating up the stone. He thought he'd eat up all that sweetness by the time Jackal got back. But before the baboon troop was out of sight, the gum got so sticky Leelikie couldn't stir. Couldn't move his hands, his legs, his head, not even his tail, and Old Jackal had turned around and was creeping closer and closer, peeping this way and that, watching the young baboon sitting as still as could be.

Jackal pranced up and down, licking his chops. "Yep, I got you now—gum and all. Look at my teeth."

Leelikie tried to yell for his daddy, but his jaws were so gummed up he couldn't open his mouth.

"You're a nice and fat little monkey. Let me feel where I'm going to take my first bite." With his right paw, Jackal pinched and poked along Leelikie's ribs, but when he tried to pull back, his paw wouldn't budge.

"Let go my hand, or I'm going to shambok you one," Jackal yelled and popped Leelikie with his left paw. It wouldn't budge either. "If you don't let go my fists, I'm going to knock the gum out of you."

"If only I *COULD* let you go," Leelikie thought. "I can't do nothing but just sit here. I can't even call for my old daddy to come get me."

Jackal's ears stuck up, and his eyes bulged out. "If you don't let my hands loose, I'll bite your head off," he groaned, as he ground his teeth. Then snarling and snapping, he dove at Leelikie's head, missed, and bit the chunk of gum in the little baboon's hand.

With head and front paws stuck tight, Jackal was now in a worse fix than ever. For out of the corner of one eye, he saw Old Baboon and the rest of his troop flying down the hill toward him, all of them barking, biting the air, and carrying on.

"It's do or die now!" Jackal squealed, and with every hair on his hide, he made one mighty tug, so that something had to give. And you know what? Something did give. Instead of yanking his hands and jaws free, he jerked so hard Leelikie sailed over his head dragging the old trickster down the hill with him. But the hide of the little baboon's behind stayed stuck to the stone.

The moment the two stopped, Old Baboon and Leelikie's brother made a jump for Jackal. But he glimpsed their dive and whirled around so that they butted into Leelikie instead. What a sight and a mix-up that was! The baboons scratching, biting, and yanking the hair out of one another. Old Baboon and his eldest son finally got situated enough to pull on Leelikie from one side while Jackal yanked on him from the other. Being the stronger tuggers, the two baboons eventually tore Leelikie loose from Jackal who popped free himself and escaped.

As a result of that gum tussle, you can still see today how baboons don't have any hair on their paws or jaws as well as on their behinds. And not a one of them has been stuck to a stone or the ground since.

COMMENTARY: This selection retold from Vaughan[29] has parallels to several other stories. In "The Leopard, Monkey, and Hare" from Heli Chatelain's 1894 *Folk-Tales of Angola*, tricksters Monkey and Hare have been stealing fruit from Leopard's tree.[30] On the advice of an oracle, Leopard decides to trap them by hanging from its branches wooden images of girls covered with gum. When Monkey and Hare greet the carvings, the dolls do not follow social protocol by speaking back. This cumulative pattern of the dolls refusing to acknowledge the two continues. Eventually, Monkey and Hare become stuck to the gummy images so that Leopard captures the two thieves. However, by using their wits, they escape—Monkey to the trees and Hare to the bushes. The story ends as a *pourquoi* which explains that these places today are where monkeys and hares seek safety from predators like leopards.

There are similarities between the plots of these African stories and Joel Chandler Harris' "The Wonderful Tar Baby Story" in which animals get stuck in a sticky trap.[31] James Mooney's work also contains two Cherokee versions titled "The Rabbit and the Tar Wolf."[32] John Reid Swanton's collection from the Creek Indians has a selection as well called "The Tar Baby" based on a manuscript of pioneering Georgia folklorist William Orrie Tuggle.[33] Folklore scholar David Elton Gay argues that such variants demonstrate the "close connection" between the traditional narratives of African American and Native American cultures during "long-term interaction" between their traditions in what is now the Southeastern United States.[34]

With respect to Vaughn's collection from South Africa, the tales are very much akin in both format and style to the plantation stories of the American South published after the Civil War. Like Harris' *Uncle Remus, His Songs and His Sayings* (1881) and Louise-Clark Pyrnelle's *Diddie, Dumps, and Tot or Plantation Child-Life* (1882), Vaughan frames his stories by having a faithful old black retainer recount his entertaining animal narratives to little white children. Instead of Harris' Uncle Remus or Pyrnelle's Uncle Bob, Vaughan's narrator is "an old Hottentot" named Uncle Hendrik, a "grey old kitchen boy" who has "long been in the service" of an "English" family consisting of an American father, an Australian mother, and their three children—one girl, eight years of age, and two boys, one ten and the other six. As with the stereotypical happy slaves of the plantation stories, Uncle Hendrik seems contented with his second-class colonial status as "a house Kaffir."[35] Nonetheless, despite these issues sometimes found in juvenile literature from earlier eras, the same might be said of Uncle Hendrik as of Harris' Uncle Remus and Pyrnelle's Uncle Bob. They are "affectionately depicted,"[36] and the stories they tell are "vibrant reminders"[37] of our diverse literary traditions.

As to style, Vaughan lards his collection with Afrikaans words to illustrate that the stories, though of so-called Hottentot origin, had passed through the Dutch of South African Boer settlers before being told in English by Old Hendrik. Since English is not the narrator's first language, Vaughan also has the narrator speak in somewhat thick dialect pronunciations. Vaughan further intersperses Hendrik's tales with numerous asides. Although such stylistic features might enhance the selections during storytelling or reading aloud by teachers, as Kiefer suggests for Uncle Remus stories,[38] Vaughan's use of nonstandard dialect spellings, Afrikaans vocabulary, and the speaker's incidental remarks will likely render the yarns of Old Hendrik difficult for contemporary young readers to comprehend. In my retellings, I have avoided such stylistic features and eliminated the structure of the framed narrative to emphasize the essential plots of both stories.

Insofar as the word "Hottentot" is concerned, it is now considered an inaccurate and derogatory term once used to designate the pastoral speakers of the Khoekhoe (Khoikhoi is an alternative spelling) language or one of its varieties. This ethnic group is sometimes referred to as the Khoisan of southwestern Africa. Historian Nicholas Hudson argues that, from the time Portuguese navigator Vasco da Gama first arrived at the Cape of Good Hope in 1497, the Khoekhoe became "the most reviled people in European thought of the early modern era" and were seen as the "most savage of all savage peoples, occupying a rung ... just above the beast."[39] According to the *Oxford English Dictionary*, the word "Hottentot" may have initially meant a "stutterer or stammerer" because of the use of "clucking," sounds in the Khoekhoe language, thus suggesting an etymology derived these linguistic features. Echoing the foregoing discussion by Hudson, one OED definition of the word, which "appears now to be very rare," is "A person of inferior intellect or culture; one degraded in the scale of civilization, or ignorant of the usages of civilized society."[40]

The word "kaffir" likewise connotes racist attitudes. Originally used by the English, Dutch, and Afrikaans, it was once a term considered neutral as a generic descriptor of several indigenous peoples of southern Africa. Today, however, the word carries such negative baggage that anyone using it in South Africa can receive a serious legal penalty. Penelope Andrews, writing for the *Mail & Guardian*, a newspaper out of Johannesburg, reports that Vicky Momberg, a real estate agent, had called several men "kaffirs" as they assisted a black police officer. For this offense, she was given a three-year prison sentence with one year suspended provided that she did not engage in the unlawful and intentional impairment of "the dignity or privacy of another person."[41]

Leopard and Monkey
(from the Kimbundu of Angola)

Leopard and Monkey lived in the same village. Leopard was known far and wide for his cruelty. He had already killed Antelope and tricked his wife so that she ate her husband and fed him to their children.

Though he had a wife, Leopard planned to marry a second time. He announced, "I am going to visit my new wife's parents." He had not yet wed the girl, but he wanted everyone to think her mother and father were already his in-laws.

Leopard grabbed his banjo, and as he started on his way to the next village, he saw Monkey. Leopard told him, "Come with me." Leopard was the chief, so Monkey agreed.

As they went along, they came upon some driver ants in the middle of the road. Leopard ordered Monkey to pick them up. Monkey said, "Mr. Leopard, these are driver ants, and they sting."

Leopard laughed. "Monkey, you are clever."

They went along further until they came to some red ants. Leopard again ordered Monkey to pick them up. Monkey answered, "These are red ants. They also sting."

Leopard laughed again. "Monkey you are too clever."

The two continued down the road until they came to a field. Leopard said, "This field belongs to others. They will be angry if you take anything ripe. You go on that side and pick green eggplants and pull up any unripe cassava roots. I'll stay on this side and do the same and meet you ahead."

Monkey went into the field and picked ripe eggplant and dug up large ripe cassava roots as well. Leopard did the same on his side. When they met later, Leopard said, "Monkey, show me what you gathered." Monkey did. "Oh, Monkey, you are shrewd." The two then rested.

After a while, they walked on until they came to a stream. Leopard took a drink of water and said, "Monkey, we will soon be at my in-laws' house in the next village. When they cook mush for us, you go and fetch water."

"How am I to carry it?" asked Monkey.

"Use this gourd," Leopard replied, and he gave Monkey a fish trap that was in the water. Monkey agreed, and the pair moved on.

When they arrived at the village, Leopard's in-laws-to-be spread mats for them to rest on in the guest house and, as it was evening, began to cook mush. Leopard told Monkey, "Go and get water." Monkey left and went outside behind the house where he stayed a short time. He then returned.

"Where is the water?" Leopard wanted to know.

"That thing you gave me is a fish trap, not a gourd. It will not dip out the water."

"All right," Leopard laughed. "Let's sit down and eat." So Monkey sat on his mat, and the two ate their meal together and then went to sleep.

During the night, Leopard got up. Monkey watched him but said nothing. Leopard thought Monkey was asleep, so he slipped out of the guest house and killed a goat. Leopard then drained its blood into a gourd and went back inside. He intended to douse Monkey with the blood, but when he raised the gourd, Monkey pushed Leopard's hand so that some of the blood splattered on him instead, although he could not see it in the dark. Leopard decided to go back to his mat and sleep.

The next morning, Monkey went outside and took Leopard's banjo. He played and sang:

> Antelope your trick deceived.
> Do you think Monkey as naïve?
> Antelope your trick deceived.
> Do you think Monkey as naïve?

Hearing the banjo and the singing, Leopard's future parents-in-law came out and asked, "Where's the chief?"

"Oh, he's still asleep."

"Well, he needs to get up. We'll go in and wake him." So the couple went into the sleeping quarters. Leopard lay on his mat completely covered up, even his head. "It's daylight already. Get up, Chief," they ordered.

Leopard just lay there and said, "I am so comfortable here lying on my mat in this little house."

His intended in-laws paid no attention to his words and uncovered his face. Leopard's head was splattered and ugly with blood. They then walked to the door to look outside to where they kept their goats. They went back inside and said, "We know your lies now. We heard Monkey sing, 'He fooled Antelope, and he wanted to fool me, too.' When Antelope came here before with you, you killed a goat and sprinkled its blood on him. To punish Antelope, we killed him. You are to be our son-in-law, but you are a wild beast. Monkey will have our daughter instead of you."

With those words, the couple killed Leopard where he lay. They then skinned him and gave one of his legs to Monkey to take back with him.

The next morning Monkey left. When he arrived at Leopard's house, his wife asked, "Where's my husband, the chief?"

"Oh, he went to collect a debt someone owed him," Monkey replied. "This leg of meat is part of what he collected. He told me to bring it for you to cook."

Leopard's wife took the leg, and Monkey returned to his own house. She set the meat over the fire and prepared some mush to go with it. When everything was done, she called to the children to come and eat. As she divided the meat, one child said, "This meat smells just like daddy."

"Don't talk like that! Your father has gone to collect a debt," snapped the wife, and she picked up the mush-stirring sick and whacked the child several times with it.

The family finished the food. Monkey came back by and went into the house. "Do you have any meat left? I would like some."

"No, we ate it all," returned the wife.

Monkey left and went to a tree on the edge of the village. He climbed up and called out, "Wife of Leopard, you think you are wise, but you have eaten your husband's leg." So saying, he climbed down and ran off into the bush.

Leopard's wife started to cry. "It is true what my little one said," and she and the children began to wail loudly.

COMMENTARY: This selection derives from the pioneering work of Swiss linguist and educator Heli Chatelain[42] who had been trained as a missionary in the late nineteenth century to bring Christianity to the natives of the Portuguese colony of Angola. While his original aim was to eliminate the "four evils" of "witchcraft, polygamy, slavery, and alcoholism," he became a champion for establishing a unifying language and literature to lead to a national identity for the colony.[43] His focus became Kimbundu, one of several varieties of the Bantu tongue. Chatelain held that the best means for understanding "the character, the moral and intellectual make-up" of the various local African populations was to "make a thorough study of their social and religious institutions, and of their unwritten, oral literature."[44]

A major outcome of Chatelain's interest was his 1894 *Folk-Tales of Angola*, a bilingual volume of fifty stories in both Kimbundu and English. In the assessment of German-American philologist and African lusophone scholar Gerald Moser, this collection reflects "African customs and oral style faithfully through almost literal transliteration."[45] Chatelain himself believed the work could serve as a "text-book for students of African languages as well as for students of comparative folk-lore."[46] He also noted how African folktales like those in his collection were models for those recounted by blacks in the Americas and had influenced Native American stories.[47] Regarding the character of Leopard in "Leopard and Monkey" and other tales in which he appears, Chatelain found he represented "vicious power combined with inferior wits."[48] As such, he is a ready dupe for Monkey's trickery.

In today's independent country of Angola, the Mbundu account for twenty-five percent of the population and are its second largest ethnic group. The Kimbundu, from which Chatelain collected his volume of talking beast tales, are a subdivision of the Mbundu and as such are a Bantu-speaking people.[49]

The Baboons and ||Xabbiten||Xabbiten
(from the San of South Africa)

Some baboons once saw ||Xabbiten||Xabbiten returning from a settlement of white men where he had gone for a visit. They had given him some flour.

"Look," said the baboons. "Uncle is coming back. Let's go and knock him down."

As the baboons approached, ||Xabbiten||Xabbiten asked them, "What are you saying to me?" He then added, "You are ugly. Your foreheads look like steep cliffs!"

Because the man mocked their appearance, the baboons grew angry, broke sticks, and threatened to beat him. Suddenly, their children ran up and yelled, "Oh, Elders, give us his head for us to play with!"

When ||Xabbiten||Xabbiten heard the demands of the little baboons, he wandered, "What can I do? There are many baboons." He ran to a quiver tree and climbed up in its branches. "If they want me, they'll have to drag me down," he said to himself.

Gathering under the tree, the baboons stared at the man. Their children chattered, "Look at ||Xabbiten||Xabbiten's big head. It is so big it likely won't break easily if we play with it. We could play with it for a long time."

But one of the elders scolded, "Why do you think you should get the head? This man is not your little cousin. He is an adult, and only we adults should have it."

||Xabbiten||Xabbiten trembled. "What can I do to rid myself of these baboons that want to attack me? Maybe I should tell the white men about them. The white men have guns, and the baboons have learned to fear a gun. Let me pretend I am talking to the white men."

So ||Xabbiten||Xabbiten sang out, "Oh, White Men, the baboons have come. They are here with me. Come and scatter them."

When the baboons heard the man's words, they darted their heads about, flashing their eyes here and there before they raced toward some cliffs. ||Xabbiten||Xabbiten quickly descended the quiver tree and escaped.

Commentary: Derived from the San of South Africa, this retelling of a rather grisly talking beast tale has as its source the 1911 anthology *Specimens of Bushman Folklore* by German linguist Wilhelm Bleek.[50] In the introduction to Bleek's volume, South African historian George McCall Theal notes how few "pure" Bushmen, or San, remained alive in the second half of the nineteenth century.[51] Pressed on all sides over the centuries by more powerful African neighbors such as the Bantu and Hottentots and by newly arriving English and Dutch colonists, Bushmen of the 1800s survived in only the most wild and remote regions of what had once been their extensive habitat throughout Africa.[52] The resulting inaccessibility of informants forced Bleek to rely on native speakers who had been convicted by the British Cape Colony for predations on sheep and cattle. After serving their sentences, these former convicts then recruited other Bushmen from more outlying areas to assist Bleek in his study of their language, but before his work could be completed, Bleek died in 1875. However, his sister-in-law, Lucy C. Lloyd, persevered with her mentor's research until the publication of their joint labors, according to Theal's account.[53]

As with other Khoisan speakers, the various forms of San dialects rely on clicks and aspirated sounds along with other distinctive features. To suggest a hint of linguistic authenticity, I have retained throughout the story Bleek's notation of ||, or two vertical lines, to accompany the name of the Bushmen trickster, ||Xabitten||Xabitten, who outwits the vicious baboons into leaving him unmolested. The double verticals represent two lateral clicks, each achieved by "placing the tongue against the side teeth and then withdrawing it," as Lloyd indicates in her preface describing Bleek's system of notation to symbolize nonalphabetic Bushmen sounds.[54] The X in Xabitten following the clicks resembles the German [ch] or "an aspirated guttural,"[55] a sound similar to the [ch] in Bach. Readers may want to imitate the lateral clicks and [ch] when they attempt to pronounce the name of the main character. Anyone interested in pursuing further Bleek's notations should consult Lloyd's preface.[56] Also of interest for its folklore is Bleek's earlier *Reynard the Fox in South Africa: Or, Hottentot Fables and Tales* (1864). It contains five baboon stories, including "The Lost Child,"[57] taken from Sir James Edward Alexander's travelogue, *An Expedition into the Wilds of Africa*. This story, untitled within the context of Alexander's journey, comes next and is discussed under the title "The Boy and the Baboons."

Like "Hottentot," the word "Bushmen" is not without controversy, with San or Saan being the preferred term over the earlier colonial designation used by Europeans. Indeed, the singular English form "Bushman" is derived from the Dutch word "bossiesman" which meant "bandit" or "outlaw,"[58] while the linguistic group, Khoisan, to which the San belong, is a compound word indicating "person" and "bush dweller."[59]

As described in *South African History Online*, the San are comprised of highly diverse ethnic and linguistic groups and are considered the first nations of southern Africa and the oldest of hunter-gatherers.[60] Few of the San today live as they once did as subsistence foragers and are now a "shattered society," most of whose members have entered Africa's contemporary world. The cost of such development has been the loss their traditional culture.[61]

The Boy and the Baboons
(from the Nama of South Africa)

One day some boys left the kraal that encircled their village. They played at some distance from it with their bows and arrows in the open countryside. As the sun began to set, the children returned to the safety of the kraal except for one boy who was five or six years old. He lingered behind the others. A troop of baboons soon surrounded him and carried him off.

As the boy had failed to return, the villagers began to search for him at first light the following morning. For days they hunted but found nothing. The baboons had disappeared into the wilds of the local mountains.

A year later, a hunter on horseback arrived at the village. In the course of speaking with the people, he reported, "On my way here, I saw baboon spoor and the small footprints of what must have been a child. These were back at the koppie with the large outcropping of high rocks just over there."

The people immediately set out in the direction where the hunter pointed. As they neared the koppie, they saw the boy sitting beside a large baboon on top of a steep rock. When the big male spotted them, he grabbed the child and fled. The villagers, though, followed in close pursuit and soon captured the boy. However, he acted wild, snapping at his captors, and would have bitten someone had he been allowed.

By the time the people returned to the kraal, the child had calmed down and regained his speech. When questioned, he replied, "The baboons were good to me. They ate scorpions and spiders they found under the rocks. I wouldn't eat their food. So they fed me roots, gum, and wild raisons. When we came to water, the baboons let me drink first. They treated me better than their own children."

COMMENTARY: This camp-fire tale comes from the second volume of Sir James Edward Alexander's 1838 *An Expedition of Discovery into the Interior of Africa*.[62] Alexander was an officer in the Forty-Second Royal Highlanders of Scotland. Under the auspices of the British government and the Royal Geographical Society, he led a year-long exploration of a part of southwestern Africa to uncover, as he says in his introduction to the first volume, "some of the secrets of the great and mysterious continent."[63] Traveling by wagon and pack-oxen, his heavily armed party consisted of seven others, including Europeans from England, Ireland, and Portugal and indigenous people from Bengal and southern Africa. Alexander's travelogue is interspersed with fascinating anecdotes of which this selection is one and which serves as the basis for this retelling.

Belonging to the category of realistic folklore, the story is similar to other tales of feral children, the most famous likely being Jean Marc Gaspard Itard's book-length work, *The Wild Boy of Aveyron*, first appearing in French in 1801. Although there is no certainty that Alexander's anecdote is true, Itard's work tells of actual events concerning the feral child Victor who appears to have undergone complete social and cultural deprivation during his time in the woods of south-central France. While Victor developed some skills in socialization after he was found, he was never able to learn speech. Anthropologist Peter Farb says, "By the time he was captured as a twelve-year-old, his ability to speak could never be recovered."[64] Fortunately for the boy taken by baboons in Alexander's account, he was only five or six at the time and was recaptured by his people a year later. At that age, his brain had not lost its capacity to learn to speak. When he returned to his village, he quickly regained the speech he had already acquired before his disappearance.

At the beginning of the story, Alexander states that baboons "sometimes annoy the Namaquas by stealing their children."[65] This assertion suggests that the anecdote originated with the Nama people who today live in Namibia, South Africa, and Botswana. This ethnic group is also part of the Khoekhoe language family described previously in the commentaries for "Why Old Baboon Has That Kink in His Tail" and "Old Jackal and Young Baboon." Many of the Nama also speak Afrikaans. They have a rich oral tradition of stories and poems. Most of the Nama still follow their traditional occupation as shepherds and live in woven mat huts called *haru oms*. These are easily disassembled to allow the Nama to migrate with their flocks to better pasturage.[66]

The Truthful Monkey
(from the Fang of equatorial Africa)

All the animals made fun of Gorilla, laughing at him and taunting him and calling him "Broken Face." So Gorilla went to the Monkey tribe and searched for little Ingenda. When Gorilla found him, he demanded, "Look carefully over my face. Just tell me the truth. Does the name fit?"

Well, this question put Ingenda in a bind. He feared to tell the truth, and he feared to refuse to tell it. So Ingenda began to climb a tree, and as he went up, he picked fruit all the while giving the excuse, "I'm hungry. I have to eat first before I can answer."

Up and up the little monkey went, and just as he got to the tree-top, he had already eaten two of the fruits. Then peering down at Gorilla, Ingenda called out, "Turn that face up, and look at me!"

Gorilla turned up his face to gaze at the now-out-of-reach monkey and asked, "Is it really true? Does the name fit? Does it really?"

Safe from Gorilla's strong arms, the small Ingenda answered. "Yes, it's true. It really is."

Angrily, Gorilla fumed, but what could he do? Nothing.

And off Ingenda went, leaping and laughing from one tree-top to the next.

COMMENTARY: Titled "Candor" in Robert H. Nassau's 1912 translation of a Fang folktale,[67] this story presents a stark contrast in which a little trickster outwits a larger and more powerful threat. Nassau says that he obtained the selections from an old man of the Banaka tribe who heard them from the Bulu.[68] According to Elizabeth Prine Pauls, the Bulu comprise one of the three major subdivisions of the Fang who are a Bantu-speaking people numbering between three and four hundred thousand and living in parts of Cameroon, Equatorial Guinea, and Gabon—all nations of West-Central Africa. Known in the past as exceptional warriors and hunters, the Fang developed a reputation for cannibalism to ward off invasion by outsiders. In colonial days, they traded ivory with Europeans but today are primarily farmers.[69]

The Woman, the Monkey, and the Child
(from the Igbo of South Nigeria)

One of the Igbo kings named Archibong owned a slave called Okun. This man lived on his master's farm near Calabar, a town lying between the Calabar and Kwa Ibo Rivers. As a hunter, Okun used to kill all kinds of antelopes and monkeys for their hides. He would dry them in the sun, and when they had cured, he sold them in the marketplace of Calabar. The monkey skins people bought for drums and the antelope skins for mats to sit on. As for the animals' flesh, Okun would smoke it over a wood fire, but unlike the hides, the meat did not bring in much money.

From his earnings, Okun paid a fee to marry Nkoyo, also a slave who belonged to another Igbo chief of the region. After they had wed, the couple returned to the farm where Okun lived. The months passed, and Nkoyo gave birth to a boy.

When the child was about four months old, Okun left to go hunting, and Nkoyo and the baby remained on the farm. As it was the dry season, Nkoyo would leave the boy in the shade of a tree and began clearing the ground for yams she would plant two months before the rains arrived.

Each day, while Nkoyo worked the soil, a large monkey came from the forest to play with the baby. A gentle beast, he would first gather the child lovingly in his arms and carry him into the tree branches above. As soon as Nkoyo completed her work, the monkey would then climb down and return the boy.

All this time, another hunter named Edem Effiong had long been in love with Nkoyo. Though he had told her of his feelings, she remained steadfast in her loyalty to Okun. When her son was born, Edem grew highly jealous and came to the farm while Okun was away.

"Where is your baby?" the hunter asked.

Nkoyo replied, "A big monkey has taken him into the tree over there and looks after him while I till the ground." Edem gazed into the branches of the tree and decided he would inform Okun.

The next day, the jealous hunter found Okun. "While you hunt, your wife goes into the forest to be with a large monkey."

At first Okun doubted the man's words until Edem said, "Follow me, and I will show you myself."

Hearing such a strong avowal, Okun without question now believed the other hunter and pledge to himself, "I will kill this monkey."

Early the following morning, the two went to the farm where Okun spied the monkey playing with his child aloft in the tree. Taking careful aim with his bow, he shot the monkey but did not quite kill it. In a savage fit, the wounded beast tore the boy apart and tossed his torso, limbs, and head to the ground before he himself dropped down dead.

So enraged was Okun at his son's mutilation that he shot his wife as she stood nearby in terror. While she lay dying, Okun hurried to King Archibong and told his master what had occurred. The king knew the murder would anger Nkoyo's owner and cause him to make war, so the king gathered his warriors. Now readied for battle, he sent a messenger informing the chief about what had happened.

"Inform King Archibong," said the chief, "that he must send his slave Okun to me so that I may punish him howsoever I please—even unto death." Upon the messenger's return, King Archibong refused and informed the chief that he would rather let arms decide the matter than submit to his demand.

Both sides now converged into the market square of Calabar and fought fiercely. Besides the many wounded, the chief lost twenty men, and King Archibong thirty. On the whole, though, Archibong won the day and drove his enemies back.

The rest of the Igbo leaders, however, did not want the battle to continue, so they sent their men out with drums to stop the slaughter. To bring the two sides to peace, the council of chiefs determined Archibong was at fault for starting the fight and ordered him to pay his foe six hundred brass rods. The king, however, declared he would rather continue to fight than pay his enemy but said he would pay the fine to the town. This offer did not satisfy the wronged chief, and the two sides prepared to commence war once again.

As rumors of ongoing hostilities spread throughout the land, the

Igbo people themselves rose up in protest. "We will have no more fighting and killing," they proclaimed.

While the hostile parties continued to meet, King Archibong argued before the Igbo chiefs that Edem Effiong's trickery had caused Okun to murder his wife Nkoyo. When Edem's master heard this evidence, he agreed to submit to a final ruling by the Igbo chiefs. They found Edem guilty of deceit and the cause of Nkoyo's death and passed sentence.

A pair of Igbo executioners, armed with whips barbed with chips of bone and metal, laid two hundred lashes on the criminal's bare back, cut off his head, and sent it to his master. This chief then set it in front of the idol he worshipped.

From that day forward, all monkeys and apes fear people, even if they are tiny children. The Igbo also declared that any marriage between the slave of one household and another would henceforth be unlawful, for such unions might lead to war and death.

COMMENTARY: This *pourquoi* legend comes from Elphinstone Dayrell's 1910 *Folk Stories from Southern Nigeria, West Africa*.[70] Perhaps the most well-known story from Dayrell's work is "Why the Sun and Moon Live in the Sky,"[71] another *pourquoi* which as a picture book won a Caldecott Honor Award in 1969 for its illustrator Blair Lent. Famed for the color fairy books, anthropologist Andrew Lang wrote an introduction to the anthology and described its selections as being "full of mentions of strange institutions, as well as of rare adventures."[72] Regarding the story retold here, Lang said it illustrated "Egbo [Igbo] juridicature very powerfully" and was "told to account for Nigerian marriage law."[73]

Originally titled "Concerning the Woman, the Ape, and the Child," the story, like the previous one, arguably belongs to the category of realistic folktales also. The large simian in the story, referred to as an "ape," a word often used interchangeably with "monkey" in older narratives not of a strictly scientific nature, does not possess anthropomorphized traits such as human speech. It does, of course, care for Nkoyo's baby in the branches of a tree, but this behavior could realistically, if somewhat implausibly, occur. Unlike many folktales with monkeys, the gentle creature in this story is neither vicious trickster nor playful prankster but an unwitting victim of Edem's deceit and Okun's suspicions about Nkoyo's behavior. The remainder of the story focuses on the quarrel between the two rival rulers and provides an explanation for an Igbo marriage custom. Lang's explanation that brass rods formed the currency of the region explains the fine imposed by the council of chiefs on Edem's owner.[74]

As for the Igbo people today, they are among the most populous

African native groups and live in southeastern and south-central Nigeria. Prior to British colonial control in the twentieth century, the Igbo, as the folktale indicates, comprised a number of chiefdoms and followed the practices of juju whereby objects (for example, Edem's head) become infused with magical properties. As explained by Ibo Cbanga and Amy Tikkanen, the principal belief is, if "two entities ... have been in close contact," they "develop similar properties even after being separated," thus allowing one entity to be manipulated "in order to reach the other."[75]

After Nigeria became independent in 1960, the Igbo developed a sense of national identity and seceded, forming the Republic of Biafra. Civil war ensued from 1967 to 1970 during which two and a half million of Biafra's citizens perished from starvation. Although the country is now one nation, articles often appear in Nigeria's online newspaper, *The Sun*, and discuss the fact that that even today Nigerian unity is far from resolved. One article states that the country's identity is still nebulous as various groups within Nigeria have maintained their long-held fears and ingrained prejudices.[76]

How Twins Entered the World
(from the Yoruba of West Central Africa)

In days long forgotten, there was a prosperous farmer famed for hunting monkeys. Because his fields always yielded abundant crops, monkeys like to come and feed in them. The creatures became so numerous they left little for the farmer and his family to eat. Even though he and his sons guarded the crops and drove the monkeys away with rocks and arrows, they returned time and time again. At last, desperate and angry, the farmer pursued the monkeys into the bush and forest to kill them.

Yet the monkeys continued to raid his crops, inventing ever more cunning ways to steal. Sometimes a few would appear in one part of a field, and while the farmer or his sons gave chase, droves of other monkeys entered another part to devour the growing grain. They even turned to juju. With their magic, they brought dark thunder clouds and rain so that those who watched the crops would leave, believing the downpours so heavy that no one, not even a monkey, would go into the fields to feed. And yet, while the rains descended, the monkeys ate.

Discovering the creatures' clever tricks, the farmer and his sons made shelters and from their cover watched the fields. Though they killed many monkeys, the survivors continued their forays.

During this time, one of the farmer's wives became pregnant. On hearing this news, an adahunse, or oracle, of the nearby town brought a warning to the farmer. "If you keep killing the monkeys, ill luck and danger wait for you," said the seer. "For monkeys are both wise and powerful. They can send an abiku into your wife. Such a child is born, lives a while, and dies. Then he will again go into the womb to be born and die. Each time the woman becomes pregnant, he will torment you this way. Do not hunt and kill the monkeys or chase them off. Let them enter your fields and eat."

The farmer heard the adahunse but would not listen. He and his sons kept driving the pests away and hunting them in the bush and forest.

The monkeys now decided to take revenge. Two of them took the form of abikus and entered the pregnant wife. They bided their time before they emerged—first the youngest, then the oldest.

Because they were the first twins of the Yoruba, they gained much attention. Some people said, "Good fortune will follow." Others said, "No, it is a bad sign. Only monkeys have twins."

But no matter what people said, the twins did not live long, suddenly dying and going back to those yet to be born. After a while, the wife became pregnant again, and again she gave birth to twins, and again they lived for a time and died.

His children's deaths made the farmer desperate. So he sought out a noted fortuneteller who lived a great distance away. The man cast palm nuts and read their meaning. "Your misfortunes," he said, "result from hunting and killing the monkeys. They have sent abikus into your wife to torment you. Allow the monkeys to feed in your fields, and your sufferings will cease."

The farmer returned home. No longer did he chase the monkeys from his fields. No longer did he hunt them in the bush and forest. Now he let them come and eat as they pleased.

After a time, his wife became pregnant and bore another set of twins. They lived and thrived. Yet the farmer was not sure his troubles had ended, so he went back to the fortuneteller who again threw his palm nuts and read the future.

"This time the monkeys have forgiven you. The twins are real children and will not die only to be reborn and die again. But know that twins are not like other children. Their power is great, and they can reward or punish other people. Their protector is the Ibeji spirit. If you abuse or neglect them, the god will punish you with sickness and poverty. But if your treat the twins well, the Ibeji will bless you with good fortune and prosperity."

The oracle then cast his palm nuts again. "Do all you can to make the twins happy. Do what they say and give them what they want. Offer sacrifices to the Ibeji for whom monkeys are sacred. The monkeys sent you the twins. Let no one in your family eat monkey flesh. The palm nuts have spoken."

The farmer went back to his wife and told her what the seer had said. From that day forward, the farmer and his wife did as the twins asked. If they wanted something sweet, they had it. If they told their mother to beg gifts for them in the marketplace, she begged. If they demanded that she dance with them there, she danced, holding them in her arms while others looked on.

In this way, the twins continued to live, growing stronger over the years. The other wives also gave birth to twins, and good fortune smiled on the farmer and all his family. From the monkeys, twins first came into the world.

COMMENTARY: Originally titled "How Twins Came Among the Yoruba," this adaptation derives from Harold Courlander's large anthology *A Treasury of African Folklore*[77] and belongs to at least two folktale categories. As a magical story, it has supernatural beings as well as a seer who casts palm nuts to learn what fate might have in store for the farmer and his wife. As a *pourquoi.* it explains why the Yoruba people regard the birth of twins as a gift from monkeys. Although some cultures in West-Central Africa consider twins to be a sign of misfortune, the Yoruba believe that twins, or *ibejis*, enjoy special capabilities of endowing their families with good luck if parents cater to their dual offspring. Parents, therefore, attempt to please them more than other children. Twins even have their own god who protects them and punishes households that do not treat them properly.[78]

Like the Igbo, the Yoruba chiefly live in Nigeria and are the second largest ethnic group found there. They constitute approximately twenty-one percent of the country's population, with the largest group being the Hausa at twenty-five percent and the Igbo at eighteen.[79] Courlander indicates that until the twentieth century the Yoruba did not think of themselves as one people and lived in different kingdoms and city states.[80]

How the Tail of the Colobus Monkey Became White
(from the Akan-Ashanti of Ghana)

One day, the elephant Esono, the monkey Kwakuo, the putty-nosed monkey named Anyinhima, and the black colobus monkey called Efuo decided to go to a village to get married. As these young men went along, they came to a pool of muddy water. The putty-nosed monkey stopped and told the others, "Be still. I have a question. Who among us is the best-looking?"

Esono the elephant answered, "Efuo, the black colobus monkey, looks the best."

The monkey Kwakuo added, "If that is true, let's beat him up and toss him into the dirty pool." So the others beat Efuo and immersed him in the water. They then continued their journey without him.

After the three had gone, Efuo got out of the pool and followed at a distance quietly behind them. He painfully walked into the village and sat down in the trash pile on its edge where everyone threw their garbage. The other two monkeys and Esono the elephant had already arrived and watched some of the unmarried girls gather beneath a Gyedua tree. Before long, they had each picked out a girl they wanted to marry.

Earlier that day, another girl had left the village and gone into the surrounding fields to work. Before leaving, she had instructed her mother, "When the young men come to select a wife, pick one and set him aside for me." She now returned. "Where's my husband?" she wanted to know.

The girl's mother replied, "When I went to the tree, the other girls had already made their choice, and no one was left."

"Oh, well, it does not matter anyway," the girl answered, and she peeled some plantains and took their skins to the trash heap.

Efuo was still sitting there, and as the girl started to throw away the skins, he cried out, "Don't toss the peelings on me."

"Who are you?" she asked.

"It is I, Efuo."

"What's the matter with you?"

Efuo explained, "The other men and I were on our way here to get married, but they thought I was too good-looking and would hurt their chances to find a wife. So they beat me and threw me into dirty water. That is why I now sit here on top of the village trash heap."

"As for me," the girl replied, "I love you. Let's go home."

So the girl and Efuo left, and she got clean water and began to wash him. After a bit, she noticed how shiny his skin was. She called to her mother, "Come and see how beautiful and glossy his skin has become."

The mother said, "Finish bathing him."

The girl did as her mother told her, and when she had finished, she put oil on Efuo to soften his skin and make him even shinier. He then put on his sandals, picked up his stringed instrument, and went out to the Gyedua tree where he began to play a tune.

The girls who had already wed saw him. One of them remarked, "I no longer love my husband but am in love with the black colobus monkey." Another girl said, "I no longer love my husband. I love this monkey, too." And thus the comments went around in a similar fashion.

Efuo, however, replied, "I love the one I have."

Upon hearing all that was said, the other animals collected their belongings. "Goodbye. It is time for us to go." They then left the village, but instead of heading home, they hid not far down the trail and waited for Efuo. They intended to beat the black colobus monkey and kill him when he came down the path.

Efuo now decided to leave as well. He gathered his things and bade the villagers goodbye before he set off down the trail. As he went along, the other animals saw him and whispered, "Here comes Efuo, the black colobus monkey." But he was too smart for them and had read their thoughts. He grabbed a tree limb and vaulted off the ground to escape.

Not to be outdone, the others grasped white clay and flung it toward him. Some of the clay stuck to his chin, and some stuck to his tail. Before, these had both been black. As a result, his chin and tail are white today.

If this story is sweet or if it is not sweet, take some of it elsewhere, but let some of it return to me.

COMMENTARY: Captain Robert Sutherland Rattray's *Akan-Ashanti Folk-Tales* (1930) is the basis[81] for this *pourquoi*. An Oxford-trained anthropologist, Rattray worked for the government of what was then the Gold Coast of East Africa which in 1900 had become part of the British Empire. Today the Gold Coast comprises the nation of Ghana, with the Ashanti people, a subdivision of the Akan, the country's largest ethnic group.[82] Their native tongue is Twi, a dialect of the Akan language.[83] In the eighteenth century, the Ashanti were partners in human trafficking with the English and Dutch, exchanging slaves for firearms.[84]

Rattray indicates that he obtained his stories firsthand in remote settlements as told "by the old folk, under the stars."[85] Unlike the method sometimes used by other collectors of folktales, he did not engage the services of collaborators who spoke both Akan and English because of their tendency "to ignore the African idiom and to omit just those apparently trivial details" that would mark the stories "with individuality and make them of value to students of languages and customs."[86] Another feature of his collection which gives further authenticity to the tales is that Rattray heard them first performed in live storytelling settings with native narrators and actors performing after dark, a time dictated by local custom for presentation. Immediately afterwards, Rattray says he recorded the tales and made emendations with the help of the performer.[87] This method is in contradistinction to that has often been used by ethnographers and anthropologists in which a native informant tells a folktale in an artificial, decontextualized setting.

One characteristic of Ashanti stories (and other African talking beast tales) that may seem curious to readers encountering them for the first time is that animals and humans appear interchangeable. For instance, in the story retold here, the black colobus monkey and the other animals traveling with him marry young women of a nearby village and are sometimes referred to as people. Rattray explains this lack of compartmentalization between animal and human worlds as part of the Ashanti storytelling tradition in which the names of animals replace those of actual people if there is satiric intent in the tale. That way, the storyteller avoids direct offense to any person present, especially one of higher social standing, and thereby escapes the native injunction against "tale-bearing and libel."[88]

Western Europe

An Aesop Sampler

The King of the Apes
(from Phaedrus, c. 18 BCE–50 CE)

Two men traveled together. One always told lies while the other spoke only the truth. The pair eventually arrived at the distant and secluded land of the apes where ruled a loud and vicious king. Upon learning about the two, he ordered his border guards to bring the men to his court. Wishing to impress the men with his splendor, he sat upon his throne where his subjects stood arrayed on either side of it in two long rows.

Eager to discover the travelers' opinion of him, the ape said to the liar, "Tell me what you think of me as a king."

The man answered, "My lord, you are a grand and mighty emperor."

"And what do think of my subjects on either side of you?"

"Your Simian Magnificence," responded the traveler, "they are all worthy apes who have the honor to be ruled by such a regal monarch." Delighted by this response, the ape at once rewarded the man with a handsome gift as all his subjects hooted in approval.

On seeing what occurred, the other man considered, "If my fellow traveler has secured such a rich present for lying, I must surely receive a gift even more grand for speaking the truth." The ape now looked at him. "Give me your opinion?" the ape demanded. "Tell me who am I and who are these, my mustered ranks that you see before you."

The lover and speaker of truth replied, "You and your court are apes and ever will be."

Instantly, the head ape cried, "He utters vicious nasty lies. Tear him to pieces."

Moral
The wicked who thrive on deceit
May kill the frank, if indiscreet.

The Ape and the Fox

Ashamed that his behind was bare, an ape went to a fox. "Your tail is long and bushy. You seem to have more than enough. Would you be willing to part with a portion of it so that my bottom might look more respectable?"

Answered the hateful fox, "Though my tail were even longer than it is now, I would let it trail through mud and brambles rather than share the tiniest part of it with you."

Moral
Even when they have too much,
The greedy never have enough.

The Lion and the Ape

When the lion became the king of beasts, he wanted his subjects to consider him a monarch noted for fairness. He, therefore, vowed to give up his former manner of eating and to limit his diet as did the other animals. He further pledged that justice and honesty would be the hallmarks of his reign. But as time passed, his promises began to falter, for he could not change his natural tendencies.

The lion, therefore, decided to take certain of his subjects aside and pose to them privately whether his breath smelled sweet or rank. No matter what the answer—whether sweet or bad—the king reacted the same way. He tore each one apart and through teeth and claws thus satisfied his craving.

After killing many in this manner, the lion turned one day to an ape and asked, "How does my breath smell?"

The ape answered, "Sire, the fragrance of your breath is like cinnamon and incense offered on the altars of the gods."

On hearing his breath thus extolled, the king felt ashamed to kill one who offered such a compliment. So he changed his tactics and pretended to be ill. His court physicians immediately entered and took his pulse. Finding it normal, they encouraged him to have a light meal that would stimulate his appetite. "For kings are allowed all things," they said.

Replied the lion, "I have never tried ape-meat. I would like to taste some of that."

No sooner had these words departed the lion's mouth than the fawning ape was slaughtered so that the king of beasts might satisfy his longing for flesh without delay.

Moral

When the mighty play their game,
For those who praise or silence keep,
The consequence turns out the same.

The Monkey and the Fox
(from Babrius, second century CE)

Traveling together, a fox and monkey began to argue with much ado about which one possessed the better lineage. They continued in this vein for quite a while until they came to cemetery with various monuments alongside the road. There, the monkey stopped. Beholding the scene, he took a long deep sigh.

Curious, the fox inquired, "Does this great sigh mask some enduring sadness of yours?"

The monkey pointed to the tombs and replied, "The numerous monuments that you see raised to the dead were put here to honor my ancestors, all eminent apes in their day." So saying, he paused as if in sympathetic reflection.

For a moment, the stunned fox remained silent, then said, "Why stop there? I'm certain none of your forebears will rise up and expose your lies?"

Jupiter and the Monkey

Jupiter, the lord of men and gods, once decided to hold a contest among the animals to see which among them had the most beautiful offspring. Among those who swelled the crowd was a monkey mother. She had proudly brought her baby—an ugly, hairy, little, flat-faced creature—to present to the judges.

Yet, when the gods and goddesses beheld the wizened wight, laughter burst from the mouth of each immortal. Venus, the goddess of beauty, laughed the loudest, while the matron goddess Juno, who presides over fertility, averted her gaze and scowled. Even Jupiter, not one to compromise his lofty dignity, tee-heed and seemed to shake the spheres.

This sport the monkey mother readily perceived. Still, she held fast to her maternal pride as she addressed the godly jury. "Although Jupiter knows who will win the prize, I know not what your standards are, but as for me, my precious one is the fairest babe of all."

The Monkeys and Their Mother

Monkey mothers will often give birth to two young. One she will nurse and fondle with overmuch care while for the other, seeing it as a superfluity, she gives no thought to its welfare and feeding. It so happens that the baby who has gained its mother's affection is undone by her excessive coddling and smothered by her fierce embraces. However, the baby she neglects as unimportant and unnecessary, that one retreats to the wilds and thrives. With us it is the same. Our purposes end differently from our intentions.

The Dancing Monkeys
(from Lucian of Samosata, c. 120 to 180 CE)

A pharaoh of Egypt once had a troop of baboons trained to dance for his entertainment. Being apt at imitation, the apes soon learned their task. Arrayed in purple robes and fine masks to look like aristocrats, they danced as well or better than any of the court dancers. Indeed, loud and long applause always followed the baboons' performances.

One day, however, a courtier, bent on a bit of mischief, tossed a handful of nuts into the middle of the dancing troop. They immediately stopped and at once pulled off their masks and tore off their robes as they beset the nuts and fought one another like savage foes. And thus the beasts heeded their true natures and forgot all their courtly breeding.

The Monkey and the Dolphin
(from Jean de La Fontaine, 1621–1695)

Passengers on Greek sailing vessels had the custom of taking a pet to amuse themselves. The animal might be a bird or a dog, but sometimes it was a monkey.

And so it happened that a passenger brought a monkey on board a ship returning from the East to Athens. As the vessel arrived near its destination near the headland of Sounion, famed for its ancient Temple of Poseidon, the winds began to blow stiffly and howl, soon becoming a violent storm that tossed all on board into the sea.

Everyone, including the ape, struggled toward the shore. Thinking him a man, a dolphin beheld his struggles and took the beast upon his back. As they neared Athens' port of Piraeus, the dolphin called out over roar of the winds and waves, "Is this your home?"

Spitting out water and seaweed, the almost drowned ape answered, "Yes, although I do not come from the common throng of the city but from its highest ranks."

"Then you must be familiar with Piraeus," said the dolphin, meaning, of course, Athens' port.

"I certainly am," replied the ape. "He's my dearest friend."

The dolphin smiled at this display of self-importance and began to scrutinize his rider. Suddenly realizing he merely resembled a man and provoked by such an obvious lie, the dolphin plunged into the depths, left the abandoned beast to the fish, and turned to save a drowning man.

Moral
If you would be what you are not,
You may be to grave danger brought.

COMMENTARY: The eight fables concerning apes and monkeys in this sampler are associated with the name of the legendary Greek slave Aesop although the number of Aesopic tales containing simians is larger than those retold here. Eminent classics scholar Ben Edwin Perry cites seven hundred and twenty-five fables in the Aesopic tradition, of which he indexes sixteen concerned with apes or monkeys.[1] A more recent volume by comparative literature expert Laura Gibbs contains six hundred selections out of which twenty-two include these primates as characters.[2]

Based on ancient historical testimony that purports to be true, little is known of Aesop personally. In summarizing what the sources from antiquity aver, Perry says he was a Thracian slave of the early sixth century BCE, lived for a while on the island of Samos, had as his master a man named Iadmon, was later freed, and developed a reputation for inventing and telling prose tales.[3] Despite these details, there is little certainty that such a person as Aesop existed. However, scholar Robert Temple presents evidence that "he did exist," based on a few scant, albeit logical, conjectures.[4]

There is also debate over whether the fable as a narrative form came from the early Greeks. Renowned fairy-tale authority Jack Zipes indicates that the brief stories likely began in Mesopotamia sometime in the 800s BCE, most often contained anthropomorphic animals as characters, dealt with the resolution of common human conflicts, and had a moral. Because the tales "adjudicated" the conflicts so as "to potentially establish ethical guidelines or principles of fair play," they "contributed to the civilizing process of all societies and the constitution of the humanities."[5]

The first three selections in the sample are based on the verse fables of the first-century Latin poet Phaedrus,[6] a freedman of Rome's first emperor, Augustus. Phaedrus holds the distinction of being the earliest surviving source for Aesop's fables and the first writer from antiquity to turn the narratives into a polished literary genre, often with a satiric edge on the foibles humanity.[7] He also varied his placement of the moral, sometimes putting it at the beginning, sometimes at the end, and sometimes embedding it within his text. The critic F.D.R. Goodyear severely judged the morals Phaedrus attached to his tales as excessively intrusive as well as "trite and wearisome."[8] Yet Phaedrus is not the only individual to receive adverse criticism on the morals yoked to Aesopic writings. Commenting on morals affixed by later collectors of the fables, Temple calls them "silly and inferior in wit and interest to the fables themselves" and finds some to be "truly appalling, even idiotic."[9]

Following Phaedrus are three retellings derived from Babrius,[10] who wrote a generation after Phaedrus. Unlike the Latin poet, who lived in the city of Rome itself, Babrius lived in the eastern Roman province of Cilicia, in what today are the countries of Armenia and Turkey. Also unlike Phaedrus, Babrius composed his fables in Greek. Even though he has a few longer and more detailed fables, his stories "tend to be brief and sometimes even terse to the point of obscurity."[11] As to his placement of a moral at the end of his fables, many authorities believe these to have been appended later and not original to Babrius.[12] To amplify Babrius' brevity for my adaptations, I consulted other versions of his fables. These include those translated in 1912 by V.S. Vernon Jones[13] as well as translations by Gibbs.[14]

The next fable, "The Dancing Monkeys," is part of a longer dialogue[15] by the second-century satirist Lucian of Samosata, who styled himself "a Syrian ... from the banks of the Euphrates."[16] Like Babrius, as a member of the Roman Empire in the east, Lucian wrote in Greek. Titled "The Dead Come to Life, Or the Fisherman," the piece is a tour de force of tongue-in-check expression, with Lucian under the guise of a character named Frankness recanting a former work in which he satirized ancient, dead philosophers such as Socrates, Plato, Aristotle, Diogenes, and others. Having taken "a brief leave of absence" from Pluto's realm of the dead, they appear before him as accusers determined to inflict upon him a painful and long-lasting death.[17] Frankness appeals to their sense of fairness, and the philosophers agree to take him to court where "Lady Philosophy" will impartially judge this " most impious of all profaners."[18] As part of his defense, Frankness relates his fable about apes "apt at imitating human ways" as an example of the false philosophers at whom he aimed his invective, not those who "truly cultivate philosophy" and adhere to her principles.[19]

Although little of Lucian life is known with any certainty, he is considered to be "one of the most gifted and entertaining of the comic satirists" and to have had a "long-lasting and pervasive" influence on later European writers from the Renaissance through the nineteenth century. These include Desiderius Erasmus, Sir Thomas More, François Rabelais, Jonathan Swift, and Walter Pater.[20]

The last adaptation, "The Monkey and the Dolphin," has its origin in the French writer La Fontaine,[21] who flourished in the second half of seventeenth century and who may have borrowed his version from an ancient source later translated into French in 1927 from Greek by the French scholar Emile Chambry.[22] In 1998, Robert and Olivia Temple rendered Chambry's collection of anonymous fables into English as *Aesop: The Complete Fables*, which Gibbs refers to as a "misleading title," likely because of many other fables not in Chambry but associated with the name of the Greek fabulist. Of course, the Temples' translation includes "The Monkey and the Dolphin."[23]

Regarding La Fontaine, like the Neoclassical authors of his own age, La Fontaine adhered to an aesthetics that had as its major aim the renewal and continuance of an artistic foundation laid in antiquity.[24] As with "The King of the Apes," "The Monkey and the Fox," and "The Dancing Monkeys," La Fontaine's fable evinces what Morris finds as a common portrayal of monkeys and apes—namely, "the impostor, the fraud, and the trickster." They especially represent "the person of lowly origin who pretends to a high position."[25]

Voltaire

Candide, the Girls, and the Two Monkeys
(Voltaire, 1694–1778)

Pursued by authorities from Portugal for alleged misdeeds, the young and innocent Candide and his valet, Cacambo, managed to escape to South America. From Buenos Aires, they traveled north through the Argentine. After several days, they arrived in a wild and unknown land just beyond the frontier of Paraguay.

Eventually, the two came to a beautiful meadow crisscrossed by rivulets and streams. There the wanderers stopped to eat. As the sun set, they heard the muffled cries of what seemed to be women. Neither master nor servant could tell whether the sounds were of delight or distress, but they rose to their feet quickly, fearing what they might find in this unexplored land.

As they peered across the field, Candide and Cacambo saw a pair of young women running along its distant edge as two large monkeys followed, both biting at the girls' buttocks. The spectacle moved Candide to pity. Being a trained marksman, he could shoot a nut off a tree and never graze a leaf. So, he aimed his double-barreled Spanish long gun and killed both apes at once.

"God be praised, Cacambo, I have saved these two wretches from great dishonor and harm. Who knows? They may be young ladies of quality, and my timely assistance may give us an advantage in this country."

About to say more, Candide suddenly turned silent. For at that moment, he beheld the young women burst into tears as they gently caressed the dead monkeys. The high pitch of lamentation echoed through the air.

Dumbfounded, Candide looked at Cacambo. "I did not expect such a tender expression of compassion for these beasts."

"Excellent marksmanship," the valet answered. "Yet you have shot and killed the lovers of the two young ladies."

"Their lovers? How so? I do not believe you! You jest, Cacambo!"

"Ah, master, you are surprised at everything. It is not so strange that in certain lands, monkeys obtain the favor of ladies, especially where there is little education. Monkeys are one-fourth human as I am one-fourth Spanish."

"Oh, my, Cacambo! My learned tutor, Dr. Pangloss, once told me that similar incidents have occurred in times past to create fauns, satyrs, and centaurs and that many great persons from ancient history had seen such creatures. Yet I had believed them the stuff of fantasy and fable."

"This event should convince you of the truth of these old tales," said the servant. "But I now fear those ladies may bring difficulties upon us."

This consideration caused Candide and Cacambo to leave the meadow as fast as they could and plunge into the nearest forest. After supper that night, they cursed all who had brought trouble upon them.

COMMENTARY: Although not a story from traditional literature, this selection from chapter 16 of Voltaire's 1759 satiric masterpiece *Candide*[26] alludes to the common folk belief of sex-crazed monkeys as part of what Morris calls "the animalistic face of humanity."[27] In this regard, the excerpt echoes the earlier "The Sultan's Daughter and the Baboon," retold from *The Thousand and One Nights*. (See the last story in the section "The Middle East and India.") Morris points out that, as far back as the ancient world, there were claims of monkeys and people copulating, with the Egyptian god Thoth depicted in statues as a baboon with an enormous penis, a portrayal that lent credence to the concept of the lustful monkey.[28]

According to Morris, this legendary belief takes two forms: sometimes the monkey engages with an all-too-willing partner and sometimes the monkey savagely rapes his victim.[29] Morris does not explicitly state that in both circumstances the monkey is a male and the partner, whether willing participant or unwilling victim, is female. The episode from *Candide* adheres to the plot of willing partner. In this case, both women are distraught that Candide has killed their lovers.

Readers will recall this same plotline occurs in "The Sultan's Daughter and the Baboon." Unlike this story, however, since the episode in *Candide* is set in Paraguay, the primates there would be New World monkeys and not Old World monkeys like the supposed baboon in the Middle Eastern tale. Among Paraguayan monkey lovers, the most likely candidate for Voltaire's story would be the black howler monkey even though it is small in comparison to a big male baboon, which has an average weight of sixty-six pounds.[30] The farthest extreme in weight for a black howler is only twenty so that it would not be as large as Voltaire's story suggests. Although referred to as the *black* howler, the color applies to the males only. Females and their young have golden-tan fur.[31]

As to the truth of the curious belief about simians having sex with people, Morris contends that the notion of a wild monkey copulating with humans is farfetched. A pet monkey, on the other hand, cared for from birth by humans, might at maturity "direct some sexual interest towards the body of its human companion, just as a pet dog will hump its owner's leg."[32] Still, if the sexual act were completed, it would "inevitably" be "hugely disappointing," for as Morris indicates, when monkeys mate in the wild, the performance normally lasts about eight seconds.[33]

Tibet, Korea, Southeast Asia, and China

The Two Monkeys
(from Tibet)

One bright, sunny day, two roving monkeys explored the area outside a village. There, they discovered a large tree heavily laden with fruit that appeared for the taking.

One monkey exclaimed, "How delicious this fruit looks. We must gather this free, luscious bounty and eat!"

The other monkey, who was wise, paused for a moment, then said, "No, no, my friend. Consider that this tree grows beside the village. If its offerings were suitable to eat, the people would already have gathered the ripe fruit. Yet no one had touched it, and neither should we."

"What nonsense," replied his companion. "Put your fears aside, and let us feast. This fruit is the same as any other."

His friend answered, "Eat if you wish. Though other trees may be farther away, I will seek fruit from them." Despite these cautions, the willful monkey was intent on satisfying his hunger then and there and devoured as much of the fruit as he could hold.

The next day, the wise monkey returned and found his friend stretched beneath the tree. There, he had breathed his last. The poison fruit had killed him.

Moral
Those who will not an urge defer
May sometimes gravest fate incur.

COMMENTARY: This story is retold from Catherine Bryce's 1910 *Fables from Afar*.[1] As with many early children's books, the author does not cite the source other than the vague attribution "Tales from the East," a heading in the table of contents. More than likely, Bryce got the story from Anton Schiefner's 1906 *Tibetan Tales Derived from Indian*

Sources.[2] Schiefner, in turn, took his stories from *The Kangyur*, an extensive collection of Buddhist writings in Sanskrit that made their way into Tibet during the seventh, ninth, and thirteenth centuries. Some of the selections toward the end of *The Kangyur* are animal fables. One such tale is Schiefner's "The Wise and Foolish Monkey Chiefs" which is essentially Bryce's "The Two Monkeys." In the original Tibetan version as given by Schiefner, there are two bands of five hundred monkeys. Each group comes to a "hill-village" where a kimpaka tree grows nearby with the fruit weighing "its branches down to the ground."[3] The monkeys of one troop long to eat the fruit, but their wise leader warns that the children of the village "have not partaken of the fruit" so that "it may be concluded that the fruit of this tree is not conducive to enjoyment."[4] The leader of the second troop allows his monkeys to feast on the fruit. Unfortunately, they "suffered agonies in consequence" of their behavior.[5]

Antedating Schiefner's tale, "Phala-Jataka"[6] has many similarities. Instead of monkeys, the story has the Bodhisattva, who has been reborn as a merchant, traveling with five hundred wagons. At the edge of a forest, he and his men near a village having a tree close by that bears fruit resembling mangoes. Some of his men arrive at the tree ahead of the rest of the caravan, and being "greedy fellows" eat the fruit.[7] Others wait for the merchant to arrive to ask his opinion. He warns that the fruit comes from the "What-fruit tree" and is poisonous.[8] Dosing with an emetic those who have already eaten, he saves all his men from death through both his medicine and wise council and concludes with a verse moral:

> When near a village grows a tree
> Not hard to climb, 'tis plain to me,
> Nor need I further proof to know,
> No wholesome fruit can thereon grow![9]

Similar to the forbidden fruit in these stories is that of the karaka tree. The tree bears large orange berries which are highly toxic if eaten before sufficiently ripe, causing violent convulsions and paralysis. The karaka tree, however, is not native to either India or Tibet but grows in coastal areas of New Zealand and the surrounding islands. A Māori word, *karaka* signifies the color orange.[10]

The Monkeys Saved from Death
(from Tibet)

Long ago, five hundred monkeys with their chief lived on a hilltop above where villagers grew grain. When it became ready to harvest, the herd would come down and eat the crop. The villagers assembled to decide what they must do. Among themselves, they asked, "How can we prevent the monkeys from devouring our food? We must do something, or we shall starve for lack of grain."

After some debate, one person said, "Let us cut down all the fruit trees that surround our fields except for one Tinduka tree. We will leave it and build a tall hedge of thorny limbs around it except for a single opening which we can quickly close. When the monkeys enter to climb the tree to eat the fruit, we can trap them inside and kill them."

The villagers agreed, and the trees were cut down with only one left standing inside the hedge of thorns. A watchman stayed hidden nearby to signal when the monkeys came.

One day, the tree hung heavy with ripened fruit, and the monkeys appealed to their leader, "The tree is full of fruit. Let us go and eat." So the chief and his troop descended from the hill and entered the hedge. They climbed into the tree and began to eat.

The watchman immediately brought word to the village. "The monkeys are in the tree and feeding."

The villagers gathered quickly. Arming themselves with bows and arrows and axes, they hurried inside the high hedge, closed the entrance, and began to cut down the Tinduka tree.

Overcome with fright, the monkeys frantically jumped from limb to limb. But their chief did not move. "Why do you sit doing nothing while we leap here and there in panic for our lives?" exclaimed his followers.

The chief calmly replied, "What happens will happen, whether I am frantic or not."

While all this ruckus was occurring, one of the chief's offspring, captured earlier by the villagers, sat lost in thought with his hand under his chin. A tame village monkey saw him and asked, "Why do you sit doing nothing, lost in thought?"

The young one answered, "How could I do otherwise? Most of the villagers have gone to kill my relatives."

Still the tame monkey questioned, "Why do you not act with courage?"

"How can a captive be courageous?" came the reply

"Then I will set you free," said the other as he removed the tether.

As soon as the young monkey was released, he set the village on fire. A thick smoke and loud crackling arose when the dwellings began to burn. The few people who had remained there made a great uproar.

When the villagers at the Tinduka tree heard the noise, they cried, "Let us run and put out the fire and then come back!" So, they hurried to fight the fire, and the monkeys scurried down the tree and escaped through the now open entrance.

COMMENTARY: As in other selections, the monkeys here partake of the often-found traits among their kind of greed and destruction. However, the monkey chief and his captive young offspring are wise enough to know that effective action is useful only when opportunity presents itself. This tale likewise has its origins in the *Kangyur*.[11]

R. Spence Hardy's 1853 *A Manual of Budhism* [sic] *in Its Modern Development* contains a variant shorter than Schiefner's.[12] Titled "The Tinduka Jataka," it has the perfunctory eighty-thousand-member monkey troop led by a wise simian king who is Buddha reincarnated. His greedy subjects do not destroy the villagers' grain but want to eat the fruit of the timberry tree. He forbids them, but they disobey. Armed with sticks, irate villagers seek to kill the monkeys. The monkey king rescues them by setting the village ablaze.

The Tinduka tree in Schiefner's and Hardy's texts is found in India and Southeast Asia. Known as the gaub tree, it is also referred to as the Indian persimmon and has medicinal uses. When ripe, its fruit is a small, round, yellow berry.[13]

The Monkeys and the Moon
(from Tibet)

Long, long ago, a band of monkeys lived in a forest. As they rambled through their land one night, they noticed that the moon had fallen into a well. Unaware that what they saw was only the moon's reflection, the monkey chieftain lamented, "Alas, the earth has lost the silver orb that lights our way by night." He then appealed to his troop, "We must rescue this kind light."

The monkeys at once agreed and through their babble formed a plan to save the moon. "Let us connect ourselves to one another by joining our arms and tails to make a long chain."

They, therefore, climbed into a tree that hung over the well. Finding a firm limb, the chieftain held onto it while another grasped his tail. The rest of the monkeys followed suit, linking themselves together above the well. Slowly, the limb began to sink from their weight. This movement made the water ripple until the moon's image wrinkled and blurred beyond recognition. The branch suddenly snapped, causing the monkeys to tumble into the well. A few escaped unhurt, but in the wild to-do to save themselves, most drowned.

An Immortal beheld the tragedy unfold and uttered the following verse:

When fools observe a fool's advice,
They should expect to pay a price.

COMMENTARY: This story, too, is adapted from Bryce[14] but originates in the Tibetan *Kangyur* and is also included in Schiefner's *Tibetan Tales Derived from Indian Sources*.[15] Along with Schiefner's text, the version in Frederick and Audrey Hyde-Chambers' anthology of Tibetan folktales served as a source text for my rendition.[16] Mark Schumacher suggests three possible lessons in the fable: a person should not foolishly attempt the impossible; appearances easily deceive the unenlightened or the restless and unfocused "monkey mind"; and when an unwise leader leads the unwise, ruin results.[17] Bryce does not explicitly state any of these morals in her version of the story. However, I have chosen to emphasis a variation of the third one by having it uttered as a verse by a deity.

Monkeys joining together to form a chain to achieve some end is factually based. In *The Land I Lost*, Nhuong describes how he observed monkeys in Vietnam drinking from a river. To avoid getting muddy paws, they linked themselves together from a branch over the water as each one took turns drinking. One chain, he says, comprised fifteen monkeys trying to reach the water when the river was low. As with the monkeys in the Tibetan tale, those from Vietnam could not swim either, according to Nhuong.[18]

The Monkey's Judgment
(from Korea)

High in the mountains near a waterfall, a hungry fox and wolf walked toward each other from the opposite ends of a path. Exactly between the two lay a large piece of meat. Both saw it at the same time, and both immediately pounced upon it, crying "It's mine! It's mine!"

Their jaws clamped tightly upon the meat, the two animals pulling back and forth trying to win the prize. This tug-o-war went on for quite a while, but neither could take the meat from the other. At last, they decided that the animal court would have to settle the matter. At that time, Judge Monkey presided. He had a reputation for deciding cases with an even hand, and all the animals considered him to be the wisest of their justices.

The fox and wolf presented their pleas. Reviewing all former cases that might have a bearing on theirs, Judge Monkey duly weighted the evidence. First, he scratched his left ear. Then he scratched his right.

Finally, after careful consideration, he broke his silence. "As both of you saw and bit down upon the meat at the same time, you both have equal rights in it. Therefore, the court rules that one-half shall go the fox and one-half shall go to the wolf."

The judge next ordered a sharp knife and scales brought into the court so that he could render the verdict fairly. Cutting the meat into two chunks, he placed the fox's part on one side of the scales and the wolf's on the other to determine whether they balanced equally. Unfortunately, one side weighted slightly more than the other. So, thinking to make the scales even, the monkey sliced off a thin strip from the heavier piece. This he ate as it would be unfair to give the extra slice to either party.

However, the former lighter piece sank lower on its side of the scales because it had now become the heavier of the two. So, with the intention of balancing the scales, the judge trimmed off a sliver from this piece. Again, to be fair, he ate it immediately, and as he did, the lighter piece of meat slowly sank on its side of the scales and became the heavier chunk.

In this way, things continued back and forth during the proceedings, the monkey trimming from one side of the scales and eating the slice and doing the same to the other side. Each time the monkey shaved off a tiny piece, no matter how wafer thin, the scales refused to balance.

After several hours, the trial concluded. Neither the wolf nor the fox received a share of the meat. It had vanished during the trial. Judge Monkey had eaten every bite.

COMMENTARY: This story appears as "The Judgment of the Monkey" in Berta Metzger's 1932 collection of Korean folktales.[19] Ernest Thompson Seton, wildlife artist and one of the founders of the Boy Scouts of America, included a variant of this selection in his 1932 *Famous Animal Stories*. "The Monkey and the Cats"[20] presents a quarrel between two cats over an oyster. A monkey who has "studied law" agrees to arbitrate the dispute, takes the oyster, and leaves the litigious cats with only the shell. To judge from the title of Seton's book, the story is purportedly a well-known folktale, yet Seton does not reveal its source or its country of origin.

Why Monkeys and People Do Not Live Together
(from the Hmong of Southeast Asia)

A long time ago, Monkey and Man lived together as best of friends. This accord came to an end, however, because of Man's envy.

The two owned fields beside each other, but Monkey's land produced more food than that of his friend. And yet the fields of Man, when viewed from the ground, appeared fertile, as if they would grow abundant crops. The fields of Monkey, though, when viewed from the trees or surrounding hills, looked poor, as though anyone foolish enough to farm them would go hungry.

This situation stirred Man's jealousy and made him want to take what Monkey had. Man showed Monkey their lands both from the ground and from the hills and trees. Monkey could clearly see the differences between their fields. So, when Man suggested that they trade with each other, Monkey readily agreed and thought that he had made the better bargain.

That spring and summer, Monkey worked hard on his new land, hoping to have a rich crop when the growing season ended. But when the harvest came, his yield turned out to be far worse even than what man had cleared when he owned the land. It seemed that Monkey and his children might starve.

So Monkey went to his friend to ask for advice and hoped that Man could recommend a way to relieve the hardships to come. But Man continued to plot and scheme, saying "My friend, I'm afraid for you to survive you'll have to kill your children. Even then, you may not have enough food for yourself."

Monkey heard these words, and his heart sank as though weighed down by a heavy burden. Full of dread, he turned toward home, and when he arrived there, he killed all his children.

That night, no moon arose to bathe the earth in soft, silver light, and in the murky darkness, Man slipped away from his house. He found Monkey's young lay dead, and he stole their flesh.

The next day, early in the morning, Monkey walked by Man's house. Outside the doorway, he saw fresh meat on spits. Some had been roasted, and some was ready for roasting in the fire nearby.

Monkey asked his friend, "What's that you have? What's that you've been roasting? What's that you've cooked today to eat?"

Man paused a moment, then said, "It's only jackdaw flesh."

But Monkey knew what Man had done. He knew how Man had forsaken their friendship, how he had killed Monkey's children, how he had stolen not only their flesh but their souls as well.

Now fear of Man in Monkey grew. He abandoned his fields and hid deep within the forest. Today he neither plants nor reaps but steals Man's rice and other crops.

COMMENTARY: In its archetype of the fall, this Hmong folktale is similar to "Irraweka and the Flood," the first story in the section titled

"The Caribbean, South America, and North America." Both narratives depict the destruction of an original and fundamental harmony that once existed between humankind and animals. Unlike the story of Irraweka, however, the primal unity in the Hmong selection is destroyed, not by a monkey's meddling, but by man's deceit and cruelty. The adaptation comes from Norma J. Livo and Dia Cha's anthology *Folk Stories of the Hmong: Peoples of Laos, Thailand, and Vietnam*.[21]

The Adventures of the Monkey King
(from China)

Birth and Early Great Deeds

In the Eastern Sea sat a little island. On the island rose the Mountain of Flowers and Fruit. And on the mountain lay a large stone. It had been there since the beginning of the world. Blessed by the powers of sky and earth and caressed by the light of the sun and moon, the stone received the spark of life. One day, the stone suddenly split apart, revealing a magical egg.

Winds fanned the egg with warmth so that the life within began to grow. At last a fully-formed stone monkey hatched. He learned to climb, run, and leap. But his first act was to bow to the north and south, east and west. His eyes flashed such light that in the High Heaven the Jade Emperor, who rules all above and below, was astonished when the rays reached his throne. He commanded his royal officials to determine the reason for the disturbance on earth, and learning the cause to be no more than a monkey, the emperor gave the matter no further thought.

As time passed, the stone monkey became companion to many animals—wolves, leopards, tigers, deer, and other monkeys. They wandered the countryside of deep valleys and high mountains and slept under overhanging rocks and in caves.

One day on their travels, they came to a large waterfall that tumbled down a cliff and seemed like a thunderous curtain. As the monkeys bathed in the sparkling stream at the bottom, they clapped their hands together and called out, "Beautiful water! Beautiful water! If one of us were brave enough to pierce the waterfall and see beyond its curtain, we would crown him our king!"

Three times the challenge went out for one of them to go beyond the water curtain when suddenly the stone monkey stepped forward and loudly cried, "I will go!" Then in one leap, he jumped through the waterfall.

And what did he find when he landed on the other side? The Cave of the Water Curtain in the Mountain of Flowers and Fruit—a world so blessed that it seemed sent from Heaven itself. There he and his companions could rest in comfort from their weary wanderings.

He returned to his friends and told them what he had found. He then led them back through the water curtain to the beautiful paradise they could now call home. Their voices rang out, "May you reign a thousand years," and they proclaimed him their ruler. He gave up his old name of Stone Monkey and took the title of Handsome Monkey King.

The Secret of Long Life

For several hundred years, he and his subjects knew only perfect peace and harmony. Over time, however, he became burdened with sorrow. One day at his birthday feast, he burst into tears. When asked why he wept, he said, "That I must grow old and weak and eventually die haunts me. I wish to escape earth's limits and live among the people of the sky."

In sympathy, the other monkeys began to weep as well. There then stepped from among them one who told the Monkey King about those who have escaped the limits of life and never die, who are as eternal as the heavens.

"Where may I find them?" he asked.

"They live here on earth among the hills in ancient caves" came the reply.

These words so delighted the Monkey King that he said, "I will learn how to become an Immortal and escape Death's doom."

The next morning, Monkey commanded his subjects to build a raft made of pine and to pile it high with all kinds of wonderful foods from the Mountain of Flowers and Fruit. He boarded his raft, pushed off, and headed into the open sea.

Upon crossing it, he came to a holy mountain which had a cave. The cave had a door, but the door was locked. So Monkey climbed into a pine tree and began eating the pine seed. He played in the branches and made much noise. After a bit, he heard a call, and the cave door opened. Out stepped a fairy lad of unusual beauty unlike any human boy Monkey had ever seen.

The boy yelled, "Who is it making all this commotion out here?"

Monkey jumped down from the tree and said, "I have come to learn the Secret of Long Life."

The boy's master had already told him that Monkey would be there. "Follow me," said the lad, and together they entered the cave.

Room after room of enormous chambers opened before them until they came to a great hall. At its end was a raised platform of green jade. On it sat a wise Immortal Master busy instructing his pupils. From this master, Monkey learned all kinds of magic to preserve a youthful appearance and to maintain long life.

But most important, he learned to perfect the art of the Seventy-Two Shapes and of Cloud Trapeze and Somersaults. After ten years of study, he vaulted over the Great Sea and lowered himself in a cloud onto the Mountain of Flowers and Fruit back home.

Triumphant Return and Grand Victory

From bushes, trees, and mountain crannies, monkeys of every shape and size gathered round to welcome their leader's return. They bowed before him and loudly cheered, "Long live the Handsome Monkey King!"

But when they were quiet, they said to him, "Why did you leave us longing for your return. A demon came to our cave, robbed us of what we had, and stole many of our children. Though we have battled with him, we cannot sleep and must be on guard day and night."

When Monkey heard his followers' fearful tale, he asked, "What kind of bandit monster is this? Where does he live and how far away? Tell me, and I will have my revenge."

The monkeys bowed low and said, "Great King, he is the Demon of Destruction, and his kingdom is north of here. He comes like wind and rain, thunder and lightning. He leaves like a mist. We do not know how far his kingdom is."

"In that case, play here and amuse yourselves. I will go and find him," replied Monkey.

He jumped into the sky toward the north and landed on a steep and rugged mountain near the monster's cave. He heard voices and walked toward the sound. At the mouth of the cave were several little imps dancing and hopping.

When they saw him, they started to run into the cave, but Monkey cried, "Stop! Go and tell your demon lord that the King of the Water Curtain Cave is here. Your master has bullied my followers and stolen their children, and I have come to deal with him."

When the Demon of Destruction heard this message, he laughed and armed himself for battle. Going to the cave entrance and catching sight of Monkey, the monster roared, "You are young and only a few feet tall. You have no weapon. Why do you strut and brag that you will deal with me?"

"Though small, I can make myself into any size I want," said Monkey. "Though weaponless, my hands can pull down the moon from heaven. Now taste Old Monkey's fists."

He leapt into the air to strike the demon's face. With his hand, the demon blocked the blow. "You are a minnow, and I a shark," howled the monster. "You fight with fists, and I with sword. Let's make the contest even."

So saying, he tossed his blade aside, and the two came to grips. Kick for kick, blow for blow, they battered each other. Monkey punched the demon below his ribs. He beat his chest and fought so hard the monster realized his mistake.

The demon grabbed his huge sword. The air sang as it sliced toward his foe. Monkey ducked aside, the sharp steel narrowly missing its mark.

Seeing that his enemy had turned more savage, Monkey used his magic. He jerked out a handful of hairs from his body. He threw them in his mouth and chewed them into tiny fragments. These he spat into the air.

"Change! Change!" he yelled.

At once the chewed-up hairs became three hundred little monkeys. They charged the monstrous demon and surrounded him. They pulled his hair. They poked his eyes. They pinched his nose. They jabbed his chest. They kicked his legs.

While they thus fought, Monkey snatched the demon's sword, pushed through the band of tiny warriors, and split the monster's skull in half. He and his little monkeys then fought their way into the cave and made an end of the imps. With his magic, he turned his soldiers back into hairs and put them on his body from where he had plucked them.

The Handsome Monkey King now gathered the young ones the demon had captured. He collected what the bandit had stolen and returned to the cave on the Mountain of Flowers and Fruit. In honor of his victory, his subjects greeted him with wild rejoicings and a grand feast.

A Powerful New Army

Monkey had taken the huge sword of the now dead demon and practiced with it each day. Yet he did not have a proper army. His soldiers had only wooden swords and bamboo canes sharpened into spears. If a human king or king of birds or beasts attacked them, these would be of little use against weapons forged from iron or steel.

As he pondered these problems, Monkey put them to his advisors.

Four old ones came forward, two with long tails and red behinds and two tailless with plain bottoms. They offered a solution.

"Great King," they said, "across a vast body of water to the east is a kingdom. On its border is a city. Its king has thousands of weapons stored there. If you get them, we will be able to defend ourselves."

So Monkey cloud-somersaulted across the water and in a flash arrived above the city. Through magic, he created a storm with strong winds that hurled sand and rocks through the air. These so alarmed the king and his subjects that they fled indoors and bolted themselves inside.

Monkey made his way straight toward the arsenal and found all sorts of weapons—axes, swords, clubs, spears, bows and arrows—far too many for him to carry by himself. As he had with the Demon of Destruction, he plucked some hairs and changed them into small monkeys. They grabbed as many weapons as they could carry. Soon the arsenal was empty.

Again through magic, Monkey created a second storm. It blew his little helpers back to the Water Curtain Cave. They brought so many of the metal weapons that his soldiers spent the rest of the day scrambling for them.

A Magical New Weapon

For a while, everything went well. The newly-armed troops marched and drilled daily, becoming ever more powerful. Yet Monkey had grown tired of his own weapon.

One day he revealed to his subjects, "The demon's sword is not to my liking. I find it too awkward. What should I do?"

The four old advisors stepped forward once more. "Great King," they said, "now that you cannot be destroyed, you need a weapon that is not of the earth. Is it possible that you could get one from those who live in the sea?"

Answered Monkey, "I can change into seventy-two shapes, become invisible, and ride the clouds. Fire cannot burn me. Neither can water drown me. What is to stop me from taking a weapon from the Sea Powers?"

"Well, if you can do it," said the old monkeys, "you must go to the palace of the Dragon King of the Eastern Sea. No doubt, there you will get a suitable weapon."

Monkey left by way of the stream flowing at the bottom of the waterfall. The stream led him across the sea to the palace of the Dragon King. A captain of the king stood guard at the gate and at first refused to admit him, but when he learned that the visitor was the handsome Monkey King, the captain ushered him into the throne room.

King Dragon greeted him. "Come in, High Immortal. Tell me. How did you gain a body beyond birth and death?"

Monkey told of his adventures and of his study. He related how his children had obtained proper arms to defend the Water Curtain Cave. Then he said, "Unfortunately, I myself do not have a suitable weapon. I hear that in your beautiful green jade palace you have many divine weapons to spare."

King Dragon did not want to refuse a fellow Immortal. So he ordered one of his captains to fetch a huge sword with a blade that resembled the silver curve of the dying moon.

Monkey declared, "I am no good with swords. What else do you have?"

Two servants next offered him a spear with nine points. "Too light," said Monkey. "Bring me something else."

"I do not understand what you mean," replied His Deep-Sea Majesty. "It weighs over three thousand pounds."

"It does not suit my hand," said Monkey.

Dragon looked frightened. He ordered larger and heavier weapons brought out for his visitor to test. None of them pleased Monkey. At last the king presented the heaviest weapon in the green-jade palace. Monkey's response remained the same. "I need more weight! Do you have something heavier?"

"There is nothing else I can show you," said the king.

"Why does the Dragon King pretend he has no treasures?" asked Monkey. "Surely you have something appropriate. You must look again."

At that moment, the Dragon Queen entered the room through a back door and whispered behind her husband's throne. "Great King, this monkey is no common fellow. In your treasury lies the giant iron rod that pressed the bed of the Milky Way flat. It has glowed with a mysterious light for the last several days. Perhaps this is a sign that you should present it to the Immortal Monkey who stands before you."

Although the rod was a thick iron pillar twenty feet long and weighed many tons, the Dragon King agreed to let Monkey have a look at it. They went to the Sea Treasury. There something beamed with numberless rays of golden light. It was the great iron rod. Monkey lifted one end with both hands.

"It is a little long and thick," he declared. "A bit smaller would be good." The rod instantly became a few feet shorter and a trifle thinner.

"Even a little smaller would help," said Monkey. Again the rod shrank.

Monkey beamed with delight. Though it weighed ten thousand three hundred pounds, he could now take it outside. In the sunlight, he noticed that each end had a handle of gold around which he could clasp his hands. In between, the rod was of black iron. Just above one of the handles were the words "Golden Wishing Staff."

"This is the best treasure one could find," he thought. "If it were yet smaller, it would be even better."

Once again, the rod shrank, this time to only two feet long. Monkey swung it through the air and thrust it forward and to each side. Golden rays shot everywhere. The court of the Dragon King marveled and trembled at Monkey's ability with the magic wishing rod.

Monkey now demanded suitable clothes to go with his new weapon. So the Dragon King summoned his brother princes—the Dragons of the northern, southern, and western seas. They offered dazzling clothes to Monkey. The Dragon of the North gave him cloud-stepping shoes. The Dragon of the South bestowed a red-gold cap with a tall plume. And the Dragon of the West presented a chain-mail vest of yellow gold.

Suitably armed and properly clothed, Monkey left. King Dragon and his brothers were happy to see him go. They had found him proud and insolent and thought that they might complain to the Powers of Heaven.

Home Again and Journey to the Kingdom of Death

On arriving home, Monkey sprang from the sea, golden and shining, without a single drop of water on him. His subjects knelt before him and cried with one voice, "How splendid you are, Great King, how splendid!"

Monkey mounted his throne. He told of his adventures in the underwater realm and showed everyone the weapon taken from the Sea Treasury. His subjects rushed forward and tried to lift the iron staff but failed.

Monkey picked it up with one hand and commanded, "Smaller!" Instantly the rod became the size of a needle. Monkey tucked it behind his ear to carry more easily.

"Please, another trick," begged the crowd.

Monkey removed the needle from behind his ear and cried, "Larger! Larger! Larger!" At once it stretched to twenty feet, and when he cried "Tall," it reached from the tops of the highest mountains to the bottoms of the deepest valleys. All creatures of the realm now trembled in awe. Tigers, leopards, wolves, along with the evil spirits of the remote hilltops and the demons of the dark caves, bowed before him.

To celebrate his success, Monkey gave a great feast to some neighboring animal kings, both great and small. When they left, he was sleepy and lay down beneath a pine tree, closed his eyes, and began to dream. In his sleep, two men walked toward him. Saying nothing, they quickly tied him up with a rope and led him away half awake.

After a while, they came to a walled city. Above its gate was an iron sign that read "Land of Darkness." The Handsome Monkey King suddenly seemed to waken. The words on the sign gave him a terrible shock as he said to himself, "This is the Kingdom of Yama, Lord of Death."

"Why am I here? I am an Immortal," Monkey protested to the two men. "Am I not beyond death?"

The two men ignored Monkey and dragged him along. He became so angry that he grabbed the needle from behind his ear and turned it into the size of a large club. He pounded the two into dust, freed himself from the rope, and marched into the city, swinging his iron rod as he went. In terror, demons with the heads of horses and bulls scurried out of his path. Ghosts fled before him and rushed into the palace of Lord Yama to warn of Monkey's violent attack.

The Ten Judges of the Dead trembled with fear when he approached. They apologized to him and claimed his arrest was all a huge mistake. Monkey would have none of it. "Bring out the lists of the living and the dead," he barked.

The judges led him to a great hall where they kept their records. A servant brought forth the books on insects, birds, and all the other animals. Because he had human traits, Monkey was not listed among them. His name was in a separate book.

"Why is my name here?" he asked. "My life has no end. I will live forever."

So saying, he demanded a brush full of thick ink and struck his name off the rolls of those who must die. He also marked off the names of all his subjects in a volume titled *Monkey*. Then forcing his way through the crowds that had gathered round, he left the Palace of Darkness.

As he went from the city, however, his foot got caught in a vine so that he tripped. When he did, he woke with a hard jolt. Everything seemed to have been a dream. The four old apes and other members of his court were standing guard over him and repeating, "You should wake up, Great King. You have been sleeping here the whole night."

Monkey told them what had happened in his dream and how through it he had entered Lord Yama's realm. "I struck our names from the lists in the Kingdom of Darkness." Monkey's subjects bowed and thanked him.

A Visit to Heaven

One morning, the Jade Emperor, Lord of Heaven and Earth, was sitting in his Cloud Palace. All the important officials of his court surrounded his heavenly throne. Standing before him were King Dragon of the Eastern Sea and Yama, Ruler of the Dead. To show their respect, each bowed so low their heads touched the golden floor of the throne room. Yet both appeared to be angry.

The Jade Emperor granted them permission to address him. King Dragon spoke first. "Your Majesty, a false Immortal from the Water Curtain Cave forced his way into my palace beneath the sea, demanded a weapon and new clothes, and insulted me and my brother Dragons of the West, North, and South." King Dragon bowed and stepped back.

Yama now came forward and made his complaint. "Death must follow life. The laws of Nature cannot be changed. Yet the haughty Monkey King beat to death my servants sent to bring him to the Land of Darkness, threatened its Ten Judges, and erased his name and the names of his subjects from our rolls. He has thoroughly upset the balance of Light and Dark, of Life and Death. My kingdom lies in chaos." Yama, too, stepped back.

Pausing for a moment, the Jade Emperor gave his judgment. "King Dragon is to return to the Eastern Sea, and the Lord of Death to the Underworld. I will send officers to arrest the troublemaker."

The Dragon King and Yama left the hall. No sooner had they gone, however, when an official rushed in, bowed, and exclaimed, "Your Majesty, a talking monkey came to your gate, demanded entrance, and is now fighting the guards."

The Jade Emperor raised a heavenly eyebrow. "This intruder must be the same unruly upstart that King Dragon and Yama complained about. We could easily subdue and arrest him."

A member of the court, though, suggested a milder course. "If Your Majesty admits this creature into Heaven and gives him a position here, we might keep a watchful eye upon him. If he causes trouble, we can easily arrest him at any time." The Jade Emperor agreed and appointed Monkey as Keeper of the Horse Stables.

On hearing about his title, Monkey mused to himself, "At last the Powers Above recognize the worth and importance of the Magnificent Monkey King of the Mountain of Flowers and Fruit."

A Challenge to Heaven

As Keeper of the Stables, Monkey had oversight of a thousand horses as well as many servants whose duty was the constant care of the animals. These had to be combed, washed, given hay and water, and exercised.

From the moment they saw Monkey, the horses took to him and came to eat food from his hand. He found the entire setting to his liking and was extremely impressed. He soon learned, however, that his title was not as important as it sounded.

Not long after Monkey arrived at the stables, the officers there held a banquet in honor of his new position. While everyone was eating and drinking, Monkey lowered his cup and asked, "Among all the Jade Emperor's officials, exactly what rank is Keeper of the Horse Stables?"

The officers looked at one other, covered their mouths with their hands, and tried not to laugh. They shook their heads as if unwilling to answer.

Again Monkey asked, "Where do I rank among the heavenly officials?" Still no answer.

As if joking, Monkey said, "No need to be shy or play games with me."

One officer finally cleared his throat and replied, "Your position has no rank."

Overjoyed, Monkey said, "It must be so high that it is not among the ordinary ranks!"

"Ah, no, Great Monkey King," the other responded. "Your position is really so low that it has no rank. That is the reason you were sent to take care of the horses. If the horses get fat, your pay will consist of the compliment 'not bad' or perhaps a little pat on the back. If they grow thin or come to any harm, you will be harshly scolded and likely fined."

At these words, Monkey's eyes blazed. "So this is how I am treated! The Lord of the Mountain of Flowers and Fruit, tricked into coming here to look after horses and stables, a job for the lowest of the low!" He knocked over the table where he sat, stormed out of the South Gate of Heaven, and cloud-somersaulted back to the Water Curtain Cave.

His subjects were horrified to learn how the Jade Emperor had treated Monkey. Two one-horned demon kings who served him said, "No one with magical powers like yours should have to take care of horses. Your title should have been Great Sage, the Equal of Heaven."

Monkey was delighted with the idea. He commanded his generals to write the title on a banner in large letters and had it raised on a pole for everyone to see. "From now on," he said, "my title will no longer be Handsome Monkey King. I will be called Great Sage, the Equal of Heaven." He had all his subjects informed of this matter, including the demon princes of the caves over whom he ruled.

A New Position in Heaven

When the Emperor heard that his Keeper of the Horse Stables thought himself too good for the job, the Lord of Heaven sent a powerful army to arrest Monkey. One commander, the Mighty Magic Spirit, was the first to reach to the Water Curtain Cave. He demanded that Monkey surrender at once.

Monkey refused. "Who do you think you are to order me? Can you not read what is on my banner? I should strike you dead with my metal club. Yet I will spare your miserable life so that you can return to the Jade Emperor. Tell him that, if he declares me Great Sage, the Equal of Heaven, I will leave him in peace. If not, I will come and drag him off his Dragon Throne."

"Call yourself whatever you will," replied the Mighty Magic Spirit, "but first eat this axe of mine."

He swung at Monkey's head, but Monkey stopped the axe with his iron rod. The two battled back and forth. Then Monkey struck at his foe's head. With his axe, the Mighty Magic Spirit caught Monkey's club as if to stop the blow. But the force with which Monkey struck was so hard that the axe split in two, and the Mighty Magic Spirit had to run for his life.

No matter who came forward to fight Monkey, the result was the same—defeat. His club was too powerful, and he could shift into too many shapes. One time he turned into a three-headed monster with six arms. Finally, the generals had to withdraw to request larger forces.

The Jade Emperor said to them, "Can a single monkey be so powerful that more troops are needed to defeat him? Must I send the whole of Heaven's army to destroy him?"

Yet one member of the court cautioned, "Perhaps Your Majesty should let him have the title Great Sage, the Equal of Heaven, and allow him to return to us. Perhaps he will then calm down and stop misbehaving so that we will have peace."

The Emperor agreed. Monkey kept his title and for good measure was put in charge of the Heavenly Peach Garden so that he might stay busy and keep out of trouble. The only condition was that he could eat none of the peaches.

When Monkey arrived at the garden, he learned from the workers that there were three kinds of peaches and thousands of trees for each kind. One peach ripened every three thousand years. Whoever ate its fruit became all-wise. The second ripened every six thousand years. Whoever tasted its fruit could float above the ground and never age. The third ripened every nine thousand years. Whoever ate its fruit would last longer than earth and heaven and be equal to the sun and the moon.

What the workers told him so delighted Monkey that he was overjoyed with his new position. He spent his days inspecting the trees and could hardly keep himself from tasting the delicious peaches. But he managed to hold himself in check—at least for a time.

One day he noticed at the top of some trees the peaches were ripe. Yet he dared not eat any because the gardeners always watched him closely. If he could only get rid of them, he could have his fill.

So he devised a scheme and said, "I am tired and am going to rest a little under some trees. Go outside the garden wall and wait for me by the gate. I will come to you shortly."

As soon as the gardeners left, Monkey scampered high into a tree and plucked the best peaches he could find. How sweet they were! He ate until he could eat no more, then went to the men, and told them he was returning to his rooms in the palace. Every few days he played the same trick, pretending to take a nap, all the while eating as many peaches as he could.

The Peach Banquet

One afternoon, Monkey was munching peaches as usual when he heard voices at the garden gate. Seven fairy maidens were there—Red Jacket, Blue Jacket, White Jacket, Black Jacket, Purple Jacket, Yellow Jacket, and Green Jacket—all bidding the gardeners to admit them. "We are here by order of the Queen to gather peaches for a feast."

"Alas, dear fairy maidens," said one of the men, "the Great Sage, the Equal of Heaven, now holds sway here, and we must ask his permission before we let you enter."

"Where is His Importance?" the maidens asked.

"He is resting in the garden," the men answered.

"Ah, you must go and find him," the seven said, "for we must collect the peaches at once."

The workers agreed and went to search for Monkey but could find him nowhere. For when he heard the voices at the gate, he had turned himself into a tiny caterpillar and hidden under a peach leaf.

The men returned without him, causing the fairy maidens to protest, "Whether the Great Sage and so forth grants us his permission or not, we have our orders and cannot return empty-handed."

"Of course, sweet beauties," replied the men. "You must do as commanded. Go and gather your fruit, and we will inform our master when he next appears."

So the maidens entered the garden. They first collected baskets of peaches that made anyone who ate them all-wise. Then they picked several baskets of those that made one rise off the ground and never grow old. But when they went to gather the peaches that rendered those who tasted them the equal of the sun and the moon and allowed them to live as long as earth and heaven, the fairies found the fruit already taken.

After searching for a long time, one of the maidens found only a single, half-ripened peach. On the twig where it hung slept Monkey, still in the form of a tiny caterpillar. When the maiden plucked the peach, the twig jerked violently, and Monkey quickly changed back into himself.

"How dare you pick my peaches!" he cried.

Terrified, the fairies immediately fell to their knees and bowed before him. "Great Sage, do not be angry. We are fairy maidens sent here by her Majesty to gather peaches for her banquet. Your guards looked everywhere for you to grant us permission, but you were nowhere to be found. We could not keep the Queen of Heaven waiting, so we began to collect the fruit. Please forgive us!"

Monkey became all smiles. "Rise, dear fairies, and tell me who will be at the banquet."

"Many gods and goddesses, princes and kings, wonder workers and great spirits—all who are important will be there," they replied.

"And will I be invited?"

"We do not know."

"How so? I, the Magnificent Monkey King, Keeper of the Heavenly Peach Garden, Great Sage and the Equal of Heaven. I, not invited?"

The fairies trembled before Monkey's wrath. "We—we do not know. We can only tell you who came the last time the banquet was held—just over a thousand years ago."

"Well," responded Monkey, "I will have to find out whether I am invited. Remain here while I scout around."

To be sure that they did not leave, he recited a magic spell. "Stay. Stay. Stay." As a result, the maidens could not move, for they were firmly fixed to the ground where they stood.

Monkey climbed atop his cloud. As he sailed out of the garden, he met an Immortal hurrying toward the Green Jade Pool. Monkey asked, "Where are you going?"

"To the Peach Banquet. Why do you ask? Have you not been invited?"

"Of course I have," said Monkey. "But have you not heard the latest news? The banquet is to take place in the Cloud Palace. Although it is a little farther away, it has more room. The Jade Emperor himself asked me to tell everyone of the change in plans."

"Ah, me, I must hurry, or I will be late." Without so much as a "thank you," the innocent creature fluttered away with a look of great distress.

Repeating another spell, Monkey transformed himself into the very same image of the Immortal and headed for the Green Jade Pool. In the banquet hall, servants ran everywhere, lighting fires, setting tables, preparing dishes, carrying jugs of wine.

Yet an aroma, more marvelous than the scents of food and drink wafting through the air, lured Monkey toward it. It smelled sweeter than honey and more delicate than a rose and seemed to come from the kitchen. However, with countless servants scurrying about, how could Monkey go there unnoticed?

He again used his magic powers. Pulling out a fistful of hairs, he stuffed them into his mouth, chewed them into fragments, spewed them into the air, and said, "Change!" The tiny hairs turned into flying insects that bit the servants' necks and faces. At once their hands sank to their sides, their eyelids closed, their heads drooped, and all fell into a deep slumber.

Now free to do as he pleased, Monkey stuffed himself with some of the finest dishes, then ran into the kitchen, seized a jug, and guzzled as much of the tasty liquid as he could before taking a breath. He drank still more and more until he felt dizzy. Loud chuckles followed soft giggles, and soon deep belly laughs followed both.

These antics continued as Monkey lost all track of time. But when the effects of the drink began to wear off, he realized that the guests would shortly arrive for the banquet. "Oh, my," he thought, "if the Jade Emperor hears of what I have done, I will have to answer for my bad behavior, and I will surely be punished. I must quickly escape."

So saying, he became invisible, mounted his cloud, and lowered himself back home onto the Mountain of Flowers and Fruit. On seeing their king, his subjects, who had been practicing for war, threw down their weapons, fell to their knees, and rejoiced.

"Great Sage, here is a bowl of wine to welcome your return," they said.

Monkey took one sip and spat it out. Frowning, he replied, "How foul tasting! I cannot drink this!"

Two of his wisest generals rushed forward. "Great Sage, the Equal of Heaven, you have drunk the wine of the gods and now cannot stomach the wine of this world. And yet surely there is no water like that of home."

"How true," said Monkey. "And truer still, there are no people like those of home either. I will return to Heaven and bring back jugs of the sweet liquid. Drink but half a cup, and none of you will ever grow old."

Monkey made himself invisible, hopped upon his cloud, and somersaulted back to Heaven. The servants in the banquet hall were still fast asleep and snoring loudly. He snatched as many jugs as he could carry and guided his cloud back to the Water Curtain Cave. At a great gathering of his subjects, he offered each a cupful or two of the drink, and everyone soon settled into perfect happiness.

The Jade Emperor Reacts

In the Peach Garden, the seven fairy maidens had remained under Monkey's spell for an entire day. When they finally could move, they went straight to the Queen of Heaven and told her how the Great Sage had worked his magic on them, causing them to be late.

"How many baskets of peaches do you have?" she asked.

"We have two baskets of the small ones and three of the medium-sized. When we got to the rear of the garden, we found that the Sage had already eaten half of the largest peaches. The rest were still green and not suitable. While the gardeners looked for him, he suddenly appeared to us, and when he found out that he had not been invited to the Peach Banquet, he made a terrible scene and froze us with his magic. We do not know where he is, and only now have we managed to come to you."

Without a word, the Queen went to her husband. As she told him the maidens' story, the officials in charge of the banquet came rushing into the throne room. "Someone has ruined the preparations for the Peach Banquet—the food eaten and the heavenly liquid drunk," they proclaimed.

Before this news could sink in, other officers appeared. One declared how Monkey had been missing for a whole day and no one knew where he was. The Immortal whom Monkey had met on leaving the Peach Garden now entered and told how Monkey had tricked her into going to the Cloud Palace for the banquet rather than to the Green Jade Pool.

The Jade Emperor's eyes flashed fire. "I shall send my best generals and a hundred thousand troops to surround the Mountain of Flowers and Fruit. This time that rascal Monkey, that no-good who claims to be my equal, shall not escape. I want him arrested and brought to me. He shall wish he had never set foot in Heaven!"

Heaven Attacks

Inside the Water Curtain Cave, Monkey and his generals were sipping the stolen drink. Suddenly, one of his imps scurried in. "Great Sage, a vast army surrounds your kingdom, and nine fierce Immortals stand outside its gates hurling insults and battle cries, calling on you to surrender."

Monkey laughed. "This drink is enough for today. Fear not what stands at the door."

As he spoke, another imp entered. "Father, the nine Immortals have burst through the gates and are coming to attack."

"They should have better manners than to disturb me," said Monkey. "I have never bothered them. I must teach them a lesson."

He ordered his generals to prepare for war. He then grabbed his iron club and ran to confront the nine Immortals. Swinging his club around his head, he threw himself into the middle of them and yelled, "Make way!"

The Immortals beat a quick retreat and formed a line. Their leader cried out, "Insolent ape, you have stolen from the Jade Emperor and ruined the Peach Banquet, not to mention your other crimes. Surrender at once, and we will spare your life. Otherwise, we will flatten your little mountain and destroy your cave."

"You are too silly," answered Monkey. "Your strength is not equal to your words. Now taste the iron of Old Monkey's club!" He then jumped upon the nine Immortals and beat them so soundly that they fled back to their tents, barely able to drag their swords and shields behind them.

Catching their breath, the Immortals reported to the Jade Emperor's generals. "The Monkey King was too powerful for us. Singlehandedly, he drove us off." The generals ordered the whole army to prepare for battle.

The struggle began early on the morning of the next day. At first the forces of Heaven overran Monkey's troops. They defeated and took as prisoners the demon kings of the caves who were Monkey's allies. The Emperor's soldiers also carried off some foxes and wolves, horned stags, tigers, and other wild cats.

Yet as the day wore on and the sun hung low in the west, Monkey turned the tide of battle. He pulled out a handful of hairs, put them in his mouth, and chewed them into tiny bits. Spitting them into the air, he commanded, "Change!"

Thousands of monkey warriors appeared and fought the Emperor's men so furiously that they withdrew from the fight. Not one monkey did his soldiers take. As night fell, both sides withdrew to await the dawn when the battle would begin anew.

The War Continues

Early the next morning, before the sun arose, Monkey and his whole host were outside the camp of the Emperor's army. Battle cry after battle cry rang out, calling on the invaders to come and fight. On hearing the noise, Prince Moksha, the second son of the chief general, told his father that he would engage the upstart ape in hand-to-hand combat. The prince had studied with the wisest and possessed all forms of magic.

With both hands, Moksha picked up his huge iron club, rushed from the camp, and called out loudly, "Where is he who claims to be the Great Sage, the Equal of Heaven?"

"Who now boldly asks for me?" answered Monkey and held his wishing staff above his head and shook it fiercely.

"I am the general's second son, Moksha, and the defender of Heaven. I arrived in the night to gain news of the war, and I have come myself to arrest you for your crimes."

"Such big talk for one who must now eat Old Monkey's club."

The prince showed no sign of fear, rushed forward, and swung his club over his head. The two stood facing each other at the bottom of the Mountain of Flowers and Fruit. Sixty times they came to blows until Moksha, his arms and shoulders too painful to fight any more, fled the scene.

Gasping for breath, the prince staggered into his father's camp. "The Monkey King is the most powerful of magicians. Try as hard as I might, I could not defeat him and left him holding the field."

The general saw no other choice than immediately to send another letter to Heaven and appeal to the Jade Emperor for more troops. When he read its words, the Emperor laughed in disbelief. "How is a single monkey so strong that one hundred thousand troops cannot overcome him? My general asks for aid, but what sort of soldiers does he expect me to supply?"

A Desperate Fight

When the Emperor had finished speaking, a member of the court stepped forward to offer new advice. "Your Majesty, your nephew Erh-lang is a great magician. He lives with his brothers in a temple at the mouth of a mighty river. He once defeated six ogres. A thousand gods with the heads of plants serve him, and each in his own right can cast powerful spells. Appeal to him, and surely we can capture this rebellious ape." The Jade Emperor nodded his head in agreement.

When Erh-lang received the message from his uncle, he was overjoyed. "I will work with all my might to bring this troublesome monkey to justice."

Erh-lang summoned his brothers and the thousand plant-headed gods and set off for the Mountain of Flowers and Fruit. Some held razor-beaked eagles on their wrists, while others led packs of hunting dogs with massive jaws and drooling jowls. A magic wind helped speed their way. Soon they arrived where the army of Heaven surrounded Monkey's kingdom.

Erh-lang asked the Emperor's commanders how things stood. When he learned that the battle was at a standstill, he said, "Keep the mountain tightly surrounded here below. Monkey and I will likely fight in the air, and I will have to shift my shape. But do not be alarmed by what goes on above. If Monkey seems to win, do not come to my aid. My brothers will assist me."

Erh-lang and his brothers then went forward to challenge Monkey. The magician ordered the remainder of his followers to keep close behind with their eagles tied to their wrists and their war dogs on a tight leash. Going to the door of the cave, he saw a huge number of monkeys drawn up for battle to look like the shape of a dragon. Some waved a giant banner with the words "Great Sage, the Equal of Heaven."

Erh-lang growled, "How dare this little monkey give himself so grand a title!"

His brothers replied, "Heed not these words, Erh-lang, but go and challenge the monster at once!"

The guards at the cave door had seen Erh-lang's approach and scurried inside to report his arrival. Monkey put on his golden breastplate and helmet, pulled on his cloud-leaping shoes, seized his iron club, and rushed outside. He glared at Erh-lang. "Who is this little fellow who challenges the Great Sage?"

"I am nephew of the Jade Emperor and by his order am here to arrest an ape who knows not his place. Your hour is now come!"

"Are you the best your uncle can send against me? Go home, little one, before someone hurts you," returned Monkey.

Erh-lang was furious. "You are rude, very rude. Now taste my steel!"

Monkey dodged Erh-lang's sword and struck back. Three hundred times the two clashed. Neither could defeat the other.

Erh-lang at last concentrated all his power and transformed himself into a giant as high as a peak capped with snow and ice. His face turned a bright blue and his hair a fiery red. Sharp fangs filled his mouth, and each arm held a three-pronged spear. He advanced toward Monkey and aimed at his head.

Yet Monkey, the master of change, turned himself into an exact replica of Erh-lang. With his club, now as thick as a massive tower, he fended off Erh-lang's thrusts. The fight became so terrible that Monkey's soldiers trembled, and their hands shook so violently they could not use their weapons.

Erh-lang's brothers ordered their plant-headed troops into the fray. These let loose their dogs and eagles, creating so much terror that Monkey's soldiers panicked. They threw down their arms and scattered before the assault. Some fled up the mountain, and some ran into the cave behind the waterfall.

When Monkey saw his followers turn tail, his heart sank. Fearing defeat and capture, he changed into a fish and jumped into the stream that flowed by the Water Curtain Cave. Still Erh-lang pursued him and changed into a fish hawk. He snapped at Monkey with his beak.

Monkey leapt into the air, turned into a water snake, and darted back into the stream. He swam until he reached its edge and wriggled into the tall grass. Now Erh-lang became a gray crane with a red-topped head and a bill like long scissors that struck swiftly, trying to swallow the snake whole.

Monkey again changed, this time into a spotted land bird that stood on the bank staring stupidly. Returning to his original form, Erh-lang took his sling and with a pebble toppled the bird over, causing Monkey to roll down to a footpath at the bottom of the mountain. From there, he sprung like a tiger and disappeared high into the clouds above. When he descended, he landed at the mouth of the river where Erh-lang's temple sat.

Weary of the chase, the great magician believed that Monkey had escaped for good. Erh-lang reported to the Emperor's generals. "My brothers are still searching for the Monkey King, but he seems to have disappeared."

The chief general replied, "Be not discouraged, Erh-lang. While flying above to see how the battle went, I watched the imp tumble down his mountain, then vault into the sky, and descend to your temple. Make haste, and you will find him there."

At once Erh-lang grabbed a three-pronged magic spear and fled homewards as fast as he could fly. Back in his original shape, Monkey saw him coming. With his spear, the magician struck at his foe's face. Monkey dodged aside, and the pair came to grips. Shouting and struggling with each other, they rose into the mists and clouds and through the air fought their way back to the Mountain of Flowers and Fruit. Erh-lang's brothers rushed to join the battle. They surrounded Monkey, now forced to defend himself on every side.

Monkey Made Prisoner

Meanwhile, the Jade Emperor and his court wondered how his nephew fared in the battle. After all, an entire day had passed without any news. So they decided to walk to the Southern Gate and look down. Below, they saw that their heavenly forces had surrounded Monkey's kingdom and that Erh-lang and his brothers hemmed in the Great Sage from all directions.

"Erh-lang seems to have done well," said one of the court. "With a bit more aid, I believe he could take Monkey prisoner."

The Emperor's advisors debated the matter briefly. Some suggested that they toss down a porcelain vase to knock Monkey on the head. However, others thought it might miss, strike his iron staff, and shattered into tiny fragments. So they finally decided to throw a snare around Monkey and capture him while he was busy fighting Erh-lang and his brothers.

Down rippled the noose, falling over Monkey and tripping him so that he lost his balance and toppled to the ground. The rope now tight, the war dogs went for him immediately, biting his legs and leaving him unable to get to his feet or to his club. This he had reduced to the size of a needle and secured behind his ear. Seeing their chance, Erh-lang's brothers closed in and bound him fast with strong ropes. The Jade Emperor commanded a demon king and a squad of soldiers to haul Monkey up and take him to the place of execution. There he would be cut into little pieces.

The soldiers tied Monkey to a column in order to lance him with spears, slice him with swords, and chop him with axes. Yet despite all their efforts, Monkey remained as whole as ever. Next they tried to burn him. No good whatsoever. Then the Thunder Spirits threw lightning bolts against him. Still no good.

One of the court said, "He has eaten the peaches of everlasting life, drunk the heavenly drink, and committed countless other pranks. His acts have made him indestructible."

During these proceedings, Monkey had had time to recover. He was now stronger than ever. He suddenly broke free and removed his iron club from behind his ear. He commanded it to enlarge and began running madly about. Charging here and there, he struck recklessly with his weapon, and everyone trembled at his might. Spirits barred themselves behind closed doors. Demon kings fled in fright. Immortals vanished behind thick fogs and shifting mists. Chaos reigned.

The Problem Solved

Sitting on his throne, the Jade Emperor heard the noise of battle and knew that Monkey must have gotten loose. The Lord of Heaven paused but a moment before he realized what he must do. He must seek the Great Buddha. So the Emperor sent two messengers to the Land of the West to ask for his aid.

When the messengers explained their purpose and told how Monkey's misdeeds were destroying Heaven, Buddha agreed to go and see what he could do. On his arrival, he heard a fearful noise and found Monkey surrounded, battling thirty-six foes.

Buddha said to them, "Put down your weapons and leave." Then he turned to Monkey and called to him to stop fighting.

With raised voice, Monkey answered, "Who are you to interrupt me in the middle of battle?"

"I am the Buddha of the West. I have heard of your misdeeds and the trouble you are causing in Heaven. Who do you think you are that you can behave in this way?"

"I am Old Monkey, born of a magical rock, blessed by the earth and the sky. I became King of the Mountain of Flowers and Fruit. My home is the Water Curtain Cave. I studied the secret of long life, learned to cloud-somersault, and can change into seventy-two shapes. I erased my name from Death's roll, ate the Peaches of Immortality, and drank the wine of Heaven. Its armies cannot defeat me. My magic is without end so that even the Jade Emperor cannot contain it. Though he is strong, I am yet stronger. Should I not sit on Heaven's throne?"

Buddha laughed. "Speak no more nonsense, Great Sage. You must prove your worth. This is your chance. Otherwise, I will have to deal harshly with you, and when I am through, there may not be much of you left to live forever."

"Now listen carefully," Buddha continued. "Here is your task. If you are so powerful, leap off the palm of my right hand. If you succeed, the Lord of Heaven will come with me to the Land of the West, and his Dragon Throne is yours. But if you fail, you must return to earth and suffer punishment for seeming years without end. Do you agree?"

Monkey thought, "This Buddha knows nothing. I can jump across the world. His palm is but inches across. The task is easy enough."

So Monkey said to Buddha, "Do you really have the power to give me the Dragon Throne of the Jade Emperor?"

"Of course I do" came the reply.

Buddha unfolded his right hand. Monkey shrunk and changed his club to the size of a sewing needle which he tucked behind his ear. He hopped onto Buddha's wrist and jumped with every ounce of strength he had. He flew faster than any ordinary eye could see. But to the wise eyes of Buddha, Monkey appeared to glide along like a disk lazily spinning and wobbling through the air.

At last Monkey came to five flesh-colored columns. "The end of the world," he said to himself. "Now I must leap back and claim the throne that is mine. But first let me leave a record here to prove what I have done."

At the base of the middle column, he wrote THE MAGNIFICENT MONKEY KING WAS HERE. He started to jump back, but first he thought he would play a clever little trick. So he peed beneath what he had written, leaving a small puddle. He then hurled himself into the air and cloud-soared once again across Buddha's hand.

"I am back," laughed Monkey in triumph. "Where is my throne?"

All around Buddha, dying stars exploded, spiral galaxies collided, new universes came into being.

"You silly little monkey," said Buddha. "You never left my palm. The great columns were only my fingers." Then he closed his hand over the Great Sage and turned his fingers into a mountain range with five snow-capped peaks. At the base of the one in the middle, Monkey lay imprisoned. He had just enough air to breathe through a small crack in the rocks.

Buddha continued, "Learn to use your magic wisely, for power is useless without wisdom. Now speak no more, but consider that, when you are truly sorry for your thoughtlessness and the troubles you have caused, someone will come to rescue you."

And so it was that, after five-hundred years had passed, Monkey changed his heart. He repented of his former mischief and was released from his prison. He turned toward the doing of good and achieved great fame for conquering evil demons and monsters until at last he became a Buddha himself.

COMMENTARY: Two translations served as sources for this abridgement and retelling about the escapades of Old Monkey: Arthur Waley's 1943 version of *Monkey*[22] and the first volume of Anthony C. Yu's 1977 more extensive rendition titled *Journey to the West.*[23] The original folk novel purported to be by Wu Ch'eng-en appeared in 1592 during the Ming dynasty (1368–1644) and was "popular among the educated elite."[24] I have provided further details on the background on this work and its main character in the section "Old Monkey of China and Hanuman of India" of my introduction.

Among significant Chinese cultural emblems related to the character of Old Monkey are aspects of the pine and peach trees. Because the pine is an evergreen, it signifies longevity,[25] an early aim of Monkey not only for himself but also for his followers. Early in his career, he longs to know the Secret of Long Life. At the outset of his quest, he travels on raft built from pine, and when he arrives at the cave of the Immortal Master who will instruct him, he waits in a pine tree and eats pine seed before he is admitted into his teacher's presence. During Monkey's study, he learns magic to keep a youthful look and to preserve long life.

A continuance of the implications of the pine is the peach tree, the fruit of which is said to have its origins in China and to symbolize springtime and everlasting life.[26] According to research of C.A.S. Williams, the peach gave the Immortals their immortality[27] and is the main ingredient of Taoism's Elixir of Life, believed to impart eternal life.[28] The god of longevity is frequently depicted as emerging from the fruit, and Chinese parents have used peach-stone amulets, cut to resemble locks, to ward off death from children.[29] To seal his immortality, Monkey eats the most prized peaches in the garden of the Jade Emperor, those which put him on par with the sun and the moon and endow him with long existence equal to that of earth and heaven. He also drinks the peach wine and serves it to his subjects when he returns to his realm of the Water Curtain Cave.

Along with the pine and the peach, jade figures as a symbol in the retelling, albeit less prominently. From ancient times in China, the scarcity and high cost of this "most precious of stones" caused it to be associated with "all that is supremely excellent" as well as the "perfection of human virtue," thus linking it with "the highest forms of matter."[30] Traditional Chinese lore further holds that, for the wearer of jade, the mineral imparts "humane, just, intelligent, brave, and pure qualities" and that the most prized hue is "a fine apple green."[31]

Another avowed quality of jade is that anyone who ingests it receives the ability to defy gravity.[32] Although there is no direct indication that the Monkey King swallows jade, when he seeks the secret of eternal life from the immortal sage early in the story and enters his inner chamber, Monkey beholds him seated upon a platform of green jade. From this master, Monkey learns the art of cloud-trapeze so that he can overcome gravity and fly immense distances. Later in the story, his signature weapon of the magical iron rod comes from the Dragon King of the Eastern Sea who lives in a green jade palace.

Ancient Chinese representations of Heaven took the form of pierced disks of jade. Because of their magical powers, these aided the earthly emperors, who were considered the Sons of Heaven, to communicate and confer with the divine realm.[33] In "The Adventures of the Monkey King," the ruler of Heaven itself holds the title of the Jade Emperor, an important mythological deity whose traits of justice, good deeds, and forbearance his counterparts on earth aspired to mirror.[34] In one account, he was born of a virgin, lived as a youth whose portents presaged his future greatness, and became the first emperor. Having achieved all his aims as an earthly ruler, he abdicated to devote himself to Taoist studies, whereupon he learned the secret of longevity, eventually attained enlightenment, and entered the pantheon of important Chinese deities.[35]

In contrasting Old Monkey, Sun Wu-kung, to the Jade Emperor, journalist Mae Hamilton finds their characters completely different in the first part of *Journey to the West*—that is, before Monkey goes on his pilgrimage to India. She says that, while Old Monkey is the "epitome of jealousy, impatience, and bitterness, the Jade Emperor is a model example of kindness, compassion, and wisdom."[36]

The Cruel Rich Couple
(from China)

In a faraway city, a rich man and his wife had lived by themselves for many, many years. And even though the old man possessed great wealth, he kept it all to himself and never did anything to help the poor. If beggars came to his gate and knocked to ask for a little money or food, he drove them away with a thick stick and gave them plenty of blows to spare. He would often shout, "You ought to die rather than beg before my gate." And, if the truth be known, his wife was just as hardhearted as he was.

As the couple had no son or daughter, one day the husband bought a girl to serve as their maid. Because of the man's stinginess and ill-temper, you can easily guess what kind of life the girl had to suffer. If anything displeased him, his anger would burn like a hot fire, and he would curse and beat the girl so badly that his lash often drew blood. His neighbors said that his house rang with his loud cursing sprees and the crack of his whip throughout the day.

When alone, the slave girl would cry and frequently sigh to herself. "Oh, Lord, why must my life be so miserable? Will it never improve? Do not the gods pity my cruel fate?"

Yet unbeknown to her, the gods had heard her cries. The day came when they sent one of their own to investigate her master and remove all doubt about her situation. Disguised as a ragged, barefooted beggar infested with fleas and lice, the Immortal left his heavenly home and came to the rich man's house. He stood before his gate and rapped upon it, making a great commotion as he called out, "Oh, Mother! Father! Please help a poor man driven here by starvation. Have pity, please! I ask for no more than a crust of bread!"

Now it happened that the girl was alone in the house that day, for the old couple had gone to buy supplies at the market. She had been heating the stove and using discarded bundles of rice straw as fuel. For a long while, she had collected the few grains of rice that sometimes clung to the straw until at last she had a sack of two thousand.

She heard the beggar's cries and went to the gate. As she stood there, her heart filled with compassion for his poverty, and she gave him all the rice she had stowed away. "Now quickly go," she said. "I dread my master might return at any moment and will beat me."

But the god refused to leave. He could see that the girl's heart was good. He learned how she had saved the grains from the cast-off straw, and he gave her a gift—a handkerchief to ease her burden. "Be sure to wash your face with this cloth each night. Let no one borrow it, and let no one see you use it"

As the Immortal spoke, abruptly to the maid's sorrow, her master and mistress returned. They saw the beggar and the girl at the door and shouted, "What have you given to him?" And with his cane, the old man tried to beat the beggar, who shunned his blows and fled. Then beside himself, as his anger hotly burned, the master began caning the girl until she fell at his feet.

Each day thereafter, when she was by herself and tears flowed from her eyes, the girl would wash her face with the handkerchief the god gave her, and slowly her face began to change. Where once there were deep creases and careworn lines, her face became smooth, and a soft glow gradually replaced the dark shadows caused by her suffering and sadness.

Her master and mistress noticed these changes, and curious to know the reason, they pulled her aside one day to question her. The girl well knew what would occur if she remained silent, so she said, "My face has lost its ashen gray and look of sorrow since that day the beggar fled from your gate. Before he left, he gave me a cloth that has washed away the grief and the grim shadows from my face."

After saying these words, she told them about the sack of rice she had given to the beggar so that he would not starve. This news made the stingy pair bray in anger, "So you gave him rice, no doubt stolen from us. Your handkerchief should pay for its cost."

The girl shuddered, fearing what might unfold. For the beggar's tone had hinted danger if anyone but herself should use the handkerchief. Yet she knew that another beating would likely be forthcoming if she denied her master and mistress the cloth. So to pacify their wrath, she paid for what they claimed she owed and handed over the beggar's gift.

The next morning, the couple rose early. They washed their faces with the cloth in the hope that youth's radiance would erase the ravages that time had traced upon them. But unlike their maid, whose looks had changed in gradual phases, beauty blessed neither of the two. For the handkerchief transformed their faces immediately as coarse hair started to sprout all over their bodies.

They scampered to a looking glass to see what their appearance had become, and beholding themselves, they each had the face and form of a hairy monkey with a long tail. Turning away in horror and chattering mindlessly, they ran from the warmth and other comforts of their home. At last, nearly dead from hunger, they came to a wasteland surrounded by barren mountains. Only scattered stones relieved the emptiness.

As for the slave girl, no one ever really knew what became of her. After the monkey couple vanished, perhaps the neighbors assumed that they had left for another city, took the girl with them, and later died. Perhaps a local official decided to investigate the pair's disappearance, ruled the maid guilty of some misdeed, had her thrown into prison, and later executed. Or maybe she escaped with the riches of the old man and woman and eventually found a better and far happier life for herself.

COMMENTARY: The commentary on the first story in this collection discusses the concept of *therianthropy*, or the transformation of humans into animals. In "The Cruel Rich Couple," the change into monkeys inflicted on the husband and wife results because of their harsh treatment of the slave girl. The Immortal in the story is her supernatural helper. Although the ending is ambiguous regarding whether the slave girl is rewarded for her goodness, the ethical truth that evil is punished is abundantly clear in the case of the old couple. *Chinese Fairy Tales and Folktales* (1938) by sociology professor and expert in classical and colloquial Chinese languages, Wolfram Eberhard, is the source for this retelling.[37]

Japan and the Philippines

The Fox, the Otter, and the Monkey
(from the Ainu of Japan)

In the land of the Ainu, when the world was young, a fox, an otter, and a monkey were the best of friends. One day, the fox said to the others, "What if we stole some food and treasure from the Japanese?"

The others readily agreed, so the three swam across the sea to a rich man's house and stole a sack of beans, a bag of salt, and a straw mat. When they returned with their booty, the fox told the otter, "You should take the bag of salt to help you preserve the fish you catch." Turning to the monkey, the fox said, "You take the mat. Your children can use it to dance on. As for me, I'll keep the beans." Each one then departed to his own house.

A bit later, the otter slid into the river, but he still had the salt with him when he took the plunge. It quickly dissolved, leaving the otter with nothing and disappointed.

With his mat, the monkey fared even worse than his friend. He spread it across the branches of a tall tree. But when his children danced on it, the mat split in two, and all the little monkeys fell to the ground and were dashed to death.

Outraged by what they considered the fox's tricks, the otter and monkey joined forces to seek revenge. But the fox discovered their plot, and before they could punish him, he chewed up many beans and made a thick paste. This he rubbed all over his himself and then lay down as if he were sick.

When the otter and monkey came to kill him, the fox groaned, "Ah, look at how ill I am. For deceiving you, I am now covered with boils and soon must die. My punishment is already upon me, saving you the trouble of killing me."

Satisfied with the story, the otter decided the fox was telling the truth and returned to the river. But the monkey became so angry that he left in a huff and swam across the sea to Japan. For this reason, the land of the Ainu has no monkeys.

COMMENTARY: The indigenous Ainu people of Japan are the source[1] for this talking beast *pourquoi* that explains why there were originally no monkeys in the land occupied by this ethnic group. Working at Tokyo University in the 1880s, linguist Basil Hall Chamberlain collected folktales from native informants in his efforts to study the Ainu language. Chamberlain rendered some of the stories as literal transcriptions as dictated by Ainu speakers, while other narratives like this one he recorded from memory a few hours after they were told to him. In both instances, he strove for "rigid exactness, even if some of concomitants of rigid exactness are such as to spoil the subject for popular treatment."[2]

Chamberlain grouped the "The Fox, the Otter, and the Monkey" in the section of his book called "Tales Accounting for the Origin of Phenomena." In his estimation, the Ainu of his time were "addicted to moralizing and speculating on the origin of things," a trait which he believed made the stories in this category the least likely to be overshadowed by influences from the dominant Japanese culture and, therefore, the more authentic of the Ainu folktales contained in his collection.[3]

Regarding the Ainu people, physical appearance and cultural differences have set them apart from the Japanese. One ancient Chinese historian described them as living in "the land of hairy men,"[4] a reference to the Ainu males' long, thick beards and hirsute bodies in contrast to the more smooth-skinned Japanese. Until Japan outlawed the practice, Ainu women tattooed their mouths, a custom which gave them the appearance of having a large moustache.[5]

The Ainu once inhabited a large portion of the Japanese archipelago, but encroachment, wars, exploitation, and suppression over the centuries by the Japanese much reduced both their territory and population. The Ainu today are primarily located in the northern part of the Japanese island of Hokkaido; the southern part of the Russian island of Sakhalin; the smaller Kuril Islands, which since World War II, have been disputed as to ownership by Russia and Japan; and the southern tip of Russia's Kamchatka Peninsula. With the end of the Japanese Shogunate and the restoration of imperial rule under the Meiji dynasty in the later part of the nineteenth century, the Ainu gained automatic Japanese citizenship with a view by the government to assimilate them into the larger culture. This policy, however, led to further marginalization as the Ainu lost indigenous status and were forced to learn Japanese, adopt Japanese names, and halt former religious practices of animal sacrifice and tattooing.[6] Recently, however, as reported in a 2019 article in the online newspaper, *The Straits Times*, the Japanese government has now officially recognized the Ainu as an indigenous people and has proposed steps to rectify past injustices committed against them.[7]

Raw Monkey Relish
(from Japan)

Near the head of a narrow valley, an old farmer went out one morning to work his rice field. As he began to dig with his hoe, a large monkey appeared and plopped down on a stone outcropping beside the edge of the man's plot. Mocking the old fellow, the monkey sang, "Swing to the left. Swing to the right. Swing behind, and bump your bottom!"

Not amused, the farmer angrily ran after the monkey, but it scooted up a tall tree on the hillside. Seeing that pursuit was useless, the old man returned to his field. As soon as he started digging, back came the monkey and began singing. "Swing to the left. Swing to the right. Swing behind, and bump your bottom!" Again, the old man chased the monkey, but once again it shinnied up a tree out of reach. This went on all morning—the monkey singing and the old man chasing it, all to no avail.

When the farmer went home at noon to eat, he made a large sticky rice cake and took it back to the rock. He spread it all over where the monkey had perched. As soon as the old fellow began digging, out came the monkey, took its seat, and once again started mocking him. But this time, when the farmer went after the monkey, it stayed stuck, flailing its arms and chattering wildly. The old man got to the rock, tossed a rope around the creature, and wound it up tight. Escape was impossible.

Nearing home, the farmer called out to his wife, "Granny, I've caught a monkey. Tonight, we'll have raw monkey relish." He then went back to work for the rest of the day.

After he had gone, his wife thought she would pound rice to cook. "Granny," said the monkey, "if you loosen this rope some, I'll pound the rice for you." Now the old woman was already feeling sorry for the monkey, so she did as it asked and loosened the rope just a little.

"I can pound better if you make the rope a little looser," said the monkey. So the old woman loosened the rope a bit more to free the monkey's hands and feet. In a flash, the beast grabbed the pestle and with it pounded the old woman to death. It then took off her clothes, cut her up, and threw the diced flesh into the mortar with the rice to make raw relish. Having finished, the monkey put on the old woman's robe and waited.

Dusk began to fall, and the farmer came home. He had worked hard all afternoon and was ready to eat. In the dim light, the monkey put a hearty helping in his bowl. The old man ate quickly and asked for more, saying it was delicious. The monkey then tore off the wife's robe and screeched, "That was Granny raw relish! Her bones are under the porch!"

Before the old man could utter a word, the monkey bounded out the door and fled into the darkness.

COMMENTARY: As told by Noda Taro, this macabre tale is adapted from Mayer's anthology of ancient Japanese folktales.[8] The monkey in the story is among the more evil of tricksters found in folklore. To repay a kindness, the beast murders the old rice farmer's wife, makes a raw relish of her, serves her to her husband, and goes unpunished. Two famous stories of serving up family members as dishes come from ancient Greek lore and are more shocking since all the participants are humans.

In the first story, Tantalus, a wicked son of Zeus, is honored by the gods and dines with them on nectar and ambrosia. To return the favor, he invites immortals to a banquet where his son is the main dish. Unfortunately for Tantalus, the gods recognize the heinous trick and sentence him to eternal torment in the Underworld. Placed in a pool of water with fruit dangling above his head, he can neither eat nor drink. When he tries to slake his thirst, the water ebbs away, and when he tries to pluck the fruit, the branches withdraw from his clasp. From his name comes the word *tantalize*, meaning to torment with unfulfilled hope.

The second tale concerns the brothers Atreus and Thyestes. Thyestes makes love to his brother's wife. Atreus learns about the betrayal, invites Thyestes to a feast, and serves him his sons whom Atreus has had butchered and then boiled to make into a stew or human ragout.

The Monkey, the Crab, and the Persimmons
(from Japan)

On a sunny fall day long ago in Japan, a monkey and a crab were playing together beside a river. One would do this, and the other would do that, and as they ran here and there, the crab came across a rice dumpling, and the monkey a persimmon seed.

"What a delicious dumpling I've got!" said the crab.

Though monkeys like persimmons, this one said nothing because he had only a hard seed he couldn't eat and he wanted the crab's dumpling.

So he paused a moment before he replied, "Why don't we trade? I'll give you my seed, and you give me your dumpling."

Well, the crab hardly thought the exchange was fair, so he asked, "Why should I give you my nice dumpling for your hard-as-a-stone persimmon seed?"

The monkey answered, "I was only thinking of your future. Once your rice dumpling is eaten, it's gone for good, but if you plant this seed, it will soon sprout and grow into a large tree in a few years. Then you can have fine yellow persimmons year after year. Naturally, I can keep the seed and plant it, but that way you'll lose out on having all the fruit for yourself."

Hearing the monkey's smooth words, the crab decided he would get the better trade and accepted the proposal. The monkey immediately swallowed the dumpling in one or two bites and made a great show of exchanging the seed, as if he were giving away something of enormous worth. The two then parted, the monkey heading home to the trees and the crab to the rocks along the river's edge. There, he dug a hole and planted the persimmon.

The next spring, the crab was overjoyed to find a tender shoot sprouting from the earth. Every year, the tree continued to grow larger and larger until one spring it burst into beautiful orange blossoms. That fall, it began to bear fruit. More than anything, the crab liked to sit under the shade and raise his little eyes on their stems to watch the persimmons ripen into luscious orange balls.

The day came when the crab thought the fruit ready. "How delicious it will be," he said to himself and stretched to reach a low-hanging persimmon with his large pinchers. But the fruit was too far away. He next tried to climb the tree. No good. His legs were only made to scurry along the ground and over rocks.

Almost at the point of giving up, the crab suddenly remembered his old friend the monkey. He could clamber up a tree as if he had been born in one. The crab set out to find him and seek his help. Walking sideways up the rocky riverbank, he reached the dim forest where he found the monkey sleeping in a tree. The crab called to his former playmate and woke him from his dreams.

When the monkey heard that the persimmon seed had grown into a tree full of fruit, he quickly climbed down, and by the time he reached the ground, he had already planned how all the persimmons would be his. "Sure," he told the crab, "I'll pick the fruit for you."

When they got back to the river, the monkey could not believe his eyes. The tree hung heavy with ripe persimmons. Before the crab could say a word, the monkey shinnied up the tree and began to eat as fast as he could the ripest and sweetest fruit he could pluck.

"Please, give me one," begged the crab. "Please, just one."

But the greedy monkey refused. Not a single persimmon would he toss down to the hungry crab and continued to gorge himself. Finally, he could eat no more, and the only persimmons left were green and hard.

"You should have climbed up and helped yourself," laughed the now-stuffed monkey and flung an unripe persimmon that grazed the crab's shell. At that instant, the monkey's limb snapped, and he tumbled to the ground.

With all the commotion, the crab ran into his hole. The monkey got to his feet and angrily began to drop a pile of turds on the burrow. But before he could complete his nasty act, the crab reached out with his large scissor claw and clamped down on the monkey's bottom.

"Ouch! Let go! Let go!" howled the monkey in pain. "Release me, and I'll give you three hairs off my behind!"

The crab unlocked his pinchers. The monkey ran into the forest. And to this day, crabs have hair on their claws, and monkeys have a red bottom.

COMMENTARY: Many variants of this folktale are found throughout Japan as a cycle of stories about ongoing monkey-crab battles, with approximately one hundred and forty cycle variations. Four texts served as sources for this retelling: Lang's "The Crab and the Monkey"; Mayer's "The Monkey, the Crab, and the Mochi"; Ozaki's "The Quarrel of the Monkey and the Crab"; and Seki's "The Monkey and the Crab."[9] The tale in Lang's *Crimson Fairy Book* is essentially a condensed parallel of Ozaki's retelling in which the monkey is more explicitly a cunning trickster, cheating the crab out of his mochi, or rice ball, and refusing to provide him persimmons once they have ripened. At the end of both stories, the monkey meets his death, though not from the same cause. The monkey's fate in the renditions in Mayer and Seki is less dire. Both are *pourquoi* tales and conclude with the crab fastening a claw tightly and painfully onto the monkey's buttocks. Mayer's version explains why monkeys have a red bottom, and Seki's gives the reason for hairs growing on the pinchers of crabs. I have included both explanations in my retelling.

The Monkey and the Wise Boar
(from Japan)

A long time ago in the district of Shinshin in Japan lived a young man who had a monkey. He had trained it to perform different entertainments. Together, they would travel through the little villages and amuse the country folk. The monkey-man would command his monkey to tumble, dance, walk on stilts, and do other tricks. The onlookers were spellbound by the little beast's antics and would drop pieces of silver onto the man's mat that he spread out whenever he and his monkey entered a village.

After just eight moons had passed, the fellow tallied up his gains and noted, "All these sacks of coins I've acquired are an invitation for thieves to rob me. I had best invest my savings in a house. I can always teach new tricks to the monkey and that way can earn more money." So he bought a cottage with a pretty garden.

After a while, he was lonely and needed help with the house, so he married the beautiful daughter of the headman of the village. After the wedding, the young man spent his days in the pleasure of his bride's company, teaching new antics to his monkey, and doing very little else other than eating and sleeping. Every few moons, he and the monkey would travel to replenish the coins that he spent. From these, he and wife thrived in prosperity and happiness. At length, the couple were blessed with a fine baby boy whom they both adored.

From the outset, the wife had been taken with the monkey and would laugh and clap her hands together as it entertained her. Now that she had a child, the monkey was more eager than ever to perform for her and the baby and to wait upon them. The mother was also generous with the monkey and smothered it with treats and affection.

And yet, when it toured the villages with its master, the monkey endured much distress. For the man lacked kindness. While he lazed upon his mat and ate and drank of the finest, his faithful little servant often went hungry and had to be satisfied with the scanty scraps that the master tossed its way.

About the time the baby was three years of age, the monkey could bear no more and began to consider how to make its life less grim. So one night, it stole away from the house and went to visit an ancient boar who lived in the wild upon a nearby mountain. The beast was famed throughout the region for great wisdom and cleverness.

The monkey approached the cool wallow where the boar lay and bowed so low as to touch the ground with its head. After relating its sad story of abuse, the monkey pled, "Oh, great clasher of sharp tusks, in your vast wisdom tell me how, how I may end the ill use my master heaps upon me."

"Well," the boar replied, "if your master abuses you beyond endurance, consider fleeing to these savage wilds. Here you may live your life as you please."

"Oh, my," answered the monkey. "I was born and bred in captivity and know not the ways of the wild. None of my kind live here, and in this savage forest I would starve."

The wise one then said, "Your case is hard. I must ponder it further. Return to me tomorrow night, when I have thought through its difficulties. I will aid you then." So the monkey did as asked and came back the following night to hear what advice the shrewd boar might offer.

"When your master next leaves behind his wife and son and goes with you upon the road, do not act as you once did. Instead, squat and gaze stupidly and do not follow his commands. Bungle all your former tricks as though your brain were in a thick fog. People will clutch their money tightly and mock your clumsy show. Your master will then be more inclined to feed you better to improve your strength and attitude."

"Your advice is hard," said the monkey almost in tears. "If I do as you say, the man will at first plead and prod, and when these encouragements fail, he will become angry and beat me. How will my life be improved if I am covered with bruises and blood from his harsh whipping?"

The boar replied, "My words come from my hard-won experience. If you cannot endure one or two blows from your master's hand, I see little likelihood for you to profit from my wisdom." And with that, the old boar rolled over on his heavy haunch and shut his eyes as if he would sleep. The monkey went away in sorrow.

For the next three moons, the master remained at home. He then decided that he would once again travel to earn some money. At the first village that he came to, he unrolled his straw mat where people might drop their coins as the monkey entertained them.

While this preparation took place, the creature thought to itself, "I had rather die and go from this world to another than endure more starvation on the road. Even if the man beats me senseless, I will follow what the boar has said. After all, there may be wisdom in his advice."

So, when the master ordered it to dance, the monkey sat motionless and seemed as if in a trance. Eighty times the man commanded the monkey to dance, and eighty times it sat still. The little beast stirred at last and danced with such awkward, oafish movements that it seemed more like a clumsy bear cub than a nimble monkey. When it had finished tripping about the street, it scratched its behind to signify that its waltz was over.

The gathered villagers booed and jeered both monkey and master during the performance, and no one dropped a single coin on the mat. At first the man scolded but soon progressed to ranting and raving. When these actions produced no improvement, he flogged the monkey with a bamboo rod.

He gave it such a violent trouncing that the people began to cry out for mercy in fear that he would kill the poor creature. Yet it continued to play its part with stupid stare and gawky spinning until the man rolled up his mat and left with the monkey in tow.

The following day at another village, the monkey acted the same way. But this time its bottom revealed welts the size of newly growing cucumbers, and it peered at the onlookers with dead fish eyes. Again, the master laid on a second beating until he grew tired and headed for home, the monkey tightly tethered to him, limping and lurching along the road.

Reaching his house at dusk, the man entered in a bad temper, kicked the creature aside, and told his wife to bring his evening meal. He ate his rice and said no word. When he finished, his wife, puzzled at his behavior, finally spoke.

"Worthy husband, you always return home in such good spirits. What makes your temper smolder as if it were about to blaze forth?"

He looked at her and said, "This day I see a future in which our happy life must end. I see a time in which poverty overtakes us and we suffer constant want and woe."

"How so?" the wife exclaimed. "Do you not have a loving wife to comfort you and a young son you hold dear? Do you not have this good house and silver saved to buy plenty of food and drink to get you through a long, lean year? And further, do you not have your pet, a wise and faithful servant, to take upon the road to gain more coin if needed?"

Hardly had she finished speaking, when the husband cried out, "This very beast, which we have pampered and handfed, brings to our door this threat of ruin. What little skill it once had is now entirely gone through age or loss of mind. It was once lively and spry as a little bird, but now it barely knows its tail from its face and cannot perform a single trick.

"I have begged and threatened. I have applied my cane to it until my arm is nearly worn out and shakes as though it has a tremor. Nothing works. I am done with it. Soon I will go to the butcher to get a price for the useless thing."

He rose to leave when his wife sobbed, "Not that! No! I beg you, no! Old age or sickness may have lessened the creature's worth. Yet mercy, please! The monkey has served you long and well. Its mind you have sharpened through your skillful training so as to set it apart from other animals.

"Our little son loves the monkey, and the monkey loves our son. Often, when I have been about my household chores, the creature has made him laugh through somersaults or funny faces and sometimes has even saved him from some fall or other harm. Surely, this ever-loyal friend you cannot so heartlessly destroy."

On hearing her plea, the husband stormed out of the house, and thinking that nothing would change his mind, the wife could not stop her tears. She went to the corner where the monkey huddled. It had understood what the man had said and shivered with fright at the thought of what would befall it.

She put her arms around it and weeping said, "Poor thing, you have no notion of what awaits you this day." And as she sobbed and heaved, the commotion woke her son who had been asleep in the room. Unaware of why his mother was upset, he began to cry in sympathy. Then tears crept from the monkey's eyes to join its sorrow with theirs for its case. After a bit, the woman rose to sooth her child back to sleep.

The husband later returned in a mood just as foul as when he had left. At once the sad wife said, "Do not tell me you have condemned our poor pet to the chopping block!"

"Not yet, but through no fault of my own. The deed still hangs in the air. When I went to butcher's shop, the wife said her husband was out. I replied that he should come to our house at noon tomorrow to take the worthless monkey away."

At these words, his wife started to cry again, but her husband glowered at her and stopped her with "Am I not master in my own house? Cease yowling or you shall have good cause for tears." He then stalked off to his quilted pallet, and she went to hers, her face blotched with red from weeping.

The monkey witnessed the whole scene and thought, "Better to starve in the forest than to be cut up by the knacker." So, waiting for the cover of darkness, when everyone in the house was fast asleep, it left at midnight to seek the lair of the wild boar.

On arriving there, the monkey bowed before the sage and told of its sufferings and the horror to come, concluding with "Only death is now left for me."

The wise one paused before answering. "What has occurred I foresaw. Return to your abode and wait until I shall visit. Now listen closely to my words.

> In the morning, the mother will place her child upon the porch so that she might perform her household duties. As usual, she will direct you to watch over her little one. You must then gaze upon your mistress with sorrowful eyes, filled with blame for your sad end. She will look at your dark and brooding face.
>
> At that moment, I will rush forth from the garden where I have hidden. I will seize what she holds most dear and snatch the child within my jaws. As

I run toward the thick woods, you must raise a loud alarm and pursue me into those depths.

There I will await and return the boy to you so that you may take him back unharmed and be justly rewarded. His parents will proclaim you the savior of their precious pearl. Your once cruel master will cherish you henceforth. You will want for nothing, and you will live out your days in happiness and ease.

With its hopes now raised, the monkey thanked the boar and left.

The wife woke up the next day a little before dawn to cook some rice and dress her son. She also set out a bowl of food for her pet. Yet it refused to touch it. She sadly mused, "It knows its fate and now grieves."

Her husband soon finished his breakfast. While he sat toying with his chopsticks, the wife led the boy onto the porch and told the monkey to watch him. However, the creature looked up at her, put one hand over its heart, and rolled its eyes as if she were the reason for its misery. But when it turned its face toward the wall and shook its head, the woman burst into tears.

To her husband, she said, "The poor thing knows more than we imagined. It is aware of your plan. See how it refuses its food and pays no attention to the child it once doted upon."

No sooner were her words out of her mouth than the wild boar darted from the garden, leapt upon the porch, and took the child into his foam-flecked jaws. Without a pause, the beast plunged into the dense forest.

Frozen where he sat, the husband could move neither hand nor foot. The monkey, though, had already given chase. The master and mistress heard its chatter sounding like furious rage. They saw it eat the boar's brisk wind as it nearly overtook the beast.

The man stirred from his stupor. With trembling hand, he searched for his spear. His wife desperately prayed for her son's life.

Then suddenly the two saw coming out of the woods the monkey hobbling on three paws. Its fourth held their child. The mother ran to hug her little one. The husband stood with his mouth wide open like a beached clam baking in the sun.

The mother cried out, "Look at our dearest pet, this creature that you would have turned over to the slaughterer to chop and grind, despite my pleas and tears. If not for this monkey's loyalty, our only son would have been torn apart by razor tusks. Take shame for your plot, and thank our savior from sure calamity."

"Ah, wife," the husband replied, "for once you seem to be in the right. Truly the monkey is our sword and shield and has restored our heart's delight. From this day forward, the little beast shall live with us as our esteemed guest. It shall dwell with us in peace and love and plenty for its remaining years. For it has earned our everlasting thanks."

These words gave the monkey such vigor that it jumped upon the porch and danced as it had never danced in its life. When it finished, the master clapped his hands in delight. The monkey then tugged upon his sleeve and looked longingly toward the road to show its willingness to travel and entertain once again. The master could not have been more overjoyed. For he saw how his sweet pet would be the means to keep his livelihood.

While everyone thus celebrated, the butcher arrived to claim the monkey. The master, though, said to him, "Prepare some boar's meat. Tomorrow we will have a feast to honor our beloved and loving pet. I shall invite my neighbors, and before all of them, I shall wish it happiness and long life."

From that day on, the monkey lived in peace and comfort, traveling and entertaining when it would. It ate the best of food and slept whenever it wanted, its life blessed by perfect love and kindness.

COMMENTARY: Post Wheeler's *Tales from the Japanese Storytellers*, a collection of twenty-four stories, is the main source for this adaptation.[10] According to the book's introduction, Wheeler had originally compiled a ten-volume work containing these selections. The title of this longer work, completed in 1938, translates into English as *Treasure-Tale-Storehouse*. Following the framed narrative format of such traditional works as *The Arabian Nights*, *The Panchatantra*, *Decameron*, *Canterbury Tales*, and others, it presents stories within the structure of a larger story. Wheeler took his tales from Japanese public storytellers whose performances had reached their final shape during the Tokugawa period (1603–1868), an era when Japan was still feudalistic. Using appropriate ceremony and wearing formal dress, the *hanasika*, with whom Wheeler was acquainted, performed their stories in the archaic style of this earlier time. Therefore, Wheeler chose to render his translations into an older style of English to give the flavor of the original Japanese versions.[11] As retold here, Wheeler's translation is condensed but retains something of his style.

In the early 1900s, Yei Theodora Ozaki translated the story somewhat loosely from a Japanese version by Sandanami Sanjin to appeal to the interests of young western readers rather than to "the technical student of folklore."[12] She also says that she added "touches of local color or description" as needed or as pleased her, sometimes using a detail from another telling of the same story.[13] Ozaki's rendering appears in *The Japanese Fairy Book*.[14] As is frequently the case with other folktales, numerous online samples of this story, without attribution, are lifted verbatim from Ozaki's translation.

Like the Brazilian tale, "How Monkey Became a Trickster," the main character is cast in the centuries old role of monkey as performer imitating human behavior. (See the section titled "The Caribbean, South America, and North America.") In the Japanese tale, the monkey's dancing, stilt-walking, and other antics amuse villagers who enjoy the comic resemblances between the simian's feats and human actions. Such displays may still be found in parts of the world today. Morris characterizes them as a type of "demeaning circus performance" by "long-suffering primates."[15]

The Monkeys and the Dragonflies
(from the Philippines)

Once when the noonday sun beat down on the forest, a dragonfly thought she would alight on a tree branch. Tired and hot, she said to herself, "Under the shade, I can rest and refresh myself." She did not realize that a troop of monkeys had made their home there and in the surrounding trees.

Fluttering her wings, she fanned her face, hoping to cool herself. One of the monkeys soon saw her, and climbing down to where she sat, he spitefully said, "Oh, wretched creature, why do you sit here? This leafy kingdom belongs to us monkeys."

"Please, sir," the dragonfly replied, "let me rest here a while. The sun is hot. The air is dry. And I am too tired to fly anymore."

Answered the monkey with scorn, "Weak things like you may not enter our shady domain. I do not know how to tell you any more directly. Now off with you." Without so much as another word, he tossed a twig toward her.

The dragonfly, though, was too fast and dodged the monkey's twiggy missile. She zipped away much offended, flew straight to her brother, who happened to be the Dragonfly King, and told him every detail of what had occurred. He became angry beyond all imagining and swore that he would make war against the monkeys for their offense. But first he decided to send three of his mightiest warriors as messengers to warn the monkey monarch of the coming war and to give him an opportunity to make amends.

The message read, "Oh, Primate King, because of the insults my dear sister received from one of your subjects, I intend to bring war to your branches. Unless you apologize immediately, I will storm your tree with might and slay you and your monkey vassals. You have been warned."

On hearing the message delivered, the monkey king burst out laughing and accepted the challenge, saying to the envoys, "Tell your little droning lord to send all the warriors he can muster. When our two armies meet, we shall see who has the superior force."

The messengers replied, "Great king, no one can know the turns of fortune. You should not judge the outcome before the fight. Fate may surprise you."

"You are fools," exclaimed the monkey monarch. "You have my answer. Away! Away!" And he shooed the insects off the royal limb.

The messengers buzzed back to their homeland to tell their ruler what they had learned. His wings instantly began thrumming, and he let loose his troops toward the monkey kingdom. Through the air they whirred and tore, and though they were a mighty multitude, their transparent wings and thin legs did not appear to foretell victory.

The monkeys, however, came to the struggle armed with heavy clubs to batter their foes and crush them. At the attack, the primate prince ordered, "Now smack and thwack these flying things and destroy them."

King Dragon heard the command and signaled to his soldiers that they land on their enemies' heads. As the monkeys rained down their clubs, the dragonflies quickly swerved from the attempted blows. These, of course, landed where unintended—on their fellow monkeys' heads. In this way, the monkey king and his whole army perished in the struggle.

COMMENTARY: In its presentation of time-honored themes found in traditional literature around the world, this Filipino story is a good example of how most folktales are "predominantly constructive" in their ethical truths.[16] Just as the small, apparently delicate, but clever dragonflies defeat the arrogant, strong, and well-armed monkeys, so intelligence can overcome brute force, and the weak can defeat the strong.

"The Monkeys and the Grasshoppers" is a parallel story with similar stark contrasts told by the Hmong of Southeast Asia.[17] In this instance, fragile grasshoppers instead of dragonflies defeat more powerful monkeys.

How Children Became Monkeys
(from the Bukidnon of the Philippines)

A woman one day went with her two children to where water buffalo had scooped out a wet shallow place from their wallowing. Here she brought some cloth, dye pots, and large spoons made from shells. The mud was a blue-black color and good for dyeing.

The woman's children helped her cover the cloth with mud. While it soaked up the dark color, she made a fire, set a pot full of water over the flames, and added leaves to complete dyeing the cloth. Her children played close by as she waited for the water to heat.

When the water reached a steady, rolling boil, she stirred it with one of her spoons, but some of it sloshed out and scalded her hand. She recoiled and cried out in pain, causing her children to laugh at her misfortune.

At once, the children turned into monkeys, and the spoons became their tails. Even today, the nails of monkeys are yet black from where the children helped their mother bury the cloth in the mud.

COMMENTARY: This adaptation comes from Mabel Cook Cole's 1916 *Philippine Folk Tales*,[18] a collection made while her husband was employed in ethnographic work for the Field Museum of Natural History. She gathered her stories from different Filipino peoples separated both by distance and varying levels of cultural development. "How Children Became Monkeys" came from what Cole termed "the Wild Tribes" of the large Philippine island of Mindanao where at the time slavery and human sacrifice were still practiced.[19]

The specific ethnic group from which Cole derived this tale were the Bukidnon, a word which signifies "mountain people." The name originated with the Bisayan, also Visayan, a lowland coastal indigenous people of Mindanao. The original name of the Bukidnon is Talaandig. This ethnic group today lives primarily by hunting and gathering food as well as by swidden farming,[20] sometimes negatively referred to as slash-and-burn agriculture thought to contribute to deforestation. In actuality, it is a rotational crop practice, with land cleared by fire, then left to regenerate for several years. As one writer on swidden cultivation in the Philippines notes, its practitioners are well aware of "the laws of letting a field lie fallow until new ground cover can restore it and preserve the soils beneath it."[21]

As a *pourquoi* tale of magical transformation, "How Children Became Monkeys" is comparable to other stories retold here about humans being changed into primates, sometimes as a punishment, sometimes because certain rituals were inadequate or were not correctly followed, sometimes for living too long among monkeys, sometimes for ingesting monkey food, and sometimes for no reason at all. See the following stories along with accompanying notes for each: "The Origin of Monkeys," "The Woman and the Monkey," "The Monkey Prince," "The Men Who Became Gibbons," "How Children Were Turned into Monkeys," "The Rich Couple Who Became Monkeys," and "The First Monkey."

The First Monkey
(from the Visayan of the Philippines)

Long ago, a village nestled at the bottom of a hill covered with trees. On the side of the hill, just above the village, lived an elderly grandmother and her grandson in a small house.

Each day, the old woman worked hard to earn her living by picking seeds from cotton. She always kept a basket nearby for the cotton and would take a long stick to spin the cotton around it.

Unlike his grandmother, the boy was lazy and never helped her. Every morning he would go down to the village and gamble, then go home where he expected his supper to be waiting. One day, after he had lost his money, he returned home and became angry because his grandmother had not prepared his meal.

His grandmother explained, "I have been working to get the seeds from the cotton. As soon as I have finished, I will sell it in the village and buy us something to eat."

Before she could say anything else, the grandson lost his temper, seized some coconut shells and tossed them at the poor woman. It was now her turn to become angry, and she grabbed her spindle and started to beat him with it. Instantly, he changed into an ugly little beast, the cotton from the spindle turning into hair which covered him while the spindle itself turned into a long tail.

Realizing that he had become an ugly animal, the boy tried to chatter a few words, then jumped out the window and scuttled down the hill to the village. When he met his fellow gamblers, he grabbed his long tail in one hand and lashed them as hard as he could. They immediately changed into ugly animals like himself.

Unwilling to let such beasts remain in the village, the people drove them into the forest. The creatures now live in the trees. Today they are called monkeys.

COMMENTARY: Another story from Cole's *Philippine Folk Tales*,[22] this brief *pourquoi* of magical transformation explains how monkeys originated—in this instance, as a punishment for laziness, disrespect, and incessant gambling. Cole indicates she obtained the story from the Visayan, or Bisayan, one of the Philippine peoples who became Christianized by the Spanish in the sixteenth century.[23] Composed primarily of three ethnolinguistic groups—the Cebuano, Hiligaynon, and Waray-Waray—most of them still occupy their original habitation of the Visayas Islands as well as the southern Luzon islands and most of the Mindanao island group, all of which compose the three geographical divisions of the Philippines. To access better economic opportunities, many Visayans have migrated to Manila's metropolitan area. They comprise the country's largest ethnic population.[24]

Readers will find a parallel between "The First Monkey" and the beginning of "Lazy Jack" from Joseph Jacob's *English Fairy Tales*.[25] "Lazy Jack" is about a boy who lives with his mother, a poor woman who gets her living by spinning like the grandmother in the Filipino tale. But there the resemblance ends. The remainder of "Lazy Jack" is a droll cumulative story which concludes with Jack marrying a rich man's daughter and his mother living with the couple "in great happiness until she died."[26]

Based on a Japanese folktale, Diane Snyder's retelling of *The Boy of the Three-Year Nap* provides a further treatment of the topic of idleness.[27] A 1989 Caldecott Honor Award book for illustrator Allen Say, it recounts how a poor widow sews silk kimonos for rich ladies while her lazy son Taro does nothing but eat and sleep. Taro decides he wants to become rich, so he disguises himself as the village deity and orders a rich merchant to have his daughter marry the widow's son. The mother realizes her son's trickery and seizes the opportunity to trick the merchant herself, persuading him to repair her house to make it fit for Taro's new bride. She also wheedles the merchant into giving her son a job. Unlike "The First Monkey," however, in which the worthless grandson is severely punished by becoming a monkey, the mother and son tricksters in *The Boy of the Three-Year Nap* are rewarded with wealth and happiness, much like the mother and son in "Lazy Jack."

The Story of a Monkey
(from the Ilocano of the Philippines)

A monkey once climbed up the tree where he made his home, and a sharp thorn became stuck in his tail. Try as he might, the thorn stuck so tightly that he could not pull it out.

So the monkey went to the barber in a nearby village. "My tail has a thorn stuck in it. If you can remove it, I'll pay you handsomely," offered the monkey.

The barber tugged and tugged on the thorn but could not pull it out. He then decided to try his razor, but it slipped in his hand and cut off the end of the monkey's tail.

The monkey cried out angrily, "Give me back my tail, or let me have your razor!"

Of course, the barber could not restore the tip of the tail. So to make amends, he let the monkey take his razor.

As he headed back to his tree, the monkey met an old woman cutting firewood and said, "That's a hard job, Grandmother. Take my razor, and you can cut the wood more easily."

Pleased by the kind offer, the old woman took the razor. But when she began to cut the wood, the razor broke.

The monkey yelled, "You've broken my razor. Now give me a new one or let me have your wood!"

Of course, the old woman did not have a new razor. So she let the monkey take all her firewood.

The monkey gathered the sticks and headed back toward the village to sell it. As he went along, he came upon another old woman making cakes by the side of the road. "Your wood is nearly gone. Why don't you take mine, Grandmother?" he kindly offered.

The old woman accepted the firewood with thanks and began to bake more cakes. However, when she burned up all the sticks, the monkey shouted, "You've used up all my wood! Now chop me more or give me your cakes as payment."

No dry wood was available to cut. So the old woman gave the monkey all her cakes. As he headed for the village to sell them, he came upon a dog. It bit the monkey so hard he died. The dog then ate the cakes.

COMMENTARY: Also adapted from Cole's anthology,[28] this talking beast story is a cumulative tale along the lines of the English folktale "The Old Woman and Her Pig."[29] Variants include Lang's "Tale of a Tortoise and a Mischievous Monkey" from the *Brown Fairy Book*[30] and "The Monkey and the Tom-Tom" from a collection of folktales from Southern India titled *Tales of the Sun*.[31]

The variant in *The Brown Fairy Book* is one among several episodes in a single story Lang indicates came from Brazil.[32] Its plot is more complex than that of "The Story of a Monkey." The plot of "The Monkey with the Tom-Tom" in *Tales of the Sun* is also more complex but concludes with an explicit moral. There, the monkey climbs to the top of a tree, beats his drum, and in triumph recaps his antics and brags about his pranks as a trickster:

> I lost my tail and got a razor: *dum dum*.
> I lost my razor and got a bundle of fuel; *dum dum*.
> I lost my fuel and got a basket of puddings; *dum dum*.
> I lost my puddings and got a tom-tom; *dum dum*.

Thus there are rogues in this innocent world, who would live to glory over their wicked tricks.[33]

Yet the cumulative episodes, except for the monkey's getting a tom-tom, more closely resemble those in Cole's Filipino selection and suggest that the Indian story traveled to the Philippines through trade with the Asian mainland. For comparison to another cumulative yarn in which a monkey loses and regains his posterior appendage, readers may find Eells' "Why the Monkey Still Has a Tail" to be of interest.[34] In this Brazilian folktale, a rabbit and an armadillo mete out punishment to a monkey for a trick he played.

Cole derived "The Story of a Monkey" from the Ilocano people who inhabited several coastal regions of the Philippines. Under Spanish influence in the 1500s, the Ilocano and other similarly situated indigenous groups like the Visayan converted to Christianity and "adopted the dress of their conquerors" but held onto their various languages and many of their native customs.[35] *Countries and Their Cultures Forum* describes the Ilocano inhabitants as making up about eleven percent of the population of the Philippines. In the nineteenth century, many of them migrated to other countries for a better life because of the harsh environment in their homeland on the island of northwestern Luzon.[36] Perhaps the most famous Ilocano was strongman Ferdinand Marcos,[37] who was president of the Philippines from 1965 to 1986 before his removal from office by the People Power Revolution.[38]

The Monkey and the Turtle
(from the Ilocano of the Philippines)

One day, as a sad and downcast monkey walked along a riverbank, he crossed paths with a turtle. Observing how woebegone the monkey looked, the turtle asked, "Is anything the matter?"

"Alas, I am famished," the monkey answered. "My fellow monkeys have stolen all the squash of a farmer, and I am nearly at death's door from lack of food."

"Oh, no need to worry, my friend," replied the turtle. "Take this sharp bolo and come with me. We'll go and steal some new banana plants."

The two then went along until they found some young plants. After digging them up with the knife, they searched for somewhere to set them out. The monkey decided to climb a tree and set out his in it. Unlike his friend, the turtle was not able to climb, so he dug a hole and set his plant in the ground. When they had finished, the pair went off and pondered about what they would do when their plants produced bananas.

The monkey said, "I'm going to take my crop and sell it so that I'll have lots of money."

The turtle said, "When my bananas are ready, I'll sell them and buy me three yards of cloth. That way, I'll have something nice to wear instead of this old cracked shell."

The monkey and turtle then left. After a few weeks had passed, they returned to check on their plants. The monkey found that his plant had died because it had no soil. The turtle's, however, had grown tall and now hung with fruit.

"I'll climb to the top of yours to get the bananas," volunteered the monkey. He scooted up the tree and began eating while the turtle remained on the ground.

"Please throw me down some," the turtle begged. But the monkey continued eating ripe fruit and tossed only one green banana to his friend. When the monkey finished, he hugged the tree with his arms and took a nap.

Now angry, the turtle gathered bamboo canes and sharpened the ends with his bolo. He then stuck the bamboo in the ground around the tree. When he had finished, he yelled in alarm, "Here comes Crocodile! Here comes Crocodile!"

The monkey woke with such a frightful jerk that he tumbled out of the banana tree and stabbed himself to death on the pointed canes. The turtle then chopped him up with the bolo, salted the pieces, and left them to dry in the sun. The next morning, he headed for the mountains and sold the meat to the monkeys who lived there. They paid him with the farmer's squash they had stolen.

Not content with his trick, the turtle called out as he was leaving, "You lazy monkeys, now you are eating yourselves!"

"Quick!" said one old monkey. "Let's catch him." Several ran and captured the turtle.

The old monkey commanded, "Grab a hatchet and chop him into little chunks."

"Good!" replied the turtle. "See all these cracks along my shell. I've been cut with a hatchet many times. Just what I prefer."

Another monkey said, "Let's toss him into the water."

"Oh, please don't throw me in the water," pled the turtle. "Please spare my life."

The monkeys, though, paid the turtle no heed whatsoever and tossed him into a deep stream nearby. He immediately settled to the bottom, caught a lobster, and swam to the surface.

Surprised to see the turtle still alive, the monkeys begged, "Show us how to catch lobsters."

The turtle explained, "Tie one end of a cord around your middle. Then tie the other end around a heavy rock to help you sink down."

Without another word, the monkeys did as the turtle said. With a cord secured around each one's middle and tied to a stone, they jumped into the stream, sank to the bottom, and never surfaced. And even so today, monkeys refuse to eat meat because they remember this story.

COMMENTARY: This story is a *pourquoi* that explains monkeys' distaste for meat. Like the previous narrative, it comes from the Ilocano in Cole's Filipino folktales.[39] Here, the monkey is a trickster who is out tricked by a turtle, not the usually expected animal such as a fox, rabbit, or jackal to outwit others. Cole, however, does note that turtles in the local lore of the Philippines were considered to have "extraordinary sagacity and cunning."[40]

The principal characters in the selection parallel those in "The Monkey, the Crab, and the Persimmons" and its variants from Japan. The greedy and foolish monkey tricksters in the Japanese and Filipino stories get their comeuppance, although admittedly the payback is much more severe for the monkeys in "The Monkey and the Turtle." Another parallel between the two stories is that the crab and the turtle are wise in planting their respective fruit trees.

There is also the parallel to stories in which a weaker, although more cunning, trickster uses reverse psychology to escape from a more powerful adversary. In this motif of stark contrasts, a trapped character begs a foe not to do what the victim really desires. The foe then performs the action, and the victim escapes. For instance, in Joel Chandler Harris' "How Mr. Rabbit Was Too Sharp for Mr. Fox," Brer Rabbit pleads, "I don't keer w'at you do wid me, Brer Fox … so you don't fling me in dat briar patch."[41] Of course, Brer Fox does exactly the opposite and sends Brer Rabbit safely on his way.

Additional examples of this motif include the West African story about the spider-man trickster Anansi and the wooden doll. Pat Perrin's adaptation is titled "Anansi & the Box of Stories."[42] Two picture book retellings with the same title as Perrin's are one by Katie Dale and Valentina Bandera[43] and a second by Stephen Krensky and Jeni Reeves.[44] James Mooney's second version of the Cherokee story "The Rabbit and the Tar Wolf" is an interesting variant from the Cherokee of the Southeastern United States[45] as is Swanton's Creek story "The Tar Baby."[46]

The Caribbean, South America, and North America

Irraweka and the Flood
(from the Carib of Guyana)

Guyana is a region in northeastern South America. Its name means "land of many waters." Large, unspoiled rainforests cover the area, many of them flooded along the major waterways. These rainforests are home to an enormous variety of plants and animals. There, long ago, animals and people lived together in peace and harmony.

Within the emerald forests or along the brown rivers, the jaguar did not fear Man's approach. Neither did the great cat run away or tense its back when man came near. No green-yellow slivers of fire flickered in its eyes, nor did its tail lash back and forth like a flailing whip.

In that time, if Man's feet crackled the leaves of the forest floor, Mapuri, the wild pig, remained where he was and refused to retreat into the undergrowth. Neither would he attack, slashing furiously with sharp tusks.

The parrots would blink in the hot sun and call out to Man to tell him what they saw from their perches high in the tops of trees. Down below, the snake would slither before Man's path and show him the best ways to get through the jungle. The bush dog and giant sloth also helped, even though the sloth would sometimes doze off to sleep.

Truly, the birds, beasts, and Man lived as friends. Man helped the animals as well. For when Kabo Tano, the Ancient One, commanded him to cut down the Great Tree that produced all fruits, Man took tender cuttings from the tree. These he gave to the animals and told them to plant the shoots near their homes. That way, the animals could find food close to the places where they lived. And for Man's kindness, they were grateful.

And yet, because he too much enjoyed his tricks, the small, brown monkey, Irraweka, did not share in the harmony. He would often pinch Mapuri hard and make him squeal, and sometimes he would jerk the tail of Abeyu, the wild cow. If the jaguar nodded drowsily or seemed off guard, Irraweka would leap upon his back and cause him to jump and growl in anger.

To disturb the parrots' rest, the little mischief maker would shake the branches where they perched. Then, in great squawking flocks they would rise into the air. He even teased the wise owl for sleeping during the day. Because of his pranks, there came a time when Irraweka nearly destroyed the animals and Man.

One day, Man found a spring flowing beneath the roots of the Great Tree that he had cut down, and as it flowed, the water rapidly swelled. It was not like a river, with a steady flow. Rather, the stream sprang swiftly, faster than a whizzing arrow so that it seemed it would soon cover the whole earth.

"Oh, Stream," asked Man, "why do you flow forth in swift outpouring from the roots of the Great Tree?"

The stream answered, "I do what I must do. Before the sun rises tomorrow, I must spread my water throughout the forest and leave not one spot dry."

On hearing these words, Man raised his hands and cried out in terror to the Ancient One. "Oh, Kabo Tano, what should I do?" And Kabo Tano put into Man's head that he should look to where some reeds grew close by, and he put into Man's heart that from the reeds he should make a basket and with it cover the source of the stream. As soon as Man put the basket over it, the gushing water ceased to rise, and Man left, now at ease.

During all this time, Irraweka had watched Man enter the forest and had followed him with movements soft and silent. From a tree, he had seen Man weave the basket and stop the water's flow. Yet from his leafy view, he could not hear what Man had said to Kabo Tano, nor could he read the fear on Man's face.

The little meddler thought, "Man is the lord of the animals, but he does not think of us and hides from us the cherished fruits in his basket. When he leaves, I will take his secret fruits and eat them." Yet, when Man left, Irraweka turned the basket over and found it empty.

Now a tide of water poured forth, and soon a roaring torrent raged. The flood rushed so hard and fast that it washed away the terrified little monkey who cried out in his loudest voice.

Sitting atop the nearby trees, the parrots saw the surging water and heard the cries of Irraweka as he was swept away. The panicked birds squawked a loud alarm, and all the animals called out as they ran trembling, "Save us, oh, Man!"

Man watched the surging flood draw ever near and knew that he and the animals might die and must find safety on higher ground. There, coconut trees, deeply rooted, soared above the forest canopy. Man shouted, "Climb these before the water covers all." And the animals climbed the trees' strong trunks which swayed in the gathering winds.

Dull-gray clouds now blotted out the bright rays of the tropical sun, and Man and the animals clung to the trees for five long days. Rain fell, and water rose. Then on the fifth night, the rumbling thunder stopped, and the forked lightning ceased. Everything became calm, and twinkling stars suddenly filled the dark sky. Yet, when dawn returned, no land could be seen, for thick mists blanketed the floor of the green world.

Now the soaked animals began to rouse themselves and stretch, but Man cautioned them to remain in the safety above until they could see better what lay below. For days on end, the mists covered all, and the only sound they could hear was lapping water.

By the tenth day, the sun had yet to penetrate the mists. So Man took a heavy coconut and dropped it. The only sound he heard was its splash below his tree, and he knew that the water was still high. For the next two days, Man let fall a coconut, and the animals listened, and each day the splashes sounded farther away than the day before.

After many days had passed, they heard a dull thud, and this made the animals want to climb down from their prison in the branches. But Man warned them that there might yet be danger below. He told the animals that he would go to the ground first.

However, the long-necked, hunched-over trumpeter bird refused to heed the warning and came down fast. As soon as he reached the ground, he stepped into a nest of stinging ants. The ants had buried themselves deep within the dry earth when the rain began. Once the flood withdrew, though, they left their snug dry hiding places and came to the surface to look for food. Savage from hunger, they bit and stung the long wading legs of the trumpeter bird and stripped off so much of its skin that its legs looked like thin sticks and still do even to this day.

Man reached the ground next, and after him the rest of the animals climbed down. The earth was cold and soaked. Although Mapuri usually liked the muddy ground, the cold made him squeal loudly and bolt for some rocks. There, he hoped to find a drier spot. The wise owl shook as if his dense, gray feathers were not enough to keep him warm. The toucan shivered so violently that his long, curved, yellow beak clacked like a pair of castanets.

Indeed, the wet and cold caused such misery that Man decided to start a fire, but the dampness made it difficult. At long last, a small coal burst into flame but vanished almost as quickly as it started. For the fat marudi bird, driven by hunger, swallowed it and wasted Man's labor. Although Man did not see who did the deed, his anger stirred. The other animals, however, blamed Alligator and said that he had eaten the little spark, leaving them cold and miserable.

None of the animals liked Alligator anyway. His wide mouth was bigger than theirs, and when he closed his jaws, he looked as if he smiled and made fun of them. He had a bad temper, too, and was always grumpy. Besides all that, he was proud of his long tongue and used it to sweep up food on every side so that, when he was around, no one else had a chance to eat. And, once he had eaten, he left so few remains that none of the other animals could get enough. Their greatest wish was that he would stay by himself and stuff his stomach alone. So they shunned his company.

When the flood waters had withdrawn, Alligator came to pay his respects to Man. All the animals shouted, "Alligator stole your ember!" In his anger, Man forced Alligator to open his wide mouth. When he did, his fear caused him to swallow his lengthy tongue. Now it is the shortest of any creature alive today.

Because of the confusion that resulted over who gobbled up the fire, the animals began to mistrust one another, and gradually they began to speak only to their own kind. Their common language vanished, and fear grew ever greater among them. Birds sang only to birds. Snakes spoke only to snakes. Parrots could only squawk, and howler monkeys could only howl. The wild cow only lowed, and the jaguar only snarled and roared. At last, nothing except noisy babbling rang throughout the forest.

Had Irraweka not removed Man's basket that kept the stream in check, none of these things would have happened. And though the trouble-maker survived the flood he had released, the peace that once prevailed among the animals and Man could not outlast the little monkey's mischief.

COMMENTARY: Derived from Carib and Arawak sources,[1] this talking animal tale[2] from South America is another account of a great flood like that told about Noah in the Bible. Such stories abound throughout the world. In the familiar role of a monkey with too much curiosity, Irraweka has become a troublemaker in the rainforest of Guyana. He unleashes a hurricane that destroys the unity and single language that once existed among its animals and between them and man.

In this sense, the tale may be read as a *pourquoi* myth that explains how the little monkey's curiosity resulted in *the fall* of the forest creatures from harmony to disharmony. The idea of the fall is a universal motif or pattern known as an *archetype*. This motif occurs throughout world literature—for example, the loss of Eden in the *Genesis* account of Adam and Eve. Embedded within the larger plot framework of Irraweka's story that explains the flood and the fall are other, briefer *pourquoi* tales such as how the trumpeter bird got its thin, sticklike legs and why the once-long tongue of the alligator is now the shortest of any animal.

As a matter of further interest, the English word *hurricane* comes from the Spanish *huracan* which has two possible borrowings from indigenous sources of the 1500s. One is that conquistadors may have derived the term from the Taino language of the West Indian Arawak who had a similar word meaning "evil spirit." Another is that the Spanish borrowed the term from *Hurakan*, the Mayan god of wind, fire, and storm.[3]

How Monkey Became a Trickster
(from Brazil)

In the tropics of Brazil, there was once a lovely garden where all kinds of fruit trees grew. Along with many other animals, a monkey lived in the garden. Often the creatures would gather for a dance, and when they did, the monkey would play his guitar to entertain them.

The trees of the garden provided food for the animals, and they could eat whenever they desired so long as they obeyed one rule. If they wanted some fruit, they had to bow low when they approached a tree, politely call its name, and say, "Please, let me taste of your fruit."

The animals had to be sure to pronounce the tree's correct name and to say "please." For instance, if they wanted figs, they had to say "Oh, Fig Tree, please give me a bite of your fruit." Otherwise, the tree would refuse to give them anything to eat. It was also important to leave fruit for other animals and not to strip the tree bare. That way, everyone would have something to eat, and there would be enough seeds left to produce new trees as the old ones became less fruitful and eventually died.

Though the fruit from every tree was delicious, in one remote corner of the garden stood the most magnificent tree of all. Standing taller than the rest, it had wide-spreading branches that hung heavy, full of luscious, round, rose-tinted fruit. It tempted all the animals to taste its offerings, but unfortunately none of them could recall its name because it was long and difficult to pronounce. Try as hard as they might to remember, when they reached the far-off tree, they could not remember its name.

In a little cottage on the opposite side of the garden lived an old woman who could name every fruit tree that grew there. Wanting to know what the special tree was called, the animals would often go to her. Yet the tree was so far away from her cottage they forgot its name by the time they came to it.

Finally, the monkey figured out what to do. Putting his guitar under his arm, he went to the old woman's cottage. When she told him the long and difficult name, he made up a little song, and strumming on his guitar, he repeated it over and over to himself as he strolled to the far corner where the fruit tree grew. As he went along, some of the other animals met him and inquired about the new ditty he was singing, but he never answered, marching on his way, playing his guitar, and singing his song that repeated the long, hard name.

At last, the monkey came to the tree. What a delicious aroma it had, filling the entire corner of the garden, and how beautiful it looked, the sun gleaming on its rose-tinted fruit! The monkey hurried to make his bow, pronounce correctly the name of the tree, and request its fruit with the word "please."

Some of the fruit fell at his feet. Eagerly he picked it up and took a huge bite. Oh, how he pinched his face in disgust. Never had anything that smelled so sweet tasted so bitter, sour, and nasty. The monkey at once tossed it away as far as he could throw it.

From that day forward, the monkey always remembered the tree's name and the little ditty he had sung to keep from forgetting it. Never did he eat the fruit again, but to amuse himself, he often gave it to the other animals just to laugh at the twisted faces they made.

COMMENTARY: From Elsie Spicer Eells' collection, a *pourquoi* in which a monkey again appears as a schemer, this time playing a guitar to help him achieve his aim.[4] His role as trickster is also combined with that of entertainer, a part which for centuries monkeys have been playing in real life for human beings though often in "unnatural ways" that are generally viewed in the West today as "relics of an ignorant past."[5] Based on its contents, this story from Brazil appears to contain a robust fusion of colonial Portuguese (*creole/crioulo*) and native elements as purportedly told by an *amah*, or nursemaid, to her young charges.[6]

The Fox and Monkey Thieves
(from the Aymara of Bolivia)

A fox and monkey left one night and came to the hut of a poor laborer. They were intent on stealing something to eat. The man inside had worked long hours that day and, much fatigued, now deeply slept. Yet on the dying embers of his fire were the still warm remnants of quinoa mush leftover from supper.

Scooping his paws inside the clay pot, the monkey ate to his fill, leaving a small amount. The fox next stuck his head into the pot's narrow opening and licked up the remains. His head, though, became caught inside, and try as he might, he could not unwedge it. In a muffled voice, he quietly begged, "Monkey, please find a rock to break the pot, or I will suffocate and die."

The monkey hurriedly felt in the darkness, but instead of a stone, his paw landed on the sleeping pongo's head. "Come here," he said to his friend in hushed tones. "I've found a large round stone perfect for you to crack the pot on."

"All right," the fox whispered.

Thwack went the pot against the pongo's head. Startled, the man woke in shock and fear but had enough presence of mind to grab the monkey crouching close by. The fox instantly ran off, leaving his friend behind.

Early the next morning, with the monkey tightly tethered, the man left for his patron's hacienda to give the monkey to his boss. The boss told the pongo, "We'll throw boiling water on him, and then we'll skin him, roll the meat in cornmeal, and fry it." They left to get the boiling water.

The fox was still lurking nearby and saw his friend tethered and tied up with strong cords. When the monkey caught sight of the fox, he cried sadly, "My troubles are beyond belief and seem to have no end. The owner of this estate has an unwed daughter and has said I must marry her today. He refuses to postpone the wedding."

"If what you say is true," replied the fox, "I'll set you free and gladly take your place for the sake of our friendship." And with those words, he quickly untied the monkey, who then tied the fox up—one, two, three—and fast fled the scene.

The sun burned almost directly overhead as the noon hour approached, and the patron and pongo returned with a pot of scalding water. The fox yelled, "Stop! I'll marry your daughter." But neither man paid the least attention, and they doused him.

Later that night, the fox regained his freedom. He gnawed the cords in two and left to bring revenge on the monkey.

Wandering through the night, the fox found the monkey on a mountainside, out in the open with no place to hide. The monkey saw the fox approaching and began to shake in fear. Then right above head, he eyed a ledge. He heard the fox shout, "I've got you now, you rascal."

The monkey reached up and put his paws against the ledge, pretending that it was about to fall. In a low, exhausted voice, he said, "Friend, I'm too tired to hold up this ledge any longer, but if I let go, we are dead. The ledge will crumble and crush us both, and what is worse, the avalanche will maim or kill the people below. You are stronger than I am. If you take my place, I'll go and bring back help in a jiffy."

The fox did as his friend asked and put his front paws along the ledge. Off ran the monkey as fast as he could, pretending to find aid to keep the rocks from sliding.

After a little time had passed, the fox grew tired from pressing against the ledge. He thought, "If I let go and the rocks start to fall, I can jump aside and not be hurt." So he let go and leapt to one side. But the ledge remained in place. "He's tricked me a second time. Now I'll surely have my revenge. I'll find the rogue and murder him or at least tear him apart."

Along a riverbank that night, he saw the monkey sitting on his haunches. A yellow half-moon had risen. By its faint light, the fox could tell that the rascal was eating something. The fox drew nearer, and the monkey said, "Ah, brother, I apologize. After I left you on the mountain path, I could find no one willing to help, even though I begged with all my might. Here, let me show I meant no harm and offer you some cheese."

The fox took the offering and swallowed it as if nothing were wrong. "Where did you steal this?" he asked.

"Swear you will do me no harm, and I'll tell you," answered the other.

The fox then promised that he would not take revenge for any of the past, and the monkey led him down to the river's fringe. The mirrored image of the half-moon glowed in the water.

"There, brother, is the stolen cheese. As you can see, I only took a small part of it. The rest I left for you." Scarcely were the monkey's words out of his mouth before the fox plunged into the river and drowned.

COMMENTARY: This talking beast story[7] presents a dubious friendship between two animals. Both are rogues, common roles for foxes and monkeys in folktales. The problem is that neither can nor should trust the other. Yet as the more gullible of the two, the fox continues to be tricked by the monkey and is incapable of profiting from experience with disastrous consequences as the result.

Quinoa is a Spanish word of Quechuan origin (*kinwa*) and refers to a seed or whole grain originating in the Andes around six thousand years ago as a key food. The Incas considered the grain sacred, calling it "chisaya mama," thus designating it "the mother of all grains."[8]

The Woman and the Monkey
(from the Arua of the Brazilian Amazon)

A husband and wife once went into the forest to set traps for monkeys and ground birds. The man imitated monkey calls, and many capuchins swarmed into the trees. He aimed an arrow toward the branches, and a monkey fell to the ground. He aimed another arrow, and a second monkey fell. Then another and another until his last arrow flew too far away and was lost.

The man collected the game he had shot and went to find his lost arrow. He told his wife to wait until he returned. To pass the time, she gathered dry grass and braided a necklace and a bracelet and wove a hat of straw. She then propped up one of the dead monkeys and decorated him with what she had made.

"How handsome," she said. "If he were human, he would look even better."

Something rustled on the ground, and when the woman turned to look in its direction, a handsome young man walked toward her. "Who are you?" she asked.

"I should ask you the same thing" came his reply.

"I was speaking with one of the monkeys and said that, if he could change into a man, he would be a very handsome fellow indeed."

"I am just that monkey! Follow me!" So she left with him.

As they made their way through the jungle, the dense tree limbs and vines seemed like a well-worn path to the monkey. He easily climbed up and down them.

A little later, the husband returned, but his wife was nowhere to be seen. He ignored the game he had shot and looked for her. When he could not find her, he went back to his home in sorrow.

He questioned everyone he met in the village. "Have you seen my wife?" Yet no one could answer him. He searched for her for a long time. One year passed. Then a second. Unbeknown to him, his wife already had hair on her hands and feet and was turning into a monkey. Even though she did not have a tail, she hoped to grow one.

One day the man came upon a sloth. He thought, "Why is this sloth on the trail in front of me, my wife now gone and I in such misery? I must kill the creature."

But the sloth read his thoughts. "Do not slay me. I can take you to your wife. She frolics with the monkeys in wild celebration. If you give me an axe and some resin for my bowstring, perhaps I could get her for you."

The husband gladly returned to his hut, got the axe and resin, and hurried back. "I am here, Grandpa!" he yelled to the sloth. Then the two went on their way and finally came upon his wife dancing with the monkeys, several of them frolicking together with her at the same time.

The sloth whispered to the man, "Wait here, and I will go and ask to dance with your wife. I'll take her down one path and another and another so they won't suspect anything. Then I will dance in your direction, and we will escape."

When the monkeys saw the sloth, they shouted, "Look! Grandpa's coming!" and they danced and hugged the woman tightly. "Come and join us!" they invited.

"Now it is my turn to dance with my granddaughter. You have danced with her long enough!" replied the sloth.

The monkeys let the sloth dance with the woman by himself, and the two danced for quite a while in the clearing. Then they went down one path and came back. Then they went down another path and came back. Soon they danced down another trail, this time going a little farther.

The dancing up and down different paths continued, with the sloth taking longer and longer to return to the clearing. After a bit, the monkeys quit paying any attention at all to the couple. The sloth and woman finally danced down the trail where the husband was waiting.

"Here is your wife," said the sloth. The three ran down the trail, the woman howling like a monkey the entire way until she fainted.

Back in the village, the shamans blew snuff over the woman and up her nostrils and through the powdered tobacco captured the woman's spirit. She came to herself, and when she revived, she explained how she had lived among the monkeys.

"I thought the monkey boy was a person, but when I followed him into the forest, I ended up among the monkeys." As soon as she spoke these words, she was forever lost to her husband.

COMMENTARY: A very earthy folktale[9] from the border region between Brazil and Bolivia,[10] this story has parallels to what anthropologist Betty Mindlin describes aa a group of indigenous myths from Amazonia in which women "allow themselves to be seduced perhaps because their men are always out hunting, always far away and inattentive."[11] Although both the husband and wife in the adaptation are together hunting for monkeys, the man does leave the woman alone in a clearing while he searches for a lost arrow. His neglect gives her an opportunity to run off with a handsome boy/monkey. This event represents a "crossing," defined as "a step across an invisible frontier that leads straight into uncharted territory."[12] In this case, the crossing is into the purely animal world of the forest.

No matter where a folktale originates, crossing a threshold has its perils. Only with difficulty can it be crossed over again, normally through the aid of a magical prescription. In the instance of the English tale "Tamlane," the title character vanishes, stolen by the Queen of Elfland. To save him, his betrothed must stand at Miles Cross between the witching night hour of twelve and one and perform certain rituals.[13] In "The Nunnehi and Other Spirit Folk,"[14] folklorist James Mooney embeds an anecdote of the Cherokee in which a hunter disappears for sixteen days during the winter. On returning to his village, he tells his friends that "the Little people had found him and taken him to their cave," where they fed and cared for him.[15] Once he had rested, they accompanied him halfway home, but when he forded a small creek to get back to the main trail, his legs froze. Not undergoing ritual purification, he died within a few days after having returned to his settlement.

It is, of course, true that indigenous stories in both South and North America do not sharply demarcate animal and human boundaries. For example, the animal world in these folktales often exhibits kinship patterns similarly found in human society. In "The Woman and the Monkey," the husband and the monkeys refer to the sloth as "Grandpa." And yet, as anthropologist Charles Hudson indicates in his study of Southeastern Indians of the United States, despite their closeness, people are still separate from animals.[16] Some action or event, however, might blur the boundary. In "The Woman and the Monkey," after running away, the wife has lived in extremely close personal contact with monkeys for an extensive period and, as a result, begins a transformation into a monkey. She sprouts hair on her hands and feet, and she wants to grow a tail. Furthermore, although this selection does not explicitly indicate how the woman survived during her time in the world of animals, she has likely eaten their food and thereby taken on a portion of their nature, making her re-crossing even more perilous once her husband captures her and the couple return to their village.

According to Mooney, standard native lore holds that those who consume anything from another realm cannot return to their own sphere and still live, unless they undergo a ritual treatment to restore them as humans and purge the desire for the other-worldly food.[17] In the Cherokee tale of "The Bear Man,"[18] Mooney recounts how a hunter has lived with a powerful bear and eaten the food it provided. When the man returns home, he must stay in isolation and not eat or drink anything for seven days. His wife, however, claims him after only four days have passed. The ritual not fully completed, he dies because his bear nature has not been purged. A similar plot occurs in another Cherokee story "The Underground Panthers."[19] Evidently, in "The Woman and the Monkey," the village shamans fail to bring back the woman's nature because, after the apparent completion of their purification ceremony, she is lost to her husband forever.

Another parallel between this Arua tale from Amazonia and North American indigenous stories is in the use of the medicinal properties of tobacco. In "The Woman and the Monkey," shamans use snuff to help the woman's spirit return to the human world after she has lived with the monkeys. The snuff fails, however, to heal her. In the Cherokee myth "Tsuwenathi: A Legend of Pilot Knob,"[20] a hunter crosses a threshold by entering a cave where kind spirit people dwell. Because he had not ritually purified himself by fasting, his legs feel "as if they were dead," causing him to stagger and fall to the ground. The cave inhabitants lift him up, and their "medicine man" revives him by rubbing "old tobacco" on his legs and makes "him smell it until he sneezed."[21]

The Monkey Who Begged for Misery
(from Haiti)

One morning, a monkey sat high up in a tree and watched a woman stroll down the path. She had a calabash perched on top of her head. Suddenly, she stumbled, and the gourd toppled off, all its sweet cane syrup spilling and spreading over the ground.

"Oh, Lord!" she cried. "What misery you've sent me! For these three days past, I've toted my gourd to sell syrup at the market. No calamity till now when it wobbled and fell." She then went on her way.

The monkey climbed down from his tree. "What meant she by this misery?" he thought and sniffed at the syrup. The sweet smell tempted him to taste it. He put in a finger and licked it. *Oh, so good!*

He stuck in his paw. The stickiness ran down his arm and mouth. He then lapped the thick liquid from the path. He clawed the ground for more, but all the tasty treat was gone. Still, the monkey craved it. So he sped as fast as he could go to Papa God.

"Good morning, Papa God. I've raced to you to beg and plead for you to send some misery my way."

"Don't you have misery enough, Brother Monkey. Why you ask for such? I know none in your condition who'd come and plead at my front door for more."

"Dear Papa God, I have tasted misery and know its sweetness. So now I come to you and beg. Do not deny me, please."

Monkey looked so sad a sight that Papa God gave in. "See those three sacks over there. No, not that one. Yes, those. Pick up the biggest and throw it over your back. That's right. You must walk and walk and walk until there are no trees along the path as far as you can see. Remember to do exactly as I say if you want more misery. When you see no trees around you in any direction, stop and open the sack. Now go away!"

Monkey thanked Papa God, hoisted the sack upon his back, and left. He walked and walked and walked, then walked some more. At last, he came to where there were no trees as far as he could see. He set down his load and patted his stomach as he longed for sweet misery. He untied the heavy sack and opened it.

RAOW RROWFF AR-ROOFF RUH-ROH and other barks and growls crescendoed from the sack, and five huge dogs jumped out, *SNARLING* and *SNAPPING.*

ZIP ZIP ZIP! Monkey took off down the road with the dogs on his heels. He soon ran out of breath and thought his end was near. He resigned himself to death when all at once a tree appeared before him. Monkey quickly scooted up its trunk, the dogs' fierce teeth nearly catching his tail. *HUH HUH HUH.* He panted fast and hard. Relieved, he rested safe on high.

And so Brother Monkey did not die from tasting too much misery. For Papa God had given him a tree.

COMMENTARY: The humor in this droll folktale derives from the monkey's misinterpretation of the word "misery." On her way to market, a woman drops her calabash (a dried gourd container) filled with cane syrup that she intends to sell. When she exclaims that the Lord has given her misery, the monkey overhears her and thinks she is referring to the syrup. After she walks away, the monkey tastes the sweet treat and begs God for more of this "misery." The optimistic theme is that, no matter how dire circumstances seem, "Papa God" will provide a way out, bringing the story to the often happy conclusion found in folktales.[22] The source for this retelling is *The Magic Orange Tree and Other Haitian Folktales.*[23]

The Monkey Girl
(from the Creek of the Southeastern United States)

An old woman had a grandson who was a great hunter. They lived together and grew corn, but raccoons and monkeys would sneak into the field and eat the crop. Although the grandson shot many of them, they continued to destroy the corn.

On day, a couple of girls came to see the old woman. They were very pretty, but she did not care for them. The young hunter, though, fell in love with one of the girls, and before long, they got married.

Every time he left to go hunting, he would ask his new bride to guard the corn until he came back, and early each day she would go out to the field to watch it. But now the hunter and his grandmother noticed the crop began to disappear faster than it had before.

Finally, the old lady told her grandson, "When your wife goes to the cornfield, follow her in secret and eye her closely."

The young man did as his grandmother directed. As he watched, his wife became a monkey and sang,

> Dungo, dungo,
> Dar-mar-lee,
> Co-dingo.
>
> Dungo, dungo,
> Dar-mar-lee,
> Co-dingo.
>
> Dungo, dungo,
> Dar-mar-lee,
> Co-dingo, dingo,
> Dar-mar-lee,
> Co-dingo.

As she sang, droves of monkeys arrived and began eating the corn.

When the young hunter returned to his grandmother, he told her what had happened. "Here," she said, "take your fiddle. When your wife comes home, play and sing the same tune she sang."

The wife soon returned from the field, and her husband said, "Here's a good song. Listen."

He began to sing,

> Dungo, dungo,
> Dar-mar-lee,
> Co-dingo.
>
> Dungo, dungo.
> Dar-mar-lee,
> Co-dingo.
>
> Dungo, dungo,
> Dar-mar-lee,
> Co-dingo, dingo,
> Dar-mar-lee,
> Co-dingo.

As the hunter sang, his bride began to cry. Then she started to howl and twist from one side to the next, all the while scratching her arms and legs. Before her husband had finished the song, course hair sprouted all over her. A tail now stuck out from under her skirt and bobbed up and down. When she saw it, she shrieked and ran chattering into the woods. She had turned into a monkey and was never heard from again.

COMMENTARY: This retelling of a tale of magical transformation comes from John R. Swanton's 1929 *Myths and Tales of the Southeastern Indians*.[24] Swanton, in turn, took the story from pioneering folklorist William Orrie Tuggle, whose unpublished work was housed in the Smithsonian Institution.[25] In the 1880s, Tuggle went to Oklahoma, then designated Indian Territory, and recorded the folklore of the Creek and Yuchi,[26] formerly the indigenous peoples of Georgia and Alabama.

Swanton acknowledges that this Creek tale is a borrowing of African origin.[27] Like stories of the trickster rabbit of the indigenous Southeast, the tale is part of what African American and Native American literature professor Jonathan Brennan describes as "overwhelming evidence" of the cultural exchanges of traditional literature between African Americans and Native Americans.[28] Brennan speculates that such fusions resulted from the time when Southeastern Native Americans such as the Creek, Cherokee, and other groups, as part of the South's plantation system, owned African American slaves.[29]

The Signifying Monkey and the Lion
(from the African American tradition)

Deep down in the jungle, so some say,
A monkey flapped his gums, both night and day,
Just looking for trouble to come his way.
Once, as he sat high up in his tree,
Strutting down the jungle trail, who should he see,
But old King Lion, proud as could be.

So up jumped the monkey and started to jabber.
"Mr. Lion," he said, "I been hearin' lots of blabber
From a brah who claims you ain't all that,
Claims you ain't no king, just some dried cat scat.
Says before he's through, he'll beat you black and blue,
Make you ache like a case of the Hong Kong flu.
And that ain't all. He says your mamma's crusty,
And your gray-headed granny smells right musty.
I could tell you more, but what's the use,
Cause that bad boy, when he cuts loose,
He'll beat your behind and cook your goose.

He'll mash your mouth and curb your purr.
He'll knock out your teeth and pull out your fur."

King Lion asked, "Who's talkin' trash? Who? Tell me who?"

The monkey signified, "He's bigger than you.
He's got long ears and a long nose, too.
He's as tall as a house with a coat of gray
And ain't worried none about no beast of prey
Cause, when his four wide feet begin to trompin',
They'll leave a cat like you half dead from the stompin'.

When he heard all that, Lion's tail kicked back,
And he bared his claws ready to attack.
He jumped through the jungle, tearin' up trees
When who should he meet but some chimpanzees.
"I ought to bite off your arms and break your knees
Just to show I'm the cat who can do what he please."

He then saw elephant on up the trail,
And he let out a roar, "I'm gonna whup your tail,
You flapped-eared, grinnin', cock-a-hoop freak,
Talkin' about me with your bull-twaddle speak."
Then he bebopped Elephant with a fast paw,
Drew a streak of blood down the pachyderm's jaw.
But that huge tusker just unrolled his trunk
And grabbed King Lion like a piece of junk.
He picked him up and slung him around
In a loop-da-loop, then flung him on the ground.

King Lion staggered up, gave a wheezy roar,
Reared on his hind legs still lookin' for more.
But Elephant blew such a trumpet blast
That Lion on his knees to the jungle floor crashed.
And when he rolled over to try and come back,
Elephant didn't cut the King of Beasts no slack.
He held him on the ground where he squirmed and gasped,
As he stomped on his belly and tromped on his face
Until he tore the King's tail clean out of place.

They fought like that till the sun sank low,
With Monkey in his tree just watchin' the show
Till the big bad bruiser let the scruffy cat go.
Then Monkey called out, "Who can that be?
I need me some glasses so I can see
If that's the King of Beasts whipped to a T,
All battered and bruised, more dead than alive—"

"Now, Monkey, I'm tired of your gate-mouth jive."

"Oh, shut your mouth. Don't even try to roar,
Or I'll come down and thrash you some more.

Get out of here. Get away from my tree,
Unless you want to feel on your head my pee."
Monkey cackled loud and jumped up and down,
Jumped so hard—*Pop Snap Break Bam*—he hit the ground.
He tried to run, but he slipped and tripped.
Like a streak of lightnin'—*Whip Zoom Zip*—
Pounced the battered old cat and the monkey gripped.
He held him down with both front feet
About to grind his behind like sausage meat.

The monkey's wife now had to have a go
And thought she'd in her two cent worth throw.
"Look here, Monkey, you deserve what you git
For bingein' on that signifyin' bit.
If I was the King, I'd reset your face
And kick your rear end up in its place."

"Now listen here," moaned the monkey in pain,
I think you the one I ought to blame
Cause, when on that limb I started to jump,
You pushed me down with a heavy thrump
And made it pop, snap clean in two
To git a mad bad cat to pay me my due."

Then before she could say a single word more,
Monkey, all pitiful to King Lion swore,
With a tear or two tricklin' out his eyes,
"Please, your majesty, I apologize.
If you in your wisdom just let me go,
I'll tell you a thing or two you ought to know."

The lion took his paws off the monkey's neck
And growled, "Make it quick, you spineless speck."
But before the cat could breathe or blink one eye.
Monkey scooted up in his tree so high,
King Lion, when he tried to pounce and snatch him,
Swatted only air and could not catch him.

"Hee! Hee!" hooted Monkey. "What I was gonna say
Is, if you ever come again and pass my way,
Growlin' and roarin' like a loud-mouth fool,
I'll enroll your ass in the elephant's school
And have him pound some sense into yourself
If I don't first knock it in myself."

"Monkey," said Lion, "there's no denyin'
You best stay put to continue signifyin',
Cause, if you come down, your trash talk's through,
For I don't aim to monkey with you!"

COMMENTARY: This anonymous poem is of African American

origin and belongs to the category of "toasts," which Robbins Burling defines as a type of oral performance art by skillful "street corner bards" in black communities.[30] Bruce Jackson emphasizes that the creation of toasts is often a communal endeavor, whereby members of the audience contribute sections of the narrative from versions of the same toast with which they are familiar.[31] Indeed, the same toast will have many versions, with performers freely borrowing from among the different renditions. In *Deep Down in the Jungle*, Roger D. Abrahams discusses several of these in relation to the escapades of the Signifying Monkey.[32] In *Get Your Ass in the Water and Swim Like Me*, Jackson offers additional renditions of the story that overlap with the toasts "The Poolshooting Monkey" and "The Partytime Monkey."[33] In my adaptation, the conclusion of variant 50D in Jackson served as a suggestion for the episode of the Signifying Monkey's wife inserting herself into his manipulation of King Lion.[34]

Besides the Abrahams' and Jackson's variants of the poem, many online versions provided additional sources for my adaptation. Musician and poet Doug Hammond has one of the few "clean" retellings.[35] Along with other artists, comedian Rudy Ray Moore[36] and the musical group Snatch and the Poontangs[37] use extremely explicit language in their performance of the poem/song on *YouTube*.

In their rough content and obscene language, poems such as toasts defy ideas of respectability and prudery embedded in both white middle-class families and the "respectable" elements of black society, according to Burling.[38] Often told through rhymed couplets, toasts recount tales of struggle by animals and men and are larded with violence and sex. Each line usually contains four stresses, although the number may be more or fewer to add variety to the meter.[39] From my reading of toasts, a consistent syllable count per line is not a strict consideration, therefore allowing for further metrical variation.

As a trickster and instigator of conflict between the lion and the elephant, the Signifying Monkey bears an interesting resemblance to the jackal Dimna in *The Fables of Bidpai*. In this story, which frames the narrative retold herein as "The Lessons of the Meddlesome Monkey and the Unheeded Bird," the jackal Dimna foments a quarrel between King Lion and the bull Shanzabeh. More severe than the lies of the Signifying Monkey, Dimna's falsehoods lead not just to a trouncing but to death— in this instance, that of Shanzabeh.

This ability of the trickster to stir up trouble where none exists gets to the heart of the meaning of "signifying." Abrahams says that the term has multiple meanings. Yet within the context of "The Signifying Monkey and the Lion," it suggests the trickster's skill to speak "with great innuendo, to carp, to cajole, to needle, and to lie" with the intent to foment discord between neighbors by telling tales.⁴⁰ Thus, through the power of speech, the Signifying Monkey trickster, even though he "rarely acts in these narrative poems," as scholar Henry Louis Gates notes, nonetheless by his language controls the actions of the more powerful characters, Lion and Elephant.⁴¹

Gates suggests correspondences between the Signifying Monkey and certain West African deities such as Eshu and Legba and their manifestations when they appear in the Western Hemisphere in countries like Haiti, Cuba, Brazil, and the United States.⁴² As described by Courlander, Eshu is a god of the Yoruba of Nigeria and is "the essence of uncertainty and accident" whose appearance brings "a flaw into the sequence of events ... that causes men to turn into unforeseen trails and trials."⁴³ Similarly, Legba of Benin's Fon people is the "spirit of accident and unaccountability."⁴⁴ In fact, an alternate name for Legba is *Aflakete*, which according to Hyde, means "I have tricked you."⁴⁵ Whether of Eshu or Legba, such attributes are applicable to the Signifying Monkey of toasts.

Chapter Notes

Preface

1. Zena Sutherland, *Children & Books*, 9th ed. (New York: Longman, 1997), 351.
2. Boria Sax, *The Mythological Zoo: Animals in Myth, Legend, and Literature* (New York: Overlook Duckworth, 2013), 16.
3. Desmond Morris, *Monkey* (London: Reaktion Books, 2013), 8–9.
4. Morris, 8.
5. "Common Spotted Cuscus," *Animalia*, n.d., pars. 1, 4, 6, and 8, https://www.animalia.bio/common-spotted-cuscus. Accessed 12 July 2023.
6. Ramon R. Ross, *Storyteller* (Columbus, OH: Charles E. Merrill, 1972), 17–18, 21, 24, 217–218.
7. Margaret Read MacDonald, *The Storyteller's Start-Up Book: Finding. Learning, Performing, and Using Folktales, Including Twelve Tellable Tales* (Little Rock, AR: August House, 1993), 11.
8. Christine Jenkins, "Concluding Our Story of Stories," *Story: From Fireplace to Cyberspace, Connecting Children and Narrative,* Papers Presented at the Allerton Park Institute, No. 39, ed. Betsy Hearne et al. (Monticello: University of Illinois, 1997), 106–107.
9. Norma J. Livo and Sandra A Rietz, *Storytelling: Process and Practice* (Littleton, CO: Libraries Unlimited, 1986), 97.
10. Jayanta Kar Sharma, "Oral Storytelling and Its Techniques," *International Journal of English Language, Literature, and Humanities* 4.2 (Feb. 2006): 273.
11. Augusta Baker and Ellin Greene, "Storytelling Preparation and Presentation," in *Jump Over the Moon: Selected Professional Readings*, ed. Pamela Barron and Jennifer Q. Burley (New York: Holt, 1984), 327.
12. Margaret Read MacDonald, *Twenty Tellable Tales: Audience Participation Folktales for the Beginning Storyteller* (New York: H.W. Wilson, 1986), 186.
13. Anne Pellowski, *The World of Storytelling* (New York: R.R. Bowker, 1977), 109.
14. MacDonald, *Twenty Tellable Tales*, viii.
15. Marjorie Y. Lipson and Karen K. Wixson, *Assessment and Instruction of Reading and Writing Difficulties: An Interactive Approach*, 4th ed. (Boston: Pearson, 2009), 40–41.
16. Baker and Greene, 327.
17. Morris, 186.
18. "Ape v. Monkey: What Are the Differences Between Apes and Monkeys?" *Safaris Africana*, n.d., par. 1, https://www.safarisafricana.com/ape-vs-monkey. Accessed 9 July 2023.
19. "Ape v. Monkey: What Are the Differences Between Apes and Monkeys?" par. 5.
20. Colin Peter Groves, "Monkey," *Britannica Online*, 27 June 2023, par. 1, https://www.britannica/animal/monkey. Accessed 10 July 2023.
21. Groves, "Monkey," par. 1.
22. "Barbary Macaque," *Folly Farm,* n.d., pars. 2, https://www.folly-farm.co.uk/.../barbary-macaque. Accessed 15 July 2023; Morris, 174.
23. "Ape v. Monkey: What are the Differences Between Apes and Monkeys?" pars. 9–11.
24. "Ape v. Monkey: What are the

Differences Between Apes and Monkeys?" par. 23.

25. "Oldest evidence of split between Old World monkeys and apes: Primate fossils are 25 million years old," *Science Daily*, 15 May 2013, pars. 2, 7, 10, https://www.sciencedaily.com. Accessed. 7 July 2023.

26. Peter Colin Groves, "Ape," *Britannica Online*, 4 May 2023, par. 1, https://www.britannica.com/animal/ape. Accessed 15 July 2023.

27. "What does it mean to be human?" *Smithsonian Institution, Museum of Natural History*, 15 August 2022, pars. 3 and 6, https://www.humanorigins.si.edu/evidence/genetics. Accessed 16 July 2023.

28. Birute M.F. Galdikas, "Orangutan," *Britannica Online*, 21 June 2023, par. 1, https://www.britannica.com/animal/orangutan. Accessed 25 July 2023.

29. John P. Rafferty, "Gibbon," *Britannica Online*, 28 Oct. 2021, pars. 1 and 3, https://www.britannica.com/animal/gibbon-primate. Accessed 25 June 2021.

30. Groves, "Ape," par. 4.
31. Morris, 177–178.
32. Groves, "Monkey," par. 1.
33. "Introduction to Monkeys," *Monkey Worlds*, n.d., par. 3, https://www.monkeyworlds.com. Accessed 12 July 2023.

Introduction

1. Max Luthi, *Once Upon a Time: On the Nature of Fairy Tales* (Bloomington: Indiana University Press, 1976), 96.

2. William Harmon, *A Handbook to Literature*, 12th ed. (Boston: Pearson, 2012), 204.

3. David L. Russell, *Literature for Children: A Short Introduction*, 5th ed. (Boston: Pearson, 2005), 197.

4. Sax, 17 and 27.
5. Charles Hudson, *The Southeastern Indians* (Knoxville: University of TN Press,1976), 139.
6. Sax, 17 and 42.
7. Sax, 17 and 36.
8. Sax, 17–18.
9. Joshua Mark, "Thoth," *World History Encyclopedia*, 26 July 2016, par. 3, https://www.worldhistory.org/Thoth. Accessed 6 Feb. 2019.

10. Phillippe Germond and Jacques Livet, *An Egyptian Bestiary: Animals in the Life and Religion in the Land of the Pharaohs*, trans. Barbara Mellor (London: Thames and Hudson, 2001), 89–90.

11. Hope B. Werness, "Monkey," in *The Continuum Encyclopedia of Animal Symbolism in Art*, illus. Joanne Benedict et al. (New York: Continuum, 2004), 279.

12. Martin Kemp, *The Human Animal in Western Art and Science* (Chicago: University of Chicago Press, 2007), 20.

13. Morris, 44–45.
14. *Pliny's Natural History*, trans. Philemon Holland, Vol 1, Book 8, Chapter 54 (London: George Barclay, 1847–48), 97–98.

15. Laura Gibbs, trans. *Aesop's Fables*, rev. ed. (New York: Oxford University Press, 2008), 229–230

16. Ben Edwin Perry, ed. and trans., *Babrius and Phaedrus* (Cambridge, MA: Harvard University Press, 1965), l.

17. *Pliny's Natural History*, vol. 1, chapter 54, book 8, 97.
18. Gibbs, 96–97.
19. Gibbs, 155–156.
20. Gibbs, 124.
21. Morris, 45.
22. Morris, 45.
23. Apuleius, *The Transformations of Lucius Otherwise Known as the Golden Ass*, trans. Robert Graves (1951; rpt. New York: Noonday, 1967), 237.

24. James Hall, *Dictionary of Subjects and Symbols in Art*, 2nd ed. (Boulder, CO: Westview Press, 2008), 23.

25. Janetta Rebold Benton, *The Medieval Menagerie: Animals in the Art of the Middle Ages* (New York: Abbeville, 1992), 90.

26. Morris, 46.
27. Hall, 23.
28. Benton, 90.
29. Hall, 23.
30. Laura Thipphawong, "Singeries: The Genre Paintings of Monkeys as Humans," *Arts Help*, 19 Nov. 2020, par. 1, https://www.artshelp.comsingeries-the-genre-paintings-of-monkeys-as-humans. Accessed 29 July 2023.

31. Thipphawong, par. 2.
32. Lucia Impelluso, *Nature and Its Symbols*, trans. Stephen Sartarelli (Los Angeles: J. Paul Getty Museum, 2003), 198.

33. "The Singerie: Monkeys Acting as Humans in Art," *The Public Domain Review*, 19 July 2016, par. 1, https://www.publicdomainreview.org/collection/the-singerie-monkeys-acting-as-humans-in-art. Accessed 19 July 2023.
34. Thipphawong, par. 3.
35. Thipphawong, par. 5.
36. Thipphawong, par. 5.
37. Thipphawong, par. 6.
38. Jean H. Duffy, *Signs and Designs: Art and Architecture in the Work of Michel Butor* (Liverpool: Liverpool University Press, 2003), 267.
39. Sax, 23.
40. Sax, 22.
41. Kemp, 185.
42. Morris, 186.
43. Morris, 187.
44. Rowena Shepherd and Rupert Shepherd, *1000 Symbols: What Shapes Mean in Art and Myth* (London: Thames and Hudson, 2002), 180.
45. Werness, 281.
46. Werness, 281.
47. Werness, 281.
48. Morris, 18.
49. Sutherland, 207.
50. Sutherland, 207.
51. H.T. Francis and E.J. Thomas, eds. *Jataka Tales Selected and Edited with Introduction and Notes* (Cambridge: Cambridge University Press, 1916), 2.
52. Sax, 21.
53. Shepherd and Shepherd, 180.
54. David Fontana, *The Secret Language of Symbols: A Visual Key to Symbols and Their Meanings* (San Francisco: Chronicle, 1993), 90.
55. Anthony C. Yu, trans., *The Journey to the West*, Vol. 1 (Chicago: University of Chicago Press, 1977), 2.
56. Yu, 6.
57. B.R. Deepak, "Hanuman and Sun Wukong: How Indian and Chinese Literary Images Integrate," *The Sunday Guardian*, 27 Dec. 2020, par. 2, https://www.sundayguardianlive.com/news/hanuman-sun-wukong-indian-chinese-literary-images-integrate. Accessed 29 Nov. 2023.
58. Yu, 10.
59. "Drawing Parallels: Are All the Monkey Gods Incarnations of Lord Hanuman?" *FormFluent*, 6 Oct. 2023, pars. 7–11, https://www.formfluent.com/blogs/blog/drawing/parallels-are-all-the-monkey-gods-incarnations-of-lord-hanuman. Accessed 29 Nov. 2023.
60. "Hanuman: The Perfect Hero," *Glorian*, n.d., par. 3, https://glorian.org/learn/courses-and-lectures/teachings-of-the-hindu-gods/hanuman-the-perfect-hero. Accessed 17 Feb. 2019.
61. Lewis Hyde, *Trickster Makes This World: Mischief, Myth, and Art* (1998; rpt. New York: Farrar, Straus, and Giroux, 2010), 353.
62. Morris, 7.
63. Morris, 8–9.

The Middle East and India

1. Inea Bushnaq, comp. and trans., in *Arab Folktales* (New York: Pantheon, 1986), 277.
2. George Herbert Palmer, trans., *The Odyssey of Homer*, ed. Howard Porter (New York: Bantam, 1962), 139.
3. Sax, 23.
4. E.F. Burton, *Reminiscences of Sport in India* (London: W. H. Allen, 1885), 123–124.
5. Charles Swynnerton, adapt., *Indian Nights' Entertainment: Or, Folk-Tales from the Upper Indus*, illus. by native hands (London: Elliot Stock, 1892), 7.
6. V.S. Vernon Jones, trans., *Aesop's Fables: A New Translation*, illus. Arthur Rackham (London: William Heinemann, 1912), 61.
7. Joseph Jacobs, ed., *Indian Fairy Tales*, illus. John D. Batten (London: David Nutt, 1892), ix.
8. Ellen C. Babbitt, adapt., *More Jataka Tales* illus. Ellsworth Young (New York: Century, 1922), 3–7.
9. Robert Chalmers, trans., *The Jataka or Stories of the Buddha's Former Births*, Vol. 1, ed. E.B. Cowell (Cambridge: Cambridge University Press, 1895), 222–227.
10. Francis and Thomas, 10.
11. Francis and Thomas, 103–107.
12. Babbitt, *More Jataka Tales*, 24–26.
13. Chalmers, 118–119.
14. W.H.D. Rouse, trans., *The Jataka or Stories of the Buddha's Former Births*, Vol. 2, ed. E.B. Cowell (Cambridge: Cambridge University Press, 1985), 237–239.
15. Rouse, 238.

16. Francis and Thomas, 45–47.
17. Rouse, 262–263.
18. Rouse, 48–49.
19. Nick Oetken, "Do monkeys throw poop in self-defense?" *TheGunZone*, 10 Dec. 2023, items 1, 4–6, 8, 11, and 13, https://www.thegunzone/do-monkeys-throw-poop-in-self-defense. Accessed 12 Dec. 2023.
20. H.T. Francis and R.A. Neil, trans., *The Jataka or Stories of the Buddha's Former Births*, Vol. 3, ed. E.B. Cowell (Cambridge: Cambridge University Press, 1987), 225–227.
21. Chalmers, 54–56
22. Francis and Thomas, 23–25.
23. Paul Lunde, "Kalila Wa Dimna: In the Fables, Wit and Wisdom," *Aramco World Magazine* 23.4 (July/Aug. 1972): 18.
24. Sir Thomas North, trans., *The earliest English version of the Fables of Bidpai, "The Morall Philosophie of Doni,"* ed. Joseph Jacobs (London: David Nutt, 1888), 73–74 and 181–184.
25. Doris Lessing, Introduction, in *Kalila and Dimna: Selected Fables of Bidpai*, adapt. Ramsey Wood, illus. Margaret Kilrenny (New York: Knopf, 1980), x.
26. Cuthbert McEvoy, *Ion Keith-Falconer: The Scholar Missionary* (London: Carey Press, 1900), 26–27, 45, and 54–56.
27. I.G.N. Keith-Falconer, trans., *Kalilah and Dimnah or The Fables of Bidpai* (Cambridge: Cambridge University Press, 1895), vii.
28. Keith-Falconer, trans., 4 and 55–56.
29. Ramsey Wood, adapt., *Kalila and Dimna: Selected Fables of Bidpai*, illus. Margaret Kilrenny (New York: Knopf, 1980), 49–53 and 160–163.
30. Wood, 261–262.
31. Kate Douglas Wiggin and Nora Archibald Smith, comps., *The Talking Beasts*, illus. Harold Nelson (New York: Grosset and Dunlap, 1911), 89.
32. G.L. Anderson, ed., *Masterpieces of the Orient, Enlarged Edition* (New York: Norton, 1977), 169.
33. B.A. van Nooten, Introduction, in *Ramayana*, adapt. William Buck, illus. Shirley Triest (Berkeley: University of California Press, 1976), xv.
34. van Nooten, xiii.
35. Robert P. Goldman, "Ramayana," *Encyclopedia of Modern Asia*, Vol. 5, ed. David Levinson and Karen Christiansen (New York: Thompson-Gale, 2002), 51.
36. van Nooten, xv.
37. van Nooten, xv–xvi.
38. R.K. Narayan, *The Ramayana: A Shortened Modern Version of the Indian Epic*, illus. R.K. Laxman (New York: Viking: 1972), x.
39. Goldman, 51.
40. van Nooten, xx.
41. Subhamoy Das, "Find Out How Hinduism Defines Dharma: Learn About the Path of Righteousness," *Learn About Religions*, 25 June 2019, pars. 2 and 4. https://www.learnreligions.com/what-is-dharma-1770048. Accessed 3 Jan. 2024.
42. van Nooten, xx.
43. Huston Smith, *The Illustrated World's Religions: A Guide Our Wisdom Traditions* (San Francisco: Harper, 1994), 49.
44. van Nooten, xvii–xviii.
45. Publisher's Preface, *Valmiki's Ramayana: King Rama's Way*, adapt. William Buck, illus. Shirley Triest (Berkeley: University of California Press, 1976), ix–x.
46. Narayan, xi.
47. P.V. Ramaswami Raju, adapt. and comp., *Indian Fables*, illus. F. Caruthers Gould (London: Swan Sonneschein, 1901), 96–98.
48. Catherine T. Bryce, comp., *Fables from Afar*, illus. Ada Budell (New York: Newson, 1910), 3–9.
49. Raju, 6–7.
50. Maive Stokes, comp. and trans., *Indian Fairy Tales* (London: Ellis and White, 1880), 41–50.
51. Stokes, Preface, v, and "The Monkey Prince," 50.
52. "Nagas: Their History, Life, and Customs," *Facts and Details*, n.d., pars. 1–4, https://www.factsanddetails.com/southeast-asia/Myanmar/sub5_5dentry-3933.html. Accessed 4 Jan. 2024.
53. Panchali Battaharyal, Tarum Tapas Mukherjee, and Swayam Prabha Satpathy, "Cultural Traditions of the Lotha Nagas: Analyzing the Folktales of Nzanmongi Jasmine Patton's *A Girl Swallowed by a Tree: Lotha Nagas Tales Retold*," *International Journal of Early*

Childhood Special Education 14.5 (2022): 4019.
54. Howard E. Hutton, Introduction, in *The Lhota Nagas*, by J.P. Mills (London: Macmillan 1922), xii.
55. J.P. Mills, *The Lhota Nagas* (London: Macmillan, 1922), 184–185.
56. Mills, 185n.2.
57. Mills, 185n.1.
58. Editors of *Encyclopedia Britannica*, "Tung Tree," *Britannica Online*, 10 April 2019, par.1, https://www.britannica.com/plant/tung-tree. Accessed 19 May 2022.
59. Mills, 222–224.
60. Mills, 26n.1.
61. "Tokhu Emong 2024—Thursday, November 7, to Friday, November 15," n.d., pars. 1–4, https://www.festivalsof India.in/tokhu_emong. Accessed 5 Jan. 2024.
62. Mills, 175.
63. Animals Network Team, "Sambur," *Animals Network*, 2018, pars. 1–2 and 10, https://www.animals.net/sambar. Accessed 5 Jan. 2024.
64. "Sambar Deer," *Wikipedia*, 29 Nov. 2023, pars. 20–21, 26, and 29–30, https://www.en.wikipedia.org/wiki/Sambar_deer. Accessed 6 Jan. 2024.
65. Max Traweek and Roy Welch, "Exotics in Texas," Texas Parks and Wildlife Department, April 1992, par.1, https://tpwd.texas.gov/publications/pwdpubs/media/pwd_bk_w7000_0206.pdf. Accessed 6 Jan. 2024.
66. Cecil Henry Bompas, trans., *Folklore of the Santal Parganas* (London: David Nutt, 1909), 212–214.
67. Editors of *Encyclopedia Britannica*, "Santhal," *Britannica Online*, 25 Sept. 2023, par. 1, https://www.britannica.com/topic/Santhal. Accessed 7 Jan 2024.
68. Bompas, 6.
69. Bompas, 128–129.
70. Bompas, 129.
71. Bompas, 56–60.
72. Bompas, 232–234.
73. Editors of *Encyclopedia Britannica*, "Sesame," *Britannica Online*, 22 Dec. 2023, pars. 1 and 4, https://www.britannica.com/plants/sesame-plant. Accessed 5 Jan. 2024.
74. "The Dhoti and Why It's So Important in India," *Get Ethnic*, n.d., par. 1, https://www.getethnic.com/blogs/dhoti-indian-outfit. Accessed 7 Jan. 2024.
75. "The Dhoti and Why It's So Important in India," pars. 6–7.
76. Vivekananda, "Sugar Palm Fruit and Its Health Benefits," *Hub Pages*, 6 Sept. 2103, pars. 1–2, https://www.discover.hubpages.com/food/Sugar_Palm_fruit_and_its_health_benefits. Accessed 7 Jan. 2024.
77. Karen Veazey, "Jaggery: Is the superfood sweetener better for you than sugar?" *Medical News Today*, 30 June 2021, pars. 1–3 and 6, https://www.medicalnewstoday.com/articles/jaggery. Accessed 6 Jan. 2024.
78. Morris, 51 and 55.
79. Morris, 56–57.
80. John Payne, trans., *The Book of the Thousand Nights and One Night: Now First Completely Done Into English Prose and Verse, From the Original Arabic*, Vol. 4 (London: The Villon Society, 1901), 141–143.
81. Morris, 57.
82. Voltaire, *Candide* in *Candide, Zadig, and Selected Stories*, trans. Donald M. Frame (New York: New American Library, 1961), 48–51.
83. Morris, 59–60.
84. Barbara G. Walker, "Crone," in *The Woman's Encyclopedia of Myths and Secrets* (San Francisco: Harper, 1996), 187.
85. Walker, "Hag," 367.

Africa

1. Vincent Muli Wa Kitutu, adapt. and comp., *East African Folktales: From the Voice of Mukamba*, illus. Kelly Matthews (Little Rock, AR: August House, 1997), 23–25.
2. Edward Steere, comp. and trans., *Swahili Tales, As Told by the Natives of Zanzibar* (London: Bell and Daldy, 1870), 1–9.
3. George W. Bateman, comp. and trans., *Zanzibar Tales Told by the Natives of the East Coast of Africa*, Walter Bobbett (Chicago: A.C. McClurg, 1901), 17–28.
4. Andrew Lang, ed., *The Lilac Fairy Book*, illus. H.J. Ford (New York: Longmans, Green, 1910), 42–53.
5. A.K. Ramanujan, comp. and trans., *Folktales from India: A Selection of Oral

Tales from Twenty-Two Languages, illus. Jenny Vandeventer (New York: Pantheon, 1991), 53–54.

6. Ellen C. Babbitt, adapt, *Jataka Tales*, illus. Ellsworth Young (New York: Century, 1912), 3–9.

7. Chalmers, 142–143.

8. Rouse, 110–112.

9. Francis and Neil, 87–88.

10. Keigo Seki, comp., *Folktales of Japan*, trans. Robert J. Adams (1956–1957; rpt. Chicago: University of Chicago Press, 1963), 25–27.

11. Seki, 26.

12. Seki, 26.

13. Yei Theodora Ozaki, comp., *The Japanese Fairy Book*, illus. Kakuzo Fujiyama (New York: E.P. Dutton, 1903), 189–202.

14. Ozaki, 202.

15. Kitutu, 67–68.

16. Huynh Quang Nhuong, *The Land I Lost: Adventures of a Boy in Vietnam*, illus. Vo Dinh Mai (New York: Harper and Row, 1982), 85–90.

17. James Honey, comp., *South-African Folk-Tales* (New York: Baylor and Taylor, 1910), 84–86.

18. Honey, 1–3.

19. Oyekan Owomoyela, *Yoruba Trickster Tales* (Lincoln: University of NE Press, 1997), ix.

20. F.A. Steel and R.C. Temple, comps., *Wide-Awake Stories: A Collection of Tales Told by Little Children, Between Sunset and Sunrise* (Bombay: Education Society's Press, 1884; London: Trubner and Co., 1884), 69–72 and 243–246.

21. Jacobs, *Indian Fairy Tales*, 17–20.

22. Francis and Neil, 199.

23. Francis and Neil, 200.

24. Joel Chandler Harris, *The Complete Tales of Uncle Remus*, ed. Richard Chase, illus. A.B. Frost et al. (Boston: Houghton Mifflin, 1955), 246–251.

25. Harris, 251.

26. Nhuong, 87–88.

27. Honey, 14–18.

28. Captain A.O. Vaughan, adapt. and comp., *Old Hendrik's Tales*, illus. F.A. Shepherd (London: Longmans, Green, 1904), 11–27.

29. Vaughan, 29–45.

30. Heli Chatelain, comp. and trans. *Folk-Tales of Angola: Fifty Tales with Ki-mbundu Text, Liberal English Translation, Introduction, and Notes* (Boston: Houghton Mifflin, 1894), 182–188.

31. Harris, 6–8.

32. James Mooney, *James Mooney's History, Myths, and Sacred Formulas of the Cherokee*, 1900 (Fairview, NC: Historical Images, 1992), 271–273.

33. John R. Swanton, *Myths and Tales of the Southeastern Indians* (Washington, D.C.: Government Printing Office, 1929), 68.

34. David Elton Gay, "On the Interaction of Traditions: Southeastern Rabbit Tales as African-Native American Folklore," in *When Brer Rabbit Meets Coyote: African-Native American Literature*, ed. Jonathan Brennan (Urbana and Chicago: University of Illinois Press, 2003), 105.

35. Vaughan, 4–5.

36. Virginia Haviland and Margaret N. Coughlan, *Yankee Doodle's Literary Sampler of Prose, Poetry, and Pictures, Being an Anthology of Diverse Works Published for the Edification and/or Entertainment of Young Readers in America Before 1900* (New York: Crowell, 1974), 277.

37. Barbara Kiefer, Susan Hepler, and Janet Hickman, *Charlotte Huck's Children's Literature*, 9th ed. (Boston: McGraw Hill, 2007), 88.

38. Kiefer, 285.

39. Nicholas Hudson, "'Hottentots,' and the Evolution of European Racism," *Journal of European Studies* 34.4 (Dec 2004): 309.

40. "Hottentot," Def. 1b, *Oxford English Dictionary*, 2nd ed., Vol. 7, 1989.

41. Penelope Andrews, "Jail time for South African woman using racial slur sets new precedent," *Mail & Guardian*, 3 April 2018, pars. 1 and 3–4, https://www.mg.coza/article/2018-04-03-jail-time-for-south-african-woman-using-racial-slur-sets-new-precedent. Accessed 22 Sept. 2023.

42. Chatelain, 168–173.

43. Gerald Moser, "Heli Chatelain: Pioneer of a National Language and Literature for Angola," *Research in African Literatures* 14.4 (Winter 1983): 516.

44. Chatelain, 16.

45. Moser, 524.

46. Chatelain, vii.

47. Chatelain, 22.

48. Chatelain, 22.
49. John Kelly Thorton and William Gervaise Clarence-Smith, "Angola," *Britannica Online*, 3 Oct. 2023, par. 11, https://www.britannica.com/place/Angola. Accessed 4 Oct. 2023.
50. W.H.I. Bleek and L.C. Lloyd, comps. and trans., *Specimens of Bushman Folklore* (London: George Allen, 1911), 254–259.
51. George McCall Theal, Introduction, in *Specimens of Bushman Folklore*, xxxiv.
52. Theal, xxxi–xxxii.
53. Theal, xxxvii–xxviii.
54. L.C. Lloyd, Preface, in *Specimens of Bushman Folklore*, ix.
55. Lloyd, viii.
56. Lloyd, vii–xvi.
57. W.H.I. Bleek, *Reynard the Fox in South Africa: Or, Hottentot Fables and Tales* (London: Trubner and Co., 1864), 42–43.
58. "San," n.d., par. 1, https://www.krugerpark.co.za/africa_bushmen.html. Accessed 15 Aug. 2019.
59. Oswin R.A. Kohler, Anthony Trail, et al. "Khoisan Languages," *Britannica Online*, 10 Oct. 2016, par. 1, https://www.britannica.com/topic/Khoisan-Languages. Accessed 19 Aug. 2019.
60. "The San," *South African History Online*, 11 Dec. 2018, pars. 1–3, 12, https://www.sahistory.org.za/article.san. Accessed 19 Aug. 2019.
61. "The San," pars. 17–20.
62. Sir James Edward Alexander, *An Expedition of Discovery into the Interior of Africa, Through the Hitherto Undescribed Countries of the Great Namaquas, Boschmans, and Hill Damaras*, Vol. 2 (London: Henry Coburn, 1838), 234–235.
63. Alexander, Vol. 1, vi.
64. Peter Farb, *Word Play: What Happens When People Talk* (New York: Vintage, 1973), 238.
65. Alexander, Vol. 2, 234.
66. "Nama People," *Exploring Africa*, n.d., pars. 1, 3–6, https://www.exploringafrica.com/en/namibia/nama/nama-people. Accessed 5 Aug. 2019.
67. Robert H. Nassau, comp. and trans., *Where Animals Talk: West African Folk Lore Tales* (1912; rpt. Westport, CT: Negro Universities Press, 1970), 233.
68. Nassau, 231.
69. Elizabeth Prine Pauls, "Fang," *Britannica Online*, 9 Feb. 2007, pars. 1–3, https://www.britannica.com/topicFang-people. Accessed 2 Aug. 2019.
70. Elphinstone Dayrell, comp., *Folk Stories from Southern Nigeria, West Africa* (London: Longmans, Green, 1910) 46–48.
71. Dayrell, 64–65.
72. Andrew Lang, Introduction, in *Folk Stories from Southern Nigeria, West Africa*, comp. Elphinstone Dayrell (London: Longmans, Green, 1910), vii.
73. Lang, Introduction, in *Folk Stories from Southern Nigeria West*, xiii.
74. Lang, Introduction, in *Folk Stories from Southern Nigeria West*, viii.
75. Ibo Cbanga and Amy Tikkanen, "Juju," *Britannica Online*, 19 July 2017, par. 2, https://www.britannicaonline.com/topic/juju-magic. Accessed 1 Aug. 2019.
76. Oluseye, Ojo, "Why Unity Is Elusive to Nigeria," *The Sun: Voice of a Nation*, 1 Oct. 2017, par. 5, https://www.sunnewsonline.com/why-unity-is-elusive-to-nigeria. Accessed 9 Sept. 2023.
77. Harold Courlander, comp., *A Treasury of African Folklore: The Oral Literature, Traditions, Myths, Epics, Tales, Recollections, Wisdom, Sayings, and Humor of Africa* (New York: Crown, 1975), 236–238.
78. Courlander, 233–234.
79. Justin Findlay, "The Largest Ethnic Groups in Nigeria," *World Atlas*, 18 July 2019, pars. 2–4, https://w.worldatlas.com/articles/largest-ethnic-groups-in-nigeria. Accessed 10 Aug. 2019.
80. Courlander, 185.
81. Robert S. Rattray, comp. and trans., *Akan-Ashanti Folk-Tales*, illus. Ashanti, Fanti, and Ewe tribe members (1930; rpt. London: Oxford University Press, 1969), 45–47.
82. Amy McKenna, "Ghana," *Britannica Online*, 28 March 2023, par. 30, https://www.britannica.com/place/Ghana. Accessed 10 April 2023.
83. Thinley Kalsang Bhutia, "Asante," *Britannica Online*, 26 Dec. 2017, par. 1, https://www.britannica.com/topic/Asante. Accessed 10 April 2023.
84. Gloria Lotha, "Asante Empire," *Britannica Online*, 19 April 2023, pars.

1 and 3, https://www.britannica,com/place/Asante-empire. Accessed 1 May 2023.
85. Rattray, vi.
86. Rattray, v.
87. Rattray, vi.
88. Rattray, xi–xii.

Western Europe

1. Ben Edwin Perry, ed. and trans., *Babrius and Phaedrus* (Cambridge, MA: Harvard University Press, 1965), 613.
2. Gibbs, 301.
3. Perry, xxxv.
4. Robert Temple, Introduction, in *Aesop: The Complete Fables*, trans. Olivia Temple and Robert Temple (London: Penguin Books, 1998), ix.
5. Jack Zipes, *The Irresistible Fairy Tale: The Cultural and Social History of a Genre* (Princeton, NJ: Princeton University Press, 2012), 10.
6. Perry, "The King of the Apes," 320–322; "The Ape and the Fox," 372–373; and "The Rule of King Lion," 322–325."
7. Gibbs, xxi–xxii.
8. F.R.D. Goodyear, "Minor Poetry: Phaedrus," in *The Cambridge History of Classical Literature: II, Latin Literature*, ed. E.J. Kenney (New York: Cambridge University Press, 1982), 626.
9. Robert Temple, Introduction, xv.
10. Perry, 50–51, 70–73, and 100–101.
11. Gibbs, xxii–xxiii.
12. Gibbs, xxiii.
13. Jones, 26–27, and 48.
14. Gibbs, 124 and 229–230.
15. Lucian, *Lucian*, trans. A.M. Harmon, Vol 3. (1913; rpt. London: William Heinemann, 1960), 1–81.
16. Lucian, 31.
17. Lucian, 9.
18. Lucian, 23–25.
19. Lucian, 55.
20. C.D.N. Costa, trans., *Lucian: Selected Dialogues* (New York: Oxford University Press, 2005), vii and xii–xiv.
21. Jean de La Fontaine, Livre IV, No. 7, *Les Fables de La Fontaine*, n.d., https://www.mesfables.com-4/07-le-singe-et-le-dauphin.html. Accessed 15 Sept. 2023.
22. Emile Chambry, trans. *Esope Fables*, 2nd ed. (Paris: Les Belles Lettres, 1927), 134–135.
23. Oliva Temple and Robert Temple, trans., *The Complete Fables: Aesop* (London: Penguin Books, 1998), 226.
24. Howard E. Hugo, "Masterpieces of Neoclassicism," Introduction, in *The Norton Anthology of World Masterpieces*, 4th ed., Vol. 2 (New York: Norton, 1979), 9.
25. Morris, 46.
26. Voltaire, 48–51.
27. Morris, 56.
28. Morris, 56.
29. Morris, 56.
30. Colin Peter Groves, "Baboon," *Britannica*, 10 March 2023, par. 1, https://britannicaonline.com/animal/baboon. Accessed 27 Sept. 2023.
31. "Black Howler Monkey," *Alexandria Zoo*, n.d., pars. 1 and 3, https://www.thealexandriazoo.com/Black/Howler/Monkey.html. Accessed 27 Sept. 2023.
32. Morris, 61.
33. Morris, 56 and 61.

Tibet, Korea, Southeast Asia, and China

1. Bryce, 45–46.
2. F. Anton Von Schiefner, trans., *Tibetan Tales Derived from Indian Sources*, trans. from German W.R.S. Ralston (London: Kegan Paul, Trench, Trubner, 1906), 352.
3. Schiefner, 352.
4. Schiefner, 352.
5. Schiefner, 352.
6. Chalmers, 135–136.
7. Chalmers, 136.
8. Chalmers, 136.
9. Chalmers, 136.
10. "Karaka (tree) facts for kids," *Kids Encyclopedia Facts*, 26 July 2023, par. 1, https://www.kids.kiddle.co/Karaka_(tree). Accessed 9 Sept. 2023.
11. Schiefner, 348–349.
12. R. Spencer Hardy, trans., *A Manual of Budhism [sic] in Its Modern Development* (London: Partridge and Oakey, 1853), 113–114.
13. "Diospyros Malabarica—Tinduka," 28 April 2020, pars. 1–2, 5, and 11, https://ayurwiki.org/Ayurwiki/Diospyros_malabarica_-_Tinduka. Accessed 11 Sept. 2023.

14. Bryce, 46–49.
15. Schiefner, 353.
16. Fredrick Hyde-Chambers and Audrey Hyde-Chambers, eds., *Tibetan Folk Tales*, illus. Kusho Ralla. (Boulder, CO: Shambala, 1981), 96.
17. Mark Schumacher, "China—Buddhist Monkey Lore," in *Monkey in Japan, Page Two—India and China Lore*, 1995–2015, par. 2, https://www.onmarkproductions.com/html/monkey-india-china-p2.html. Accessed 27 Sept. 2017.
18. Nhuong, 93.
19. Berta Metzger, comp., *Tales Told in Korea*, illus. Arthur Y. Park (New York: Frederick A. Stokes, 1932), 176–177.
20. Ernest Thompson Seton, comp., *Famous Animal Stories: Animal Myths, Fables, Fairy Tales, Stories of Real Animals* (New York: Brentano's, 1932), 80.
21. Norma J. Livo and Dia Cha, eds., *Folk Stories of the Hmong: Peoples of Laos, Thailand, and Vietnam*, illus. Anthony Chan, photo. Michael Mancarella (Englewood, CO: Libraries Unlimited, 1991), 44.
22. Wu Ch'eng-en, *Monkey*, trans., Arthur Waley (New York: John Day, 1943), 11–84.
23. Yu, 65–197.
24. Robert E. Hegel, "Literature—China," *Encyclopedia of Modern Asia*, Vol. 3, ed. David Levinson and Karen Christiansen (New York: Thompson-Gale, 2002), 486.
25. C.A.S. Williams, *Outlines of Chinese Symbolism and Art Motives*, 3rd rev. ed. (New York: Dover, 1976), 327.
26. Williams, 315–316.
27. Williams, 316.
28. Williams, 171.
29. Williams, 316.
30. Williams, 235–236.
31. Williams, 236.
32. Williams, 236.
33. Williams, 235.
34. Mae Hamilton, "Jade Emperor," *Mythopedia*, par. 1, 1 Dec. 2022, https://www.mythopedia.com/topics/jade-emperor. Accessed 20 Jan. 2024.
35. Hamilton, pars. 10–12.
36. Hamiliton, par. 15.
37. Wolfram Eberhard, ed. and trans., *Chinese Fairy Tales and Folk Tales* (New York: Dutton, 1938), 139–140.

Japan and the Philippines

1. Basil Hall Chamberlain, comp. and trans. *Aino Folk-Tales* (London: The Folk-Lore Society, 1888), 17–18.
2. Chamberlain, 4.
3. Chamberlain, 3.
4. qtd. in Edward B. Tylor, Introduction, in *Aino Folk-Tales*, comp. and trans. Basil Hall Chamberlain (London: The Folk-Lore Society, 1888), v.
5. "The Ainu: The little-known indigenous people of Japan and Russia," *The Vintage News*, 4 Oct. 2016, par. 6, https://www.thevintagenews.com2016/10/4theainu. Accessed 7 Aug. 2019.
6. Kristen Refring, "Ainu," *Encyclopedia of Modern Asia*, ed. David Levinson and Karen Christiansen, Vol. 1 (New York: Scribner's, 2002), 72.
7. "Japan to recognize indigenous Ainu people for first time," *The Straits Times*, 15 Feb. 2019, pars. 1 and 6, https://www.straitstimes.com/asia/east-asia/japan-to-recognize-indigenous-ainu-people-for-first-time. Accessed 6 Aug. 2019.
8. Fanny Hagin Mayer, ed. and trans., *Ancient Tales in Modern Japan* (Bloomington: Indiana University Press, 1984), 302–303.
9. Andrew Lang, ed., *The Crimson Fairy Book*, illus. H.J. Ford (1903; rpt. New York: Longmans, Green, 1947), 187–190; Mayer, 294; Ozaki, 202–213; Seki, 15–16.
10. Post Wheeler, trans., *Tales from the Japanese Storytellers*, comp. and ed. Harold G. Henderson (Rutland, VT: Tuttle, 1964), 11–19.
11. Harold G. Henderson, comp. and ed., Introduction, in *Tales from the Japanese Storytellers*, trans. Post Wheeler (Rutland, VT: Tuttle, 1964), ix.
12. Ozaki, vi.
13. Ozaki, vi.
14. Ozaki, 148–152.
15. Morris, 83.
16. Sutherland, 180.
17. Norma J. Livo and Dia Cha, eds., 67–68.
18. Mabel Cook Cole, comp., *Philippine Folk Tales*, illus. Fay-Cooper Cole (Chicago: A.C. McClurg, 1916), 130.
19. Cole, viii–ix.

20. "The Bukidnon People (Talaandig Tribe) of the Philippines: History, Culture, Customs, and Tradition," *Yodisphere,* Aug. 2022, pars. 1–2 and 17, https://www.yodisphere.com/2022/08/Bukidnon-Tribe-Talaandig-.html#google_vignette. Accessed 16 Oct. 2023.
21. David Joel Steinberg, *The Philippines: A Singular and A Plural Place* (Boulder, CO: Westview Press, 1982), 20.
22. Cole, 202–203.
23. Cole, ix.
24. "Visayans," *Alchetron: Free Social Encyclopedia,* 18 Oct. 2022, pars. 1 and 10, https://www.alchetron.com/Visayans. Accessed 16 Oct. 2023.
25. Joseph Jacobs, ed., *English Fairy Tales,* illus. John D. Batten (London: David Nutt, 1890), 152–153.
26. Jacobs, *English Fairy Tales,* 153.
27. Diane Synder, adapt., *The Boy of the Three-Year Nap,* illus. Allen Say (New York: Houghton, 1988), sic passim.
28. Cole, 183–184.
29. Jacobs, *English Fairy Tales,* 20–23.
30. Andrew Lang, ed., *The Brown Fairy Book,* illus. H.J. Ford (1904; rpt. New York: Longmans, Green, 1910), 327–342.
31. Georgiana Kingscote and Pandit Natesa Sastri, comps., *Tales of the Sun or Folklore of Southern India* (London and Calcutta: W.H. Allen, 1890), 187–189.
32. Lang, *The Brown Fairy Book,* 342.
33. Kingscote and Sastri, 189.
34. Elsie Spicer Eells, comp., *Fairy Tales from Brazil: How and Why Tales from Brazilian Folk-Lore,* illus. Helen M. Barton (New York: Dodd, Mead, 1917), 145–151.
35. Cole, 175.
36. "Ilocanos," *Countries and Their Cultures Forum,* n.d., pars. 1–3, https://www.everycluture.com/wc/Norway-to-Russia/Ilocanos.html. Accessed 26 Aug. 2019.
37. "Ilocanos," par. 2.
38. Mark John Sanchez, "The People Power Revolution, Philippines 1986," *Origins: Cultural Events in Historical Perspectives,* Feb. 2021, par. 2, https://www.origins.osu.edu/milestones/people-power-revolution-philippines-1986. Accessed 1 Nov. 2023.
39. Cole, 176–178.
40. Cole, 178, n.1.
41. Harris, 13.
42. Pat Perrin, adapt., "Anansi and the Box of Stories," 2007, 1–5, *Archive.org, 2007,* https://www.archives.org/AnansiAndTheBoxOfStories/mode/2up. Accessed 30 Aug. 2019.
43. Katie Dale and Valentina Bandera, adapts., *Anansi and the Box of Stories* (London: Franklin Watts, 2019), sic passim.
44. Stephen Krensky and Jeni Reeves, adapts., *Anansi and the Box of Stories: A West African Folktale* (Minneapolis: Millbrook Press, 2008), sic passim.
45. Mooney, 272–273.
46. Swanton, 68.

The Caribbean, South America, and North America

1. Philip Sherlock, adapt., *West Indian Folk-Tales,* illus. Joan Kiddell-Monroe (London: Oxford University Press, 1966), 1.
2. Sherlock, 21–26.
3. Rachelle Oblack, "Where Does the Word 'Hurricane' Come From?" *ThoughtCo,* 17 Oct. 2019, pars. 2–3, https://www.thoughtco.com/where-does-the-word-hurricane-come-from-3443911. Accessed 15 Nov. 2022.
4. Eells, 87–91.
5. Morris, 71 and 77.
6. Eells, viii–ix.
7. Weston La Barre, "Aymara Folktales," *International Journal of American Linguistics* 16.1 (Jan. 1950): 40–45 [#37].
8. "Quinoa," *New World Encyclopedia,* 7 Dec. 2022, pars. 5–7, https://www.newworldencyclopedia.org/p/incex.php?title=Quinoa&oldid=1090803. Accessed 20 Nov. 2023.
9. Betty Mindlin, ed., *Barbecued Husbands and Other Stories from the Amazon,* trans. Donald Slatoff (London: Verso, 2002), 236–238.
10. Mindlin, 297.
11. Mindlin, 262.
12. Sheldon Cashdan, *The Witch Must Die: The Hidden Meaning of Fairy Tales* (New York: Basic Books, 1999) 31–32.
13. Joseph Jacobs, ed., *More English Fairy Tales,* illus. John D. Batten.

(New York: G.P. Putnam's Sons, 1922), 172–176.
14. Mooney, 330–335.
15. Mooney, 334.
16. Charles Hudson, 160.
17. Mooney, 474n.76.
18. Mooney, 327–329.
19. Mooney, 324.
20. Mooney, 343–345.
21. Mooney, 344.
22. Russell, 160.
23. Diane Wolkstein, comp. *The Magic Orange Tree and Other Haitian Folktales*, illus. Elsa Henriquez (1978; rpt. New York: Schocken Books, 1997), 113–116.
24. Swanton, 85–86.
25. Eugene Current-Garcia and Dorothy B. Hatfield, eds., *Shem Ham & Japeth: The Papers of W.O. Tuggle* (Athens: University of Georgia Press, 1973), 282.
26. Current-Garcia and Hatfield, 3.
27. Swanton, 85.
28. Johnathan Brennan, Introduction: Recognition of the African-Native American Tradition, in *When Brer Rabbit Meets Coyote: African-Native American Literature*, ed. Johnathan Brennan (Urbana: University of Illinois Press, 2003), 17.
29. Brennan, 10.
30. Robbins Burling, *English in Black and White* (New York: Holt, 1973), 78–79.
31. Bruce Jackson, *"Get Your Ass in the Water and Swim Like Me": Narrative Poetry from Black Oral Tradition* (Cambridge: Harvard University Press, 1974), 5.
32. Roger D. Abrahams, *Deep Down in the Jungle: Negro Folklore from the Streets of Philadelphia*, 2nd ed. (Chicago: Aldine, 1970), 146–156.
33. Jackson, 161–179.
34. Jackson, 177–178.
35. Doug Hammond, "The Signifying Monkey," *YouTube*, uploaded by Schoenleitner, 27 Jan. 2008, https://youtube.com. Accessed 12 Dec. 2022.
36. Rudy Ray Moore, "Signifying Monkey," *YouTube*, uploaded by The Orchard Enterprises, 9 Nov. 2014, https://www.youtube.com. Accessed 12 Dec. 2022.
37. Snatch and the Poontangs, "The Signifying Monkey 1 & 2." *YouTube*, uploaded by Chabrot Liveshere, 8 Dec. 2010, https://www.youtube.com/watch?v=n-oA3U-Sc8w. Accessed 12 Dec. 2022.
38. Burling, 79.
39. Burling, 80.
40. Abrahams, 51–52.
41. Henry Louis Gates, "The Blackness of Black: A Critique of the Sign and the Signifying Monkey," in *Literary Theory: An Anthology*, 2nd ed. ed. Julie Rivkin and Michael Ryan (Malden, MA: Blackwell, 2004), 991.
42. Gates, 988.
43. Courlander, 186.
44. Courlander, 159.
45. Hyde, 7.

Bibliography

Abrahams, Roger D. *Deep Down in the Jungle: Negro Narrative Folklore from the Streets of Philadelphia*. 2nd ed. Chicago: Aldine, 1970. Print.

"The Ainu: The little-known indigenous people of Japan and Russia." *The Vintage News*, 4 Oct. 2016, https://www.thevintagenews.com/2016/10/4the-ainu. Accessed 7 Aug. 2019.

Alexander, Sir James Edward. *An Expedition of Discovery into the Interior of Africa, Through the Hitherto Undescribed Countries of the Great Namaquas, Boschmans, and Hill Damaras.* 2 vols. London: Henry Coburn, 1838. Print.

Anderson, G.L., ed. *Masterpieces of the Orient, Enlarged Edition.* New York: Norton, 1977. Print.

Andrews, Penelope. "Jail time for South African woman using racist slur sets new precedent." *Mail & Guardian*, 3 April 2018, https://www.mg.coza/article/2018-04-03-jail-time-for-south-african-woman-using-racial-slur-sets-new-precedent. Accessed 22 Sept. 2023.

Animals Network Team. "Cuscus." *Animals Network*, 2018, https://www.animals.net/cuscus. Accessed 10 July 2023.

_____. "Sambar." *Animals Network*, 2018, https://www.animals.net/sambar. Accessed 6 Jan. 2024.

"Ape v. Monkey: What Are the Differences Between Apes and Monkeys?" *Safaris Africana*, n.d., https://www.safarisafricana.com/ape-vs-monkey. Accessed 9 July 2023.

Apuleius. *The Transformations of Lucius Otherwise Known as The Golden Ass.* Trans. Robert Graves. 1951; rpt. New York: Noonday, 1967. Print.

Babbitt, Ellen C., adapt. *Jataka Tales.* Illus. Ellsworth Young. New York: Century, 1912. Print.

_____. *More Jataka Tales.* Illus. Ellsworth Young. New York: Century, 1922. Print.

Baker, Augusta, and Ellin Greene. "Storytelling: Preparation and Presentation." *Jump Over the Moon: Selected Professional Readings.* Ed. Pamela Barron and Jennifer Q. Burley. New York: Holt, 1984. 325–332. Print.

"Barbary Macaque," n.d., https://www.folly-farm.co.uk/meet-the-zoo-animals/barbary-macaque. Accessed 15 July 2025.

Bateman, George W., comp. and trans. *Zanzibar Tales Told by the Natives of the East Coast of Africa.* Illus. Walter Bobbett. Chicago: A.C. McClurg, 1901. Print.

Battaharyal, Panchali, Tarun Tapas Mukherjee, and Swayam Prabha Satpathy. "Cultural Traditions of the Lotha Nagas: Analyzing the Folktales in Nzanmongi Jasmine Patton's *A Girl Swallowed by a Tree: Lotha Nagas Tales Retold.*" *International Journal of Early Childhood Special Education* 14.5 (2022): 4019–4023. Print.

Benton, Janetta Rebold. *The Medieval Menagerie: Animals in the Art of the Middle Ages.* New York: Abbeville, 1992. Print.

Bhutia, Thinley Kalsang. "Asante." *Britannica Online*, 26 Dec. 2017, https://www.britannica.com/topic/Asante. Accessed 10 April 2023.

Bierhorst, John, ed. *Latin American Folktales: Stories from Hispanic and Indian*

Traditions. New York: Pantheon, 2002. Print.

"Black Howler Monkey." *Alexandria Zoo,* n.d., https://www.thealexandriazoo.com/Black/Howler/Monkey.html. Accessed 27 Sept. 2023.

Bleek, W.H.I., and L.C. Lloyd, comp. and trans. *Specimens of Bushman Folklore.* London: George Allen, 1911. Print.

Bleek, W.H.I., trans. *Reynard the Fox in South Africa; or, Hottentot Fables and Tales.* London: Trubner and Co., 1864. Print.

Bompas, Cecil Henry, trans. *Folklore of the Santal Parganas.* London: David Nutt, 1909. Print.

Brennan, Jonathan. Introduction: Recognition of the African-Native American Literary Tradition. *When Brer Rabbit Meets Coyote: African-Native American Literature.* Ed Jonathan Brennan. Urbana and Chicago: University of Illinois Press, 2003. 1–97. Print.

Bryce, Catherine T., comp. *Fables from Afar.* Illus. Ada Budell. New York: Newson, 1910. Print.

Buck, William, adapt. *Valmiki's Ramayana: King Rama's Way.* Illus. Shirley Triest. Los Angeles: University of California Press, 1976. Print.

"The Bukidnon People (Talaandig Tribe) of the Philippines: History, Culture, Customs, and Tradition." *Yodisphere,* Aug. 2022, https://www.yodisphere.com/2022/08/Bukidnon-Tribe-Talaandig-.html#google_vignette. Accessed 16 Oct. 2023.

Burling, Robbins. *English in Black and White.* New York: Holt, 1973. Print.

Burton, E.F. *Reminiscences of Sport in India.* London: W.H. Allen, 1885. Print.

Bushnaq, Inea, ed. and trans. *Arab Folktales.* New York: Pantheon: 1986. Print.

Cashdan, Sheldon. *The Witch Must Die: The Hidden Meaning of Fairy Tales.* New York: Basic Books, 1999. Print.

Cbanga, Ibo, and Amy Tikkanen. "Juju." *Britannica Online,*19 July 2017, https://www.britannica.com/topic/juju-magic. Accessed 1 Aug. 2019.

Chamberlain, Basil Hall, comp. and trans. *Aino Folk-Tales.* London: The Folk-Lore Society, 1888. Print.

Chambry, Emile, trans. *Esope Fables.* 2nd ed. Paris: Les Belles Lettres, 1927. Print.

Chatelain, Heli, comp. and trans. *Folktales of Angola: Fifty Tales with Ki-mbundu Text, Liberal English Translation, Introduction, and Notes.* Boston: Houghton Mifflin, 1894. Print.

Cole, Mabel Cook, comp. *Philippine Folk Tales.* Illus. Fay-Cooper Cole. Chicago: A.C. McClurg, 1916. Print.

"Common Spotted Cuscus." *Animalia,* n.d., https://www.animalia.bio/common-spotted-cuscus. Accessed 12 July 2023.

Costa, C.D.N. trans. *Lucian: Selected Dialogues.* New York: Oxford University Press, 2005. vii–xiv. Print.

Courlander, Harold, comp. *A Treasury of African Folklore: The Oral Literature, Traditions, Myths, Legends, Epics, Tales, Recollections, Wisdom, Sayings, and Humor of Africa.* New York: Crown, 1975. Print.

Cowell, E.B., ed. *The Jataka or Stories of the Buddha's Former Births.* Vols. I–V. Cambridge: Cambridge UP, 1895, 1897, 1901, 1905. Print.

Current-Garcia, Eugene, and Dorothy B. Hatfield, eds. *Shem Ham & Japeth: The Papers of W.O. Tuggle.* Athens: University of Georgia Press, 1973. Print.

Dale, Kate, and Valentina Bandera, adapts. *Anansi and the Box of Stories.* London: Franklin Watts, 2019. Print.

Das, Subhamoy. "Find Out How Hinduism Defines Dharma: Learn About the Path of Righteousness." *Learn Religions,* 25 June 2019, https://www.learnreligions.com/what-is-dharma-1770048. Accessed 3 Jan. 2024.

Dayrell, Elphinstone, comp. *Folk Stories from Southern Nigeria, West Africa.* London: Longmans, Green, 1910. Print.

Deepak, B.R. "Hanuman and Sun Wukong: How Indian and Chinese Literary Images Integrate." *The Sunday Guardian,* 27 Dec. 2020, https://wwwsundayguardianlive.com/hanuman-sun-wudong-indian-chinese-literary-images-integrate. Accessed 29 Nov. 2023.

"The Dhoti and Why It's So Important in India." *Get Ethnic,* n.d., https://www.getethnic.com/blogs/dhoti-indian-outfit. Accessed 7 Jan. 2024.

"Diospyros Malabarica—Tinduka." 28 April 2020, https://www.Ayurwiki/Diospyros_malabarica_-_Tinduka. Accessed 11 Sept. 2023.

Bibliography

"Drawing Parallels: Are All the Monkey Gods Incarnations of Lord Hanuman?" *FormFluent*, 6 Oct. 2023, https://formfluent.com.blogs/blog/drawing-parallels-are-all-the-monkey-gods-incarnations-of-lord-hanuman. Accessed 29 Nov. 2023.

Duffy, Jean H. *Signs and Designs: Art and Architecture in the Work of Michel Butor*. Liverpool: Liverpool University Press, 2003. Print.

Eberhard, Wolfram, ed. and trans. *Chinese Fairy Tales and Folk Tales*. New York: Dutton, 1938. Print.

Editors of Encyclopedia Britannica. "Santhal." *Britannica Online*. 25 Sept. 2023, https://www.britannica.com/topic/Santhal. Accessed 7 Jan. 2024.

———. "Sesame." *Britannica Online*, 22 Dec. 2023, https://www.britannica.com/plant/sesame-plant. Accessed 5 Jan. 2024. Accessed 5 Feb. 2024.

———. "Tung Tree." *Britannica Online*, 10 April 2019, https://www.britannica.com/plant/tung-tree. Accessed 19 May 2022.

Eells, Elsie Spicer, comp. *Fairy Tales from Brazil: How and Why Tales from Brazilian Folk-Lore*. Illus. Helen M. Barton. New York: Dodd, Mead, 1917. Print.

Fansler, Dean S. comp. and ed. *Filipino Popular Tales*. Lancaster, PA: American Folk-Lore Society, 1921. Print.

Farb, Peter. *Word Play: What Happens When People Talk*. New York: Vintage, 1973. Print.

Findlay, Justin. "Largest Ethnic Groups in Nigeria." *World Atlas*, 18 July 2019, https://www.worldatlas.com/articles/largest-ethnic-groups-in-nigeria. Accessed 10 Aug. 2019.

Fontana, David. *The Secret Language of Symbols: A Visual Key to Symbols and Their Meanings*. San Francisco: Chronicle, 1993. Print.

Francis, H.T., and E.J. Thomas, eds. *Jataka Tales Selected and Edited with Introduction and Notes*. Cambridge: Cambridge University Press, 1916. Print.

Galda, Lee, and Bernice E. Cullinan. 6th ed. *Literature and the Child*. Belmont, CA: Wadsworth, 2006. Print.

Galdikas, Birute M.F. "Orangutan Primate." *Britannica Online*, 21 June 2023, https://www.britannica.com/animal/orangutan. Accessed 25 July 2023.

Gates, Henry Louis. "The Blackness of Black: A Critique of the Sign and the Signifying Monkey." *Literary Theory: An Anthology*. 2nd ed. Ed. Julie Rivkin and Michael Ryan. Malden, MA: Blackwell, 2004. 987–1004. Print.

Gay, David Elton. "On the Interaction of Traditions: Southeastern Rabbit Tales as African-Native American Folklore." *When Brer Rabbit Meets Coyote: African-Native American Literature*. Ed. Jonathan Brennan. Urbana and Chicago: University of Illinois Press, 2003. 101–113. Print.

Germond, Phillippe, and Jacques Livet. *An Egyptian Bestiary: Animals in the Life and Religion in the Land of the Pharaohs*. Trans. Barbara Mellor. London: Thames and Hudson, 2001. Print.

Gibbs, Laura, trans. *Aesop's Fables*. Rev ed. Oxford: Oxford University Press, 2008. Print.

Goldman, Robert P. "Ramayana." *Encyclopedia of Modern Asia*. Vol. 5. Ed. David Levinson and Karen Christiansen. New York: Thompson-Gale, 2002. 51–52. Print.

Goodyear, F.R.D. "Minor Poetry: Phaedrus." *The Cambridge History of Classical Literature: II, Latin Literature*. Ed. E.J. Kenney. New York: Cambridge University Press, 1982. 624–626. Print.

Groves, Colin Peter. "Ape." *Britannica Online*, 4 May 2023, https://www.britannica.com/animal/ape. Accessed 15 July 2023.

———. "Baboon." *Britannica Online*, 10 March 2023, https://www.britannicaonline.com/animal/baboon. Accessed 27 Sept. 2023.

———. "Monkey." *Britannica Online*, 27 June 2023, https://www.britannica.com/animal/monkey. Accessed 10 July 2023.

Hall, James. *Dictionary of Subjects and Symbols in Art*. 2nd ed. Boulder, CO: Westview Press, 2008. Print.

Hamilton, Mae. "Jade Emperor," *Mythopedia*, 1 Dec. 2022, https:/www.mythopedia.com/topics/jade-emperor. Accessed 20 Jan. 2024.

Hammond, Doug. "The Signifying Monkey." *YouTube*, uploaded by Schoenleitner, 27 Jan. 2008, https://www.youtube.com. Accessed 12 Dec. 2022.

"Hanuman: The Perfect Hero." *Glorian*,

n.d., https://www.glorian.org/learn/courses-and-lectures/teachings-of-the-hindu-gods/hanuman-the-perfect-hero. Accessed 17 Feb. 2019.

Hardy, R. Spencer, trans. *A Manual of Budhism [sic] in Its Modern Development*. London: Partridge and Oakey, 1853. Print.

Harman, William. *A Handbook to Literature*. 12th ed. Boston: Pearson, 2012. Print.

Harris, Joel Chandler. *The Complete Tales of Uncle Remus*. Ed. Richard Chase. Illus. A.B. Frost et al. Boston: Houghton Mifflin, 1955. Print.

Haviland, Virginia, and Margaret N. Coughlan. *Yankee Doodle's Literary Sampler of Prose, Poetry, and Pictures, Being an Anthology of Diverse Works Published for the Edification and/or Entertainment of Young Readers in America Before 1900*. New York: Crowell, 1974. Print.

Hegel, Robert E. "Literature—China." *Encyclopedia of Modern Asia*. Vol. 3. Ed. David Levinson and Karen Christiansen. New York: Thompson-Gale, 2002. 482–488. Print.

Henderson, Harold G., comp. and ed. Introduction. *Tales from the Japanese Storytellers*. Trans. Post Wheeler. Rutland, VT: Tuttle, 1964. vii–x.

Honey, James A., comp. *South-African Folk-Tales*. New York: Baylor and Taylor, 1910. Print.

"Hottentot." Def 1b. *Oxford English Dictionary*. 2nd ed. Vol. 7. 1989. Print.

Hudson, Charles. *The Southeastern Indians*. Knoxville: University of Tennessee Press, 1976. Print.

Hudson, Nicolas. "'Hottentots' and the Evolution of European Racism." *Journal of European Studies* 34.4 (Dec. 2004): 308–332. Print.

Hugo, Howard E. "Masterpieces of Neoclassicism." Introduction. *The Norton Anthology of World Masterpieces*. 4th ed. Vol. 2. New York: Norton, 1979. 1–22. Print.

Hutton, J. Howard. Introduction. *The Lhota Nagas*. By J.P. Mills. London: Macmillan, 1922: xi–xxxix. Print.

Hyde, Lewis. *Trickster Makes This World: Mischief, Myth, and Art*. 1998. New York: Farrar, Straus, and Giroux, 2010. Print.

Hyde-Chambers, Fredrick, and Audrey Hyde-Chambers, eds. *Tibetan Folk Tales*. Illus. Kusho Ralla. Boulder, CO: Shambala, 1981. Print.

"Ilocanos." *Countries and Their Cultures Forum*, n.d., https://www.everyculture.com/wc/Norway-to-Russia/Ilocanos.html. Accessed 26 Aug. 2019.

Impelluso, Lucia. *Nature and Its Symbols*. Trans. Stephen Sartarelli. Los Angeles: J. Paul Getty Museum, 2003. Print.

"Introduction to Monkeys." *Monkey Worlds*, n.d., https://www.monleyworlds.com. Accessed 12 July 2023.

Jackson, Bruce. *"Get Your Ass in the Water and Swim Like Me": Narrative Poetry from the Black Oral Tradition*. Cambridge, MA: Harvard University Press, 1974. Print.

Jacobs, Joseph, ed. *English Fairy Tales*. Illus. John D. Batten. London: David Nutt, 1890. Print.

———. *Indian Fairy Tales*. Illus. John D. Batten. London: David Nutt, 1892. Print.

———. *More English Fairy Tales*. Illus. John D. Batten. New York: G.P. Putnam's Sons, 1922. Print.

"Japan to recognize indigenous Ainu people for first time." *The Straits Times*, 15 Feb 2019, https://www.straitstimes.com/asia/-east-asia/japan-to-recognize-indigenous-ainu-people-for-first-time. Accessed 6 Aug. 2019.

Jenkins, Christine. "Concluding Our Story of Stories." *Story: From Fireplace to Cyberspace, Connecting Children and Narrative*. Papers Presented at the Allerton Park Institute, No. 39. Ed. Betsy Hearne et al. Monticello: University of Illinois Press, 1997. 106–107. Print.

Jokinen, Anniinna. "Monkeys and Monkey Gods in Mythology, Folklore, and Religion." *Luminarium*. 8 Mar. 2007, www.luminarium.org/mythology/monkeygods. Accessed 8 Sept. 2017.

Jones, V.S. Vernon, trans. *Aesop's Fables: A New Translation*. Illus. Arthur Rackham. London: William Heinemann, 1912. Print.

"Karaka (tree) facts for kids." *Kids Encyclopedia Facts*, 26 July 2023. https://www.kids,kiddle,co/Karaka_(tree). Accessed 9 Sept. 2023.

Keith-Falconer, I.G.N., trans. *Kalilah and Dimnah or The Fables of Bidpai*.

Cambridge: Cambridge University Press, 1885. Print.

Kemp, Martin. *The Human Animal in Western Art and Science*. Chicago: University of Chicago Press, 2007. Print.

Kiefer, Barbara Z., Susan Hepler, and Janet Hickman. *Charlotte Huck's Children's Literature*. 9th ed. Boston: McGraw-Hill, 2007. Print.

Kingscote, Georgiana, and Pandit Natesa Sastri, comps. *Tales of the Sun or Folklore of Southern India*. London and Calcutta: W.H. Allen, 1890. Print.

Kituku, Vincent Muli Wa, adapt. and comp. *East African Folktales: From the Voice of Mukamba*. Illus. Kelly Matthews. Little Rock, AR: August House, 1997. Print.

Kohler, Oswin R.A., Anthony Traill, et al. "Khoisan Languages." *Britannica Online*, 10 Oct. 2016, www.britannica.com/topic/Khoisan-Languages. Accessed 19 Aug. 2019.

Krensky, Stephen, and Jeni Reeves, adapts. *Anansi and the Box of Stories: A West African Folktale*. Minneapolis, MN: Millbrook Press, 2008. Print.

La Barre, Weston. "Aymara Folktales." *International Journal of American Linguistics* 16.1 (Jan. 1950): 40–45 [# 37]. Print.

La Fontaine, Jean de. Livre IV. No. 7. *Les Fables de La Fontaine*. n.d., https://www.mesfables.com-4/07-le-singe-et-le-dauphin.html. Accessed 15 Sept. 2023.

Lang, Andrew, ed. *The Brown Fairy Book*. Illus. H.J. Ford. 1904. New York: Longmans, Green, 1910. Print.

———. *The Crimson Fairy Book*. Illus. H.J. Ford. 1903. New York: Longmans, Green, 1947. Print.

———. *The Lilac Fairy Book*. Illus. H.J. Ford. New York: Longmans, Green, 1910. Print.

Lang, Andrew. Introduction. *Folk Stories from Southern Nigeria, West Africa*. Comp. Elphinstone Dayrell. London: Longmans, Green 1910. vii–xvi. Print.

Lessing, Doris. Introduction. *Kalila and Dimna: Selected Fables of Bidpai*. Adapt. Ramsey Wood. Illus. Margaret Kilrenny. New York: Knopf, 1980. ix–xix. Print.

Lipson, Marjorie Y., and Karen K. Wixson. *Assessment and Instruction of Reading and Writing Difficulties: An Interactive Approach*. 4th ed. Boston: Pearson, 2009. Print.

Livo, Norma J., and Dia Cha, eds. *Folk Stories of the Hmong: Peoples of Laos, Thailand, and Vietnam*. Illus. Anthony Chan. Photo. Michael Mancarella. Englewood, CO: Libraries Unlimited, 1991. Print.

Livo, Norma J., and Sandra A. Rietz. *Storytelling: Process and Practice*. Littleton, CO: Libraries Unlimited, 1986. Print.

Lloyd, Lucy C. Preface. *Specimens of Bushman Folklore*. Comp. and trans. W.H.I. Bleek and L.C. Lloyd. London: George Allen, 1911. vii–xvi. Print.

Lotha, Gloria. "Asante Empire." *Britannica Online*, 19 April 2023, https://www.britannica.com/place/Asante-empire. Accessed 1 May 2023.

Lucian. *Lucian*. 1913. Trans. A.M. Harmon. Vol. 3. London: William Heinemann, 1960. Print.

Lunde, Paul. "Kalila Wa Dimna: In the Fables, Wit and Wisdom." *Aramco World Magazine* 23.4 (July/Aug. 1972): 18–21. Print.

Luthi, Max. *Once Upon a Time: On the Nature of Fairy Tales*. Bloomington: Indiana University Press, 1976. Print.

MacDonald, Margaret Read. *The Storyteller's Start-Up Book: Finding, Learning, Performing, and Using Folktales, Including Twelve Tellable Tales*. Little Rock, AR: August House, 1993. Print.

———. *Twenty Tellable Tales: Audience Participation Folktales for the Beginning Storyteller*. New York: H.W. Wilson, 1986. Print.

Mark, Joshua. "Thoth." *World History Encyclopedia*. 26 July 2016, http://www.worldhistory.org/Thoth. Accessed 6 Feb. 2019.

Mayer, Fanny Hagin, ed. and trans. *Ancient Tales in Modern Japan: An Anthology of Japanese Folk Tales*. Bloomington, IN: Indiana University Press, 1984. 302–303. Print.

McEvoy, Cuthbert. *Ion Keith-Falconer: The Scholar Missionary*. London: Carey Press, 1900. Print.

McKenna, Amy. "Ghana." *Britannica Online*, 28 March 2023, https://www.britannica.com/place/Ghana. Accessed 10 April 2023.

Metzger, Berta, comp. *Tales Told in Korea*. Illus. Arthur Y. Park. New York: Frederick A. Stokes, 1932. Print.

Mills, J.P. *The Lhota Nagas*. London: Macmillan, 1922. Print.

Mindlin, Betty, ed. *Barbecued Husbands and Other Stories from the Amazon*. Trans. Donald Slatoff. London: Verso, 2002. Print.

"Monkey Species." *MonkeyWorlds,* n.d., https://www.monkeyworlds.com/types-of-monkeys. Accessed 10 July 2023.

Mooney, James. *Myths of the Cherokee*. 1900. *James Mooney's History, Myths, and Sacred Formulas of the Cherokees*. Fairview, NC: Historical Images, 1992. 5–576. Print.

Moore, Rudy Ray. "Signifying Monkey." *YouTube*, uploaded by The Orchard Enterprises, 9 Nov. 2014, https://www.youtube. Accessed 12 Dec. 2022.

Morris, Desmond. *Monkey*. London: Reaktion Books, 2013. Print.

Moser, Gerald. "Heli Chatelain: Pioneer of a National Language and Literature for Angola." *Research in African Literatures* 14.4 (Winter 1983): 516–537. Print.

"Nagas: Their History, Life, and Customs." *Facts and Details,* n.d., https://www.factsanddetails.com/southeast-asia/Myanmar/sub_5_5d/entry-3933.html. Accessed 4 Jan. 2024.

"Nama People." *Exploring Africa,* n.d., https://www.exploring-africa.com/en/namibia/nama/nama-people. Accessed 5 Aug. 2019.

Narayan, R.K., adapt. *The Ramayana: A Shortened Modern Version of the Indian Epic*. Illus. R.K. Laxman. New York: Viking, 1972. Print.

Nassau, Robert H., comp. and trans. *Where Animals Talk: West African Folk Lore Tales*. 1912. Westport, CT: Negro Universities Press, 1970. Print.

Nhuong, Huynh Quang. *The Land I Lost: Adventures of a Boy in Vietnam*. Illus. Vo Dinh Mai. New York: Harper and Row, 1982. Print.

North, Sir Thomas, trans. *The earliest English version of the Fables of Bidpai, "The Morall Philosophie of Doni."* Ed. Joseph Jacobs. London: David Nutt, 1888. Print.

Oblack, Rachelle. "Where Does the Word 'Hurricane' Come From?" *Thought Co.,* 17 Oct. 2019, https://www.thoughtco.com/where-does-the-word-huricane-come-from-3443911. Accessed 15 Nov. 2022.

Oetken, Nick. "Do monkeys throw poop in self-defense?" *TheGunZone,* 10 Dec. 2023, https://www.thegunzone.do-monkeys-throw-poop-in-self-defense. Accessed 12 Dec. 2023.

Ojo, Oluseye. "Why Unity Is Elusive to Nigeria." *The Sun: Voice of a Nation,* 1 Oct. 2017, https://sunnewsonline.com/why-unity-is-elusive-to-nigeria. Accessed 9 Sept. 2023.

"Oldest evidence of split between Old World monkeys and apes: Primate fossils are 25 million years old." *Science Daily,* 15 May 2013, https://www.sciencedaily.com. Accessed 7 July 2023.

Onyanga-Omara, Jane. "Stephen Hawking's Memorable Quotes: 'We are just an advanced breed of monkeys.'" *USA Today.* 14 Mar. 2018, www.usatoday.com. Accessed 9 Feb. 2019.

Owomoyela, Oyekan. *Yoruba Trickster Tales*. Lincoln: University of Nebraska Press, 1997. Print.

Ozaki, Yei Theodora, comp. *The Japanese Fairy Book*. Illus. Kakuzo Fujiyama. New York: E.P. Dutton, 1903. Print.

Palmer, George Herbert, trans. *The Odyssey of Homer*. Ed. Howard Porter. New York: Bantam, 1962. Print.

Pauls, Elizabeth Prine. "Fang." *Britannica Online,* 9 Feb. 2007, https://www.britannicaonline.com/topicFang-people. Accessed 2 Aug. 2019.

Payne, John, trans. *The Book of the Thousand Nights and One Night: Now First Completely Done into English Prose and Verse, From the Original Arabic*. Vol. 4. London: The Villon Society, 1901. Print.

Pei, Fang Jing. *Symbols and Rebuses in Chinese Art: Figures, Bugs, Beasts, and Flowers*. Berkeley, CA: Ten Speed Press, 2004. Print.

Pellowski, Anne. *The World of Storytelling*. New York: R.R. Bowker, 1977. Print.

Perrin, Pat, adapt. "Anansi and the Box of Stories." *Archive.org,* 2007, https://www.archive.org/AnansiAndTheBoxOfStories/mode/2up. Accessed 30 Aug. 2019.

Perry, Ben Edwin, ed and trans. *Babrius*

and Phaedrus. Cambridge, MA: Harvard University Press, 1965. Print.

Pliny's Natural History. Trans. Philemon Holland. Vol. 1. London: George Barclay, 1847–48. Print.

"Quinoa." *New World Encyclopedia*, 7 Dec. 2022, https://www.newworldencyclopedia.org/p/index?title=Quinoa&oldid+1090803. Accessed 20 Nov. 2023.

Rafferty, John P. "Gibbon." *Britannica Online*, 28 Oct. 2021, https://www.britannica.com/animal/gibbon-primate. Accessed 25 July 2021.

Raju, P.V. Ramaswami, adapt. and comp. *Indian Fables*. Illus. F. Caruthers Gould. London: Swan Sonneschein, 1901. Print.

Ralston, W.R.S. Introduction. *Tibetan Tales Derived from Indian Sources*. Comp. and trans. F. Anton Von Schiefner. London: Kegan Paul, Trench, Trubner, 1906. vii–lxv. Print.

Ramanujan, A.K., comp. and trans. *Folktales from India: A Selection of Oral Tales from Twenty-Two Languages*. Illus. Jenny Vandeventer. New York: Pantheon, 1991. Print.

Rattray, Robert S. comp. and trans. *Akan-Ashanti Folk-Tales*. 1930. Illus. Ashanti, Fanti, and Ewe tribe members. London: Oxford University Press, 1969. Print.

Refring, Kristen. "Ainu." *Encyclopedia of Modern Asia*. Ed. David Levinson and Karen Christiansen. Vol. 1. New York: Scribner's, 2002. 70–73. Print.

Ross, Ramon R. *Storyteller*. Columbus, OH: Charles E. Merrill, 1972. Print.

Russell David L. *Literature for Children: A Short Introduction*. 5th ed. Boston: Pearson, 2005. Print.

"Sambar Deer." *Wikipedia*, 29 Nov. 2023, https://www.enwikipedia.org/wiki/Sambar_deer. Accessed 6 Jan. 2024.

"San," n.d., https://www.krugerpark.co.za/africa_bushmen.html. Accessed 15 August 2019.

"The San." *South African History Online*, 11 Dec. 2018, https://www.sahistory.orgza/article.san. Accessed 19 Aug. 2019.

Sanchez, Mark John. "The People Power Revolution, Philippines 1986." *Origins: Cultural Events in Historical Perspectives*, Feb. 2021, https://www.origins.osu.edu/milestones/people-power-revolution-philippines-1986. Accessed 1 Nov. 2023.

Sax, Boria. *The Mythological Zoo: Animals in Myth, Legend, and Literature*. New York: Overlook Duckworth, 2013. Print.

Schiefner, F. Anton Von, trans. *Tibetan Tales Derived from Indian Sources*. Trans. from German W.R.S. Ralston. London: Kegan Paul, Trench, Trubner, 1906. Print.

Schumacher, Mark. "China—Buddhist Monkey Lore," in *Monkey in Japan, Page Two—India and China Lore*, https://onmarkproductions.com/html/monkey-india-china-p2.html. Accessed 27 Sept. 2017.

Seki, Keigo, comp. *Folktales of Japan*. 1956–1957. Trans. Robert J. Adams. Chicago: University of Chicago Press, 1963. Print.

Seton, Ernest Thompson, ed. *Famous Animal Stories: Animal Myths, Fables, Fairy Tales, Stories of Real Animals*. New York: Brentano's, 1932. Print.

Sharma, Jayanta Kar. "Oral Storytelling and Its Techniques." *International Journal of English Language, Literature, and Humanities* 4.2 (Feb. 2006): 269–281. Print.

Shelton, A.L., trans. *Tibetan Folk Tales*. Illus. Mildred Bryant. St. Louis, MO: United Christian Missionary Society, 1925.

Shepherd, Rowena, and Rupert Shepherd. *1000 Symbols: What Shapes Mean in Art and Myth*. London: Thames and Hudson, 2002. Print.

Sherlock, Philip, adapt. *West Indian Folk-Tales*. Illus. Joan Kiddell-Monroe. London: Oxford University Press, 1966. Print.

"The Singerie: Monkeys Acting as Humans in Art." *The Public Domain Review*, 19 July 2016, https://www.publicdomainreview.org/collection/the-singerie-monkeys-acting-as-humans-in-art. Accessed 19 July 2023.

Smith, Huston. *The Illustrated World's Religions: A Guide to Our Wisdom Traditions*. San Francisco: Harper, 1994. Print.

Snatch and the Poontangs. "Signifying Monkey 1 & 2." *YouTube*, uploaded by Chabrot Liveshere, 8 Dec. 2010, https://www.youtube.com/watch?v=-n-oA3U-Sc8w. Accessed 12 Dec. 2022.

Snyder, Dianne, adapt. *The Boy of the Three-Year Nap.* Illus. Allen Say. New York: Houghton, 1988. Print.

Steel, F.A., and R.C. Temple, comps. *Wide-Awake Stories: A Collection of Tales Told by Little Children, Between Sunset and Sunrise.* Bombay: Education Society's Press; London: Trubner and Co., 1884. Print.

Steere, Edward, comp. and trans. *Swahili Tales, As Told by the Natives of Zanzibar.* London: Bell and Daldy, 1870. Print.

Steinberg, David Joel. *The Philippines: A Singular and a Plural Place.* Boulder, CO: Westview Press, 1982. Print.

Stokes, Maive, comp. and trans. *Indian Fairy Tales.* London: Ellis and White, 1880. Print.

Sutherland, Zena. *Children and Books.* 9th ed. New York: Longman, 1997. Print.

Swanton, John R. *Myths and Tales of the Southeastern Indians.* Washington, D.C.: United States Government Printing Office, 1929. Print.

Swynnerton, Charles, adapt. *Indian Nights' Entertainment: Or, Folk-Tales from the Upper Indus.* Illus. by Native Hands. London: Elliot Stock, 1892. Print.

Temple, Olivia, and Robert Temple, trans. *The Complete Fables: Aesop.* London: Penguin Books, 1998. Print.

Temple, Robert. Introduction. *The Compete Fables: Aesop.* Trans. Olivia Temple and Robert Temple. London: Penguin Books, 1998. ix–xxiii. Print.

Theal, George McCall. Introduction. *Specimens of Bushman Folklore.* Comp. and trans. W.H.I. Bleek and L.C. Lloyd. London: George Allen, 1911. xxv–xl. Print.

Thipphawong, Laura. "Singeries: The Genre Paintings of Monkeys as Humans." *Arts Help,* 19 Nov. 2020, https://www.artshelp.com/singeries-the-genre-paintings-of-monkeys-as-humans. Accessed 29 July 2023.

Thorton, John Kelly, and William Gervase Clarence-Smith. "Angola." *Britannica Online,* 3 Oct. 2023, https://www.britannica.com/place/Angola. Accessed 4 Oct. 2023.

"Tokhu Emong 2024—Thursday, November 7, to Friday, November 15," n.d., https://www.festivalsofIndia.in/tokhu_emong. Accessed 5 Jan. 2024.

Traweek, Max, and Roy Welch. "Exotics in Texas." Texas Parks and Wildlife Department, April 1992, https://tpwd.texas.gov/publications/pwdpubs/mediapwd_bk_w7000_0206.pdf. Accessed 6 Jan. 2024.

Tylor, Edward B. Introduction. *Aino Folk-Tales.* Comp. and trans. Basil Hall Chamberlain. London: The Folk-Lore Society, 1888: v–viii. Print.

van Nooten, B.A. Introduction. *Valmiki's Ramayana: King Rama's Way.* Adapt. William Buck. Illus. Shirley Triest. Berkeley: University of California Press, 1976. xiii–xxii. Print.

Vaughan, Captain A.O., adapt. and comp. *Old Hendrik's Tales.* Illus. F.A. Shepherd. London: Longmans, Green, 1904. Print.

Veazey, Karen. "Jaggery: Is the superfood sweetener better for you than sugar?" *Medical News Today,* 30 June 2021, https://www.medicalnewstoday.com/articles/jaggery. Accessed 6 Jan. 2024.

"Visayans." *Alchetron: Free Social Encyclopedia,* 18 Oct. 2022, https://www.alchetron.com/Visayans. Accessed 16 Oct. 2023.

Vivekananda, "Sugar Palm Fruit and Its Health Benefits," *Hub Pages,* 6 Sept. 2017, https://www.discover.hubpages.com/food/Sugar_Palm_fruit_and_its_health_benefits. Accessed 7 Jan. 2024.

Voltaire. *Candide, Zadig, and Selected Stories.* Trans. Donald M. Frame. New York: New American Library, 1961. Print.

Walker, Barbara G. *The Woman's Encyclopedia of Myths and Secrets.* San Francisco: Harper, 1996. Print.

Werness, Hope B. "Monkey." *The Continuum Encyclopedia of Animal Symbolism in Art.* Illus. Joanne H. Benedict et al. New York: Continuum, 2004. Print.

"What does it mean to be human?" *Smithsonian Institution, Museum of Natural History,* 15 Aug. 2022, http://www.humanorigins.si.edu/evidence/genetics. Accessed 16 July 2023.

Wheeler, Post, trans. *Tales from the*

Japanese Storytellers. Comp. and ed. Harold G. Henderson. Rutland, VT: Tuttle, 1964. Print.

Wiggin, Kate Douglas, and Nora Archibald Smith, comps. *The Talking Beasts: A Book of Fable Wisdom.* Illus. Harold Nelson. New York: Grosset and Dunlap, 1911. Print.

Williams, C.A.S. *Outlines of Chinese Symbolism and Art Motives.* 3rd rev. ed. New York: Dover, 1976. Print.

Wolkstein, Diane, comp. *The Magic Orange Tree and Other Haitian Folktales.* Illus. Elsa Henriquez. 1978. New York: Schocken, 1997. Print.

Wood, Ramsey, adapt. *Kalila and Dimna: Selected Fables of Bidpai.* Illus. Margaret Kilrenny. New York: Knopf, 1980. Print.

Wu Ch'eng-en. *Monkey.* Trans. Arthur Waley. New York: John Day, 1943. Print.

Yu, Anthony C., trans. *The Journey to the West.* Vol. 1. Chicago: University of Chicago Press, 1977. Print.

Zipes, Jack. *The Irresistible Fairy Tale: The Cultural and Social History of a Genre.* Princeton, NJ: Princeton UP, 2012. Print.

Index

Abrahams, Roger D. 214
adversary *see* folklore motifs
Aesop 9, 19, 134, 138–140; *see also* Gibbs, Laura; Jones, V.S. Vernon
Afrikaans 104, 116–117, 124
Agni (fire god) 75
Ahura Mazda   11; *see also* Zoroastrians
Ainu people 176–178
Akan-Ashanti Folk-Tales see Rattray, Robert S.
Akan people 132
Alexander, Sir James Edward 122–124
Amazonia 206
Ananda (Buddha's disciple) 21
Ananse the spider 104, 196
Anansi *see* Ananse
Andersen, Hans Christian 7
anthropoids 4
appearance v. reality 85, 147
Apuleius (Latin author) 10
Arab Folktales see Busnaq, Inea
Arabian Nights see *One Thousand and One Nights*
Arawak people 197, 201
archetypes *see* folklore motifs
Arua people 205, 208
Aryans 75
Ashanti people 130, 132–133
Athena *see* goddesses of wisdom
Atreus   179
Aztec view of monkeys 12

Babbitt, Ellen C. 21–23, 101
baboon as adversary 120–121
Babrius 9, 136, 139
Bandera, Valentina 196
Bantu people 120–121, 125
Bateman George W. 100
bear (human qualities) 7–8
beaver (human qualities) 8

bestiaries and monkeys 10
Bisayan people 190–192, 194
Bleek, W.H.I. 121–122
boar as helper 182–183, 185–186
Bodhisattva 2, 22–25, 104, 144
Boers 103–105, 116
Bompas, Cecil Henry 90–91, 94
The Boy of the Three-Year Nap see Snyder, Diane
Brer Fox 105, 115, 196
Brer Rabbit 105, 115, 196
The Brown Fairy Book 193; *see also* Lang, Andrew
Bryce, Catherine 77, 143–144, 147
Buck, William 75
Buddhism 13–15, 19, 21–25, 27–29, 104–105, 144, 146
Bukidnon people 189–190
Bulu people 125
Burton, E.F. 19
Bushmen 103–105, 121–122
Busnaq, Inea 17

Caldecott Award 127, 192
Candide see Voltaire
cannibalism 125
Canterbury Tales 187
Carib people 197, 200
Cha, Dia 150, 189
Chamberlain, Basil Hall 177
Chambry, Emile 140
Chatelain, Heli 115, 120
Cherokee Indians 115, 196, 208, 211
Chinese Fairy and Folktales see Eberhard, Wolfram
Chinese Zodiac 13
Circe and magical transformation 18
Cole, Mabel Cook 190–191, 193–194, 196
colobus monkey 130, 133
"considerate text" 3

239

240 Index

Courlander, Harold 130, 215
Cowell, E.B. 21–22, 101
crab 103, 179. 181, 196; *see also* monkey-crab battles
Creek Indians 115, 196, 209, 211
The Crimson Fairy Book 181; *see also* Lang, Andrew
crone *see* folktale motifs (wise crone)
crossing thresholds *see* folktale motifs
cumulative tale *see* folktale types
cuscus (marsupial mistaken for monkey) 2

Dale, Kate 196
Darwin, Charles 8
Dayrell, Elphinstone 127
"The Dead Come to Life, Or the Fisherman" *see* Lucian of Samosata
Decameron 187
Demon King *see* Ravana
Deschamps, Alexandre Gabriel 11; *see also* singeries
Devadatta (Buddha's adversary) 25
dharma (moral law of the universe) 24, 28, 74–75
Diddie, Dumps, and Tot or Plantation Child Life see Pyrnelle, Louise
dog (human qualities) 8
dolphin as helper 137–138
Doni, Anton Francesco *see* North, Sir Thomas
Dravidians 75
droll tale *see* folktale types

East African Folktales see Kitutu, Vincent Muli Wa
Eberhard, Wolfram 175
Eells, Elsie Spicer 194, 202
Egbo people *see* Igbo people
Elixir of Life (Taoist belief) 172
emong (Lotha festival) *see* Tokhu Emong
English Fairy Tales see Jacobs, Joseph
Erasmus, Desiderius 140
Eshu (African trickster god) 215; *see also* Legba
ethical truths of folktales 175, 189, 209
An Expedition of Discovery into the Interior of Africa see Alexander, Sir James Edward

The Fables of Bidpai 13, 33–34, 214
fakir (holy man) as helper 85
the fall *see* folklore motifs
Famous Animal Stories see Seton, Ernest Thompson

Fang people 124–125
feral children 123–124
flood stories 197, 200
Folk Stories of the Hmong Peoples of Laos, Thailand, and Vietnam see Cha, Dia; Livo, Norma J.
Folk-Tales of Angola see Chatelain, Heli
folklore adapters, collectors, compilers, editors, and translators of ape and monkey tales (includes pages from *Chapter Notes* and *Bibliography*): Africa (Alexander, Sir Edward 122–124, 223, 229; Bandera, Valentina 196, 226, 230; Bateman, George W. 100, 221, 229; Bleek, W.H.I. 122, 223, 230; Chatelain, Heli 115, 120, 222–223, 230; Courlander, Harold 130, 215, 230; Dale, Katie 196, 226, 230; Dayrell, Elphinstone 127, 223, 230; Honey, James 104, 107, 110, 222, 232; Krensky, Stephen 196, 226, 233; Kitutu, Vincent Muli Wa 100, 103, 221–222, 233; Lang, Andrew (*The Lilac Fairy Book*) 100, 221, 233; Lloyd, L.C. 121–122, 223, 230; Nassau, Robert H. 125, 223, 234; Perrin, Pat 196, 226, 234–235; Rattray, Robert S. 132–133, 223, 235; Reeves, Jeni 196, 226, 233; Steere, Edward 100, 221, 236; Vaughan, Capt. Arthur Owen 110–111, 115–116, 222, 236); Caribbean (Haiti) (Wolkstein, Diane 209, 227, 237); China (Eberhard, Wolfram 175, 225, 231; Waley, Arthur 171, 225, 237; Yu, Anthony C. 14, 171, 225, 237); India (Babbitt, Ellen C. 21–22, 101, 219, 229; Bompas, Cecil Henry 90–91, 94, 221, 230; Bryce, Catherine 77, 220, 230; Buck, William 75, 220, 230; Burton, E.F. 19, 219, 230; Chalmers, Robert 219–220 [*see also* Cowell, E.B.]; Cowell, E.B. 21–22, 101, 219–220, 230; Francis, H.T. 13, 21, 23, 29, 219–220, 231; Jacobs, Joseph 7, 104, 219, 232; Kingscote, Georgiana 193, 226, 233; Mills, J.P. 86–87, 221, 234; Narayan, R.K. 74, 220, 234; Raju, P.V. Ramaswami 77, 220, 235; Ramanujan, A.K. 100–101, 222, 235; Rouse, W.H.D. 219–220 [*see also* Cowell, E.B.]; Sastri, Pandit Natesa 193, 226, 233; Steel, F.A. 104, 222, 236; Stokes, Maive 85, 220, 236; Swynnerton, Charles 19, 219, 236; Temple R.C. 104, 222, 236; Thomas, E.J. 13, 21, 23, 29, 219–220, 231); Japan (Chamberlain, Basil Hall 177, 225, 230; Henderson, Harold G.

Index

187, 225–226, 232; Lang, Andrew (*The Crimson Fairy Book*) 181, 225, 233; Mayer, Fanny Hagin 179, 181, 225, 233; Ozaki, Yei Theodora 102, 181, 187, 226, 234; Seki, Keigo 181, 222, 235); Korea (Metzger, Berta 148, 225, 234); Middle East (Bushnaq, Inea 17, 219, 230; Jacobs, Joseph 33, 220, 234; Keith-Falconer, I.G.N. 33, 220, 232–233; North, Sir Thomas 33, 220, 234; Payne, John 97, 221, 234; Wiggin and Smith 34, 220, 237; Wood, Ramsey 33, 220, 237); North America (Abrahams, Roger D. 214, 227, 229; Hammond, Doug 214, 227, 231; Jackson, Bruce 214, 227, 232; Moore, Rudy Ray 214, 227, 234; Snatch and the Poontangs 214, 227, 236; Swanton, John Reid 115, 196, 211, 227, 236; Tuggle, William Orrie 115, 211 [*see also* Swanton, John Reid]); Philippines (Cole, Mabel Cook 190–191, 193–194, 196, 226, 230; Fansler, Dean S. 231; Lang, Andrew (*The Brown Fairy Book* and *The Crimson Fairy Book*) 181, 193, 226, 233); South America (Eells, Elsie Spicer 194, 202, 226, 231; La Barre, Weston 204, 226, 233; Lang, Andrew (*The Brown Fairy Book*) 193, 226, 233; Mindlin, Betty 206, 227, 234; Southeast Asia (Hmong) (Cha, Dia 150, 189, 225, 233; Livo, Norma J. 150, 189, 225, 233); Tibet (Bryce, Catherine 143–144, 147, 224–225, 230; Hardy, Spence R. 146, 225, 232; Hyde-Chambers, Audrey 147, 225, 232; Hyde-Chambers, Frederick 147, 225, 232; *The Kangyur* 144, 146–147; Schiefner, Anton 143–144, 146–147, 224–225, 235; Shelton, A.L. 235); Western Europe (Chambry, Emile 140, 224, 230; Frame, Donald M. 221, 224, 236; Gibbs, Laura 138–140, 218, 224, 231; Harmon, A.M. 224, 233 [*see also* Lucian]; Jones, V.S. Vernon 19, 219, 239; La Fontaine, Jean de 140, 224, 233; Perry, Ben Edwin 138, 218, 235; Temple, Olivia 138–140, 224, 236; Temple, Robert 138–140, 224, 236

folklore motifs: adversary 107, 196; crossing thresholds 206–207; the fall 149–150, 200–201; hag *see* wise crone; helper 18, 75, 85, 98, 107, 175; hero 12–13, 15, 25, 27, 74 (*see also* Hanuman); journey *see* quest; magical transformation 17–18, 85–86, 88, 175, 190–191, 207, 209 (*see also* therianthropy; zoanthropy); outcast 92; quest 85; stark contrast 77, 85, 92, 94, 111, 125, 189, 196; trickster 15, 19, 33, 92, 94, 100–102, 104, 107, 110, 115, 120, 122, 125, 127, 140, 179, 181, 188, 192–194, 196, 201–202, 204, 211, 214–215; underdog 85; wise crone 97–98; wise fool 92

Folklore of the Santhal People see Bompas, Cecil Henry

folktale types: cumulative 192–194; droll 110, 209; magical 94, 97–98, 130; *pourquoi* 17, 86, 88, 101–102, 110, 115, 127, 130, 132, 177, 181, 190–191, 196, 200–202; realistic 123; romantic 97; talking beast 34, 77, 120, 134, 200, 204; trickster *see* folklore motifs

Folktales from India see Ramanujan, A.K.

Folktales from Southern Nigeria, West Africa see Dayrell, Elphinstone

Fon people 215

fox 103–104, 135–136, 176–177, 196, 202; *see also* Brer Fox

Francis, H.T 13, 21, 23, 29

Gama, Vasco da 116
gaub tree 146
Gautama Siddhartha 13, 27
Gibbs, Laura 138–140
goddesses of wisdom 98
The Golden Ass see Apuleius
great apes 4

hag *see* folklore motifs (wise crone)
hagiology 98
Hammond, Doug 214
hanasika (Japanese storytellers) 187
Hanuman 12–15, 27, 75, 88, 171
Hardy, R. Spencer 146
Harris, Joel Chandler 105, 115–116, 196
Hausa people 130
helper *see* folklore motifs
Henderson, Harold G. 187
hero *see* folklore motifs
Herodotus on the *dhoti* 94
Hinduism 74–75
Hippocrates on apes and monkeys 8–9
The Hitopadesa 32
Hmong people 148–150, 189
Honey, James 104, 107, 110
Hottentot (negative implications) 116–117, 121–122
howler monkey 142
hurricane etymology 201
Hyde-Chambers, Audrey 147
Hyde-Chambers, Frederick 147

Index

ibejis (Yoruba name for twins) 130
Igbo people 125, 127–128, 130
Ilocano people 192, 194, 196
Indian Fables see Raju, P.V. Ramaswami
Indian Fairy Tales (1880) see Stokes, Maive
Indian Fairy Tales (1892) see Jacobs, Joseph
Itard, Jean Marc Gaspard 123–124

jackal 103–105, 110–111, 196
Jackson, Bruce 214
Jacobs, Joseph 19, 33, 104, 192
Jade Emperor 15, 172–173
jade symbolism 172
The Japanese Fairy Book see Ozaki, Yei Theodora
The Jataka or Stories of the Buddha's Former Births see Cowell, E.B.
Jataka Tales see Babbitt, Ellen C.
Jatakas 13, 19, 21–22, 24–25, 27–29, 33, 104–105, 144
Jones, V.S. Vernon 19, 139
journey see folklore motifs
Journey to the West 3, 14–15, 171, 173

kaffir (negative implications) 116–117
Kalila and Dimna (characters in *The Fables of Bidpai*) 33–34, 214
Kamba people 99, 102
The Kangyur (Tibetan Buddhist text) 144, 146–147
karaka tree 144
karma 74–75
Keith-Falconer, I.G.N. 33
Khoekhoe people 107, 111, 116–117, 122, 124
Khoikhoi people see Khoekhoe people
Kimbundu people 117, 120
kimpaka tree 144
Kingscote, Georgiana 193
Kitutu, Vincent Muli Wa 100, 103
Kokoschla, Oskar 11; see also singeries
Krensky, Stephen 196
Kupla, Frank 11; see also singeries

La Fontaine, Jean de 137, 140
The Land I Lost see Nhuong, Huynh Quang
Landseer, Sir Edwin Henry 77; see also singeries
Lang, Andrew 100, 127, 181, 193
langur monkey 75, 88, 91, 94
Legba (African trickster god) 215; see also Eshu

Lent, Blair 127
leopard as adversary 115, 117–120
lesser apes 5
Lhota people see Lotha people
The Lilac Fairy Book 100; see also Lang, Andrew
lion as adversary 107, 135–136, 211–215
Little people (Cherokee magic makers) 207
Livo, Norma J. 150, 189
Lloyd, Lucy C. 121–122
The Lotha Nagas see Mills, J.P.
Lotha people 86–88
Lucian of Samosata (ancient classical author) 137, 139
Lucifer see Satan
lustful monkey 97, 141–142

The Magic Orange Tree and Other Haitian Folktales see Wolkstein, Diane
magical tale see folktale types
magical transformation see folklore motifs
The Mahabharata 74
A Manual of Budhism [sic] in Its Modern Development see Hardy, R. Spencer
Mayan view of monkeys 12
Mayer, Fanny Hagin 179, 181
Meiji dynasty 177
Metamorphoses see Ovid
Metzger, Berta 148
Mills, J.P. 86–87
Mindlin, Betty 206
Minerva see goddesses of wisdom
Ming dynasty 171
mochi (rice ball) 181
Monkey (novel) see Waley, Arthur
monkey-crab battles (story cycle) 181
Monkey King 14–15, 75, 150, 171–173
"monkey mind" 147
Monkey Painter see Deschamps, Alexandre Gabriel
monkey paintings see singeries
The Monkey Sculptor see Watteau, Antoine
monkeys as pests 1, 103, 128, 146
Mooney, James 115, 196, 207
Moore, Rudy Ray 214
moral law of the universe see dharma
More, Sir Thomas 140
More Jataka Tales see Babbitt, Ellen C.
Morris, Desmond (zoologist) 1, 5, 9–10, 12, 15, 97, 140–142, 188
The Mythological Zoo see Sax, Boria
Myths and Tales of the Southeastern Indians see Swanton, John Reid

Myths of the Cherokee see Mooney, James

Nagaland 86, 88
Nama people 122, 124
Narayan, R.K. 74
Nassau, Robert H. 125
Natural History see Pliny the Elder
Nhuong, Huynh Quang 103, 105
Noah *see* flood story
North, Sir Thomas 33

Odysseus *see The Odyssey*
The Odyssey 18
Old Hendrik's Tales see Vaughan, Captain A.O.
Old Monkey *see* Monkey King
On the Nature of Man see Hippocrates
One Thousand and One Nights 97, 142, 187
orangutan as helper 107
outcast *see* folklore motifs
Ovid 17
Ozaki, Yei Theodora 102, 181, 187

Palmyra fruit *see* toddy palm fruit
The Panchatantra 32–33, 187; *see also The Talking Beasts: A Book of Fable Wisdom*
Pater, Walter 140
Payne, John 97
peach tree symbolism 171–172
Perrin, Pat 196, 226
Perry, Ben Edwin 138
persimmon 104, 179
Phaedrus 134, 139
Philippine Folk Tales see Cole, Mabel Cook
Picasso, Pablo 11; *see also* singeries
pig (human qualities) 8
pine tree symbolism 171–172
Pliny the Elder 9
pourquoi tale *see* folktale types
Pyrnelle, Louise 116

Queen of Elfland 207
quest *see* folklore motifs
quinoa etymology 204

Rabbi Joel 33
rabbit 194, 196, 211; *see also* Brer Rabbit; Zomo the rabbit
Rabelais, François 140
rainbow folktale series of Andrew Lang 100
Raju, P.V. Ramaswami 77

Rakshasas (demons in *The Ramayana*) 75
Rama *see The Ramayana*
Ramanujan, A.K. 100–101
The Ramayana 3, 12–15, 27, 34, 74–75
Rattray, Capt. Robert Sutherland 132–133
Ravana (Demon King of Lanka) 15, 75
Reeves, Jeni 196
Reff, Theodore 11; *see also* singeries
The Reflection, the Monkey and the Looking Glass see Landseer, Sir Edwin Henry
Reminiscences of Sport in India see Burton, E.F.
Republic of Biafra 128
Reynard the Fox in South Africa see Bleek, W.H.I.
rice ball *see* mochi
ritual purification 207–208
Ross, Ramon R. 2

sambar deer 88–89
sambhur deer *see* sambar deer
San people 120–122
Santal people *see* Santhal people
Santhal people 89–92
Sastri, Pandit Natesa 193
Satan and monkeys 10
Sax, Boria 1, 7, 11, 13, 18
Say, Allen 192
Schiefner, F. Anton Von 143–144, 146–147
Seki, Keigo 181
sesamum (plant) 94
Seton, Ernest Thompson 148
Shanzabeh (character in *The Fables of Bidpai*) 33, 214
shark as adversary 99–101
Shogunate 177
sinful monkey *see* lustful monkey
Singeries (monkey paintings) 10–11
Sita *see The Ramayana*
sloth as helper 206–207
Smith, Nora Archibald 34
Snatch and the Poontangs 214
Snyder, Diane 192
Son of the Wind *see* Hanuman
Sophia *see* goddesses of wisdom
South-African Folk-Tales see Honey, James
"spank the monkey" 12
Specimens of Bushman Folklore see Bleek, W.H.I.
stark contrast *see* folklore motifs
Steel, F.A. 104

Steere, Edward 100
Stokes, Maive 85
Storyteller see Ross, Ramon R.
storytelling 2–3, 104, 132–133, 187
Sun Wu-Kung see Monkey King
suttee (custom of ritual suicide by a grieving Hindu widow) 91
Swahili Tales see Steere, Edward
Swanton, John Reid 115, 196, 211
swidden farming 190
Swift, Jonathan 140
Swynnerton, Charles 19

Taino people 201
Talaandig people see Bukidnon people
Tales from the Japanese Storytellers see Wheeler, Post
Tales of the Sun see Kingscote, Georgiana; Sastri, Pandit Natesa
talking beast tale see folktale types
The Talking Beasts: A Book of Fable Wisdom see Smith, Nora Archibald; Wiggin, Kate Douglas
Tantalus 179
Taoism 172–173
tar baby stories 115
Taro, Noda 179; see also Mayer, Fanny Hagin
Temple, Olivia 140
Temple, R.C. 104
Temple, Robert 138–140
therianthropy 18, 175
Thomas, E.J. 13, 21, 23, 29
Thoth 8, 142
Thutmose III 8
Thyestes 179
Tibetan Tales Derived from Indian Sources see Schiefner, F. Anton Von
Tinduka tree see gaub tree
toasts (African American poetry genre) 214–215
tobacco (healing and magical properties of) 208
toddy palm fruit 94
Tokhu Emong (Lotha festival) 88
Tokugawa period 187
Tower of Babel 11
Treasure-Tale-Storehouse see Wheeler, Post

A Treasury of African Folklore see Courlander, Harold
trickster see folklore motifs
Tuggle, William Orrie 115, 211; see also Swanton, John Reid
tung tree 87
turtle as trickster 196
twins see *ibejis*

Uncle Bob 116
Uncle Hendrick 116
Uncle Remus 105, 116
underdog see folklore motifs

Valmiki 74; see also *The Ramayana*
Vaughan, Captain Arther Owen 110–111, 115–116
Victor see Itard, Jean Marc Gaspard
Visayan people see Bisayan people
Voltaire 97, 140–142

Waley, Arthur (translator) 171
Watteau, Antoine 11; see also singeries
Wheeler, Post 187, 225, 237
Why the Sun and the Moon Live in the Sky 127; see also Dayrell, Elphinstone; Lent, Blair
Wideawake Stories see Steel, F.A.; Temple, R.C.
Wiggin, Kate Douglas 34
The Wild Boy of Averyon see Itard, Jean Marc Gaspard
wise crone see folklore motifs
wolf as adversary 107, 110–111
Wolkstein, Diane 209
Wood, Ramsey 33
Wu Cheng'en see *Journey to the West*; Waley, Arthur

Year of the Monkey 13
Yoruba people 128, 130, 215
Yu, Anthony C. 14, 171
Yuchi Indians 211

Zanzibar Tales see Bateman, George W.
Zeus 179
Zipes, Jack 138–139
Zomo the rabbit 104
Zoroastrians on monkeys 11

www.ingramcontent.com/pod-product-compliance
Ingram Content Group UK Ltd.
Pitfield, Milton Keynes, MK11 3LW, UK
UKHW041938210426
5322IPUK00016B/237

9 781476 695426